THE CLOSING

A NOVEL BY

KEN ODER

This book is a work of fiction. Any references to historical events,
real people, or real places are used fictitiously. Other names, characters,
places, and events are products of the author's imagination, and any
resemblance to actual events, places, or persons, living or dead,
is entirely coincidental.

ISBN: 978-1-939889-16-4 (SkipJack Publishing)
First Edition: February, 2014

Editor: Meghan Pinson

Cover: *Double Sunset, 2009* by Devon Oder

To Cindy

Contents

Chapter 1

The Prisoner
May 5, 1968

A prison guard ushered Nate Abbitt into a room marked Visit A – Max Sec and closed the door. The room was divided by soundproof glass, with desks snug to the pane and telephones bolted to the walls on each side. Nate sat at the desk and withdrew documents from his briefcase. He heard the crackle of lightning and felt the rumble of thunder as it passed under the cell block and subsided in the distance. He closed his eyes and ran his hand over his close-cropped gray hair.

The barred door on the other side of the divider rolled open and Kenneth Deatherage entered the room. Dressed in a khaki prison jumpsuit, he was in his mid-twenties, average height, with a round florid face and oily red hair that fell to his shoulders. Manacles were chained to his ankles and his wrists were cuffed behind his back. A guard closed and locked the door. Deatherage backed up to it, stuck his hands through the bars, and stared at Nate while the guard uncuffed him. Deatherage's pale blue eyes betrayed no hint of the crimes he was accused of – assault, rape, murder. The guard walked away, and Deatherage sat in the chair and grabbed the phone. Nate picked up the phone on his side.

"Who are you?" Deatherage said.

"Nate Abbitt."

"What do you want?"

"Did you receive my letter of introduction?"

"I won't sign for the mail. They won't give it to me without me signin for it."

"I'm a lawyer. The court asked me to represent you."

"What happened to Swiller?"

"Randolph Swiller died of a heart attack last month."

Deatherage paused. "Did he file the appeal before he died?"

"No."

"Have they set a new execution date?"

"No. Your execution date was postponed indefinitely. Swiller explained that to you, didn't he?"

"I haven't seen Swiller since they threw me in this hole. The warden told me they put off my date, but he didn't say why."

"Cases are pending before the United States Supreme Court challenging the constitutionality of the death penalty. There's a nationwide moratorium on executions until the court rules. All execution dates in Virginia were suspended indefinitely."

Deatherage seemed surprised. "How long will they hold off on the killins?"

"The court won't render a decision for at least a year or two."

"A year or two." Deatherage's heavy body settled into his chair. He chuckled. "I'll be damned. A year or two."

Nate placed a court pleading, a letter, and a pen in a metal tray in a slot below the window and shoved the tray through to Deatherage. "The court asked me to take your case, but it's subject to your consent. I prepared these documents. The court pleading says you want me to represent you. If you sign it, I'll file it with the court and begin reviewing the case. The letter is from you to Swiller's estate, telling the executor to send me Swiller's files. His estate can't release his files to me without your consent because they're protected from disclosure by the attorney-client privilege."

Deatherage's eyes traced the path of a scar that slashed across Nate's forehead and down the side of his jaw. "What happened to your face?"

"I was in a car accident." Nate pointed to the pleading and the letter. "Read the documents and tell me what you want to do."

Deatherage stared at Nate's scar for a few moments and then looked at the documents. He moved his lips as he ran his finger under each line. When he came to the last page, he squinted at Nate's name. "Nathan A. Abbitt. I've heard your name somewhere."

"I was a prosecutor. I prosecuted some of the men in here with you."

Deatherage furrowed his brow. "You're that crooked lawyer, the one from Selk County, the one they ran out of the county lawyer's job."

Nate showed Deatherage nothing, no change in expression, no color in his face, no discomfort.

"You're the one who sent Jimmy Deeks to death row."

Nate didn't say anything.

"They claim Jimmy Deeks put a bullet through his daddy's head while he was sleepin, but Deeks says he didn't do it."

"Deeks is lying." Nate pointed to the documents again. "Decide what you want to do."

Deatherage leaned forward and jabbed his finger at Nate. "Deeks says you're crooked. Says you framed a man, a ree-tard. Says you talked the retard into signin a phony confession that said he killed somebody when he didn't do it. Deeks told me that tough old judge in Selk County caught you and threw you out of the county lawyer's job. The old judge tried to keep what you did secret, but Deeks says everybody in Selk County knows about it."

"That case has nothing to do with you."

"Don't I have a right to know if you framed a man?"

"You have a right to reject my appointment. Turn me down and I'll be on my way. The court will send you another lawyer."

Deatherage stared at Nate for a long time.

"Make your choice," Nate said.

"You were a big-time county lawyer. Why did you switch sides?"

"I have to make a living."

"Why did you agree to take my case?"

"You have a constitutional right to counsel."

"You think I killed her, don't you?"

"I don't know. I don't care."

Deatherage fell silent.

"Make up your mind," Nate said.

"I don't know, mister. You look beat down. How old are you?"

"Fifty-six."

"You look older than that. You look tired and worn out, like you don't have much fight left in you. How long were you the county lawyer?"

"Twenty-six years."

"How many men did you send down the river to this hellhole?"

"I didn't keep count."

"How many did you send to death row?"

Nate considered whether to answer the question. He said, "Four."

"They die in the chair?"

"All but Deeks. He got the benefit of the moratorium, the same as you."

"You watch the killins?"

"Two of them."

Deatherage's eyes settled into the trench of Nate's scar. "You've seen em do the deed. That's somethin in your favor, I suppose. You know what it's like when they pull the lever and shoot the juice into a man. Nobody could watch em fry a man and not want to put a stop to it."

Nate returned Deatherage's stare evenly and said nothing.

Deatherage said, "If you framed the retard, you know how it's done. That's another point in your favor. And you can't be workin for em. They threw you out of the county lawyer's job so they can't trust you. You're probably the only one they could send here who can't be workin for em."

"Make your choice," Nate said.

Deatherage looked at the documents. Thunder sounded faintly in the distance. He signed the pleading and the letter and shoved them through the slot. Nate looked at the pleading that placed him between Deatherage and the electric chair.

"They framed me," Deatherage said. "Swiller and Judge Herring and the sheriff and God knows who else, the whole Buck County crew, they rigged the trial to put it on me. I didn't kill her."

Nate placed the documents in his briefcase. "I'll meet with you again after I review the files." He hung up the phone. Deatherage said something into the phone but Nate couldn't hear him through the soundproof divider. He didn't care what Deatherage had to say.

Nate left Visit A – Max Sec and walked back to the guard's desk. The guard was a short, stocky man with bushy eyebrows. He pushed a ledger across his desk to Nate, and Nate signed it and entered the time of his departure.

"One of your clients do it to you?" the guard said.

"What?"

"That big old scar. One of your clients cut you?"

Nate turned away from the guard, opened the prison door, and emerged from the penitentiary into a pouring rain.

Chapter 2
The Trial

Nate rented an office in Jeetersburg, Virginia, on the second floor of a residential home that had been converted to an office building after World War II. From his office window, Nate had a good view of the courthouse across Lighthorse Street. A week after he met with Deatherage, he sat at his desk, stared at the courthouse, and thought about the cases he had tried there as Selk County commonwealth's attorney. He missed the challenges, the accomplishments, and the sense of purpose of his twenty-six years as the county's chief prosecutor. He longed to prosecute again, but the court's discovery of his professional malfeasance a year and a half earlier on January 12, 1967, made that impossible.

The first matter on circuit court judge Harry Blackwell's morning calendar that day had been the arraignment of Jack Tin, a mentally impaired defendant charged with murder. Nate was drunk when he stood to enter his appearance on behalf of the commonwealth, but no one noticed. By then, he had mastered the art of appearing sober while drinking throughout the day. He gripped the lectern firmly, stood straight, and spoke in a strong, clear voice. The arraignment proceeded smoothly until he offered in evidence Tin's signed confession. At that point, the judge cut Nate off in midsentence, adjourned the hearing, and summoned Nate to his chambers.

In chambers the judge sat at his desk dressed in a black suit. He was eighty years old, tall and gaunt, with snow-white hair and a handlebar moustache. His face was flushed; his expression stern. There was a tape recorder on his desk.

"What's going on, Harry?"

The judge flipped a switch on the recorder, and the reels of the tape turned. Nate heard his voice and the voice of his secretary, Rosaline Partlow. Nate asked Rosaline to sign an affidavit swearing she'd witnessed Tin confess to the murder of his own free will. She refused at first, but Nate persisted and she agreed. His voice and Rosaline's voice droned on.

Nate went to a window that looked out on the town square. It was snowing big wet flakes that blotted out the sunlight and darkened the room. The soft light of the judge's desk lamp and the scent of his cherry pipe tobacco gave the room an atmosphere of peacefulness that seemed ironic to Nate, given the circumstances. The voices on the tape fell silent. The judge turned off the recorder and sat with his arms crossed over his chest.

After a long silence, Nate said, "Where did you get the tape?"

"The sheriff gave it to me."

"Are you going to have me indicted?"

"I persuaded the sheriff not to press charges. He assured me there are no copies of the tape recording. I intend to destroy the original."

Nate swallowed hard. "Thank you, Harry."

"My forbearance is based on requirements that are not negotiable. You will submit your resignation to the board of supervisors this morning. You will notify the bar association you wish to go on inactive status for personal reasons. You will not practice law again until and unless I allow you to do so."

Nate struggled to control his emotions. It was all he could do not to reach for the flask of whiskey he had concealed in the breast pocket of his suit jacket. It took him a while to find his voice. Then he said, "All right. I'll do as you say."

The judge stared at Nate, disappointment etched on his face. Nate couldn't bear to return his gaze. The judge said, "I'll try to keep your malfeasance confidential, Nathan, but I can only do so much. Too many people in the sheriff's office know about it."

Nate nodded. "I understand."

The judge stood, crossed the room, and opened the door. "Go home. Think about what you've done. When you understand the reasons you betrayed the trust so many of us placed in you, perhaps you can find a way to redeem yourself."

Nate walked out of the room, and the judge closed the door behind him. He found a spot in the shadows at the other end of the hall, leaned against the wall, took several deep breaths, and tried to slow the beating of his heart. With a trembling hand, he withdrew the flask from his pocket, turned it up, and drained it.

Later that day, Judge Blackwell's clerk found Nate nursing a glass of whiskey in a back room of Michie's Place, a restaurant that served alcohol under the table. The clerk said the judge wanted to see him in chambers again.

Nate trudged through the snow to the courthouse. In chambers Judge Blackwell asked him about other prosecutions, and he answered the questions truthfully. At the end of the meeting, the judge looked over his notes and said, "I count four cases plus the Tin case. Five tainted prosecutions in all."

Nate nodded.

"Have you told me everything?"

"Yes."

Judge Blackwell leaned back in his chair and put his hand over his eyes. Nate returned to Michie's Place.

As the judge predicted, he was unable to keep confidential the reasons for Nate's resignation. Someone talked and the truth about him spread throughout the state. When the judge finally agreed to allow Nate to resume practicing law, no county or city in Virginia would hire him as a prosecutor. He turned to criminal defense, a role he detested, but as he told Deatherage, he had to make a living.

He turned away from his office window and his view of the court-house. His eyes fell on a cardboard box that sat on the floor near his desk. Someone, probably a file clerk, had scrawled on its side *"Commonwealth v. Deatherage."* The box contained the record of the criminal proceedings. He forced himself to open the box, spread its contents on his desk, and begin to review the file. He soon became engrossed in the story of the case.

Deatherage was arrested on June 3, 1967, in Bloxton, Buck County's seat of government. He was charged with murder and rape. A Buck County general district court judge had ruled that Deatherage was indigent and appointed Randolph Swiller to represent him. The case worked its way up to the Buck County Circuit Court, where Deatherage was arraigned on an indictment that accused him of willful, deliberate, and premedi-tated murder in the commission of rape. Deatherage pled not guilty and was tried on January 29, 1968, before Buck County Circuit Court Judge Edbert Herring.

Nate found the trial transcript and turned to the commonwealth's opening statement. The Buck County commonwealth's attorney, George Maupin, was Nate's lifelong friend. George's opening provided a clear roadmap to the prosecution's case, but it gave the jury almost no informa-tion about the victim, Darlene Updike, a young woman from New York. The colorless opening statement in the Deatherage case seemed odd to Nate because it was out of character for George.

Randolph Swiller waived his opening statement; Nate was surprised. In his thirty years of experience he had never seen a defense counsel waive the opening statement. He could think of no strategic justification for forfeiting the opportunity to explain the facts and law to the jurors in the light most favorable to the defendant.

The commonwealth's first witness was Willis Odoms, who testified that he lived next door to an abandoned warehouse in Bloxton. He and his wife returned home from a party before dawn on June 3, 1967. It was a hot night. When he opened his bedroom window for air, he heard a woman's voice coming from the warehouse: "Please don't. Oh, don't. Please stop. Please."

While Odoms' wife called the police, he approached the warehouse with a handgun and a flashlight. He pointed his light at a warehouse window and saw Deatherage. "That son of a bitch peeked through the window. I could tell by the look on his face he was the cause of the trouble. He ducked down and I figured he would run out the back to get away. There's a twelve-foot wall behind the warehouse and I knew he'd have to come around the front to get off the property, so I waited for him. Sure enough, he came sneakin alongside the building and took off down the road. I chased him and knocked him off his feet. I stuck my gun in his ribs and held him down till the sheriff's man came along."

On cross-examination, Swiller asked Odoms one question: "Did you see the defendant kill Darlene Updike?" Odoms said he didn't see the killing.

George called Buck County Deputy Sheriff Darby Jones to the stand. Jones said he arrived at the warehouse at 5:25 a.m. and found Odoms standing in a dirt road that ran between the warehouse and a motel, holding a gun on Deatherage. Jones cuffed Deatherage and searched him. "I found a scarf in Deatherage's pants pocket. It was the type of scarf a woman would wear over her head or around her neck. There was a stain on the scarf that appeared to be fresh blood."

After questioning Odoms, Jones entered the warehouse and found a woman's corpse sprawled on the floor under the window where Odoms first saw Deatherage. Jones radioed the Buck County sheriff's office and told the dispatcher to notify the medical examiner. Jones then conducted a thorough search of the warehouse and found a rag, which appeared to have fresh blood on it, on the floor at the rear of the warehouse under an open window.

It seemed to Nate that a victim of rape and murder would have fought for her life during the assault, but George Maupin asked Jones no questions about the state of Deatherage's clothing or his physical condition. Nate guessed this was because Deatherage bore no signs of a struggle. If Nate was right, Swiller should have asked Jones if there were scratches or bruises on Deatherage's body or tears or rips in his clothing, but when the judge turned to Swiller for cross, Swiller said, "No questions, Your Honor."

The next witness was the local medical examiner, Malcolm Somers. He testified that Updike was a young white female, five feet one inch tall, one hundred five pounds. He described the condition of the corpse upon his arrival at the warehouse. Her blouse was ripped open, and she was naked from the waist down. A bra, torn skirt, and panties lay on the floor near the corpse. Updike's left eye was swollen shut. Her lip was split and two upper front teeth had been dislodged. There were abrasions on her hands, elbows, thighs, and knees. Her vaginal wall was torn and there was blood on her thighs. A rope was wound around her neck, and a stick was twisted in the coil of the rope. There were three bloody rings of broken flesh around her neck. A rag was lodged in her throat.

Somers estimated the time of death as between 4:00 a.m. and 5:00 a.m. He said the cause of death was "asphyxiation due to compression of her neck and obstruction of her airway." He notified the Virginia chief medical examiner's office that Updike was the victim of a homicide.

Swiller asked no questions of Somers.

George then called Shirley West to the stand. West worked for the Virginia chief medical examiner's western district office, based in Roanoke. The state's chief medical examiner's office was responsible for conducting investigations when a local medical examiner determined a death was the result of homicide. West was a forensic pathologist, and Nate had worked with her on many cases. She was a middle-aged single woman with no children. Her job was her life, and she was an excellent expert witness.

West confirmed the wounds Somers described and his determination of the cause of death, but she stated it more plainly: "Miss Updike's assailant tightened a rope around her throat while she was in the process of swallowing a rag he stuffed in her mouth. She couldn't breathe."

The rag Somers found in Updike's throat was white, six inches square, frayed on two edges. West said, "I established a match between dust on the rag and particles of concrete from the warehouse floor."

West said the rope and stick found wrapped around Updike's throat were a "makeshift garrote" used to strangle her. "The rope was a thirty-six-inch length of a common type. It was half-inch three-strand laid rope with a right-handed twist. It was made of hemp. It had been cut at both ends from a larger coil. The fraying at the ends and the discoloration of the rope indicated that it was not newly store-bought."

"The assailant used the stick to tighten the rope gradually by twisting it. The stick was ten inches long, three quarters of an inch wide, and flat on all four sides. There was a vertical indentation along one side with small shards of glass embedded in the crevice. In the warehouse I found several broken window mullions under the window where Deputy Jones found the victim's body. This stick matched those mullions."

West had dusted the mullion for fingerprints. "There were prints along one end of the mullion that were too distorted to be identifiable. There was one clear partial print in its center. This print matched a portion of the defendant's thumb print." George Maupin's direct examination of West left unclear the extent of the print that was found on the mullion.

Nate thought Swiller should have attacked the reliability of the match on cross because its accuracy depended in part upon the portion of the print not recovered. He flipped ahead in the transcript to see what Swiller did with the issue. By then, he was not surprised to find Swiller's familiar refrain: "No questions, Your Honor."

Nate grimaced and turned back to West's direct testimony. West analyzed the blood evidence. Her tests revealed Updike's blood type as B+ and Deatherage's as O+. "There was a large bloodstain low on the front side of the defendant's shirt. This blood was type B+. The scarf Deputy Jones found in the defendant's pants pocket was also stained with B+ blood, and the blood on the rag Jones found on the floor in the back of the warehouse under an open window was the same blood type."

West said Somers found semen in Updike's vaginal cavity and on her thighs. West testified that the semen was deposited by an O+ secretor. Secretors secrete antigens of their blood type into body fluids. Non-secretors secrete very little of their antigens. West determined that Deatherage was an O+ secretor. From his days as a prosecutor, Nate knew that about eighty-five percent of the male population is comprised of secretors and O+ is the most common blood type, about forty percent of the general population, but George did not ask West questions that revealed these statistics to the jurors and Swiller did not clarify these weaknesses on cross.

West said she found on Updike's corpse thirteen hair follicles, which appeared red to the naked eye. Under microscopic analysis she determined the follicles contained the pigment, pheomelanin, which is only present in red and yellow hair. Updike's hair was black. Deatherage's hair was red. West compared the follicles found on the corpse to samples of Deatherage's hair. She observed a high degree of similarity in the thickness and presence of pigment in the cuticle, or outer layer, of the hair shaft. In the cortex, or middle layer, the organization, density, and distribution of pigment granules were also very similar. West opined that it was highly likely the hair follicles found on the corpse came from Deatherage.

Nate knew that critics of perceived hair follicle matches argue that comparing the characteristics of hair is similar to comparing facial features and concluding that two people who look alike are in fact the same person. He assumed that Swiller could not have hired an expert witness within the state's budget to present this criticism, but there were anti-death-penalty groups that provided private funding to attack this type of analysis. Nevertheless, Swiller had not called an expert to rebut the evidence.

The prosecution rested after West testified. The defense rested without calling a witness. The court recessed for lunch.

After the break, George Maupin delivered a powerful closing statement, pulling all the evidence together to tell a vivid story. George said Deatherage encountered Darlene Updike somewhere away from the warehouse. He beat her savagely to subdue her, dragged her to the seclusion of the warehouse, and ripped off her clothing. He choked her with a rope while he raped her. With the tightening of the rope, he brought her to the edge of death, and she passed out. Then he loosened the rope to allow her to breathe. She regained consciousness and he started in again. He did this three times, creating three bloody rings around her neck.

Somewhere along the way she made too much noise and Deatherage stuffed a rag in her mouth to gag her. Gasping for air, she swallowed the rag and it blocked her air passage. That obstruction and the constriction of the rope choked her to death. Odoms flashed a light in the warehouse window and saw Deatherage in the spot where Updike's corpse was found. Deatherage panicked. He wiped off her blood with another rag while he ran to the rear of the warehouse. He tossed the rag on the floor, climbed out a back window, and ran toward his truck. Odoms caught Deatherage before he reached his truck and held him down until Deputy Jones arrived and found Updike's scarf in Deatherage's pocket. George argued that there was no reasonable doubt that Deatherage killed Updike. All the evidence pointed to him as the killer and to no one else.

In Swiller's closing, he stammered through a vague explanation of reasonable doubt, but he gave the jury nothing to hang on that peg.

The jurors retired to the jury room at two thirty. They returned at four fifteen and rendered a verdict of guilty. The next morning George presented evidence in support of the death penalty. Swiller offered no evidence against it. The jury retired and returned shortly before noon with a unanimous vote in favor of a death sentence. Judge Herring entered a sentence of death in a hearing on February 23 and set the execution for

July 12. The Virginia Supreme Court of Appeals postponed the execution
date indefinitely and extended the deadline for filing an appeal to August
10 due to Swiller's sudden death.

Nate returned the file to the cardboard box, looked out his office
window, and thought about the case. He was convinced Deatherage was
guilty. A competent defense counsel could have weakened the impact
of each separate piece of evidence against Deatherage, but Nate could
imagine no coincidence of innocent occurrences that could explain all the
evidence taken together. But he was also convinced there was a strong
argument for overturning Deatherage's conviction because Swiller did
nothing to defend him. Appellate courts rarely overturned convictions
based on inadequate representation at trial, but Swiller's passivity was in
a class by itself. A successful appeal based on the denial of Deatherage's
Sixth Amendment right to competent counsel would force the Virginia
Supreme Court of Appeals to remand the case to the Buck County Circuit
Court for a new trial, and Nate would be required to defend Deatherage there. The question hanging over Nate like a poisonous cloud was
whether he could force himself to do his best for Deatherage, knowing
that he was a murderer.

Chapter 3

The Truth

An attorney's opinion about guilt or innocence is not supposed to affect his representation of his client, but Nate was having difficulty adjusting his sentiments to his new role as a criminal defense lawyer. He wanted to believe Deatherage was innocent. The day after reviewing the case file, Nate returned to the state penitentiary, hoping to find information that would change his conclusion about Deatherage's guilt.

The air in Visit A – Max Sec was hot and close. Sweat beaded Deatherage's brow and upper lip. Nate mopped his own face with a handkerchief. "I want to know the facts surrounding the murder," Nate said. "Don't hold anything back. I want to know everything. And no lies. That's a hard and fast rule with me. If I find out you've lied to me, I'll withdraw from your case. Do you understand me?"

Deatherage nodded. "What do you want to know?"

"Had you ever met Darlene Updike before the night of the murder?"

"I saw her once or twice, but I never met her."

"Where did you see her?"

"I saw her in a restaurant in Bloxton called the Coal Bin."

"Did you talk to her?"

"No. I didn't even know her name till they charged me with the murder."

"When did you first see Updike the night of the murder?"

"I found her body in the warehouse after she was killed."

"What were you doing in the warehouse?"

"I had a fight with my old lady. I ran off and bought a jug of white lightnin. I went to the warehouse to drink my hooch where nobody would bother me."

"What time did you have the fight with your wife?"

"About eight or nine o'clock the night before I was arrested for killin the girl. I lost my temper. The damn baby was cryin. I told my old lady to shut him up, but she wouldn't do it. That kid squalls all the time, and she won't ever shut his damn mouth. That night I lost it and hauled off and hit her. Busted her teeth. I'm not proud of it, but I couldn't help it. I went plum crazy there for a second or two."

"Where did you go after you fought with your wife?"

"I drove out to Cecil Garrison's house. He's a moonshiner. I bought a jar of white lightnin and drove back to Bloxton. I parked next to the warehouse and sat in my truck and drank."

"Why did you choose to park at the warehouse to drink?"

"It was a good place to pull a big drunk. There was nobody around."

"When did you go inside the warehouse?"

"By midnight I was snookered. I went inside to find a place to sleep. I went upstairs, sat under a window, and drank the rest of my hooch. I stretched out on the floor and passed out. I was there all night, sleepin it off."

"What time did you wake up?"

"I don't know exactly. It was still dark. About five in the mornin, I guess."

"What did you do then?"

"When I woke, I heard the woman. 'Please. Please don't. Please stop.'"

"Where did the cries come from?"

"Downstairs."

"What did you do?"

"I got up to go see what was goin on, but I had a sour belly from that hooch. I puked up most of my guts. I sat down to get my strength back. I don't know how long I sat there, but it was a long spell. When I got up,

I didn't hear the woman's cries, and I kind of forgot about her. I decided to go home. When I came downstairs, I saw the woman lyin on the mattresses under a window at the front wall."

Nate paused. "There was no mention of mattresses in the case file."

"She was on top of a pile of four or five old mattresses when I saw her."

Nate was skeptical. "No mattresses were mentioned in the deputy sheriff's report or the medical examiner's testimony."

"I know what I saw. She was sprawled on top of a pile of mattresses."

"Why would there be mattresses in an abandoned warehouse?"

"Callao Coal Company used to own the warehouse. Before they closed the coal mine and pulled out of Buck County, there were beds in the upstairs rooms because the managers from up north stayed in the warehouse when they came to town. After the coal company left town for good, somebody hauled the old mattresses down to that window where I found the girl. They been piled up there for years."

Nate studied Deatherage's demeanor. He seemed truthful. Nate decided to move on. "All right. What did you do when you saw Updike?"

"I was rattled by the sight of the girl. She was in awful shape. Clothes torn off of her. Blood comin out her mouth. Bloody cuts around her neck. Face beat up. I wanted to help her awful bad."

"What did you do?"

"I tried to loosen the rope that was tied around her neck. I fiddled with the stick that was twisted up in the rope, but I couldn't do any good because my hands shook too bad. I leaned over too far and I fell on the girl. I sank down into those old mattresses and I had a hard time gettin off her and I rolled around on her. When I finally got off her, I had blood on my shirt. I figure that's how my hair got on her body, too. It was damn dumb to fall on her like that."

Nate was amazed. Deatherage provided a simple explanation for the partial fingerprint on the mullion, the blood on his shirt, and the presence of his hair on Updike's corpse. He didn't believe him, but he gave him credit for resourcefulness. "Did you tell Swiller about falling on Updike?"

"I told Swiller, Darby Jones, Sheriff Feedlow, the sheriff's secretary, the damn county lawyer, and everybody else I saw, but nobody would listen to me. They were too busy settin me up for the electric chair."

There was no sign of dissemblance in Deatherage's face, but Nate's experience was that deceit did not always show through a practiced mask. "Was Updike alive when you found her?"

"I ran off before I could tell."

"Why did you run?"

"I saw a light in the window, and I heard sirens. I figured the man with the light was the law, and I knew the law was comin for the girl. I was right there beside her and I figured they'd blame me for it. I ran out the back, came around the warehouse, and high-tailed it toward my truck. I would've made it, but Willis Odoms ran me down and stuck a gun in my craw."

"Why did you have a woman's scarf in your pocket when Jones arrested you?"

"I didn't have no scarf in my pocket."

"Deputy Jones said he found a bloody scarf in your pocket."

Deatherage shook his finger at Nate. "Now that was a damned lie. I didn't take that scarf off the girl. She didn't have no scarf on her when I saw her."

"Why would the deputy lie?"

"He was part of it. They had it wired to put it on me. Think about it, lawyer. If I killed the woman, I sure as hell wouldn't run off with her scarf in my pocket. I might as well pin a sign on my chest says 'Killer.'"

"Some killers take trophies from their victims and use them to revive memories of a killing."

"Well, I didn't take no trophy. I didn't kill her."

"It's convenient for you to say Jones planted the scarf. The scarf had blood on it matching Updike's blood type. It's damning and you can't explain it."

"That's why Darby Jones told that lie. He set me up. He was part of it."

"Part of what?"

"Part of the bunch that decided to put the girl's murder on me. They used that lie to do it. When I told em I fell on the girl, they knew I could explain the blood and hairs so they phonied up that scarf to nail me, and they gave me Swiller as my lawyer to make sure I'd go down without a fight. Judge Herring, the sheriff, Swiller, Odoms, Darby Jones – they were all part of it. They set me up."

"Why would the authorities in Buck County want to pin the murder on you?"

"Maybe one of em did it or maybe they're hidin somethin about the murder that makes em look bad. I don't know. All I know is I was an easy mark. I had nobody to help me and no way to fight back."

"Why would public officials risk their careers to frame you?"

"You tell me. You did it. You framed the retard, didn't you?"

Nate put his pen and pad in his briefcase, snapped it shut, and prepared to leave.

"Wait," Deatherage said. "I'm sorry I said that. I don't know what you did in Selk County and I don't care. Don't walk out on me. Please. Help me fight the bastards in Buck County." Deatherage leaned forward. "Look. I don't know who was in on it and I don't have no way to figure it out because I've been locked up since the killin. All I know is Darby Jones lied about that scarf and Swiller wasn't worth a damn because he didn't do anything to help me at the trial and Judge Herring just sat there and watched him throw me over. I don't know who else was part of it but you're smart and you know how it's done. Go to Buck County. Talk to em. You can figure out how they did it to me."

Nate searched Deatherage's face one last time. He seemed to be telling the truth, but Nate had convicted good liars on less evidence than confronted Deatherage. "I'll see what I can find out." He hung up the phone and closed his briefcase.

Deatherage's expression was hopeful. He raised his hand in a silent farewell. Nate returned the gesture with a tentative wave.

Chapter 4

The Divorce

One morning several days later the trial transcript was open before Nate on his desk when Howard Raines walked in. He was an attorney who had opposed Nate many times when Nate was commonwealth's attorney, and he owned the office building. His office was on the first floor, and he rented Nate's to him at a low rate to help him get back on his feet. He and Nate were about the same age, but where Nate was tall, lean, and had a full head of hair, Howard was short, stout, and bald.

Although Howard's specialty was criminal defense, Nate's wife, Christine, had hired him to file a bill of complaint for divorce against Nate. Nate was representing himself in the proceedings.

"Brought you the mail," Howard said. He tossed a manila envelope on the desk, shoved his hands in his pockets, and looked out the window. "Pretty day. One of the last cool days before the summer rolls in." Neither of them said anything for a while. Then Howard said, "You and I need to come to an understanding."

"About what?"

"Your divorce. You need to face reality."

Nate turned his back on Howard, looked out the window, and said nothing.

"Look," Howard said. "I understand what happened. You had a midlife crisis. It was a doozy. Your father was fifty-three when he got cancer and died. You hit fifty-three and you got nervous, I guess."

"Don't try to analyze me, Howard. You're not a psychiatrist."

"My point is you messed up pretty badly, you drank too much, you did terrible things, things you would never have done sober, and you lost everything. Now you're trying to regain your reputation and rebuild your legal career. That's all fine and good, but you can't regain Christine. You have to let her go."

Nate turned and faced Howard. "Drop it, Howard. I don't want to discuss this with you."

"That's too bad, damn it. I'm in the thick of your personal problems with you, and believe me, I don't like it any more than you do."

"I told you before. I'd much rather have you representing Christine than some stranger who doesn't care what happens to us. I'm glad you took Christine's case."

"Well, I'm not." Howard sighed heavily. "You broke Christine's heart, you know."

"I wish I could take back everything I did, but I can't change the past."

"You can control the present. You can agree to finalize your divorce and allow Christine to move on with her life."

Nate didn't respond.

Howard said, "Are there any terms you would accept to settle the case?"

"I don't know."

"It's high time to end this ordeal, Nate. Christine's done everything she can to accommodate you. All she's received in return is truculence. She made a reasonable settlement offer. You rejected it out of hand. She improved her offer, and you rejected that. She wants to be shed of the marriage, but you seem determined to drag out this divorce to no apparent purpose."

"I'm doing what I have to do."

"What does that mean?"

"It means I'm not ready to settle."

Howard grimaced. "I owe Christine my best effort, Nate."

"I wouldn't expect you to do any less."

"I hope you understand where this thing is headed if we don't resolve it. The settlement conference is next Monday. We'll make a settlement offer to you then. It will be our last offer. If you reject it, I'll be forced to destroy you at trial. Don't make me do it." Howard went to the door and stopped. He stood there with his back to Nate for a few moments and then turned. His eyes glistened. "I know how hard it must be to let her go. You still love her. I can see that, but she doesn't love you any more, Nate. Prolonging the divorce proceedings won't save your marriage. You're only causing her more pain."

Tears welled in Nate's eyes. He swiveled his chair around so Howard couldn't see them. Behind him, he heard Howard's steps walking away down the hall. Nate wiped his eyes and took a deep breath. He knew Howard was right about his marriage. There was no realistic possibility he could save it. He had hurt Christine in too many ways before they separated, and his actions since their separation had only made matters much worse.

They'd separated the day Judge Blackwell forced Nate to resign from his position as commonwealth's attorney. He didn't go home until two in the morning that night, and he was drunk when he parked his car in the driveway of his farm in Whippoorwill Hollow. His home was a two-story yellow frame house. A fist tightened around his heart when he saw a light in the downstairs window. No amount of whiskey could ease the pain of the loss he knew he was about to suffer.

He had broken her heart many times before that night. Christine complained about his drinking, and he lashed out at her. Her criticism intensified and he pushed back harder, belittling and demeaning her. Two years of lying and hiding and bullying had taken their toll. By the time he sat in his driveway staring at the house, Christine's patience was exhausted; her loyalty destroyed; her faith breeched. The revelation of Nate's crimes would merely confirm what she already knew: he was no longer the man she loved.

His short confrontation with her that night was seared into his memory. He got out of the car and walked toward the house. The sky had begun to clear and a pale yellow three-quarter moon peeked through a veil of mist, casting a tall blue shadow of Nate across the snow-covered pasture to the barn. As he climbed the porch steps, Christine opened the door and stood in the doorway. Her raven hair was streaked with gray. She was trim and fit and beautiful, even though her eyes were red-rimmed and filled with hurt.

"Is it true?"

Nate didn't answer.

"What they're saying about you, is it true?"

"I'm sorry."

Christine's eyes brimmed with tears. She turned and ran upstairs. The next day she told him to get out.

That night he gathered all the bottles of whiskey in the house, packed them in a box, and lugged it out to the car. The previous day's snow had frozen into a crust and his steps broke through it unevenly when he crossed the yard. Down at the barn, the mare trotted to the corral's fence and stared at Nate, jets of steam blowing from her nostrils. Chloe was Nate's present to Christine on her fiftieth birthday. He'd blindfolded Christine and led her to Chloe's stall. When he took off the blindfold, Christine let out a little cry and grabbed Chloe's neck and kissed her. Then she threw her arms around Nate and kissed him.

Nate looked down at the beautiful bay bathed in moonlight. He wiped a tear away, took a last look at the house and farm, and drove away. Sometime after midnight, about a hundred miles south, he crossed the Starkey County line and drove into the town of Hayesboro, rented a room, and drank until he passed out.

In the coming weeks, he was too ashamed to go home and face all the people he had disappointed, so he hid in Hayesboro and tried to forget all the trappings of his former life – the practice of law, his friends, the farm, his home. And Christine.

When he ran out of cash, he took a job as a night shift desk clerk in a run-down hotel on the edge of Hayesboro's slums. The pay was meager but it covered his limited needs: room, board, and enough whiskey to numb his pain.

Late at night, six months into Nate's stay, Howard Raines found him at the hotel's front desk. Howard withdrew a document from his valise and handed it to Nate. "Christine retained me to file this bill of complaint for divorce." Nate leafed through it.

"You'll represent yourself, I suppose," Howard said.

"I guess so."

"What do you want to do?"

"I don't know. I'll think about it."

"All right. When you're ready to talk, give me a call." Howard started to leave, but halfway across the lobby he stopped and looked back at Nate. "I guess you heard about Jack Tin," he said.

Jack Tin, the mentally impaired defendant he had convinced to sign a confession to murder, was one of the many memories Nate had tried to kill with whiskey. "No," he said. "I haven't followed the case."

"The sheriff solved the case. Tin is innocent. He didn't murder any-one." Nate didn't say anything. "I'm sorry I brought it up," Howard said. "I didn't mean to embarrass you."

Nate folded his hands on top of the counter and looked down at them.

Howard said, "Listen, Nate, you have a great gift. You're an excellent lawyer. You made a mistake, a big one, but don't throw your talent away. Come back to Jeetersburg and the practice of law. You have a lot of friends who'll forgive and forget. There's still a place for you in Selk County." Howard turned and walked out the door.

That night in bed Nate gazed at the moonshadows on the ceiling, sipped from a bottle of whiskey, and thought about Howard's words. A sea of whiskey had pooled in his cells and deadened most of his feelings. He didn't care about his talent as a lawyer or his friends who might forgive and forget. Whiskey had drowned all that. It was the pain of losing Christine that no anesthesia seemed capable of easing. He still loved her. He loved her more than anything, more than life itself.

The next morning, he packed his bag and drove back to Jeetersburg. He leased a one-room apartment above Sally's Diner on Lee Street, met with Judge Blackwell, and convinced him to allow Nate to practice law again. Howard rented Nate the office in his building, and the legal work trickled in, but there wasn't enough to fill Nate's day. During his downtime, he reviewed Christine's complaint for divorce, searching for a defense. But there was no defense. If the case moved all the way to a conclusion, a divorce decree would be entered and he would lose her forever. He thought his only hope was to circumvent the court proceedings by persuading her to withdraw the complaint and take him back. She had loved him once. He had to convince her to love him again.

He drafted a presentation to her, similar to a closing argument he would present to a jury at the conclusion of a trial. In his closing, he argued that the burden of years of prosecutions had broken him down and distorted his judgment, but he admitted these were merely mitigating circumstances. They didn't excuse his behavior. He'd betrayed the public's trust and destroyed her faith in him. He was abusive, cruel, and selfish. He agreed he deserved to be punished, but the thrust of his argument was that his punishment did not fit his crime. He conceded that losing his position as commonwealth's attorney, the respect of his peers and the citizenry, and his reputation and good name was fair and just, but he argued that losing Christine was too harsh a penalty.

He argued that he had rested and healed and regained his moral sensibilities during his penance of dark days in Hayesboro, and he contended that he was once again the man he had been before he betrayed Christine's trust. He begged her to grant him a probationary reconciliation, with full reconciliation to be based upon his good behavior. He would submit to any conditions she desired. He would live in a separate bedroom in their home or in the tack room in the barn. He would agree not to approach her unless invited. She could reacquaint herself with him at her own pace and according to her own standards. She could decide at her sole discretion whether she could trust him again.

Nate became obsessed with his closing. He worked on nothing else for weeks. He revised it, polished it, and rehearsed it. One rainy night in October, he thought he was ready to make his case to Christine, but he was afraid. His life was on the line. He drank a bottle of whiskey to calm his nerves, but his hands still shook. Halfway through a second bottle he got in his car. The rain came down in sheets and lightning flashed like bursts of artillery along the road through Whippoorwill Hollow. Nate's fear overwhelmed him again when he reached the farm, so he parked beside the road just short of the driveway and finished off the rest of the whiskey.

His memory of what transpired after that was blurred. He remembered Christine meeting him at the door and trying to lock him out, but he shoved his way in. He recalled that she tried to call the sheriff's office and he snatched the phone out of her hands. The exact sequence of events immediately after that was jumbled and confused. He recalled his great frustration that she wouldn't listen to his closing and that she kept trying to get away. He remembered grabbing her and trying to hold her in place while she kicked and screamed at him. A lamp fell to the floor and a chair tumbled over.

She slapped him and raked her nails down his face, and rage rose up inside him. In his mind's eye, he saw himself hit her.

Shaken, he let her go and stepped back and stared at her fearfully. He hadn't hit her, but he had come close. He loved her more than life itself, but he had come to the very edge of striking her. In that moment, he realized he was lost. The impenetrable shields of denial erected by his alcoholism fell away, and he knew he was not the man he claimed to be in his closing. He had not reformed. He was still a drunk, a liar, and a felon. And he had been on the verge of hitting Christine to bend her to his will, to get what he wanted.

She must have seen in his eyes what he was thinking, because she backed away from him and ran to the door. She opened it and turned back to him. "I hate you!" she said. "I hate you!" And she ran outside.

He staggered out to the porch. In a flash of lightning he saw Christine running down the hill to the barn. His mental faculties receded into an alcoholic fog after that. Only a few disjointed segments of the remainder of the night survived. He recalled wrestling with the steering wheel as his car crashed through a fence and skated down a steep slope. He saw the massive trunk of a fallen tree across the path of the car, but high enough that he thought he might pass under it unharmed. He remembered being alone on his back in a field of grass in pouring rain and seeing red and blue lights flashing above him.

When he regained his senses, he was in bed on his back. A soft light emanated from a bowl-shaped fixture above him. Bandages swathed his head and face and smelled of disinfectant. Tubes ran from his nose and arms to machines standing sentry beside him. To the left of the bed, Judge Blackwell sat slumped in a chair, his head lolling to one side.

Nate swallowed to moisten his powder-dry throat. "Harry," he said. He saw Judge Blackwell's eyes open and saw him sit up straight. "Christine," Nate said. "I want to see Christine. I need to tell her I'm sorry." His throat closed over and he wept.

He saw tears in the judge's eyes, too. "Thank God, son," he said. "I was afraid we'd lost you."

Sitting at his desk in his office ten months later, Nate traced the path of his scar with his fingertips and took a deep breath. That was the worst night of Nate's life. It was the night that extinguished any realistic hope of regaining Christine's love. He knew Howard was right. Prolonging the divorce proceedings served no purpose. He'd known it that awful night when she said she hated him, but he had not been able to force himself to give her up. He would never voluntarily consent to the entry of a divorce decree. He would stall and hope for a miracle. He would fight for her until the law said he could fight no longer.

Chapter 5

Swiller's Cases

Nate's recuperation from the accident was slow and painful. The trunk of the fallen tree Nate had seen as he sped down the slope had peeled off the top of the car and struck Nate at his hairline, scalping him and splitting open one side of his face. The surgeon found Nate's scalp folded up at the back of his head. He'd slid it forward to its proper place and sewed Nate's face back together. The wound healed badly. Tissue on both sides of a crimson gash melded back together unevenly to form a jagged scar that sliced across his forehead just below the hairline and plunged down the side of his face.

Nate thought the events of that night would inflict an indelible scar on his legal career as well. He expected to be prosecuted for assault and trespass for breaking into the house, forcing himself on Christine, grabbing her, and pushing her, and he assumed the Virginia State Bar's Disciplinary Committee would initiate proceedings to disbar him for those felonies, but Judge Blackwell stepped in again. He persuaded Christine that Nate was so drunk he didn't know what he was doing. She agreed not to press charges in exchange for Nate's stipulation to a restraining order. He was forbidden from contacting her outside of meetings required by the divorce proceedings, and the judge again convinced the county sheriff and the commonwealth's attorney not to file criminal charges. As a result, no one reported the assault and trespass to the disciplinary committee, and there were no disbarment proceedings.

The judge's favors came with a price: "From this day forward, you will not drink alcohol. You will meet with me weekly. In each meeting you will affirm that you have remained sober." Nate did not resist the judge's demands. There was no argument to be made. The evidence of his alcoholism was incontrovertible. Days after the accident, he had pulled the tubes out of his arms and staggered down the hospital hallway in search of whiskey. The orderlies tied him down. For days he fought against the restraints, begged the doctors for whiskey, and cursed them for not giving it to him. Nate's body purged the poison from his system during his stay in the hospital, but his craving for alcohol did not abate. Months after his accident, it was all he could think about.

In one of his weekly meetings with Judge Blackwell, Nate said, "The craving is relentless. It gives me no peace."

"Turn to your work to occupy your mind. Immerse yourself in your caseload."

"I don't have a caseload. No one will hire a disgraced ex-prosecutor."

"You have the court appointments I gave you."

"A handful of small cases requiring no skill. I sleepwalk through them."

"What about that death penalty appeal the chief justice called me about? Did you take that case?"

"I took it."

"Pour your energy into that case."

"I hate the case."

"Why?"

"I have the wrong side of it."

"You're a lawyer, Nathan, not a judge. Give the defendant your best effort and leave it to the court to decide the case."

Nate was trying to follow the judge's advice, but his instincts were those of a prosecutor. Those instincts told him Deatherage was a sadistic rapist and murderer. The morning Howard came to Nate's office and spoke to him about his divorce, Nate had been trying to concentrate on the Deatherage case despite his revulsion for his client. After Howard left, thoughts of Christine and the mess Nate had made of both their lives crowded everything else out of his mind. A long time passed before he was able to force himself to return his attention to his work.

Nate picked up the envelope Howard had tossed on his desk when he brought Nate the mail and opened it. It contained a legal file and an enclosure letter from Carol Ergenbright of Bloxton. Her letter said the Buck County Circuit Court had appointed her the executrix of Randolph Swiller's estate and that Swiller's Deatherage case file was enclosed.

Nate looked through a thin folder. There were copies of a few pleadings from the court file and three pages of notepaper. The first page contained a crude sketch of a judge sitting on the bench and a black man in a witness chair. The second page contained the words "Reasonable Doubt" written in ink in script so large that it filled the entire page. There were elaborate swirls and curlicues adorning the characters of the two words. They had been traced over many times. The only writing on the third page was "Eva Deatherage" and a phone number.

Nate called Carol Ergenbright. "I received your packet. These papers aren't of much use to me. I need the case file."

"You have it."

"That's impossible. There's nothing in this file. This is a capital case. The real case file must be voluminous."

"I'm sorry, Mister Abbitt. I sent you every scrap of paper I could find."

"There must be more work product somewhere. Are you sure you've found all Swiller's files?"

"I've tried my best, but I'm not certain. No one knows where Mister Swiller kept his files. I didn't know him and I can't find anyone who knows anything about his business. No one in town seems to have known him well."

"How did you become the administrator of his estate?"

"He died in testate. The court couldn't locate any of his relatives.

Judge Herring asked me to administer Mister Swiller's estate in order to close his legal business and transfer his cases to other lawyers. If I'd known how difficult that task would be, I would have refused the assignment. I've tried my best to satisfy the needs of Mister Swiller's clients, but I can't find complete files. I scoured his office and his apartment, but I found almost nothing. I don't know what else to do."

"Did you speak with his secretary?"

"Mister Swiller practiced law alone with no staff. He used an off-site service to answer his phone. The people there didn't know anything about him. He rented an office in a building near the freight yard where there are no other law offices. None of the lawyers in town socialized with him. He lived in a boarding house near the coal mine. The other boarders didn't know him. He seems to have had no friends in town. No one has been able to give me any information about him."

"There should be notes of his witness interviews, information about Deatherage's background, research of case law about the death penalty. This file you sent me contains nothing but doodles."

"I understand your concern, Mister Abbitt. I've explained the situation over and over again to the other lawyers and they're just as upset as you are, but I've done my best and I don't know what else to do."

"What other lawyers?"

"The lawyers the court appointed to replace Mister Swiller on his death penalty cases, Mister Campbell from Appomattox and Mister Garth here in town. Mister Driscoll from Waynesboro. They've all said the same thing. There must be more files, but I can't find them."

"You mean Swiller represented other capital defendants?"

"Three others."

Nate stared at the tracings. "Were all Swiller's capital cases tried in Bloxton?"

"Yes, sir. In the Buck County Circuit Court before Judge Herring."

"What's the status of the other cases?"

"They're in various stages of the death penalty appeal process."

"Were all Swiller's capital defendants sentenced to death?"

"Yes, sir. They're all on death row."

Nate was troubled. Swiller had offered no defense in the Deatherage case. He appeared to be grossly incompetent, but he had tried three other capital cases.

"Mister Abbitt? Are you there?"

"Yes, I'm sorry. Mrs. Ergenbright, when were the other capital cases tried?"

"Well, let me look at my notes. Let's see. The first one was Otis Banks. He shot the men at the gas station. I believe that was about three years ago. Yes. It says here the Banks case was tried on November 8, 1965. Carl Gibson killed his wife about that same time, but his trial was later on, I think. That's right. It was February 16, 1966. Then they tried James Washington for killing Mister Hitt in the spring of 1967, I believe. Here it is. April 13, 1967. Then your case, Kenneth Deatherage. That one was tried last winter."

"Have any other death penalty cases been tried in Buck County since 1965?"

"I don't think so. I don't remember hearing about any other murder trials."

Nate fell silent.

"Is there anything else I can help you with, Mister Abbitt?"

"No, ma'am. Not at the moment."

Nate hung up the phone. Buck County was a sparsely populated rural county. There were four capital cases tried there in three years. Swiller represented all four defendants. They were all convicted and sentenced to death. Nate wondered what sort of defense, if any, Swiller had provided the other defendants.

Chapter 6

The Black Gold Motel

Appellate counsel often accepts the facts presented at trial and concentrates on legal issues, but the Deatherage case required a different approach. Swiller had done nothing to develop the facts of the case. To prepare the strongest possible appeal, Nate felt he should investigate the facts anew, as if he were preparing the case for trial. After lunch that same day, he called the office of the Buck County commonwealth's attorney, George Maupin, spoke with George's secretary, and scheduled a meeting with him for the next morning. Nate then found Swiller's note about Eva Deatherage and dialed her number.

"Hello."

"Mrs. Deatherage?"

"That's my name. What do you want?" Her voice was gruff and sounded older than he expected.

"I'm Nate Abbitt. I'm a lawyer. I represent your husband."

"My husband left me near-on to thirty years ago."

Nate hesitated. "I represent Kenneth Deatherage."

"Kenny's my son."

"I'm sorry, ma'am. I misunderstood."

"What do you want?"

"Your son's lawyer died of a heart attack. I've taken his place. I'll be in Buck County tomorrow. I'd like to meet with you and your son's wife and any other family members you think could be helpful to me."

"What for?"

"Well, to be frank, ma'am, your son's first lawyer didn't leave me much to work with. He didn't present any information to the jury about your son's background. I want to talk with you about what type of young man he was before this tragedy occurred."

"You get with Kenny yet?"

"Yes, ma'am. I met with him twice."

"Then you know what kind he is. You don't need no help from me, and you won't get none. You won't get no help from his wife neither. You're diggin a dry well."

"Yes, ma'am. Well, I'd appreciate the chance to talk to you about him."

"No use in talkin about him. I told Judge Herring he killed that girl. There's nothin more I can do."

"You talked to Judge Herring about your son?"

"Yes, sir. I told him there's no doubt Kenny killed that poor girl."

"How do you know he killed her?"

"Oh, I didn't see it or anything like that, but I know he killed her. It's in his nature to cause pain to every livin soul around him. I'm sorry for what happened to that girl, but it ain't my fault. There was nothin I could do about the way Kenny turned out. He was a bad seed from birth, and it's a mighty sore point with me. I won't talk about Kenny to you or no one else, and that's my last word." Eva Deatherage hung up the phone.

Mrs. Deatherage's comments about talking with Judge Herring puzzled Nate even more than her callousness toward her son. Nate's review of the record revealed that she didn't testify at any of the hearings or at the trial. If she spoke to Judge Herring, the trial judge, their conversation was outside the court proceedings. Nate had once disqualified a trial judge for conversing with a witness off the record outside the presence of counsel. The rule against *ex parte* conversations applied to Judge Herring's contact with Eva Deatherage and should have caused the judge to recuse himself from the trial. Nate was beginning to think Deatherage's claims of bias were not totally frivolous.

As Nate drove out of Jeetersburg late that afternoon and headed the hundred and thirty miles west to Bloxton, a thunderstorm swept through the region and the temperature fell into the fifties. A steady rain followed the storm and made the mountain road dark, slick, and treacherous.

Buck County lay along the Virginia-West Virginia border, and Bloxton, its county seat, was a small town at the base of Skink Mountain. When geologists discovered a massive vein of coal there in the 1850s, Callao Coal Company bought all the property on the mountain, and Norfolk and Western Railway ran a rail line from Bluefield, Virginia, to the mines, linking them to Roanoke and points east all the way to Norfolk. The town of Bloxton had grown up around the freight depot.

The coal vein was a major supplier of fuel to the nation and to Europe for many years until production petered out in the 1930s and Callao Coal Company shut down its mines, laid off all the miners, and pulled out of Bloxton. In 1968, Buck County was sparsely populated. There were few jobs. Its people were dirt poor, and the county suffered from one of the highest *per capita* crime rates in the state.

The conditions required Nate to drive slowly and he didn't reach Bloxton until ten that night. It was still drizzling when he turned off the state highway to the town's main thoroughfare, Ewell Street. George's secretary had told Nate the only place in Bloxton that rented rooms to travelers was the Black Gold Motel. The windshield wipers pumped back and forth, whining and thumping as Nate peered through the fogged-up windshield searching for the motel.

Ewell Street dead-ended at the foot of Skink Mountain at the mouth of an abandoned coal mine. The old freight yard stretched out along one side of the street and a five-story dilapidated gray building stood on the other side. In front of the building sat a motel and a signpost with neon tubes that flashed "Bla k Gold otel."

Nate pulled into a gravel parking lot. A sign over a door in the middle of a line of rooms said "Office" and a placard in its window said "Check In." He got out of his car, approached the office, and opened its screen door. Its top hinge was detached and the door scraped against the stoop. He pushed the main door open, stepped inside, found a light switch on the wall, and flicked it. An overhead light cast a gray pallor over a sparsely furnished room. A chair with cracked leather upholstery sat beside the door. A plywood counter stood on the other side of the room. A dust-covered rolltop desk rested behind the counter. There was no one in the office. Nate looked out the window. There was no one in sight. There were no cars parked in the lot, and all the motel rooms were dark. There was an Esso station across Ewell Street. The station was closed, but a light shone in a second-floor window above it. Otherwise, the street was dark.

Nate waited, but no one came. Time passed. He didn't know what to do. He noticed a row of boxes containing room keys in the mouth of the rolltop desk. He rounded the counter to look at the keys and stepped on some papers strewn on the floor. He picked up the papers. They were carbon copies of receipts for renting rooms, dated weeks earlier. "Paid $10. April 18, 1968. Lawrence Driscoll." Nate knew Driscoll. He was a defense lawyer from Waynesboro. Carol Ergenbright had mentioned that Driscoll took one of Swiller's death penalty appeals. Nate glanced at the other receipts.

The screen door scraped against the front stoop, the door opened, and a short, squatty old man wearing bib overalls and a red ball cap stepped inside. "What the hell are you doin?"

Nate dropped the receipts onto the desk. "I didn't know what to do. No one was here."

"I came soon's I saw your car. Now get the hell outta there. You ain't supposed to go behind the counter."

Nate rounded the counter.

The stumpy old man limped to the desk behind the counter, grabbed a big black book, and plopped it on the countertop. "Ten dollars a night for number three. It's the one's got the clean sheets. Five dollars for the other ones. There's a coin laundry two blocks up Ewell Street if you want to wash the sheets yourself." The man placed his stubby forearms on the counter and looked at him. The man flinched. He gawked at Nate's scar until he noticed Nate staring back at him. He looked down at the registration book and then at the window. When he turned back to Nate, his eyes darted back and forth from his scar to his eyes. "So what'll it be, lawyer? Number three or one of the other ones?"

"How do you know I'm a lawyer?"

"Ain't you Abbitt? The one who wants em to turn Kenny Deatherage loose?"

"How do you know who I am?"

The old man smiled. Two bottom front teeth were missing and the old man's tongue rolled into the blank space. "George Maupin's secretary, Miss Lucy, told me you was comin. Said you'd need a room, so I told Gladys to put the clean sheets in number three."

"I see. I'll take number three then."

The old man handed him the key, and Nate signed the book.

"Name's W. D. Drinkard. Live across the street above the gas station. You need somethin when I ain't here, go to the station and tell one of the boys who runs it. Them boys can always find me."

Nate gave Drinkard a ten-dollar bill. Drinkard retrieved a booklet from the desk and scrawled a receipt. He tore the original receipt and a carbon copy from the booklet, handed the original to Nate, and tossed the copy on the desk.

Nate looked out the window. The rain had slackened to a mist. A tall gray building loomed in the dark beside the motel.

"You're lookin at the place where he did it."

"What?"

"That's where Kenny Deatherage killed the girl. Old warehouse. Callao Coal used the top floors for offices for the big shots and the bottom floor to store equipment and supplies for the coal mine, but they moved out years ago. It's a stinkin old rattrap today. Walls buckled down. Roof leaks."

Nate squinted into the darkness. "What's that little building next to it?"

"Used to be the mine superintendent's house. Willis Odoms lives in it now. Big old colored boy. Strong as a bull. Willis caught Kenny Deatherage in the dirt road behind this here motel, right behind number three. I saw it all from my window over the gas station. Break of dawn Darby Jones came barrelin down Ewell Street in his patrol car, lights flashin and sirens wailin. Willis had Deatherage down on his belly in the dirt. Darby jumped outta the car, fell on top a Deatherage, and slapped the cuffs on the sumbitch. Then Darby went in the warehouse and found the girl, dead as a mackerel."

"Did you know Kenneth Deatherage before he was arrested?"

"Everybody knows everybody in Bloxton."

"What do you think of him?"

"He killed the woman, if that's what you mean. No slick lawyer can get the bastard off. You're wastin your time."

"What did you think of him before he was arrested?"

"He was a good-for-nothin drunkard, but that's no crime. Lots of drunkards round these parts. I never heard about no serious trouble with Kenny."

Nate thought about Deatherage's allegation that Deputy Jones lied about finding a bloody scarf on Deatherage when Jones arrested him. "What's Deputy Jones' reputation?" Nate said.

"Good boy. His daddy's the preacher at Mount Zion Baptist Church. Made him walk the straight and narrow when he was a boy, but Darby loosened up some since then. He drinks a little, cusses some, chases the girls once in a while. Nothin bad. Nothin I didn't do when I was a young buck."

"What kind of deputy is he?"

"He's all right. Only been a lawman a couple years."

"What did he do before he became a deputy?"

"Army drafted him and sent him off to Vietnam. He was a big hero over there. Came home with a chest full a medals. He was with a bunch got ambushed. Most of em was cut to shreds, but he shot his way out. Took a bullet in his leg, but he kept fightin. When it was all over, his leg was hurt so bad they wouldn't let him fight no more. Sheriff Feedlow snapped him up soon's he got back, and he's been a deputy ever since."

"Have you heard any complaints about his conduct as a deputy?"

"No complaints about him from the decent folk. I heard tell the bad ones whine to the sheriff about him some."

"What do they say?"

"The usual malarkey. Slaps em around, kicks em when they're cuffed, smacks em when they smart-mouth. Nothin worth listenin to."

A preacher's son and a war hero, Nate thought. Jones didn't fit the profile of a corrupt policeman. On the other hand, Nate didn't fit the profile of a corrupt prosecutor either.

Nate wondered what Drinkard might know about the victim. "Did you know Darlene Updike?"

"Never met the young lady." Drinkard smiled. His tongue fell into the gap in his teeth.

"I thought everybody knew everybody in Bloxton."

"She wasn't from Bloxton." Drinkard chuckled.

Nate wondered what he thought was humorous. He stared at the registration book on the counter. The motel was the only place to stay in Bloxton and Darlene Updike was from New York. He stepped over to the counter and turned back a page in the registration book. He pointed to an entry. "Darlene Updike signed your book."

Drinkard closed the book and tossed it on the desk behind him out of

Nate's reach. "I don't remember nothin about her." He laughed.

"You don't seem to do much business here at the Black Gold Motel."

"People don't come to Bloxton much these days. We was busy when Callao Coal ran the mine, but they shut her down a long time ago. Now that the coal's all gone, people don't have cause to come here no more."

"With so few guests it seems you'd remember Miss Updike."

"Gettin old, lawyer. Forgot more'n I ever knew." Drinkard laughed again.

"Mind if I take another look at your registration book?"

"Can't do it, lawyer." Drinkard rolled the top of the desk down to cover the book and the receipts. He locked the rolltop and put the key in his pocket. "People stay at the Black Gold don't want no lawyers messin in their business. You got to get out now. I got to lock her up and go to bed."

Nate went outside. A light mist still fell. Drinkard pulled the door shut, locked it, and headed to the gas station.

"She stayed here the night she was murdered, didn't she?" Nate said.

Drinkard stopped and looked at Nate. He laughed. "Told you, lawyer. Forgot more'n I ever knew." He squinted at the sky, hustled across Ewell Street, and disappeared from sight behind the gas station.

Nate went to number three. The room was small and bare. The bed smelled of mildew. A naked light bulb hung from the center of the ceiling. No carpet. No wall hangings. The bathroom was a sink with a leaking faucet, a urine-stained toilet, and a shower stall barely large enough to accommodate a man standing sideways.

Once Nate settled in, he pulled the curtain back from the window. Dust billowed from its folds. He looked up and down Ewell Street. The light was still on in the room above the gas station. Otherwise Ewell Street was dark. He gazed at the abandoned warehouse and thought about Deatherage's claim that he found Updike's corpse on top of mattresses. Nate turned up his collar against the drizzle and went outside. He retrieved a flashlight from his car, walked across the gravel lot to the warehouse, and stood in a dirt road in front of the building. The warehouse was five stories tall.

Its walls were streaked with black stains and most of its windows were broken. He pointed his light at a row of windows on the ground floor. Odoms said he saw Deatherage peering out of one of those windows. Nate walked to a window, flashed his light inside, and moved the light along the floor under the windows. He saw no mattresses. Of course, a year had passed since the murder. Someone could have disposed of the mattresses, if they ever existed.

A loud clank sounded to Nate's left. He flashed the light that way. The front door, a metal door, had swung open and closed in the wind. He walked to the door, stepped inside, and flashed his light around. The first floor was one big room, high ceiling, no partitions, cinderblock walls, and concrete floor. Water dripped from cracks in the ceiling and pooled in puddles on the floor. Concrete steps began their climb in a corner of the room and hugged the front wall up to the second floor. The row of windows was beneath the stairwell. Deatherage said he slept in a room on the second floor. From there he could have heard cries from someone under the stairwell. He would have come down the steps and turned to the door. He would have seen Updike's body lying under the windows, just as he told Nate.

Nate turned his light on the rear of the vast first floor and saw a dark mass in a far back corner. Something moved there. "I told you to leave me be. I didn't see nothin." The voice was hoarse. The words were slurred. Nate focused his light on the corner and saw a man on top of a pile of mattresses. Nate walked toward the man. The sound of his steps echoed off the walls, giving him the impression someone was walking along behind him. He stopped and flashed the light behind him. He saw no one.

"Go away. Leave me be."

Nate turned back to the man and saw him prop himself up on his elbow. Nate walked closer. The man's face was bearded and covered with grime. His hair was long and matted. He reeked of body odor and whiskey. "Leave me be. I did what you said. I didn't tell nobody. You got no call to roust me out again." His voice rattled with phlegm. He held up his hand to block Nate's light and squinted at him between filthy, scabrous fingers. The man looked surprised. "Who the hell are you?" His gaze shifted to a spot above Nate's shoulder and his eyes widened.

Chapter 7

The Big Boss

Nate's thoughts were sluggish, his mind numb. He was lying on his belly. He rolled over on his back and groaned. He sat up and held his head in his hands. Pain pounded his skull above his ear. He rubbed the spot. It was tender. He crawled to his hands and knees. When the floor stopped whirling, he picked up his flashlight, rose to a crouch, and flashed the light around the warehouse. No one was there. He struggled to his feet and leaned against a wall. He pointed the light at the corner. The bearded man and the mattresses were gone.

Nate walked unsteadily across the warehouse floor and out the front door. He pointed his light down the dirt road. There was no one in sight. He touched the tender spot above his ear. It was swollen and oozing blood. He pressed a handkerchief to it and looked at his watch. It was just after eleven. He guessed he entered the warehouse about ten thirty, so he'd been out for twenty to thirty minutes. He searched his pockets. He still had his wallet and cash. His mugger was not a thief.

Someone must have seen him leave his motel room and enter the warehouse. He looked at the dark motel rooms. His car was the only one in the lot. Willis Odoms' house was dark and quiet. All of Ewell Street was dark except for the light in the room above the gas station. That window overlooked the motel and the entry to the warehouse. Either Drinkard was Nate's assailant or he saw who followed Nate from that window.

Drinkard was a liar. Nate thought about how he'd smiled with his tongue rolling in the gap in his teeth, and his temper flared.

In happier times Nate had been a patient man, careful, cautious. He'd had something to protect – his precious privileged life. Those times were gone. He jogged to the motel's office, jerked open the screen door, and threw his shoulder against the main door. It gave way. Nate shoved his way inside and walked over to the desk. He found scissors in the middle drawer, wedged the scissor blade under the rolltop, and busted its lock.

Nate found copies of seven receipts made out to Darlene Updike, all dated April and May, 1967, except the last one. It was dated June 2, 1967, the night before the morning of the murder. He leafed through the registration book. All seven entries in the book matched the dates of the receipts. He put the receipts in his pocket and walked out of the check-in shack, across the street, and around the gas station. He flashed his light inside the window of a back door. Stairs led to a second-floor room. Nate tried the door. It was locked. He raised his fist to pound on it, but he stopped. If he confronted Drinkard at that moment, he would thrash him. Beating the old man would accomplish nothing.

Nate stepped back from the door and waited for the surge of adrenaline to pass. When he regained control, he analyzed the events of the night more logically. Drinkard was too old to have attacked Nate, but he probably knew who did it. He knew a lot more about Updike than he wanted to reveal, too. He wasn't smart or sophisticated, and he probably didn't know much about the law. It shouldn't be difficult to intimidate him and force him to tell Nate what he knew.

Nate rapped on the door. "Drinkard! Open up!" A door opened at the top of the steps, a wedge of light fell across the stairway, and Drinkard limped down the stairs. He tripped the lock and opened the door.

"What you doing up so late, lawyer?"

Nate withdrew the receipts from his pocket and held them up for Drinkard to see. "You lied to me. Darlene Updike stayed in the motel seven nights, including the night before she was murdered."

Drinkard stared at the documents and said nothing.

"You're in a lot of trouble, Mister Drinkard." Nate pushed past Drinkard and climbed the stairs. Drinkard followed him. Nate stepped into a small room with worn, scuffed hardwood floors and faded wallpaper. A single bed rested on the back wall. Stacks of old newspapers and magazines lined the other walls. A desk and a chair sat in front of a window. A phone sat on the desk.

Drinkard crossed the room and stood in front of the bed. "What do you mean I'm in trouble?" he said.

"You've broken the law. You've committed serious felonies."

"I didn't break no laws."

"Did you tell the sheriff's office about the nights Darlene Updike stayed in the motel? Did you show the sheriff the receipts and the registration book entries?"

Drinkard started to answer but stopped short. He swallowed hard.

Nate said, "Withholding information material to a homicide investigation constitutes obstruction of justice."

"I didn't withhold nothin. No one asked me about the girl."

"That doesn't matter. You knew she stayed here seven nights and you didn't come forward. Failure to volunteer material information is the same as withholding it. Obstruction of justice is a felony. It carries a minimum five-year jail term."

"I didn't mean to do nothin wrong. I didn't know I was breakin the law."

"Ignorance of the law is no defense."

Drinkard sat on the bed, took off his ball cap, and ran his hand through his hair.

Nate said, "I've scheduled a meeting with George Maupin in the morning about the Deatherage case. Unless you and I work something out, I'll have no choice but to tell him you withheld evidence."

Drinkard looked at Nate hopefully. "What do you mean by work somethin out?"

Nate paused for a long time, making Drinkard sweat. "You have information, Mister Drinkard. If you tell me what you know, I'll consider giving you a pass on obstruction of justice."

"What kind of information?"

"You were sitting at this desk, waiting for me, when I arrived tonight. It took you more than ten minutes to cross the street and check me in. You spent that time calling someone on the phone and telling him I was here. Who did you call?"

"I didn't call nobody. I came soon as I saw you."

"You're lying."

"I didn't call no one. Swear to God."

Nate shrugged. "It's your neck." He headed toward the door.

"Wait," Drinkard said. "You don't understand. Talkin to you could buy me more trouble than five years in jail. If I agree to talk to you, I don't want people to know. I want you to promise to keep my name out of it."

"I can't promise you secrecy. Developments in the case may force me to reveal you as a source of information. I'll try to keep our conversation confidential, but I can't guarantee it."

"That's not good enough."

"If I tell George what you've done, there's no doubt you'll be locked away for at least five years. You're not a young man, Mister Drinkard. You'll be in jail for the better part of the time you have left, but if you tell me what you know, there's a reasonable chance I won't have to reveal our conversation to anyone and you won't suffer any adverse consequences. Seems like a clear choice to me."

Drinkard stroked his jaw.

Nate waited a long time, but Drinkard didn't volunteer anything. Nate said, "Who did you call when I arrived here?"

Drinkard looked askance at Nate. "Judge Herring," he said in a small voice.

Nate was surprised. He had appeared in court before the judge. The judge was not in the best of health and walked with a limp. He wasn't physically capable of attacking Nate, but he could have told someone to do it. "Why did you call the judge?"

"He told me to call him when you got here."

"Why did he want to know when I arrived?"

"How the hell do I know? I don't ask him no questions. He's the big boss. He owns the motel. The gas station, too. He says do somethin, I do it."

"What did the judge say when you told him I was here?"

"Said thanks for tellin him. That was it. Swear to God."

"Someone followed me into the warehouse. You were watching from this window. Who followed me?"

"I didn't see. I went to bed after you checked in."

"Your light was on when I left my room, and it was on when I came out of the warehouse. Your bed's still made. You're still dressed."

"I laid down on top of the covers to read the papers. Sleep don't come easy when you're old. You'll see when you're old as me. I turned on the light to read the papers. I didn't watch the motel."

Nate saw newspapers strewn on the floor next to Drinkard's bed. Maybe he was telling the truth. Nate wanted to be sure. He pointed to the wound over his ear. "See this? The person who followed me attacked me and knocked me out, and I'm damned good and mad about it. Tell me who followed me or I'll turn you in to George Maupin in the morning."

Drinkard scooted up on the edge of the bed. "I don't know who hit you. If I knew, I'd tell you. I don't want to go to jail."

Nate searched Drinkard's face. He seemed to be telling the truth. "All right. Tell me about the night before Darlene Updike was killed. What time did she check in?"

Drinkard hesitated and then said, "Supper time. About six."

"Did you know she was coming to stay here that night?"

"You're messin with fire now, lawyer. You'd best back off."

"Answer me or I'll turn you in for obstruction of justice."

Drinkard closed down. He sat back on the bed, crossed his arms over his chest, and set his jaw. "I'll do the five years."

Nate was surprised. Drinkard was obviously afraid of someone. It seemed likely he was afraid of the "big boss." "Answer my questions or I'll call Judge Herring on that phone and tell him you ratted on him."

Drinkard stood. "You can't do that. You'll get me in a world of trouble. You'll be in big trouble, too. You don't know what you're up against. You call the judge and you'll stir up more trouble than you can imagine."

"I'm not afraid of the judge."

"You should be. Don't call him."

Nate picked up the phone.

"Wait."

"Did you know Updike was coming to the motel the night before she was murdered?"

Drinkard sat on the bed and heaved a sigh.

"Answer my question."

"Judge Herring told me she was comin."

Nate replaced the phone in its cradle, sat in the desk chair, and pondered Drinkard's second big surprise of the night. "How did Judge Herring know her?"

"I don't know. He didn't say. I didn't ask. It was none of my business."

"Did you call the judge when she checked in?"

"He told me to call him when she got here, and I did what he told me."

"Did you watch her room that night?"

Drinkard nodded.

"What did you see?"

"Don't make me say, lawyer. Leave it be."

"Tell me or I'll call the judge."

"You're makin a big mistake, lawyer."

Nate reached for the phone.

Drinkard held up his hands. "Don't."

Nate sat back.

After a long silence, Drinkard said, "Judge Herring came to her room."

Nate paused to consider the implications of the judge's presence in Updike's room the night before her murder. "What time did the judge arrive?"

"About nine."

"How long did he stay?"

"About an hour."

"What's the judge's reputation for faithfulness to his wife?"

"Aw, hell, lawyer, you're chasin the wrong rabbit. The judge wouldn't cheat on Betsy. They been sweethearts since high school. The judge wouldn't know how to play around if he tried."

"What was he doing in Updike's room?"

"I don't know, but he wasn't sparkin her. Other men did, but not the judge."

"Did you see other men come to her room?"

"Damn straight."

"Who?"

"Kenny Deatherage, for one."

Drinkard was full of surprises. Deatherage said he didn't know Updike, but Drinkard had no reason to lie about it. "When did Deatherage visit her room?"

"That same night, the night before she was killed."

"What time was he there?"

"Not long before the judge got there. About half past eight. Looked like Kenny meant to stay a while. He had a jug of liquor with him, but he was only in the room a couple minutes. He came out mad. Drove off in a hurry, tires squealin."

"Did he come back to her room that night?"

"Not as far as I know."

"Did you see anyone else go to her room that night?"

"No. I went to bed after the judge left her room."

"Did the judge or Deatherage visit her the other nights she stayed here?"

"No."

"Did anyone else visit her?"

"She came here drunk most nights. Different men stayed with her each time."

"Who were they?"

"Married men who didn't want people to know they were with her."

"Tell me their names."

"I don't want to get them in trouble."

"Tell me their names."

Drinkard sighed. "Frank Gentry, Larry Lamb, Herman Doyle. They could barely walk when they snuck in her room, drunk as skunks, just like her."

"Did you tell the sheriff any of this?"

"Those men didn't want their funny business spread around. Besides, what they did with the girl was none of my business."

"Did you tell the sheriff about Deatherage's visit to Darlene's room?"

"Hell, no."

"Why not?"

"The judge came to her room right after Kenny left. I was afraid I'd get tripped up and spill the beans on the judge. The sheriff had the goods on Kenny. He didn't need me to tell him nothin." Drinkard looked at Nate fearfully. "I told you all I know. Now you got to protect me. I'm an old man, lawyer. I can't afford to lose my job. Ain't no jobs in Bloxton even for the young men. I lose this one, I won't have me no job and there ain't nobody to take care of me. Anybody finds out I told you about the judge, I'm done for."

"I'll do what I can to keep your name out of the case, but I have to defend Deatherage. If that requires me to reveal our conversation, so be it."

Drinkard grimaced. Nate headed to the door.

Drinkard said, "You get it in a knife fight?"

"What?"

"That big old scar. Maybe you pushed somebody too far. He came at you with a knife. That how you got it?"

"I was injured in a car accident."

"Well, I'll be damned. I would've bet good money somebody cut you on purpose. Somebody you treated poorly. Maybe caught you when you wasn't ready, when you was sleepin." Drinkard held Nate's eyes for a moment and looked away.

Nate went back to number three. Drinkard's thinly veiled threat worried him. He took the tire iron from the trunk of his car and carried it into the room. He locked the door, propped the back of a chair under the knob, and lay on the bed fully clothed with the tire iron in his hand at his side.

Nate guessed that his attacker knocked him out to prevent him from talking to the derelict. The bum must know something about the case. Deatherage had lied to Nate when he said he didn't know Updike, but his claims that the judge and others plotted against him appeared to be valid. Sleep didn't come to Nate that night.

Chapter 8

The Prosecutor

The next morning the wound over Nate's ear was scabbed over and the swelling was down. He decided not to see a doctor about it. He drove to the town square to meet with George Maupin. Nate knew George well. George grew up in Bloxton, the son of a coal miner who couldn't find work after the mine was closed. After his father drank himself to death when George was six years old, his family lived on welfare benefits and handouts. George put himself through college and law school at Jefferson State on student loans and earnings from part-time jobs.

Nate and George met in law school and became fast friends. They studied together, debated on the same team as moot court advocates, and walked down Jefferson State's lawn side by side to receive their diplomas. They sat for the bar together and celebrated when they were admitted. They went into private practice about the same time, and George was elected commonwealth's attorney shortly after Nate was.

A year after his election, George married Gracie Sandridge. The next summer when the couples vacationed together at Virginia Beach it was obvious that Gracie and Christine weren't a good match. There was no animosity between them, they simply had nothing in common. Gracie was a farm girl who hadn't gone to college. Christine had earned a doctorate. Christine's passions were medieval literature and horseback riding; Gracie liked quilting bees and canning. Social interaction between Nate and George fell away as a result, but they'd stayed in touch on a professional level and maintained their friendship through three decades.

Defense counsel would not normally seek the assistance of a prosecutor in preparing a case for appeal, but Nate felt he could approach George. He only wanted to sound out George about Swiller, Judge Herring, and a few procedural issues.

The county offices were on the edge of the Bloxton town square in an old building with oak floors and cream-colored plaster walls. George met Nate at his office door on the second floor. George, a tall, bald, heavyset bear of a man, hugged Nate, held him at arm's length, and stared at his scar. "They told me you busted your head in a car wreck, but I had no idea it was so serious." He squinted. "What's that knot over your ear? That looks like a fresh wound."

"Someone knocked me out last night in the warehouse by the motel."

George looked surprised and concerned. "You have a doctor take a look at it?"

"It's not serious. I feel fine this morning."

"Did you report the assault to the sheriff?"

"No."

"Damn it, Nate, you know better than that. The longer you wait the less chance you have of recovering what they stole."

"Whoever hit me didn't steal anything."

George shook his head. "There are some damned bad people in this county. I guess one of them hit you for the pure pleasure of it. You should report it to the sheriff."

George led Nate into his office. An antique desk, a captain's chair, and two barrel chairs sat in front of a wall adorned with paintings of Patrick Henry, Thomas Jefferson, and Robert E. Lee. Bookcases with leatherbound volumes of Virginia statutes and case law lined a side wall, and a cabinet displaying a silver tray and crystal glasses stood on the opposite wall. A conference table sat in front of a floor-to-ceiling window that overlooked the town square. The sweet scents of pipe tobacco and bourbon lingered in the air. George led Nate to the table and they sat down across from one another. Nate gazed out the window. The rain had stopped and the sky had cleared. Across the square the Buck County courthouse gleamed in the sun.

"What were you doing in the warehouse in the middle of the night?" George said.

"I wanted to see the crime scene."

"All sorts of drunks and vagrants crawl into that dark hole at night. You shouldn't have gone there by yourself. What did you think you'd find? We gathered all the evidence about the Deatherage case a year ago. It's in the court file."

"I wanted to see the scene of the murder, but it was a mistake to go there alone at night. I guess I'm still feeling my way along as a defense counsel."

"How did you get saddled with the Deatherage case in the first place?"

"I volunteered for court appointments to capital punishment cases. The chief justice called Judge Blackwell about the Deatherage case. Harry recommended me."

"Old Harry Blackwell didn't do you any favors. Deatherage is a stone-cold murderer, and if the communists on the Supreme Court keep their noses out of our business, he'll pay for it with his life."

"I guess it's my job to keep that from happening."

"It's my job to make sure it does happen. You won't gain anything by talking with me. We're good friends, but I can't help you with the appeal."

"I understand, but Swiller didn't keep a file on the case. It's hard to understand a case working with nothing but the pleading clip. I hoped you'd be willing to answer some questions about uncontested matters, background information, and procedure and the like."

"Fire away."

"There's almost nothing in the record about Darlene Updike. Who was she?"

"We don't know much about her. She was a stranger in Bloxton. The sheriff's men found a New York driver's license on her body and tracked the address on it to her parents' home in Albany. I talked with her father by phone. He said she left there a couple months before she was killed, but he didn't know what she was doing in Bloxton."

"Did you investigate her background?"

George looked out the window, avoiding Nate's stare. "Randy Swiller made a motion *in limine* to exclude all evidence about Updike's personal life. Judge Herring granted the motion on the grounds that the prejudicial impact outweighed the probative value. It wasn't worth my time to flesh out her background. I couldn't use it at trial."

Nate was shocked. "There's no record of any such motion in the pleadings."

"Swiller made the motion orally in the judge's chambers. The court reporter wasn't there. Swiller sprang that motion on me after the arraignment and the judge granted it before I had a chance to say anything."

"Why didn't you object?"

"It doesn't always pay to make objections in Eddy Herring's courtroom."

"The judge granted an unnoticed motion off the record without a full briefing and you didn't object."

"I opposed Randy in a host of cases, and he never made a motion *in limine*. The judge is a stickler for procedure, but he ran roughshod over the rules on that motion. The whole thing threw me off balance. Later, when I had time to think, I decided to let it go. The case against Deatherage was open and shut. I didn't need Updike's background to convict him. I thought the judge understood the strength of my case and granted Randy's motion so Deatherage wouldn't have any basis for an appeal. It didn't seem to matter to the outcome of the case. The jury found Deatherage guilty. He was sentenced to death."

"So you didn't investigate Updike's background."

"My resources are limited and Albany is a long way off. Besides, no investigation was warranted after the judge granted Randy's motion."

Nate was puzzled by George's concession of the issue. He was an aggressive litigator. Docility was out of character for him, but Nate decided not to press the point. "Tell me about Swiller. No one in town seems to have known him."

"That doesn't surprise me. He moved here from Charlottesville a few years back. Buck County doesn't warm up to strangers easily, and Randy wasn't sociable."

"I understand Swiller represented four capital defendants in Buck County."

George was quiet. Then he said, "Swiller had five capital cases."

"Carol Ergenbright told me there were four appeals from Swiller's trials."

"Swiller represented Creighton Long. There was no appeal in that case."

"Creighton Long, the serial killer?"

Nate had heard about the Long case. Four or five years earlier, the case experienced a brief period of notoriety due to the brutality of Long's crimes. It received statewide media coverage for a few days and then dropped out of the news after Long was convicted. "Long was executed," Nate said.

"Damned straight. Creighton Long was the best argument for the death penalty I ever saw. He murdered five little boys. Tortured and sodomized them before he killed them. He worked on them with a pair of pliers, for pity's sake."

"How did Swiller get within a country mile of a high profile case like that?"

"I don't know what you mean."

"Be straight with me, George. I read the record of the Deatherage case. I saw Swiller's handiwork. Deatherage would have fared better if he represented himself."

George shrugged. "Swiller did the best he could with a hard case."

"If that was Swiller's best, he wasn't fit to handle criminal misdemeanors, much less capital cases."

"Swiller was no genius, but I've seen worse lawyers."

"Name one."

George didn't respond, and he seemed uncomfortable.

Nate decided to move on again. He knew from his review of the record that Deatherage was first charged with crimes in Buck County General District Court. District Court Judge Tobias Gwathmey was responsible for appointing Swiller to represent Deatherage and he would have been similarly responsible for appointing counsel for the other Buck County capital defendants. Nate said, "What sort of procedure does Judge Gwathmey follow to select lawyers to represent indigent defendants?"

George looked out the window. "In capital cases, Toby takes his cues from Judge Herring."

"What do you mean by that?"

"Most district court judges check with the chief judge of their circuit before they appoint a lawyer to represent a defendant in a capital case. Toby Gwathmey is no exception. Eddy Herring is the chief judge of our circuit. He told Toby to appoint Randy Swiller to those capital cases and Toby did what Eddy said."

"Why in hell would Judge Herring want Gwathmey to appoint a lawyer as bad as Swiller to represent all the capital defendants in Buck County?"

"There are no rich clients in Buck County to pay the big fees that attract the cream of the crop. There are only a few lawyers in Bloxton, and none of them would give F. Lee Bailey a run for his money. I'll grant you, it's curious that Randy was appointed to all the capital cases in the county, but the judge didn't have much to choose from."

Nate could see that George was growing more uncomfortable with each question he asked. He worried that George might shut down if he didn't shift to a less contentious subject. "What's Judge Herring like?" he asked.

"He's like every judge. He puts the black robe on in the morning and he thinks he's God until he takes it off at supper time."

"Is he as smart as I've heard?"

"He finished law school at the top of his class. He practiced law in Richmond and made a fortune speculating in real estate. He got elected as a judge in this circuit twenty years ago, and he became the circuit's chief judge in 1960. He owns half of Buck County. He's nobody's fool."

"People wonder why Judge Herring came here to take the bench," Nate said. "They say he could have been elected to a circuit judgeship in Henrico County. I don't mean to be rude, George, but we both know the Henrico County judgeship is a lot more influential than the Buck County seat."

"Eddy grew up in Bloxton, like I did. People here respect a local boy who makes good. Respect means a lot to Eddy. He's the biggest fish in this small pond. He's decided every significant criminal and civil matter here for twenty years, and he's touched the lives of everybody in the county. Nobody makes a move without his say-so. Eddy calls the shots in this county, and he likes it that way."

"Does he call the shots for you?"

"I'm the commonwealth's attorney. I've got some clout, but Eddy's the only circuit court judge in the county. He could make my life miserable if he wanted to."

"I understand."

"I hope you do, Nate. It would be a mistake to accuse Judge Herring of wrongdoing unless you have solid proof, and you don't. Even if Eddy convinced Judge Gwathmey to appoint Swiller to represent all the murdering bastards in the county in an effort to grease the skids on their pathway to hell, that's not illegal. It's not even grounds for appeal. There are no bullets in your gun, Nate, so don't point it at Eddy. He's the king of Buck County, and you know what they say. Don't take aim at the king unless you're certain you'll kill him."

Nate considered this. He had watched George confront and defeat every economic hardship in his difficult life. Until that moment Nate had considered George to be fearless, but it was clear he was afraid of Judge Herring.

"Thanks for the advice," Nate said. "I'll be careful."

George's bloodshot eyes looked bone-tired. "How about a drink?"

Nate struggled with the question. "No thanks. I'm on the wagon."

"Well, I need one." George lumbered across the room to the cabinet. "The sight of a good man like you defending a son of a bitch like Deatherage jangles my nerves." George carried a bottle of bourbon and two glasses back to the table and sat down. He poured himself a drink and held the bottle out to Nate. "Sure you don't want a taste?"

Nate looked away from the bottle. "No thanks."

George took a sip of whiskey and blew out a long breath. "I never got the straight scoop, Nate. Why did you resign?"

Nate didn't answer.

"Come on, Nate. You spent your whole career putting bad people where they belong. You never hinted to me you might hang up your spurs. I had to read about your resignation in the newspaper. I haven't heard a word from you in more than a year. Now you waltz in here and grill me about the Deatherage case. You owe an old friend an explanation. Why did you resign?"

"I set up an innocent man."

"The gossips told me that much, but nobody seems to know the details. Exactly what did you do to the man?"

George was one of the few people Nate trusted with ugly truths. "A man was killed in Selk County. Sheriff Grundy arrested a man who worked with the victim." Nate hesitated and looked at the whiskey bottle. "I was confident he was the murderer. I wrote out a confession. The man had limited mental ability. I convinced him to sign it with his mark before the district court appointed counsel for him. The judge eventually appointed a kid fresh out of law school as defense counsel. I sprang the confession on him and used it to bully him into agreeing to a guilty plea to a lesser offense. Judge Blackwell knew the defendant's lawyer hadn't protected him, and he refused to accept the plea."

"Old Harry has always been quick to make allowances for a weak lawyer."

"Harry was right. Later on, the sheriff found the real killer. The defendant was innocent."

"You made a mistake. You pushed too hard to get a conviction. That's understandable in this business. I don't see why that cost you your job."

"There was a lot more to it."

George paused. Then he said, "We go way back together, Nate. You know you can trust me."

"All right, George. Here's the truth. Because of the man's limited capacity, his confession was worthless without a witness to verify that he confessed of his own free will. I convinced my secretary to sign a statement swearing that the man volunteered the incriminating statements."

"She wasn't there when you questioned him?"

"That's right."

"She committed perjury. You suborned perjury."

Nate nodded.

George emitted a low whistle.

Nate wanted a drink in the worst way. He stared at the bottle. "That case wasn't the only time I crossed the line."

"How many cases did you mess with?"

"Five, including the Tin case."

"Does Harry Blackwell know about the other cases?"

"He asked me and I told him."

"What did he do about those?"

"Tin was released when the sheriff found the real murderer. The other cases were retried. One defendant was acquitted. Three were convicted a second time. The judge tried to keep my malfeasance quiet, but too many people knew. Most of it's common knowledge in the legal community. I'm surprised you haven't heard the rumors."

"I imagine people were reluctant to spread such dirt my way because of my friendship with you. They were right to stay away from me. I might have popped some self-righteous prick in the mouth for talking trash about you."

A tight smile crossed Nate's lips. "You're a good friend, George."

George frowned. "To tell you the truth, I'm surprised Harry didn't have you indicted. Harry's a tough old bird. How did you talk him out of jailing you?"

"I didn't talk him out of it. I don't know the reason he spared me."

"How did Harry keep the sheriff and the new commonwealth's attorney off your back?"

"He said I wouldn't be prosecuted, and he kept his word. I don't know how he did it."

"Well, needless to say, I agree with his forbearance."

"You're kind to say so, George, whether you really believe it or not."

"No. I mean it. I understand what you did. Prosecution is a heavy responsibility. It grinds you down after so many years. Frustration with the criminal justice system can drive a good man to do bad deeds. What you did was wrong, but I don't hold it against you." George turned up his glass of bourbon and drained it.

"Was someone in law enforcement in Buck County driven to do bad deeds in the Deatherage case?"

George filled his glass again. "There were some odd quirks in that case, but no bad deeds I'm aware of."

"What sort of odd quirks?"

"That motion *in limine* was odd." George ran his hand down his face and sighed.

"What else?"

George shrugged. "I've said all I care to say about the Deatherage case."

Nate had never seen George look so tired. "What about you, George? Have you yielded to frustration with the justice system?"

A wan smile crossed George's face. "Not me, Nate. I'll admit I've been tempted. The burden on the prosecution is too great. The appellate courts interpret the Constitution to ignore the rights of victims and to protect the guilty from the slightest risk of unfairness. You know what they say: Better a hundred guilty men go free than one innocent man be jailed." George made a wry face. "Tell that to the victims of the hundred guilty men. I'm frustrated, but I haven't given in to it. I stay inside the lines. I don't bend the laws." George glanced at Nate's scar. "I guess I'm afraid of the consequences." George extended the bottle to Nate. "You sure you don't want a drink?"

Nate thought about the bracing fire of straight whiskey. It took all his strength of will to turn away. "No thanks. I'd better be going."

They stood and shook hands. George said, "Be careful. If you need help, call me."

Chapter 9

The Judge

Nate walked across the town square toward his car. He stopped in front of a statue of a Confederate officer. Carved in the stone at its base was the inscription "Captain Josiah Bloxton, January 18, 1828 – July 3, 1863." The legend of Captain Bloxton was common knowledge in southwestern Virginia. He led a unit of fifty Buck County rebels up Cemetery Hill at Gettysburg as part of General Pickett's charge, and he and most of his men paid for their bravery with their lives.

Nate looked up at the towering piece of carved stone, gunmetal gray with green resting in the crevices. Billowing cotton clouds moved across the sky behind a plumed cocked hat and a stern face. The captain leaned forward, one foot raised in midstride, his arm extended over his head waving to his troops to follow him, leading his men to their deaths, fighting for a losing cause, an unjust cause.

The statue made Nate uneasy. He felt an unwelcome kinship with the captain. Despite the possibility of corruption in Buck County's justice system, Nate thought Deatherage was guilty. The forensic evidence against him was damning. Like Josiah Bloxton, Nate's cause was unjust, but unlike Bloxton, if Nate fought hard enough, he might win the war. Deatherage could go free. He could kill again.

"Good day, Mister Abbitt."

Nate looked up. Judge Herring was walking across the square toward him. The judge was in his mid-sixties, tall and heavyset with white hair parted in the middle. His complexion was gray. He puffed on a cigar and walked with a limp. The judge extended his hand and Nate shook it.

"Welcome to Buck County. It's good to see you again."

"Thank you, Your Honor."

"I was sorry to hear about your automobile accident. You've recovered fully from your injuries, I trust."

"Yes, I'm fine."

The judge adjusted his wire-rimmed glasses and squinted at Nate's scar. "I see it left you with a mark. From what Harry Blackwell told me, you're fortunate you survived. That scar is a small price to pay for the mercy the fates bestowed upon you that night."

"I guess so."

"I hear you suffered another blow to the head in the old Callao Coal warehouse."

Nate was surprised by the comment. He'd assumed only Drinkard, George Maupin, and the man who assaulted him knew about that. Drinkard seemed too afraid of the judge to have told anyone about it and George hadn't known long enough to tell anyone. "Who told you about my injury, Your Honor?"

The judge puffed on his cigar and narrowed his eyes. "I don't recall. Such colorful news travels at the speed of light in Bloxton. Everyone seems to know about it." The judge blew a stream of smoke at the statue and a low rattle rolled up from deep inside his chest. He covered his mouth and succumbed to a string of phlegmy coughs. When the coughing passed, he took a rasping breath and cleared his throat. "You must be careful where you go at night in this town, Mister Abbitt. This isn't Selk County. We have a distressed economy here. Thievery is rampant."

"I wasn't robbed."

The judge wiped his lips with a handkerchief and shook his head.

"There are hooligans in this region who engage in acts of violence for recreational pleasure. We've taken strong measures to clean up, but we still have a long way to go. I apologize to you, Mister Abbitt, on behalf of Buck County's decent people."

"Thank you for your concern."

The judge rolled the cigar around in his mouth. "Speaking of Buck County's hooligans, I understand you represent one of them. I received the notice of your appearance in the Deatherage case. I'm pleased someone of your mindset agreed to represent the man."

"My mindset, Your Honor? I don't take your meaning."

"Mindset isn't the most specific of terms, I suppose. I meant I'm pleased to see a former prosecutor representing Deatherage. A prosecutor's perspective is what the case requires." There was an uncomfortable silence. The judge seemed to be watching Nate closely, measuring his reaction. "So, tell me, what's your assessment of how we conducted the trial? How did we do?"

Nate wasn't certain what the rules of ethics required concerning a conversation between appellate counsel and the trial judge. It seemed inappropriate, without his adversary present. "I'm not sure it's ethical for me to discuss the case with you outside the presence of George Maupin, Your Honor."

"Yes, of course, you're probably right. It wouldn't be ethical, I suppose. Thank you for reminding me." The judge tossed the butt of his cigar on the lawn. It smoldered in the grass. He cast a stern look at Nate. "You're an expert on legal ethics, I suppose, Mister Abbitt." The judge turned abruptly, walked across the town square, and entered the county office building.

Chapter 10

The Witness

Nate drove down Ewell Street and parked near the warehouse in front of the old house where Willis Odoms lived. Drinkard had described Odoms as "a big old colored boy" and "strong as a bull."

Nate was apprehensive about approaching him. Race relations in Virginia and the nation had been especially tense since Dr. Martin Luther King was shot and killed in April. Riots had broken out in most large cities, and even though rural southwest Virginia was insulated enough from the turmoil that no overt violence had taken place, a change in attitudes on both sides of the color divide was palpable. Anger, fear, and distrust lurked beneath a thin veneer of civility. Nate needed to ask Odoms some hard questions, questions Swiller should have used to cross-examine Odoms and to undermine his credibility.

Nate got out of the car and waded through tall weeds to the house. Its paint had long since peeled away and the front porch leaned to one side. Nate stepped up on the porch and knocked on the door.

"Go way. Leave me be."

"Mister Odoms?"

"I told you she ran off with it." The door swung open. A middle-aged black man stood in the doorway wearing nothing but undershorts. He was huge. He looked like he belonged on the cover of a body-builders' magazine. His face was angry.

"I told you on the phone Rita ran off with the Ford. You want it, you go catch Rita."

"I don't know what you're talking about, Mister Odoms."

"You're the ree-po man, Hansen, right?"

"I'm Nate Abbitt. I'm an attorney. I represent Kenneth Deatherage."

Odoms smirked. "You'd be better off you was the repo man."

"I'd like to ask you some questions about the murder."

"I told it all to the judge at the trial."

"I'm interested in the circumstances surrounding your testimony. Would you mind walking through the crime scene with me and explaining what you saw?"

Odoms stared at Nate. "Ugly scar."

"I was in a car accident."

"Musta been a bad one."

"It was."

Odoms studied Nate's face. Nate waited. Odoms turned away and disappeared inside the house. In a few minutes, he returned clad in a khaki work shirt and jeans and stepped out on the porch. "What you want to know?"

"You testified you came home from a party the night of the murder? Had you been drinking?"

"It was Friday night. Everybody was drinkin."

"How many drinks?"

"I drink em. I don't count em. I see what you're gettin at and I don't appreciate it. I wasn't drunk. I know what I saw."

"All right, Mister Odoms. I'm not accusing you of anything. You and your wife got home. What happened then?"

"We went to bed. I had my time with Rita, only thing she's good for. I opened the window cause it was hotter'n hell. A little bit later, Rita and me heard the woman cry out." Odoms said he told Rita to call the sheriff. He got his gun and a flashlight and headed to the warehouse.

"Why do you own a handgun, Mister Odoms?"

"I'd be a damned fool not to own a gun."

"Why is that?"

"Good old boys, white boys with the Confederate flag plastered across the back window of their pickup trucks, have their high old times in the warehouse late at night. They get drunk and rowdy and think they're man enough to beat up on somebody, but they don't ever get so drunk as to pester a man owns a gun."

"Have you ever had trouble with the law, Mister Odoms?"

"There ain't a colored man in Buck County hadn't been roughed up by Sheriff Feedlow and his boys."

"Any criminal charges?"

"Long time ago they locked me up for beatin up Rolly Jackson when I was drunk and he came on to a girl I was with. The Buck County jail didn't suit me. I ain't been back, and I ain't goin back. I watch my step. I stay away from trouble."

"Did you know Darlene Updike?"

"I didn't know her. I never seen her till they hauled her dead body out the warehouse and put it in the truck."

"You ever have trouble with Deatherage?"

"Him and me didn't mix."

"I get the impression you don't like Deatherage."

"Nobody likes Deatherage."

"Why do you say that?"

"He's a mean drunk. Beats up on people smaller and weaker than him, like his wife and his little boy. He's the kind of white boy can get a colored man in trouble. I stayed away from him. There was nothin between us. I saw him in the warehouse window. He ran. I chased him and caught him. That's all there was to it."

Nate was impressed with Odoms' straightforward manner. His take on his position in Buck County society seemed honest and credible.

Nate said, "Would you mind showing me where you were when you saw Deatherage?"

Odoms led Nate through the yard to the front of the warehouse. He stopped about fifteen feet from the front door. The noonday sun glanced off a puddle of rainwater under the warehouse windows. Honeysuckle vines climbed the wall. Yellow jackets swarmed over a hole in the mud by the door. It was a blazing hot day. Nate wiped sweat from his face with a handkerchief.

Odoms pointed at a window in the center of the wall. "I flashed my light at that row of windows. When my light hit that one there, I saw the white boy peekin out at me like a scared rabbit. He dove down and I figured he would run. I started to go inside, but I stopped when Henry came out the door."

"Someone came out of the building?"

"Henry Crawford. He's an old bum who sleeps in the warehouse."

"This man came out of the building after you saw Deatherage?"

"Henry came out carryin his stinkin old shoes. Barefoot. Grinnin at me like a fool. Walked down the dirt road and sat in a foldin chair in front of the motel."

Nate was shocked. "Why did you let the man walk away? He could have been the killer."

"Henry's harmless. He wouldn't hurt a livin soul."

"Did you tell the police about this man?"

"When Deputy Jones drove up, he saw Henry sittin in the chair down there at the motel. Everybody knows Henry sleeps off his drunks in the warehouse."

"Did Jones question him?"

"Jones talked to Henry, but Henry didn't know anything. He was drunk on rotgut. I could smell it on him strong enough to knock me back."

Deputy Jones' report about the arrest was an exhibit at Deatherage's arraignment. The report did not mention Crawford. "Did Randolph Swiller ask you about Crawford?"

"First time I ever saw the lawyer was in the courtroom when I testified."

"Why didn't you tell the court about Crawford during your testimony?"

"Deputy Jones told me to answer the questions the lawyers asked me and to keep my big mouth shut otherwise. I did what he said. Nobody asked me about Henry."

Nate was amazed. Crawford's presence in the warehouse might have created a reasonable doubt in a juror's mind about Deatherage's guilt. "Where can I find this Henry Crawford?"

"Daytime you find him drunk in a ditch somewhere or lookin for pop bottles to turn in for drinkin money. Most nights you find him sleepin on some old mattresses in the warehouse."

"I saw a man in the warehouse last night. His beard was down to his waist."

"That's Henry."

Nate stared at the warehouse window. If Crawford normally slept on the mattresses, his hair and fibers from his clothing would have remained on them. If Updike was murdered on the mattresses, as Deatherage claimed, that evidence and Crawford's presence in the warehouse would have made Crawford a suspect for the murder. If Nate's attacker was "part of it," to use Deatherage's phrase, he'd attacked Nate because he didn't want him to learn Crawford was in the warehouse the night of the murder.

Odoms wiped sweat from his brow and flicked it away with a jerk of his hand. "Let's get this over with. Hot as hell out here."

"You mentioned that Crawford slept on mattresses in the warehouse. Where were the mattresses the night of the murder?"

"Piled up under the window where I saw Deatherage."

"You're sure of that."

"I didn't actually see em there that night. I didn't go in the warehouse and look, but those old mattresses were piled up under that same window for years."

"Last night the mattresses were stacked against the rear wall of the warehouse."

"Henry dragged em back there after the killin. He was scared to sleep up front near the windows."

"Why was he scared?"

"Henry said he saw the dead girl's ghost by the windows. He's afraid she wants to take him across the river Jordan. He said the girl blames him for not helpin her and the law blames him, too."

Nate stiffened. "Did he say how he knew the law blames him?"

"He said he told the law he was too drunk to know what happened to the girl but they wouldn't leave him alone about it. Said they pestered him somethin fierce and kept askin him what he knew."

"Who talked to him? Deputy Jones?"

"I doubt anybody talked to Henry about the girl. He sees people that ain't there, hears voices that ain't talkin to him."

"Did he name anyone from the law he thought talked to him?"

"No. He just raved about the law and how they were pesterin him. He's crazy drunk all the time and I didn't believe a word of it." Odoms wiped sweat from his face and sighed. "Get on with it, lawyer. It's mighty hot in the sun."

"Let's go inside the warehouse for a moment." Odoms pulled open the rusty door and Nate followed him inside. Nate pointed to the back wall. "That's where I saw Crawford and the mattresses."

Odoms looked around the room. "Where'd they go?"

"Somebody removed them from the warehouse last night," Nate said.

"Why would anybody steal those old mattresses?"

"Did you see anyone around the warehouse last night?"

"Some men were here late, about eleven or so."

"Did you see who they were?"

"I didn't see em, but I heard their foolishness," Odoms said. "They yelled and hollered so loud they woke me from a dead sleep. I turned on my porch light and I saw a pickup parked by the warehouse, but I didn't see anyone. They got quiet, and I went back to bed. They must be the ones who stole Henry's mattresses."

"What kind of truck was it?"

"A junkheap. Beat-up old Chevy. Red. Big dent in the driver's door."

Nate looked around the warehouse. The passage of time had washed away all traces of the murder. If Swiller had inspected the warehouse after the murder, there was no record of it in his file. Nate would never know what a competent investigation would have revealed.

"Are we done?" Odoms said.

"Just a few more questions. Deatherage ran from the warehouse and you caught him and held him until Deputy Jones arrived, right?"

"Yeah."

"Did Jones search him?"

"Yeah."

"Did he find anything?"

"The white boy was clean. No gun. No knife. Nothin."

"Did Jones find a scarf in Deatherage's pocket?"

"He didn't find anything on Deatherage."

"You're sure?"

"I was standin next to them. The white boy didn't have anything in his pockets."

Nate thanked Odoms for his help. Odoms went inside his house and Nate went to his car. He sat in the car and took stock of what he had learned. The nature of Judge Herring's relationship with Darlene Updike was unclear, but his visit to her motel room the night before she was killed should have caused him to recuse himself from the trial. What's more, if Odoms was telling the truth, Deputy Jones' testimony about the scarf was perjurious. Deatherage was apparently correct; he had been framed. The question troubling Nate was whether Buck County had framed a guilty man.

Chapter 11

The Promise

It took Nate three hours to drive back home to Jeetersburg that night. He parked behind Sally's Diner and walked down Lighthorse Street to Michie's Place, his favorite watering hole when he was drinking. He stood outside, looking in the window and thinking about whiskey. After a long while he turned away from the window, crossed the street to Beauregard Park, and sat down on a bench.

It was a warm, humid night. He gazed at a fountain to the right of the park bench. Water spouted from the mouth of a lion's head mounted on a stone wall and splashed in a circular pool below it. The sound of the water was peaceful, but Nate found no peace. He was lonely and steeped in self-pity. He wanted a drink.

At his lowest points, his thoughts always turned to Christine. He sought refuge from the miserable present in memories of his past. His favorite memories were his first experiences with her, when they were young, long before he hurt her, when she loved him completely, without reservations.

The first time he saw Christine he was a senior on the Jefferson State University cross-country team. It was the first meet of the fall season. He stood at the finish line of the women's team race. The forest at the edge of a grass field was splashed with burnt orange, gold, and cardinal. A girl ran out of the trees wearing the colors of Jefferson State, a red top and blue shorts. She was short with long black hair that fanned out behind her as she ran. Her legs were spattered with mud from the stream beds that crisscrossed the course. She had the build of a sprinter and her stride was a sprinter's stride – short, choppy, and powerful.

Two runners came out of the trees behind her. They were classic distance runners, tall with long, gliding, effortless strides. They pulled even with the short girl about twenty yards from the finish line, and she struggled to stay with them. Her running form broke down, but she mustered a final burst of speed and fell across the tape just ahead of the others.

She lay on the ground while her coach knelt beside her and tried to help her recover. Time passed. Most of the runners crossed the finish line, but the girl could not stand. After a long while, the coach helped her struggle to her feet and the two made their way toward the locker room. When the girl walked by Nate, she swept a strand of raven hair away from her face and her eyes met Nate's. Her eyes were big and brown and filled with tears and wild with pride, anger, and pain. Nate felt something stir inside his chest.

They dated through the fall and winter, and Nate fell in love with her in the spring. He could pinpoint the exact moment when he realized he was in love. In April they spent a weekend together at his father's log cabin on Jasper Lake. They lay together on the bed on a warm night. They made love. Later that night it rained. Nate got up and opened the window so they could hear the rain fall. The patter of the rain was steady and gentle and peaceful. The smell of it was fresh and clean.

He stood at the window and looked at Christine as she lay on the bed. There was no moon. He could barely see the outline of her hair spread over the pillow and the gentle curves of her body against the night-gray of the bedsheets. He lay down beside her, she on her back, he on his side. He draped his leg across her legs, rested his head on her breast, and listened to the beat of her heart. A sense of bliss and contentment came over him. In that moment he was whole, complete, fulfilled. There was nothing more he wanted in life than to be with her. So this is what it's like to love someone, he thought. This is it.

The rain slowed and then stopped. For a while there was the sound of water dripping from the leaves to the ground, but that eventually stopped, too, and the night was still except for the beat of Christine's heart.

"This is nice," she said.

Nate rolled over and lay on his back beside her, their bodies touching all along one side. "I want you to meet my father." It was a wish borne out of the realization that he was in love with her. It escaped his lips before he thought about it.

He felt her body tense. "That's a big step. I'm not sure I'm ready for that."

Nate worried that he was pushing her too hard, that he might scare her away, but what he had said was true. He wanted her to meet his father. He pressed on. "There's not much time."

"What do you mean?"

"There's something I haven't told you. I didn't want to put pressure on you."

"I don't understand."

"My father has cancer. He's dying."

Christine drew her leg up to rest across Nate's thighs and placed the palm of her hand on his chest. "I'm so sorry, Nate."

"He's very near the end. I told him about you. He asked to meet you. I know it's unfair to you, but it would mean a lot to him . . . it would mean a lot to me if you would go with me to see him."

She stroked his cheek. "How long before your father . . ."

"A month at best."

He felt her warm tears on his chest.

The following Monday in the late afternoon they stood together in the hospital at one end of a long hall. Christine wore a beige blouse buttoned at the neck and a gray skirt that came to her knees. She clutched Nate's arm. They walked down the corridor. His stomach was tight as it always was on these visits, and it grew tighter when they approached the doorway. The door was open. They stepped inside.

Nate's father lay on a bed beside the window. The bed was cranked to an angle to enable him to see outside. A sheet was pulled up to his chest. The sunlight fell across his face. His face was a translucent leathery mask stretched thin over knobby bones. His gray hair was the consistency of a spider's web. An oxygen mask covered his nose and mouth. Nate would not have recognized him if he hadn't watched the cancer suck the life out of him over the past year.

Nate's father gazed at them through half-closed lids. His eyes fixed on Christine. Nate led her across the room. "This is Christine Smith, Dad."

"I'm so happy to meet you, Mister Abbitt."

Nate held his father's hand. It felt like a crow's claw. The cold hand squeezed Nate's hand ever so weakly, but his father's eyes never left Christine.

"Nate has told me so much about you," she said.

Nate's father looked at the oxygen mask and then at him.

"I guess it's all right," Nate said. He removed the mask.

Nate's father said something but his voice was so low Nate could barely hear him. He leaned toward his father. "What did you say, Dad?"

"Want to talk to her alone."

Nate was afraid for Christine. His father's veins ran full with morphine. His mind wasn't always clear. "You two don't know each other," Nate said.

"Please."

"I don't know, Dad."

"It's all right," Christine said.

Nate wanted to protect Christine but did not know how to dismiss his father's request. "Are you sure?"

"It's all right," she said again.

Nate walked to the door and looked back at them. Christine took his father's hand and leaned over him. He spoke to her. She said something in low tones and his father nodded.

Nate stepped outside. He was worried that he shouldn't have done this. Christine's feelings for him were not clear. She had mentioned other men she knew before she met him. She'd slept with a few of them and one of those relationships lasted for a while, but she didn't view any of her prior relationships as serious. Nate knew she enjoyed his company, but he didn't think she loved him. A private deathbed conversation seemed likely to frighten her away.

Christine came to the door. "He's asleep now."

Nate looked in the room. Christine had replaced the mask. His father's eyes were closed, and his chest rose and fell steadily.

"He's resting," Christine said. She took Nate's arm and led him down the hall. She looked straight ahead. Tears slid down her cheeks. They walked to the parking lot in silence and got in the car.

"What did he say to you?"

"Let's go back to the cabin. I'll tell you there."

They drove to the lake house. Christine stared straight ahead and didn't say anything to Nate along the way. Several times her eyes pooled with tears and her lips trembled. Each time she clenched her fists and regained her composure. It was dusk when he stopped the car in front of the cabin. The sun hung low over the mountains, casting a long glistening silver streak across the surface of the lake. Cicadas clacked their din. A cool breeze swayed pine boughs.

"What did my father say to you?"

"He said you brought more joy to his life than he deserved. He said you are his proudest achievement. He said he loves you."

Nate's breath caught in his throat. When he could speak, he said, "I'm sorry I asked you to do this. I didn't know he would want to talk to you alone."

"It's all right."

"I shoved you into the middle of our relationship at our saddest moment. It was unfair to you. I know my father loves me. He's told me so many times. He didn't need to send a message to me through you. If he'd known what he was doing, he wouldn't have put you through that. The morphine warps his thinking."

"The morphine had nothing to do with it. He was thinking clearly. He had a reason to tell me about his love for you."

"What reason?"

"He said he feared there would come a time in your life when you might doubt him, when you might need reassurance about his love for you. By asking me to tell you, he said he thought you would believe him no matter what happens in the future."

Nate was surprised and perplexed. "Did he say why he thought I might question his feelings for me?"

"He said only that you might need reassurance, and he thought telling me would help you believe the sincerity of his love for you when that time came."

Nate stared at the lake, unable to imagine an explanation for his father's concern. "Did he say anything else?"

"There was one thing more."

"What?"

Christine paused. "I can't tell you about that."

"Why?"

"It's too awkward to discuss."

"Awkward in what way?"

"Maybe some day I'll tell you about it, but I can't tell you now. I won't. You'll have to trust my judgment about this."

Nate reluctantly dropped the subject, but he didn't forget it.

Six years after his father's death and five years after he and Christine married, they vacationed at the lake house in the winter. It snowed for two days. A crusty shelf of snow-covered ice extended from the shoreline a few feet into the lake. A blanket of white down covered the ground around the cabin and ice hung from the pine branches. The road to the house was impassable.

They had stocked the refrigerator and the liquor cabinet at the beginning of the week. They lit a fire in the fireplace. The cabin was warm and cozy, and they were happy to be snowed in. They ate, drank, laughed, and talked. On the day after the snowstorm, they made love twice – once in the morning when they awoke and once in the afternoon when he caught her up in his arms and carried her into the bedroom with her kicking and screaming in mock protest.

That night they sat in easy chairs on either side of the fireplace. The pine logs popped and cracked and the flames licked high in the chimney. Nate was reading a murder mystery. He looked at Christine curled up in her chair writing an analysis of Chaucer for a class she taught at Jefferson State. She wore jeans, a black turtleneck sweater, Nate's hunting socks, and the scent of jasmine. He was thinking about holding her again when he noticed the scene outside the window behind her. A dim outline of the car was visible through the falling snow. It was parked in the same place where she'd told him six years earlier about her private conversation with his father, and Nate was reminded of the unanswered question.

"What did my father tell you that day in the hospital?"

Christine looked up from her work. "What made you think about that?"

"In the car out there six years ago, you said you would tell me someday."

"I said I *might* tell you someday."

"I've held nothing back from you. It's unfair for you to withhold my father's last thoughts from me."

"Your father said he loved you."

"You told me that before. I want to know what else he said, the part you said was too awkward to discuss with me."

Christine looked at the fire. "Sometimes there are things about people we love that we might be better off not knowing. This may be one of those times."

"I want to know what he said to you, Christine."

She set her work aside, pulled her knees up to her chest, and wrapped her arms around them. "Your father said you were in love with me. He asked me if I loved you."

Nate paused, surprised and a little fearful. "What did you say?"

"I said I liked you."

"But you didn't love me?"

"No."

Nate's uneasiness increased. "What did my father say when you told him you didn't love me?"

"He asked me how long I planned to stay with you."

"What did you say?"

"I told him I didn't know how long we would be together. I told him I enjoyed passing time with you, but I didn't see us staying together in the long term. He asked me to be patient, to give you time to show me who you are before I made a decision to leave you."

"So you agreed to wait."

"Yes."

Nate felt unsure of himself for the first time since they married. "Why did you agree to wait?"

"I felt sorry for him." She looked away from Nate and stared into the fire. "I felt sorry for you, too."

A flood of emotions ran through him. Love for his father filled his heart. His father used his last reservoir of energy and guile to bind Christine to Nate until he could win her over. A sense of guilt also washed over him because he realized that on some level he'd known he was likely to gain her sympathy, and therefore more time with her, from that meeting. But mostly he was fearful. He was afraid her pity might be the reason she married him. He didn't want that. He wanted her to love him, not pity him.

"You told my father you didn't love me," he said. "Do you love me now?"

Christine stared at him for a moment. Then she arose and stood in front of him. She took off her clothes, put her hands on her hips, and looked down at him, her big brown eyes shining. She leaned forward, placed her hands on his shoulders, and kissed him long and hard. She sat on his lap and put her arms around his neck. "Well, I certainly like you. At least I like some things about you."

"What do you like about me?" he said, feeling a lot better.

She squirmed in his lap. He was aroused. "Well, you're . . . tall." She kissed him deep and probing.

"Let's go to bed," Nate said.

"Let's stay here."

He clicked off the lamp. The soft glow from the fire flickered on her bare shoulders. She undressed him and sat on his lap again. She kissed him and touched him and teased him and held him off until he felt he would explode. At the end of it, she straddled him as he sat in the chair. Her hands clasped behind his neck, she leaned back until her arms were straight. She tilted her head back as far as she could. When he burst inside her, she said through clenched teeth, "I love you. Oh, yes. I love you. I love you."

Lost in his memories, Nate sat on the bench in Beauregard Park beside the lion-head fountain until Michie's Place cut off its lights and locked its doors. He went to his apartment where there was no whiskey and went to bed, but sleep didn't come. He wanted a drink. He needed a drink. He arose before dawn, walked to the courthouse, and sat on the courthouse steps. Judge Blackwell was always the first to arrive, and so it was that morning. His old Cadillac pulled into the parking lot. The judge got out of his car, crossed the lot, and stopped at the steps to look at Nate. Nate was pale and covered with sweat. No words passed between them. The judge unlocked the courthouse door, and Nate followed him to his chambers. Nate sat in the chair across from the judge's desk. The judge made a pot of coffee and gave Nate a cup. Nate's hands trembled so badly he couldn't bring it to his mouth.

"Fold your hands, place them on the desk, and press them together. Breathe deeply."

Nate did as he was told.

"Think about something you care about. What do you most want to gain by remaining sober?"

Nate's tongue was dry, his voice hoarse. "I want Christine to take me back."

The judge was quiet for a long time. "All right. Think about Christine."

Nate closed his eyes. Through an alcoholic blur, he could see her face and hear her voice: *I hate you.* "So do I," Nate said. He covered his face and sobbed.

"Let it out, son."

After a long time, Nate calmed. He wiped away the sweat and tears, leaned back in the chair, and sipped coffee from the cup.

"Do you want me to talk with Doctor Davis about readmitting you to the hospital?"

"For what?"

"You can't drink there."

Nate shook his head. "I can't hide from the whiskey forever."

The judge and Nate sat together for a long time without saying anything. Nate finished the coffee. "Thanks," he said. He stood to leave.

"Are you all right?"

"I don't know." He headed toward the door.

"She'll probably never take you back, Nathan, but if there's any chance at all, whiskey will kill it for you."

Nate paused at the door. As always, the judge had done the right things to fortify him, and he had said the only words that could give Nate the strength to resist for a while longer. He turned and looked at the judge. A question had rolled around in his mind for a long time. "Why do you protect me, Harry?"

"What?"

"You convinced the sheriff and the commonwealth's attorney not to indict me for the crimes I committed as a prosecutor. You recused yourself from our divorce proceedings, but you stepped in and convinced Christine not to press charges against me for forcing my way into the house and you again persuaded the sheriff and the commonwealth's attorney to back off. You meet with me weekly to help me stay sober. What's your interest in me? Why do you keep stepping in to save me? I didn't ask for your help. You're not my keeper."

The judge folded his hands in his lap and looked down at them. "You served the county well for almost thirty years. We owe you some consideration for your good work."

"That's not enough to cause you to go to so much trouble. There has to be something more. What is it, Harry?"

The judge was quiet for a long time. Then he said, "I suppose there's no harm in telling you. Before your father died, I promised him I'd watch over you and step in if you ever needed help."

Nate was surprised. "You and my father were friends?"

"We were good friends once, before you were born. I was his attorney."

"My mother never mentioned your friendship."

"She may not know we were friends. We drifted apart after he married your mother, but I went to see him at the hospital before he died. He asked me to watch over you. I promised him I would do my best. Your mother wasn't there when I visited him. I doubt he told her I came by."

"Why is it you never told me about this promise?"

"It was a private pledge. Until recently, your conduct was above reproach. You didn't need my help and there was no point in telling you, but your recent string of self-destructive acts has brought my old promise into play."

Nate studied the judge. "Harry – "

"I have nothing more to say about this." The judge seemed suddenly irritated. "Take my advice and immerse yourself in your work, stay out of trouble, and stay sober. You're correct that I've invested a lot of time and energy in helping you, and my well of patience has run dry. It's time you took responsibility for your actions. Don't slip and fall again. You'll face the harsh consequences of your misconduct alone from here on. I won't step in to save you again. Leave me now. I must prepare for this morning's calendar."

Nate pulled the door closed behind him, puzzled by the judge's revelations. On his deathbed, Nate's father sent a message of reassurance to him through Christine. Now he knew his father had extracted a promise of help and protection from the judge. Despite the judge's claim of friendship with his father, Nate was skeptical. Nate and his father were very close, and his father had never mentioned the judge. Nate stared at the door, thinking there was something still unsaid.

Chapter 12

The Whole Truth

For the third time during the month of May, Nate sat in the little sweatbox that was labeled Visit A – Max Sec, but this encounter was different. It was a come-to-Jesus meeting. Deatherage sat on his side of the divider with his elbows propped on the desk, one hand pressing the phone to his ear, the other fiddling with a lock of greasy red hair. "Okay. I'll admit it. I lied to you about the girl. I lied because I was scared. I told the sheriff and Darby Jones and Swiller I didn't know her. I was afraid if I told you different, you'd walk out on me."

"It works the other way. I'm withdrawing as your lawyer because you lied to me."

"I'm not a liar. I mean I lied this one time, but I'm not a regular liar."

"You lie when it suits you."

"No, that's not fair. Listen, I understand you're mad at me, but put yourself in my place. If your life was on the line and the whole Buck County crew framed you for killin the girl, would you admit you knew her?"

"I'm done with you." Nate gathered his papers and put them in his briefcase.

"Wait. Give me a chance and I'll tell you the God's-honest truth."

"You had your chance." Nate snapped his briefcase shut.

"Hear me out, lawyer. Please. I'll tell you the whole truth. No more lies. I promise."

"You'll tell me a fresh pack of lies."

"No. Nothin but the truth this time. I promise."

Nate stood.

"Please, lawyer. I don't stand a chance against em without you. Please stay. Give me one more chance to come clean. Please."

Nate hesitated. Then he said, "This better be good. More to the point, it better be the truth." He sat down.

Deatherage wiped sweat from his face and leaned back in his chair, visibly relieved.

"When did you first meet Updike?" Nate said.

"Okay. Here's the God's-honest truth. I was tomcattin around Bloxton one night about two weeks before the girl was killed. I rolled into a restaurant on Water Street name of the Coal Bin. They sell liquor under the table. She was at the counter by herself, drinkin straight whiskey. She had that look, you know, good lookin, but with a bit a trash to her. Smooth and soft, but kinda rough too. You know what I mean?"

Nate said nothing.

"I guess a man like you wouldn't know about that. You probably like high-class women. I don't. I like the ones who drink with me, cuss at me some, talk some trash. She had a nasty streak to her, the way I like. And she was little. I like em little."

"Did you approach her that night?"

"I sat down next to her. She was pretty far-gone drunk when I started in on her. I poured a few more drinks down her, and she was ready to roll." A smile came across Deatherage's lips. "That little girl was good at it. She was real good. We had us a time, we did. All night long." He stroked his chin. His smile widened.

"Where did you take her?"

"We went to the Black Gold Motel. She told me to stay in the car while she checked in with old man Drinkard. She sneaked me into her room, and we went at it all night."

"Was that the only time you were with her?"

"You find one as good as she was, you come back for more, but she wouldn't tell me her name or where she lived or her phone number. I looked for her the next night at the motel, but she was gone and Drinkard claimed he didn't know anything about her. I looked for her every night, but she wasn't at the Coal Bin or the motel or anywhere else I looked. Then I had that fight with my old lady I told you about. I bought a jar of moonshine. It was Friday night and I wanted to party. I drove around Bloxton lookin for someone to party with. I was fillin my tank at the Esso station across from the motel and I saw that little girl drive up and go inside the office. I watched her lug a bag into one of the rooms. She looked mighty good, tight red blouse with a black bra peekin through, a short black skirt came near-on up to her butt cheeks, a little piece a trash showin off what she had." Deatherage gazed at nothing and smiled.

"What did you do?"

"I banged on her door and she opened up and I told her I wanted to party again, and I kind of shoved my way inside. That's when things went bad."

"What happened?"

"She said she didn't know who I was. I reminded her about what we did in that same room a couple weeks before. She claimed she didn't remember. I didn't believe her at first, but she kept sayin she didn't know me. I guess she was blind drunk the night I rolled all over her."

"What did you do?"

"I got kinda hot. I don't care how drunk she was. A woman shouldn't do the things she did with me and then tell me she don't remember. It hurts a man's pride."

"Did you hit her?"

"I slapped her around a little."

"The medical examiner's report said she had a swollen eye and a busted lip."

"I didn't do that to her. I didn't hit her hard enough to leave a bruise. I didn't get the chance. She pulled a gun on me."

"She had a gun?"

"She had a little black pistol. She put the barrel snug to my chest and told me to get the hell out. Said she was meetin another man later on and he was the kind that would put me in a world of hurt if I didn't get out. That was it for me. I wanted to lay with her awful bad, but I didn't want it bad enough to get shot. I took off lickety-split."

"Where did you go?"

"I drove around Bloxton, poppin wheelies and cussin, mad as hell. I decided I needed more than one jar a shine to get over all my setbacks, so I drove out to Cecil Garrison's place and bought another jug. I sat on Cecil's porch drinkin hooch until Cecil told me to move along."

"What time did you leave this man's house?"

"About eleven."

"Where did you go?"

"I drove to the warehouse, parked my truck on the dirt road behind the motel, and started in on that second jar a shine. About midnight I went inside the warehouse, finished off my hooch, and passed out."

"You didn't bother Updike any more that night?"

"I didn't see her again until I found her on those old mattresses just before dawn."

Nate thought about the story of the murder George Maupin presented to the jury. The murderer choked Updike to the point of death and allowed her to revive twice before he killed her. He took great pleasure in her pain. According to Deatherage's story, Updike insulted his virility and he wanted to punish her for that. Nate thought he had sufficient motive. "You were drunk and angry at Updike. You say you didn't go to her room and have it out with her, but it sounds more like you drank in your truck behind the motel to build up your courage to attack her."

"I know it looks bad. Hell, that's why I lied about knowin her, but the truth is I stayed away from that little girl. I don't have a death wish. She had a gun. She said she was waitin for a man would do me in if he got his hands on me. I didn't go to her room because I was afraid."

Deatherage told his story in a convincing manner, but Nate was skeptical. He decided to test Deatherage by surprising him. "Did you see Henry Crawford that night?"

"I didn't see him."

"He was in the warehouse."

Deatherage didn't flinch. "Did you talk to him?" he said.

"Not yet."

"Well, if Henry was there, he might have seen who killed the girl, but he's drunk out of his mind pretty much all the time so I don't think anyone will believe him. It's still worth a try for you to track him down. He sleeps in the warehouse most nights. Come to think of it, he used to sleep on those mattresses where I found the girl."

Nate had questioned a lot of liars over the years. Most of them showed some sign of deception. They looked away from their listener, fidgeted with their hands, shifted in their seats, or watched their listener too eagerly. Deatherage was looking directly into Nate's eyes and telling his story in a relaxed manner. He volunteered details that were unflattering to him. Either he was telling the truth or he was a very good liar.

"I'll give you one more chance," Nate said. "I'll go to Bloxton again to investigate your story. If you lied to me this time, I'm done with you."

"Thanks for stickin with me. I'm sorry I lied to you. It won't happen again. I told you the truth this time, the whole truth."

Chapter 13

The Expert

Nate wanted to discuss the case with a forensic pathologist before he returned to Bloxton, but the state's budget didn't provide enough money to hire an expert and Nate didn't think the volunteer experts available to him were strong enough to meet his needs. The best forensic pathologist he knew was Shirley West. She and Nate were old friends. They had won a lot of cases together and she owed him favors, but he didn't think she would talk to him about Deatherage because she'd testified for the commonwealth at the trial. Nate decided to give her a try anyway. When he called her, she answered on the first ring.

"This is Shirley West. Can I help you?"

"You can help me, but my guess is you don't want to."

"Who is this?"

"Nate Abbitt."

There was a pause. "Long time no see."

"Yeah, well, I got fired."

Another pause. "I heard you resigned."

"No point in being delicate with me, Shirley. I got fired, and I deserved it."

"I don't believe much of what I hear in the rumor mill."

"Whatever you heard about me can't be any worse than what I did."

Shirley fell silent.

"I'm working the other side of the courtroom now," Nate said. "I represent Kenneth Deatherage. I'd like to talk to you about the case. Can we get together?"

"George Maupin told me you took the appeal. He also told me to stay away from you. You're on the opposing team now, Nate."

"I got fired because I ignored the fact I had an obligation to be fair to the defendants. Don't follow my bad example."

There was a long silence.

Nate said, "Come on, Shirley. Help me out. I promise I won't ask you to compromise your duty to the state."

There was another pause. Then she said, "Where do you want to meet?"

"Is that coffee shop down the street from your office still in business?"

"Jane's Kitchen Table. Still there."

"I'll meet you there in two hours."

It took Nate an hour and a half to drive from Jeetersburg to Roanoke. He arrived at Jane's Kitchen Table at two thirty, went inside, and ordered two coffees and three glazed donuts dripping with syrup and sugar. Outside the shop a red brick patio with tables bordered the sidewalk. Nate found a table in the shade of a beech tree, sipped coffee, and waited.

Shirley trundled down the sidewalk a few minutes later. She was a stout woman of average height dressed in a frumpy dark brown tent dress. Her brown hair was short and stiff. She wore no makeup. She smiled when she saw Nate. He stood and they hugged. She glanced at his scar and looked away. They sat at the table.

Nate set the three donuts in front of her. She clapped her hands and laughed. "I haven't eaten one of these fat bombs since you resigned."

"The first case you and I worked together, your old boss, Clancy Tilden, clued me in on your addiction."

"Good old Clancy. He used to bring a box of glazed donuts to the lab every morning. I couldn't keep my hands off them. If Clancy hadn't kicked the bucket in 1954, I'd weigh two hundred and fifty pounds."

"Maybe, but you look like you've lost weight. You on a diet?"

"Always. One eighty-six and falling. Till I inhale these bellybusters." Shirley bit into a donut and closed her eyes, savoring the moment. "Okay, I'm yours." She laughed and took another bite. "Ply me with sugar dough and I'll give you anything." She laughed raucously and took another bite. With a full mouth she said, "Oh my God. What do you want from me?"

"I want perspective."

"Speak plainly, Mister JD degree. I'm a scientist."

"Did anything look strange to you in the Deatherage case?"

Shirley was quiet for a while. "Take a close look at the exhibits."

"The scarf?"

Shirley shrugged and bit into the donut.

"What am I looking for?"

"You'll know when you see that scarf."

"Deatherage claims Jones didn't find the scarf on him. What do you think?"

Shirley swallowed a chunk of donut and paused. "George will kill me, but then again, he doesn't bring me sugar-glazed donuts." She smiled. "I'll die happy at least." Her smile lingered and then gradually fell away. "Think about it, Nate. It was strange the victim was wearing a scarf in the first place."

"How so?"

"She was murdered in June during a hot spell, too hot to tie a scarf around your neck. No rain that week, so she wasn't wearing it as a head cover." Shirley took another bite and chewed, looking contemplative. "Another thing that puzzled me. If Deatherage needed to gag her to silence her cries, why not stuff the scarf in her mouth instead of grabbing a cast-off rag on the warehouse floor?"

"Unless Updike wasn't wearing a scarf."

"Maybe. Take a close look at that scarf. It will interest you for other reasons."

"Maybe you can help me with another question. At trial George didn't ask Jones about Deatherage's physical condition. I'm guessing he avoided those questions because Deatherage didn't bear any signs of a struggle."

"Don't bother to go down that blind alley. George had no evidence to work with because we blew it. When Jones arrested Deatherage, Sheriff Feedlow was out of town. Jones was green, only a couple years as a deputy, and you know Feedlow's training program. 'Here's your service revolver, son. Don't shoot yourself with it.' Jones didn't examine Deatherage for wounds and didn't take pictures of him. Somers is a passable medical examiner, but he's a plodder. It didn't occur to Mac to examine him. I'm to blame, too. I didn't think to ask them if they'd examined him until we got to the preliminary hearing. Deatherage's wounds, if there were any wounds, had healed by then. George was livid, but there was nothing he could do about it. We failed to gather the evidence, pure and simple."

"Too bad. It would have been a strong indication of guilt or innocence."

"I agree, but there was plenty of evidence of guilt."

"Deatherage claims he found Updike's body after she was assaulted. He says the forensic evidence against him is the result of his attempt to help her."

"Deatherage doesn't seem like the Good Samaritan type."

"He's a hardscrabble character, but he says he was rattled by the appearance of the body. He says he leaned over Updike to untie the rope and he fell on her. Could the forensic evidence against him be the result of his falling on her?"

"It's not likely."

"Is it possible?"

"The prevalence of hair on a corpse depends on the pressure and duration of contact with the victim's body and clothing. The hair follicles we found on Updike required more contact than a single brushup against her."

"Suppose he struggled to get off her, rolled around on her a bit."

Shirley frowned and sighed. "It's possible. That kind of action might cause enough contact and pressure to produce the hair I found on her."

"He says he found her body sprawled on a pile of mattresses. What do you know about the location of the body when she died?"

"Jones said he found her body on the warehouse floor. He didn't say anything about mattresses."

"Maybe Jones didn't want you to test them."

"Why?"

"It's a long story. Tell me this. If she was raped and murdered on a mattress, is there any evidence that would survive the passage of time since the crime?"

"It's been almost a year. You could probably still see a bloodstain on the fabric if it hasn't been cleaned, but the blood is degraded by now to the point where I wouldn't be able to determine if it was human, much less its type. Of course, semen degrades within days." Shirley started in on the second donut. She looked pensive as she chewed and swallowed. "Hair is robust. It retains comparable microscopic characteristics for a long time. Updike had jet-black hair, coarse, thick. If the mattress has hair on it, I could probably determine if the hair was a close match to Updike's even after a year's time. The problem with hair is it doesn't have great persistence. Hair doesn't cling to fabric. If the mattress has been moved or jostled about or if it was exposed to wind and weather, her hair likely won't be there."

"What about fibers from her clothing?"

"Fibers retain their characteristics for a long time, too. She was wearing a black skirt and a red knit blouse with relatively distinctive fibers, but fibers don't cling to most fabric either. My guess is we won't find her hair or fibers of her clothing on the mattress. Do you have it?"

"I saw four or five mattresses stacked against a wall in the warehouse, but someone removed them, maybe to prevent me from finding evidence of her on them, but I guess I'm wrong."

"Not necessarily. There's at least a remote possibility it would still retain hair and fiber. Maybe someone's playing it safe."

Nate nodded thoughtfully.

Shirley picked up the third donut, looked at it longingly, put it down, and frowned at it. "That's interesting about the mattresses. You know, Nate, I inspected the warehouse. I thought I would find a bloodstain on the floor. Deatherage tore her vaginal wall when he raped her and that wound bled on the inside of her thighs and pelvis. Blood should have pooled on the floor under her hips, but there was no stain."

"Maybe he's telling the truth about the mattresses."

Shirley didn't respond.

"That reminds me of another question," Nate said. "You inspected his clothing. If she bled so much, his trousers and underwear should have had blood on them. You only testified about blood on his shirt."

"The stain on his shirt was on the front tail down near his crotch. I figured he took off his pants and underwear but wore his shirt when he raped her. Jones found a bloody rag at the rear of the warehouse near an open window. I guessed Deatherage used the rag to wipe the blood off his legs and hands before he fled."

"Makes sense."

Shirley stared at the last donut. "I'll be eating carrots and celery for a month because I ate those first two sugar bombs. I eat this last one and I'll have to cut out the carrots." Shirley took a last swig of coffee and stood. "I've got to get back to the lab before I break down and eat that."

Nate stood. "Thanks for talking to me, Shirley."

"I'll do anything for a sugar-glazed donut."

Nate grinned. "Anything?"

Shirley grinned back at him. "Most anything." She turned and walked away.

Chapter 14

The Stain

Nate returned to Jeetersburg after his meeting with Shirley, and the next morning he began the three-hour drive from Jeetersburg west to Buck County. His mother's house was along the road on the outskirts of Jeetersburg. Nate slowed his car as he passed it. A little farther along he turned around and drove back. No one answered when he rapped on the door. It was unlocked, and he went inside. His mother wasn't there.

He went out back and saw movement behind the translucent plastic sheeting of the makeshift greenhouse at the far end of the vegetable garden. He walked past rows of staked-up tomato plants and snap beans and picked his way through melon and cucumber vines. Bees droned in the blossoms at his feet.

Nate's mother was eighty. She was vigorous and healthy, and she'd built the greenhouse herself. It was a flimsy structure, plastic sheeting stretched over pine studs. Nate opened the rickety door. His mother stood by a workbench with her gloved hands in the soil of a potted geranium, a straw sun hat tilted back. Strands of white hair fell across her face. She looked up when she heard the creak of the door. She glanced at Nate's scar and a look of disappointment darkened her aspect for a fleeting moment. Then she smiled. "Nathan. What a pleasant surprise."

Inside the greenhouse the heat was stifling and the air was as close as a wet blanket. The acrid odors of pesticide and fertilizer fought for dominance with the fragrances of the flowers. Nate mopped sweat from his brow. "It's sweltering in here, Ma. You shouldn't be in this hothouse at the worst part of the day."

"Best place to be. I've got my jug of ice water and my flowers. What more could I want, other than a surprise visit from a handsome lawyer?" She hugged him. The back of her dress was damp with perspiration. Her cheek brushed against his scar.

She stepped back and smiled at him. Her eyes fell on his chest and she frowned. She looked down at her soiled gloves. "Look at that. I left marks on your clean white shirt. I've got potting soil all over my gloves." She took off her gardening gloves and tossed them on the bench. "Come in the house and I'll clean that spot."

Nate took her arm and walked with her to the house. She limped slightly. He noticed it. "How did you hurt yourself, Ma?"

"Oh, it's nothing."

"Tell me what happened."

"Nothing. Really. Oh, I might have twisted my ankle a little when I stepped off the back stoop. I've lived in this house fifty years, and I still forget that last step every now and then." She laughed.

"It's not a laughing matter. I don't like you living here alone. What if you fall and can't get up? There's no one here to help you."

"If something happens, I'll live through it or I won't. Either way, I'm ready. I won't waste precious time worrying about all the ways I could get hurt."

"I wish you'd consider moving to that home I told you about."

"If you came here to badger me about the home for the living dead, you can walk right on out of here and take your shirt to the cleaners."

"Okay. Okay. I just worry about you. That's all."

"Well, cut it out." She steered him into the house, took off her straw hat, and washed her hands in the sink. She used a dish towel to mop the sweat off her face and neck. "Take off that shirt and give it here."

He took off his shirt, handed it to her, and sat at the kitchen table. His mother put the shirt under the tap and scrubbed the soiled spot with a stiff brush. "I was surprised to see you. I'm used to visits from you way after the sun goes down. You're a workaholic, you know. This is the first time you've come here during business hours since you were in law school." There was an awkward silence. "Are you busy these days?"

"I have enough work to pay the bills."

"What are you working on today?"

"A murder case. My client's on death row."

"Who did he murder?"

"He's accused of raping and murdering a young woman in Bloxton over in Buck County."

Nate's mother frowned. "Is that the sort of work you want to do, Nathan?"

"I don't have a choice. I can't prosecute."

Nate's mother stared at him. He looked away.

She held the shirt up to the light. "I'll hang it on the porch and let the sun dry it out. In this heat, it'll only take a few minutes." She got a hanger from the wash room and hung the shirt outside, then poured them each a glass of lemonade.

"Hits the spot on a hot day like this." She sat at the table with Nate and frowned at his scar. "Does your wound still hurt?"

"No."

"It looks like it hasn't healed."

"It's healed, but the scar won't go away."

She placed her hand over his hand. "Are you doing all right, Nathan?"

"I'm getting by."

"You look sad. You miss Christine, don't you?"

Nate's eyes glistened.

"Lately, I've thought about you and your father a lot. He died when you were so young. You've needed his guidance these past few years."

"I wasn't a little boy when he passed on, Ma. I was a senior in college."

"I know, but your father was still young when he passed. He wasn't here to show you the way to live out the later stages of your life, to teach you how a man grows old. I've thought about that a lot since you got into so much trouble."

"I made a mess of things, but Dad couldn't have done anything about it."

They fell silent, remembering his father. Then Nate said, "Dad's name came up the other day. That's why I dropped by. I heard something about him I didn't know. I heard he and Judge Blackwell were close friends."

He felt his mother's hand flinch just a little. She lifted it off his and brushed a wisp of hair from her face. "Who told you that?"

"Judge Blackwell."

She sipped from her glass. She seemed uneasy. He grew uneasy, too. She said, "What did Harry Blackwell say about your father?"

"Just before Dad died, he asked the judge to promise to watch over me and help me if I ever got in trouble."

His mother pursed her lips and started to say something, but she stopped.

"Did Dad tell you about Judge Blackwell's promise?" Nate said.

"No."

"Did you know Dad and the judge were close friends?"

"Harry Blackwell was your father's lawyer before you were born. I didn't know he and your father were close, but it's possible they were."

"I'm surprised Dad didn't tell you he asked the judge to watch over me. It seems odd that Dad would ask someone for a family favor and not tell you about it."

"Cancer dragged your father to his death slowly. The judge and many others sat by his deathbed near the end. I don't know everything he said to his visitors. He and I loved each other, but he had his secrets and I had mine."

Nate's mother got up and walked out on the porch. She brought the shirt back to him. "It's dried out. There's no stain. Your old mom's still good for something, I guess." She laughed, too loudly. She ironed the shirt. They remained silent as she did so, and his uneasiness grew. He knew his mother well. She was hiding something.

She handed the shirt to him.

"What's the matter, Ma? Why don't you want to talk about Dad and the judge?"

"Your father died hard. It hurts to think about it, even after all these years. I'd rather not take myself back to those painful times."

Nate buttoned his shirt.

His mother brushed her hand over his chest where the stain had been. "Good as new." She patted his chest and looked up at him. "The best-looking fifty-six-year-old man in the United States of America." She chuckled, but she glanced at his scar.

She kissed his cheek, put on her straw hat, took his arm, and walked him to his car. He got in and she smiled at him, a stiff, forced smile. Then she turned away and walked back to the greenhouse.

Chapter 15

The Scarf

To take a close look at the scarf and the other exhibits in the case, Nate arrived at the Buck County courthouse in the early afternoon and found the file room in the basement of the building. The file clerk was a young black man who led Nate through rows of cardboard boxes and metal bins to a conference room. Its walls were off-white and bare. A paper-thin gray carpet covered the floor and a conference table sat under a fluorescent light that flickered intermittently. The room was warm and stank of cigarette smoke.

"Deatherage case has six boxes of exhibits," the clerk said. He brought the first box into the room. Nate rummaged through it and found a folder containing the photographs of Updike's corpse taken by the local medical examiner, Malcolm Somers. Nate reviewed the photographs while the clerk came and went with the other boxes.

The first photograph of the corpse was taken from a distance of about fifteen feet. The image was paled by light coming in through a warehouse window, but it was clear that Updike's body lay sprawled on the warehouse floor. There were no mattresses.

The second photograph was a full-length frontal body shot taken from a position standing over the body. The image was clear. Nate's breath caught in his throat. Darlene Updike bore a striking resemblance to Christine when Christine was in her twenties. In the photograph, Updike was nude except for her blouse, which was open. She lay on her back, her legs spread wide. Her face was swollen, bruised, and abraded, and blood ran from her mouth down one side of her face to her ear. The rope was tight around her neck, embedded in a groove of bloody flesh. Her thighs and crotch were smeared with blood. Updike's hair was jet black, thick and coarse, like Christine's hair. She was short. Taut breasts, strong legs. She could have been Christine's sister.

The physical resemblance between them shocked him, but even more disturbing was the jarring thought that there was a similarity between Updike's assailant and Nate. Nate tried hard to suppress the comparison. We are not the same, he assured himself. It was true that he'd almost hit Christine when she wouldn't listen to his closing. Anger and frustration had swelled up inside him, but he had stepped back that night, horrified by the violence he saw lurking in a dark corner of his mind. He looked again at the photograph of Darlene Updike's ravaged body. Nate was not like the monster who unleashed his rage on this poor girl. Nate could not have done this to Christine, to Darlene Updike, to anyone.

He took a deep breath and thought about all the sorrow and misery he had caused over the last few years, and his defenses slowly crumbled. He hadn't beaten Christine, thank God, but he had abused her emotionally. He had belittled her and bullied her and lied to her. He had broken her heart.

Nate set the photograph on the table, slumped in his chair, and covered his eyes. He felt nauseous. Perversely, a vision of the first time he made love to Christine burst into his mind. He saw himself on a blanket spread in a clearing by the dam at Jasper Lake on a summer day. Christine sat with her legs to one side, wearing a yellow two-piece bathing suit. He leaned toward her and kissed her. Her tongue flicked in and out. He put his hand behind her head, pulled her to him, and kissed her hard. He unhooked the top of her bathing suit. He thought she would stop him, but she didn't resist. The top fell away. She rested her head on his shoulder and kissed his neck while he caressed her breasts.

He guided her down on her back. She raised her hips and he slipped the bottom of her bathing suit down her legs and tossed it away. He took off his shorts and threw off his shirt. He lay on top of her and kissed her. They made love. She cried out at the moment of climax. He fell away and they lay naked together on the blanket, breathless.

"Jesus," he'd said.

She laughed a quiet, throaty laugh.

He propped himself up on an elbow and looked at her. She lay on her back, naked, with her eyes closed, basking in the sun. She made no move to cover herself. Her breasts were small and taut, her stomach flat, her legs tan and athletic. He moved his hand over her breasts, hips, and thighs. She lay still and did nothing to stop him. His fingers traced her lips. She had a pert mouth with full lips and big wideset brown eyes framed by thick, straight, raven hair.

"You're beautiful," he said.

Nate opened his eyes and looked at the photograph of Darlene Updike. She was Christine. Her body was Christine's body. Her face was Christine's face. He was lightheaded. He leaned back in the chair and breathed deeply.

"You all right, sir?" The file clerk was standing at the conference table, watching him.

"I'm recovering from the flu. Could you bring me a glass of water, please?"

The clerk left the room. Nate put the photographs in the folder. His hands shook. He thought he might faint. He leaned forward, his head between his knees.

The clerk returned with a glass of water. Nate drank it down and leaned back in the chair again.

"You want me to call a doctor?"

"I'll be fine in a moment." Nate looked at the boxes of exhibits. He needed to finish quickly and get away from the photographs. "I'm interested in Commonwealth's Exhibit D. Can you find that exhibit for me?"

"You sure you're all right?"

"I'll be fine once I concentrate on the case. Can you find that exhibit for me?"

The clerk withdrew a transparent plastic pouch from a file box and handed it to Nate. Nate leaned over the table, gripping the pouch with both hands. He closed his eyes.

"You sure you're all right, sir?"

Nate took more deep breaths and gathered his wits. "I'll be fine. Thank you for your concern."

Nate forced himself to focus on the scarf inside the pouch. The scarf was square, about three feet long on each side. It was royal blue with a yellow border. In its center there was an image of a yellow lily. There was a single splotch of blood near a corner of the scarf. The stain was shaped like an egg, about two inches at its widest point and about four inches long. The stain was as dark on its borders as it was in its center.

Nate stared at the bloodstain for a long time. When the shock of the photograph finally subsided and his mind cleared, it dawned on him why Shirley West told him to inspect the scarf carefully. Even in his diminished state of mind, he could see the problem with the bloodstain. It was too neat. The blood bled into the scarf evenly across the whole stain. There was no other visible sign of blood on the scarf – no splatters, no smears. The appearance of the stain didn't fit the violent character of the crime or the nature of Updike's wounds. Nate was unable to imagine circumstances consistent with a crazed strangulation, rape, and beating that could have resulted in this perfectly oval-shaped bloodstain.

The design of the scarf caught his eye, too. The yellow lily was centered, but it wasn't symmetrical. It was slightly larger on the left side. The yellow border wasn't a straight line all the way around the scarf. It strayed too far to the outside on its top and left sides. No manufacturer would have sent such a flawed pattern into mass production. The scarf was handmade.

Nate said, "Is there a craft shop in Bloxton where people sell handmade goods, quilts and pillows, things like that?"

"I don't know of such a shop in Bloxton, but my wife crochets sweaters and shawls and such. Sometimes she sells em at a shop name of Country Faire near the county line in Dealeton."

Nate handed the pouch to the clerk, who withdrew a logbook from a drawer in the table and entered the exhibit number, date, and time. Nate signed his name and looked at the other entries. Swiller's name wasn't there. George Maupin had viewed the exhibits on January 3, 1968, shortly before the trial, and again on May 20, probably in preparation for the appeal. Daryl Garth looked at the exhibits on April 23. Nate had heard of Garth. He was a lawyer in private practice in Bloxton. As far as Nate knew, Garth had no connection to the case.

"Were you on duty the day Mister Garth viewed the exhibits in this case?"

"Yes, sir."

"Do you know why he looked at them?"

"Mister Garth took over Jimmy Washington's case after Mister Swiller died. He asked to see the exhibits in all four of Mister Swiller's death row cases."

"Jimmy Washington is one of the defendants on death row?"

"Yes, sir." The clerk's fists were clenched. The nameplate pinned over the breast pocket of his county uniform said "F. Washington."

"Is Jimmy Washington your brother?"

"He's my cousin."

The hard edge in Washington's voice was unmistakable. Nate was mindful that the vast majority of defendants executed in Virginia in modern times were black men. Virginia juries were almost always all white. As a court clerk, Washington would be aware of that. Nate said, "I'm sorry. It must be difficult for you."

"Yes, sir."

"Do you know why Mister Garth looked at the files of all the capital cases?"

"No, sir."

Washington's tone of voice caught Nate's attention. Nate thought he was holding something back. "You know something about these cases, don't you, Mister Washington?"

"You done lookin at the exhibits?"

"Yes."

Washington lifted a box and left the room. He came and went, removing all the other boxes without looking Nate in the eye. When he was done, he said, "I'll show you out now."

Nate stood, but Washington didn't move toward the door. "Is there something you want to tell me?" Nate said.

"Jimmy got a raw deal. When Mister Swiller died, the others on death row got good lawyers, lawyers who work outside Buck County, lawyers like you. Jimmy got Mister Garth. Mister Garth feeds his family by tryin cases in Judge Herring's courtroom." Washington went to the door. He opened it and held it for Nate.

Nate stopped at the door and faced Washington. "Help me find the truth, Mister Washington. Tell me what you know."

"I know I have to feed my family, just like Mister Garth."

"I might be able to help your cousin if you tell me what you know."

Washington stared at Nate. He seemed to be considering whether he could trust him. Nate waited. Washington looked around. No one was in sight. In a quiet voice, he said, "Judge Herring came here and reviewed the Deatherage file last month after you filed the papers said you were on the case."

"Does the judge normally review files of cases on appeal?"

"This was the first time he came here in the eleven years I worked the file room."

"Why didn't you enter the judge's name in the log?"

"He told me not to log him in and not to tell anyone." Washington lowered his voice even more. "He came here just before closin time. Told me to put the Deatherage file in the conference room and wait out front. Said he'd make sure the county paid me for the overtime. I pulled the file for him and he was here till eight thirty."

"More than three hours."

"Yes, sir."

"Do you know if the judge looked at the scarf?"

"He didn't look at the exhibits. He looked at the written record. I went to the conference room about seven and asked him how much longer he'd be. When I opened the door, he was lookin at the transcript and writin notes on a pad."

"Did he say anything to you about the transcript?"

"Said he wanted to know when anyone asked to see the Deatherage file. Gave me the number of his private line and told me to call him if anyone asked to see it."

"Did he ask you to tell him if anyone looked at the files of the other death penalty cases?"

"The Deatherage file was the only file he wanted to know about."

"Have you called him to tell him I was here?"

"I'll call him when you leave."

"How do I get to that shop, Country Faire?"

"Take state road 677 to Dealeton. Before you get to the state line, you'll see a Texaco station on your right. The shop is across the road from that station."

"How long will it take me to get there?"

"Bout thirty minutes."

"Maybe you could do me a couple favors, Mister Washington. When you talk to the judge, maybe you could tell him I looked at the scarf and I didn't look at any other exhibits. Tell him I asked you about handmade scarves and I asked you for directions to Country Faire."

"I can do that."

"I need one more favor. I need you to wait an hour before you call him."

Washington nodded. "I'll make the call one hour from now."

Chapter 16

The Change-of-Life Baby

Dealeton was twenty miles west of Bloxton, on the border between Virginia and West Virginia. The little town was a row of ten shacks clustered around a gas station on a narrow country road. The shack across the road from the Texaco station was draped in the shadows of tall white pines. A thick layer of pinetags covered its felt roof. "Country Faire" was painted in crude brushstrokes on a sign over the open door.

Nate parked in front and climbed the porch steps. The shop was small and dark and smelled like mothballs. Quilts hung from racks in the shadows along the wall to his left. Items of clothing lay on a plywood table against the opposite wall. A glass-top counter stood in the back. No one was in the shop.

He looked around. The garments on the table were cast-off clothing – old dresses, blouses, shirts, and pants. Some were soiled. A blouse was ripped at the shoulder. He could barely make out a small selection of cheap jewelry caked with dust through the film of grime on the glass-top case. He turned to the quilts hanging on racks. There were about a dozen, all handmade, with distinctive patterns. Most had big square patches sewn together with the same image in a different color inside each square. One was multicolored roosters. Another was butterflies. He pulled the quilts apart to get a better view of those hanging in the back. Dust billowed from them. His eyes watered. When his vision cleared, he saw a red lily.

The quilt had lilies of a different color in each square – red, blue, green, and yellow. The yellow lily was identical to the one on the scarf.

Nate heard steps at the doorway. He turned to see an obese old woman. "I don't tolerate no looky-loos. You make me walk all the way over here from the house in my condition, you got to buy somethin."

The old woman's hair was white. Her face was round and flushed. She leaned on a cane and puffed and blew as she struggled to walk across the room. Something about her seemed familiar to Nate, but he was certain he had never met her.

The old woman sat on a stool at the end of the counter and wiped her face with a rag. "Shewee. Hotter'n hell. Gimme a minute." She clutched her chest, wheezed and frowned at Nate. "You're a stranger. Who told you bout my shop?"

"I heard about it in Bloxton. I'm looking for a scarf."

"I don't have no scarves. You'll have to buy somethin else." She thrust her cane at the wall of quilts. "Buy one a them quilts. Handmade. Sadie Biggs made em. Twenty dollars cash on the barrelhead."

"I'm looking for a special scarf. It's a blue scarf with a yellow lily." Nate pulled the quilt out for the woman to see. "A yellow lily like this one."

The woman scowled at him. "Who the hell are you?"

"I'm Nathan Abbitt."

"I've heard that name somewhere before. Where you from?"

"Selk County. Jeetersburg."

The woman squinted at Nate. "Mighty bad cut you got on your face. You look like you might be a bad un. You won't do me no harm, I hope."

"No, ma'am. I was injured in a car accident."

The old woman wiped her mouth with the rag. She thrust the rag toward a telephone on the glass-top counter. "I can call the sheriff on that phone there. His men'll be here in a jiffy."

"There's no need. I won't harm you. I came here to find the scarf."

"What did you say your name was?"

"Abbitt. Nate Abbitt."

"I know I've heard your name, but my memory don't work too good no more. Truth be told, nothin I got works too good no more." She seemed to relax about Nate's scar. "I had three of them yeller lily scarves last spring. Sadie Biggs made em. Only ones she ever made. I don't have no more of em."

"Who bought them?"

"Nobody bought em. Somebody broke in here in the middle of the night and stole em. Stole all my quilts, half my hand-me-downs, and all three of them scarves. Don't know why they didn't take my jewelry. I had the case locked. They didn't want to break the glass and make a big ruckus, I reckon."

"Did you report the break-in to the sheriff?"

"Might as well tell my dog about it. Sheriff Feedlow made me fill out a form. Went away and I never heard from him again. Hubert Feedlow's bout as shiftless as the crooks he's supposed to catch, and truth be told, he don't catch very damn many of em."

"When were the scarves stolen?"

"Last summer. Hot day like this un. June. July maybe."

"Did you keep a copy of the complaint form?"

"Why the hell you want those scarves so bad?"

"I'm a lawyer. The scarves may be important to one of my cases."

The old woman's eyes narrowed. "A lawyer. Lordy. You're that lawyer called me bout Kenny."

The familiarity of the old woman's features came together. She resembled an aged Kenneth Deatherage. "You're Eva Deatherage."

The woman struggled to her feet. "I could tell by that ugly scar you was no good. You tricked me. You got no right to pester me. I told you I wouldn't talk to you."

"No, ma'am. I didn't trick you. I didn't know you were Kenny's mother. I came to your shop to find the scarf, but I didn't know you were the owner."

"I told you I won't talk about Kenny." She caned to the door.

"Please, ma'am, I need your help." Eva walked on. "Wait. I'll buy the quilt, the one with the lilies."

She stopped. "That one costs more. Thirty dollars for that one."

"That'll be fine."

Eva held out her hand. Nate gave her the money. She stuffed the bills in a pocket of her dress. She limped back to the stool, sat on it, and wiped her face with the rag. "You'll have to fetch it yourself. I can't manage it." The quilt was bound to the rack too high for Nate to reach the clasps. Eva pointed her cane at a chair in the corner. "Best way is to stand on that chair and unhook the quilt from the rack." Nate carried the chair to the quilt rack. "You're wastin your time, you know. Kenny killed that girl." Nate set the chair beside the quilts and looked at her. "Don't look at me that way, mister. I'm not a bad mother. It ain't my fault Kenny turned so mean."

"He says he didn't kill the girl."

"That don't mean nothin. Kenny always lied about the killins."

"What killings?"

"All of em. My chickens, my cat, Sadie Biggs' beagle pup. He always lied. I went three months with a shotgun propped by the door watchin for the fox he claimed was killin the chickens. The chickens made a big ruckus one afternoon. When I got to the coop, he was standin inside, wringin the neck of one of my guinea hens. Three others was already dead. Blood all over his hands. Goony grin on his face. I switched him till he bled, but it didn't do no good. Nothin did no good with Kenny. He's got too much of his daddy in him."

Nate climbed carefully onto the chair, balanced himself on its straw seat, and began to unhook the quilt. "Any chance I could talk with Kenny's father?"

"Good luck. Nobody round here's seen him in twenty-eight years. Run off right after I got pregnant with Kenny." Eva dabbed her brow with the rag. "Jake ran off with Lucy Morris. Some says they went to Tennessee. Others says Missouri. Truth be told, I don't care where Jake is in this life, long as he ends up in hell in the next."

Nate freed the quilt from the rack and stepped off the chair. He set the quilt on the counter and folded it. "Did Kenny tell you what happened the night of the murder?"

"Kenny and me ain't talked since he was fourteen."

"I don't mean to pry, ma'am, but why is that?"

Eva fiddled with her cane. Her eyes darted around the room, at the quilts, the wall, the floor. "I caught him in his bedroom with one of them girly magazines. I'd whupped him for it before, but Kenny didn't mind me. I whupped him all the time for every kind of sin and it never did no good. I beat him somethin terrible that day, though." She raised her cane to Nate. "I beat him with my hickory stick, by God." She mopped her face with the rag and wheezed. "He wouldn't take his whuppin like a man. He slapped down his own momma. Knocked me on the floor and got on top of me. Choked me near to death. He woulda killed me, but my stick was on the floor within reach, thank the good Lord. I hit him on the noggin hard as I could and knocked him out cold. The sheriff took him off to reform school. When Kenny got out, he didn't come home. I ain't talked to him since he tried to kill me, and I ain't missed him one bit. No, sir." Eva stared at the floor, lost in her bad memories.

Nate allowed a respectful time to pass. "Do you have a copy of your complaint about the theft of the scarves?"

"I suppose so. Sheriff Feedlow gave me a copy. It's around here somewhere."

"Can I see it?"

Eva looked around the shop and frowned. "It's in that drawer over there, I think. Help me up."

Nate helped Eva stand. She limped behind the glass counter and rummaged through a drawer. She withdrew a paper and handed it to Nate.

The form was a carbon copy that listed the stolen goods as seven quilts, three blouses, six dresses, four pairs of shoes, and three scarves, noting the prices of each item. "This document says the theft took place on June 12."

"Sounds bout right."

"Mind if I take it?"

"Suit yourself."

"Thank you, ma'am, and thanks for talking to me about Kenny."

"No need thankin me for worthless jabber. Like I said, you wastin your time. Kenny killed that girl sure as I'm standin here jawin with you."

"From what I've learned so far, he may not have killed her."

"That girl was choked to death, right?"

"Yes, ma'am."

"Then Kenny was her killer. Chokin was Kenny's way. He wrung my chickens' necks. He hanged the cat. He strangled Sadie's pup. And he tried to choke the life out of me. I saw that goony smile on his face when he had his hands wrapped around my throat, that same smile I saw the day I caught him in the chicken coop. Chokin was his special pleasure, mister. You'd know if you seen that smile of his. He killed that poor girl. I know he did." Eva sighed. "Kenny was my last child. A change-of-life baby. They're supposed to be special. Precious." Eva's eyes glistened. "Wish to God he'd never been born."

Nate gave Eva time. Then he said, "When I spoke with you on the telephone, you said you told Judge Herring that Kenny killed Darlene Updike."

"I told the judge what I told you. Kenny's special pleasure is chokin the life outta helpless creatures."

"When did you talk with the judge?"

"He came to my house the day of the girl's killin and asked me about Kenny. As soon as he said the girl was choked, I told him Kenny killed her."

"Did the judge come with the sheriff or the prosecutor?"

"He came alone."

"Did he say why he wanted to know your opinion about the murder?"

"The judge said he wanted to be certain they hadn't made a mistake by arrestin Kenny because if he wasn't the killer, then some other killer was runnin loose in the county fixin to kill more girls. Judge Herring is a good man. He stood in my house and cried like a baby for that poor girl. I tell you what, mister. There's no better man than the judge when it comes to watchin out for the decent people in Buck County."

Nate left Eva Deatherage in her shop. He went to his car, sat behind the wheel, and withdrew the pleading clip of the Deatherage file from his briefcase. He turned to the indictment. It recited that Updike was murdered before dawn on June 3, 1967. Kenneth Deatherage was arrested and incarcerated that day. He was held in jail without bail until the trial took place the following January.

The scarf marked as Exhibit D was in Country Faire until June 11. Jones could not have found the scarf in Deatherage's pocket on June 3. He, or someone working with him, must have stolen it to make sure no sale could be traced back to Jones. By stealing other items with the scarf, Jones further obscured the scarf's trail. Nate figured that Jones poured type B+ blood on the scarf, which would explain the even pattern of the stain. The source of the blood could have been the medical examiner, Somers. Another possibility was that Jones stole Updike's blood from Somers' lab, although the logistics of such a theft would be difficult. Jones could also have acquired blood from a source other than Updike's corpse, stained the scarf and placed it in an evidence pouch some time after June 11, and backdated the log to June 3.

Nate was troubled. Deputy Jones' reputation as a war hero did not square with a corrupt scheme to steal a scarf and plant it on Deatherage, but Odoms' statement that Jones didn't find the scarf on Deatherage and the date of its theft from Country Faire left no room for doubt that Jones had framed Deatherage.

If Deatherage was innocent, who killed Updike? Before talking with Eva Deatherage, Nate thought Judge Herring was the most likely suspect, but Eva said the judge cried when he spoke about the murder and seemed to be trying to confirm that Deatherage killed her. Nate could think of no reason the judge would have taken the risk of approaching Eva if he was the real murderer.

Nate looked at his watch. It was four in the afternoon. He had left the Buck County file room a little over an hour earlier. By now, Washington had called Judge Herring. If someone was conspiring with the judge, that person should soon appear. Nate drove across the road to the Texaco station, which was a gas pump and a little store on a dirt lot. He parked behind the store, went inside, bought a soda, and stood at a window where he had a good view of Eva's shop.

In a short while, a Buck County patrol car came along the road and parked at Country Faire. A deputy sheriff stepped out of the car. He took off his hat and wiped sweat from his face with a kerchief. He was young, in his twenties. His blond hair was cut in a military style, a close-cropped flat top with the sides and back shaved. He was fit and strong, with broad shoulders and a weightlifter's chest. The deputy walked to the store with his back straight in measured strides with a slight hitch in his gait that favored his left leg. Nate knew this was the young Vietnam veteran, Darby Jones.

Chapter 17

The Relapse

Nate returned to Jeetersburg Friday night. Maybe it was the similarity between the corruption in Buck County and Nate's malfeasance as commonwealth's attorney that broke him down. Or perhaps it was Darlene Updike's striking resemblance to Christine. Or Nate's concern about the settlement conference in his divorce proceedings scheduled for Monday morning. Later, upon reflection, he thought it was more likely that nothing in particular caused his relapse. His addiction was powerful and his will to resist was simply exhausted. Whatever the cause, he broke the seal on a bottle of whiskey at noon on Saturday. That night, when he was three fingers from the bottom of a second bottle, he dialed the home number of his former secretary. Her mother answered the phone. Nate asked to speak with Rosaline.

"Who's calling?"

"It's Nate Abbitt, Mrs. Partlow."

"Rosaline doesn't want to speak to you."

"I'd appreciate it if you'd tell her I'm on the line."

Nate heard Rosaline's mother say, "It's that man again."

Rosaline's voice came through the line. "I told you not to call."

"I want to see you."

"I don't ever want to see you again."

"I made a mistake. Give me a chance to make it up to you."

"Mistake? Is that what you call it? You talked me into committing a crime."

"I didn't mean to put you at risk."

"You told me everybody would be better off if I signed that document. You said that man was guilty of the murder. You lied to me."

"I didn't lie. I thought he was guilty."

"You told me I couldn't get in trouble for signing that paper. That was a lie. Judge Blackwell said I committed perjury. He said he could have sent me to jail for five years."

"I didn't think things through. I'm sorry."

"Sorry's not good enough." There was a long silence. Then Rosaline said, "You said you needed time to tell Christine about us. I waited a whole year. You still hadn't told her when this big mess came along. Have you ever told Christine about us? Have you told her what you were doing all those nights and weekends when we were together?"

Nate didn't answer.

"Our time together, it was all a lie, wasn't it? You never meant to leave Christine, did you? You didn't love me. You loved what we did together when we were alone." Her voice broke. She took a deep breath. "Well, you got what you wanted from me." Her voice broke again and she hung up the phone. Nate drained the bottle and passed out.

On Sunday before dawn, he vomited. He struggled through a series of dry heaves until midmorning. Sunday evening he kept down tomato soup. Monday morning he awoke early, sat on the edge of his bed, rubbed his temples to soothe a dull headache, and looked around his apartment. His bed rested against the back wall. A stove, icebox, and sink stood against adjoining walls. In between were a kitchen table and folding chairs. The room stank of cigarette smoke that seeped through the floor from Sally's Diner below it. Nate hated the squalid little room. He hated all the trappings of his broken life.

He went to the window and looked across Lee Street at Beauregard

Park. A squirrel foraged for food under an oak tree. Nate watched it scamper across the lawn and thought about the settlement conference scheduled for that morning and the train of events that led to Christine's complaint for divorce. With money he inherited from his father, Nate and Christine bought their farm in Whippoorwill Hollow shortly after they married. Nate was elected commonwealth's attorney. Christine earned a doctorate in English literature at Jefferson State. The college hired her to teach, and she made full professor. They agreed they didn't want children, but in her mid-thirties, she pressed him to change his mind. He resisted, and her interest in children waned. They went on with their lives and never regretted their decision. They were dedicated to each other and to their professions and they were happy and successful.

The first signs of trouble came with the approach of Nate's fifty-third birthday, his father's age when he contracted cancer. Nate found himself dwelling on his father's final days, the suffering, and the physical deterioration. Christine's birthday gift was a candlelight dinner at Jeetersburg's finest restaurant followed by a romantic evening at home with wine, a fire in the fireplace, and Christine in a negligee. Uneasiness had plagued Nate throughout the day, and when she embraced him that night, he was unable to perform. She tried to console him. "It's nothing to worry about. You probably drank too much wine. Besides, it's natural. We're getting older."

Nate brooded over Christine's comment. She was right, he thought. His youth had slipped away from him when he wasn't looking. Twenty-five years of sitting behind a desk and the stress of his heavy caseload had taken their toll. The cross-country athlete had given way to a flabby middle-aged man with jowls and a paunch, a man who resembled Nate's father near the end of his life, a man who was old enough to die.

Nate's preoccupation with aging and death caused him to take stock of his life. He felt he had squandered his talent prosecuting cases of no significance beyond the borders of Selk County. If he died tomorrow, his achievements would be forgotten, and if he lived another twenty years, he would achieve nothing more meaningful because he would never be more than a local prosecutor.

His assessment of his life's work robbed him of his professional energy. His cases suddenly seemed mundane, resembling cases he had tried twenty years earlier. The faces of the criminals and victims were different, but the issues were the same. One day in court, he lost his presence of mind and forgot the name of the defendant and the facts of the case, and he was forced to request a recess to review the file.

A relentless malaise came over him. He worried that he had inherited his father's cancer and that a time bomb of diseased cells lurked inside him. The sense that he was rapidly running out of time made him desperate, constantly in search of excitement, a jolt to his system, a thrill, something to make him feel young again.

Nate turned to alcohol to calm his fears. It seemed to work, at first, but over time he needed more and more whiskey to quell his anxieties. He drank pints, then fifths, then gallons, but the whiskey always wore off, and when it receded his fears returned, like rats scurrying across a basement floor when the lights have gone out. Only a continuous flow of whiskey through his veins kept the rats quiet, so he reorganized his life to allow him to function while he drank. At work, Nate sipped bourbon from a Coca-Cola can, refilling it from whiskey bottles he stowed in a desk drawer. When he was away from his office, he drank from a flask he concealed in his jacket breast pocket. On breaks during hearings and trials, he guzzled whiskey in a courthouse bathroom stall.

Nate manipulated Christine to prevent her from becoming an obstacle to his drinking. He told her he was working late when he was actually sitting at a table in Michie's Place. He came home most nights after she had gone to bed and left in the morning before she arose. She challenged him about his absences and his drinking. He thought he would lose her if she knew he was weak and afraid, so he blamed his caseload. His lies kept her at bay for a while, but she eventually insisted that he hire help to staff his cases and cut down on his drinking. He put her off but she wouldn't drop the subject. He exploded and attacked her for not being supportive. She pushed back. He reacted belligerently, insulting and berating her. Confused and hurt, Christine backed off and gave up, and Nate lost her trust and respect in the process. She stopped complaining because she stopped caring, but he was too dependent on alcohol by then to realize the severity of her wounds.

Through all the turmoil it never crossed Nate's mind that he was an alcoholic. He told himself he was a social drinker, someone who drank to relax. By the time he met Rosaline Partlow, he needed more than a fifth of liquor before noon to relax. She was a receptionist in a law office in Jeetersburg. He went there to negotiate a plea agreement. When he approached her desk, she looked up and smiled and he felt the spark of excitement he had been searching for. At first, he wasn't sure what attracted him to her. She was thirty-five, tall and slender, with blue eyes framed by shoulder-length brown hair. She was pretty, but not stunning. He had met more attractive women over the years and had never been tempted to betray Christine, but later, with the clear eyes of sobriety, he understood his infatuation with Rosaline. She was on the rebound from her second divorce. She had no children and no close friends. She was lonely and frightened and desperate for affection. She stood at the dead end of a dark road, lost and hopeless, and Nate became her savior. He took her hand and led her into the sunshine, and she repaid him with her passion. Their lovemaking restored his sexual confidence and fed his ego. She was young and she made him feel young again, and for a while, he lost himself in the taste, smell, and feel of her.

If Nate was bored with his work before he met Rosaline, after she came along it became an intolerable burden. The first steps he took to free himself from his responsibilities were small ones, unethical perhaps, but not illegal. He gave defendants generous plea agreements in cases he could have won. This alone wasn't sufficient to clear his calendar, so he ventured further across the line to compel more defendants to plead out. He withheld exculpatory evidence. He claimed to have evidence he had not yet gathered. Sometimes, he lied outright about evidence. Each breach of his oath made the next one seem less important, and whiskey overcame his moral reservations. In the end, the law's bright lines disappeared in an alcoholic haze, but Nate got what he wanted. He disposed of his cases with little or no effort, and no one was the wiser. Until the Jack Tin case.

It was Nate's obsession with Rosaline that brought him down. Six months into their affair Rosaline asked him to leave Christine. His relationship with Christine was broken, but he still loved her, or at least he loved his memory of his love for her. By then, Nate's interest in Rosaline had become purely sexual – robotic, mechanical, and addictive. He didn't want to leave Christine and he didn't want to end his affair with Rosaline, so he stalled. And he drank. Rosaline waited. Nate drifted, hoping something would extricate him from his dilemma. Rosaline's complaints that they didn't spend enough time together became more vehement, and she threatened to break off their affair. To appease her, he fired his secretary of twenty years, Marthy Critzer, and hired Rosaline.

Marthy was in her mid-fifties. She had never married and Nate suspected she had always carried a secret torch for him. She was hurt and obsessed with the injustice of her discharge. She called him on the phone every day. She lurked outside the office building and confronted him every time he went in or out. He assumed she secreted the recording device in his office in hopes of capturing evidence that would prove he was having an affair with Rosaline. What Marthy discovered was much worse.

Nate turned away from the window and got dressed for the settlement conference. He chose a blue suit that Christine had always liked and stood before the bathroom mirror and thought about the mess he had made of his life. After his accident, when all the alcohol had passed out of his system, he understood what he had been through. His fifty-third birthday had triggered a midlife crisis. His father's early death raised the specter of Nate's own mortality and the resultant fear was part of the cause of his downfall. Mourning the passage of his youth was in the mix, too. The loss of a sense of purpose, the self-loathing, chronic depression, and alienation from Christine changed him. But alcohol was the primary cause of his destruction. He had been a good man for thirty years. He loved his wife. He was one of the best prosecutors in the state. He was sensible, honest, and happy. He had the tools he needed to combat and survive a midlife crisis, even a severe one, but alcoholism washed those tools away. He had destroyed his career and had broken Christine's heart. Now he was trying hard to regain what he had lost, but alcoholism was a predator that never rested. He would never be free of it.

Nate left the apartment and walked down Lighthorse Street to the Selk County courthouse. The courtroom's floor-to-ceiling windows spilled sunlight over rows of oak pews. He went to the front of the courtroom and approached Howard Raines. The parties to the complaint for divorce were required to attend the settlement conference, but Christine was not at counsel's table with Howard that morning.

"Where is Christine?" Nate said.

"I couldn't persuade her to attend. She said she couldn't face you." Howard handed a court pleading to Nate. "I filed this motion asking Judge Greene to excuse her. I apologize for the lack of notice, but when we started to come over here, she couldn't do it and I had to throw this motion together."

Nate read the pleading. The motion said Christine was afraid to attend the hearing because Nate broke into her house and threatened her last fall.

The bailiff called the court to order, and Judge Luther Greene took the bench. Judge Blackwell normally presided over Selk County criminal and civil matters, including divorce cases, but he'd recused himself because of his close association with Christine and Nate. The circuit's chief judge assigned settlement discussions in the case to Judge Greene. Luther Greene had toiled in obscurity as a divorce lawyer in Jeetersburg for twenty years, but a close friendship with the local member of the House of Delegates led to Greene's election by the general assembly as a circuit court judge. Judge Greene was short and had a receding hairline and a sparse red goatee. His black robe swallowed his small frame, and the judge's high bench dwarfed him.

Judge Greene opened the hearing by acknowledging Howard's motion to excuse Christine's appearance and asked Nate if he wished to object to its lateness or otherwise reply. Nate said he didn't oppose the motion and the judge granted it. The judge suggested they go off the record and retire to chambers. "I'll meet with each of you separately. I'll see Mister Raines first."

They all exited the courtroom, and Howard went into chambers with the judge. Nate sat on a bench in the hallway and waited. A clock on the wall marked the time, its long hand lurching forward at the end of each passing minute. Twenty minutes passed slowly. Howard emerged and Nate entered chambers.

Judge Greene sat at a conference table beside a window. He wore his black robe even in the informal surroundings. Nate took a seat across from him. The room smelled like a doctor's office. A jar of Vick's vapor rub and a roll of cough drops sat on the table. Judge Greene popped a cough drop in his mouth. "Mentholated throat lozenges. Allergies to pollen. Menthol's the only thing that gives me relief during the growing season." Judge Greene folded his hands on the table and smiled at Nate. "I had a long talk with Howard. Christine authorized him to make a very fair offer. She's willing to sell the farm and house and split the proceeds down the middle. She'll release you from any obligation to pay alimony. Howard characterized this offer as Christine's last, best, and final offer of settlement."

"I won't agree to it."

The judge's smile disappeared. "How would you propose to resolve your differences?"

"I don't know, but I don't want to sell our home."

The judge dabbed at his forehead with a handkerchief. He glanced at Nate self-consciously. "The allergies give me a fever." He rubbed his temples and straightened his glasses. "If you don't accept Christine's offer, you'll go to trial. Are you sure that's what you want? A trial could be quite unpleasant for you."

"A trial won't make things any worse."

"You couldn't be more wrong." Judge Greene took off his glasses and wiped them with his handkerchief. "What do you think you'll achieve in a trial that you can't accomplish by accepting Christine's settlement proposal?"

"I'm not certain, but I know I don't want to sell our home."

The judge coughed and rubbed his throat. "Howard tells me you had an affair."

Nate's stomach turned over, but he did his best to show the judge nothing.

"A Miss Rosaline Partlow." The judge looked at Nate, waiting.

Nate had taken great pains to conduct his affair with Rosaline in the dark. Up to that moment, he'd assumed no one knew about it.

"Do you know this Miss Partlow?"

"She was my secretary."

"Howard says his investigator spoke with Miss Partlow yesterday. She said she had an affair with you. Is this true?"

"Christine and I have been married for thirty years. I may have made a mistake along the way. So what?"

"Well, of course, an affair with this woman is quite significant to your case. Howard says this affair lasted more than a year and ended only after your separation from Christine. Is that true?"

"I don't see the relevance of these allegations to this proceeding."

"Howard says this affair is the reason the differences between you and Christine are irreconcilable."

"I haven't seen Rosaline Partlow in more than a year. She means nothing to me. Christine broke off our relationship because of my resignation from my position as commonwealth's attorney. Rosaline is irrelevant to the issues of the divorce."

Judge Greene cupped his hand over his goatee and squinted at Nate. "Perhaps you don't know what's in store for you. You were busy prosecuting criminals all those years you were commonwealth's attorney. You probably never had occasion to observe a divorce trial. Perhaps you don't know what a good divorce lawyer can do to a man."

Judge Greene waited. Nate said nothing.

The judge continued. "Howard will call Miss Partlow to the stand. He'll ask her questions about how and when the affair began, how long it lasted, dates and times of your encounters, what you did with her, where you did it, what you promised her, what you told her about Christine. Howard will spread every tawdry detail before us in open court. Nothing is sacred. Nothing is private."

Nate was shaken, but he tried to project unwavering determination. "I repeat. Whatever I may have done with Rosaline Partlow is irrelevant to this proceeding."

"You're too smart to hold such a naïve view. You may not be a divorce lawyer, but you know the basics. A few states have a no-fault statute where your affair with Miss Partlow would not be relevant, but Virginia considers fault. This affair is central to the issue of fault. If Howard succeeds in proving fault against you, which seems almost certain, the trial judge will consider it in rendering his decision and it will weigh heavily against you."

Nate could think of nothing to say.

"Christine wants to settle the case on generous terms rather than go to trial," the judge said. "Believe me, her generosity in the face of this affair is quite rare. If you decline her offer, you'll force Howard to hang you out to dry in open court. As a former commonwealth's attorney, you are a figure of interest to the press. Your private life will be the lead story in newspapers and television broadcasts throughout the state."

"I don't care. I won't agree to sell our home. We lived there for thirty years. It's our home, damn it. I know I did some bad deeds. I know I hurt Christine. I know I have no right, but . . ." Emotion choked off Nate's words. "I don't want this divorce, Luther. I want to go back . . ." Nate's throat tightened and he couldn't speak.

Judge Greene sat back in his chair and made a wry face. "So that's why you've rejected Christine's offers. You're stalling. You don't want a final decree to be entered. You're hoping some sort of *deus ex machina* will save your marriage." The judge put his hand on Nate's arm. Nate pulled it away. "I know you don't value my advice, Nate. I understand. You're a good lawyer. You think I was mediocre at best."

"I didn't say that."

"You don't have to say it. I know what you think of me. I'm not offended. I can't compare my pedestrian achievements to your storied career. You were one of the best prosecutors in the state. You were at the top of the profession, and it meant a great deal to you. It was your identity, but you've lost all that. Your career as a prosecutor has met its demise. You confronted that awful reality and moved on as best you could. It had to be very difficult for you, but you faced up to it."

"I don't want to discuss the collapse of my career with you, Luther."

"I know. You're proud, and you don't want help, least of all from me, but you need good advice now and I'm your best resource for advice about your divorce. Despite what you may think, I was a good divorce lawyer, and I know how to adjudicate disputes between people who once loved each other and now hate each other. I'm the best referee you can find in this corner of hell." Judge Greene put his hand on Nate's arm again. "Your career and your marriage are at the same place in the road. You accepted the demise of your career. Now you must face the truth about your marriage. Your marriage is over. You must accept the death of your relationship with Christine and move on."

"I won't accept it. I can't, and I won't agree to sell our home. I won't agree to anything." Nate fumbled with his briefcase, pushed away from the table, and walked to the door. He turned back to the judge. He wanted to say something more. He wanted to proclaim the salient point that would turn the tide in the case. He wanted to deliver the brilliant argument that would save his marriage, but no words came to him.

"You're too smart to deceive yourself," the judge said. "You know I'm right."

Nate wanted to walk out the door, but he stood there, unable to move.

"What will you do, Nate? Will you accept Christine's offer or shall I give you a trial date?"

Tears welled in Nate's eyes. "I don't know what to do. I can't get Christine back, and I can't let her go. I don't know what to do."

"I understand and I'm sorry, but you have to make a choice."

Nate struggled to rein in his emotions. The judge stood up and went to Nate's side. "I understand, Nate. You need time to come to grips with this loss. I'll give you two weeks. I'll schedule a trial-setting conference for Monday after next. I'll tell Howard he'll have to wait until then for your response to Christine's offer."

Nate let out a long breath. "Thank you, Luther. I appreciate your patience." He stood at the door for a moment. Then he looked Judge Greene in the eye. "I apologize for my disrespect, Luther. You're right. You're good at this."

"Thank you, Nate. Take my advice. Use this time wisely. This will be your last chance to settle with Christine. Given what she knows about your affair, I'm surprised she's willing to settle on any terms. Her good will isn't typical and it won't last. Trust me. I've been down this unhappy road many times."

Nate went back to his office and gazed out the window. Storm clouds had clustered at the peaks of the mountains. The sky darkened. Splinters of lightning flashed on the blue slopes. Thunder rolled across Whippoorwill Hollow to Jeetersburg. The rain came down lightly at first and grew in intensity until it fell in sheets. Nate thought about the judge's advice. He tried to imagine a future worth living without Christine. He could not.

"Judge Greene says you need two weeks to consider our offer." Nate turned to see Howard walk into his office and sit down. "We can't wait two weeks. Respond now or the offer is off the table."

"Why?"

"You didn't have much in your favor in this case to start with. Rosaline Partlow removes all doubt about fault."

Nate turned his back to Howard and looked outside. The rain smelled fresh and clean. "How did you find out about Rosaline?"

"I always do a background check in divorce cases. I hired Clarence Shifflett to do a check on you. I didn't expect him to find anything except the bad prosecutions, but he talked to your old secretary, Marthy Critzer. She suspected you'd had an affair with Rosaline. Clarence confronted Rosaline as though he already knew about it. She fell into his trap and admitted it, but she wouldn't give him any details. Yesterday she changed her mind and told Clarence everything. She offered to testify for Christine."

The rain eased off. A cardinal alit on a maple tree branch just outside the window. Wind ruffled his feathers and beads of water coursed down his back. He rippled his wings and flicked off the rain.

"I need your response to our offer now, Nate."

"I'm sorry, Howard. I can't accept your offer."

"You'll lose everything."

"I don't care. I can't give her up."

There was a long silence. Howard said, "There's something you should know before you turn down my offer." Howard swiped his hand over his bald pate. "I lied to you and Judge Greene this morning. My motion to excuse Christine's appearance was a contrivance. She didn't refuse to appear. I told her to stay home."

Nate turned to Howard, surprised. "Why?"

"Christine doesn't know about Rosaline Partlow. I didn't tell her."

Nate absorbed the import of Howard's confession. Howard had advised Christine to make the settlement offer without telling her the most damning fact against Nate. Howard had breached his duty to Christine and defrauded the court in the process.

Howard said, "I met with Christine last night, fully intending to tell her about Rosaline, but I couldn't do it. I know too much. I know you spent countless nights and weekends with her when you told Christine you were working. You told Rosaline you loved her. You told her you intended to leave Christine for her. I know enough to break Christine's heart in two." Howard's eyes brimmed with tears. "So I didn't tell her about Rosaline, but I'm not like you. I'm no good at breaking the rules. I'm no good at deceiving my client and lying to the court. I can't hold it together. If you don't accept my settlement offer now, I'll break down and tell her everything."

Nate struggled. He was confronted with two bad alternatives. If he accepted Howard's offer, he would lose all hope of a reunion with Christine. If he turned it down, Christine would suffer another grievous wound at Nate's hand.

Howard leaned forward, desperation etched on his face. "Don't put her through this, Nate. She loved you with all her heart. If she learns you lied and cheated and betrayed her for more than a year, I don't know what she'll do. Don't make me tell her."

Nate tried to think of a way out of the dilemma, but there was none. After a long silence, he said, "All right. I'll agree to the settlement. I'll accept the divorce."

"Thank God. I'll call her now. My secretary will bring you my draft of the settlement agreement." Howard hurried out of the room.

Nate looked out the window again. A light rain still fell, but shafts of sunlight speared through the clouds. He thought about good times with Christine. With his back turned to the door, he cried softly. Howard's secretary brought Nate the agreement. He signed it without reading it.

Much later, he was still staring out the window when he heard someone behind him. He wiped his eyes, pulled himself together, and turned to see Howard sitting in the chair across from Nate's desk. Howard was pale and his eyes were red. "Rosaline Partlow called Christine this morning. Christine knows everything. She won't agree to the settlement."

Nate felt a surge of relief. His marriage was not yet dead. But despair quickly overwhelmed the relief. He had hurt Christine again. "How is she?"

"She's in shock."

"Go to her, Howard. She needs your help."

"She may not want my help. I lied to her and betrayed her."

"Go to her. She'll understand you were trying to protect her."

"I suppose, but that doesn't make it right."

Howard stood and went to the door.

"Tell her I'm sorry," Nate said.

Howard glared at Nate. "It's way too late for that."

Howard walked out, and Nate was alone. He recalled again Judge Blackwell's warning. "Christine will probably never take you back, Nathan, but if there's any chance at all, whiskey will kill it for you."

Nate had given in to his craving, he'd turned to Rosaline, he'd hurt her, and she'd called Christine. He had turned to whiskey and had broken Christine's heart yet again. "Christine," Nate said in a whisper. "I'm so sorry."

Chapter 18

The Investigator

The next morning Nate met with Judge Blackwell in chambers and told him about the relapse. The judge's reaction was stern, but measured. "Alcoholism is a cunning disease. You let your guard down, and it seized you."

"The craving is as intense as it ever has been."

"Abstinence is your only hope. Put this setback behind you. You must not drink again. Turn to your caseload. Apply your skills. Use your talent."

"What good will it do? I can't regain what I lost."

"When you were sober, you were a success and Christine loved you. When you became a drunk, you lost it all. Who's to say you can't regain what you lost by staying sober and concentrating on your work? Why not try to prove to everyone you're still the man you were before you started drinking?"

"That man is dead. I killed him when I lied to Christine and cheated on her. I can't forgive myself for what I did. Certainly no one else will forgive me, least of all Christine."

"The chance of recovering what you've lost may be slim, but it's all you've got. Work hard and see what happens."

Nate did not believe he could gain redemption through his work, but he had no other alternatives, and anyway, work was his only distraction from his grief. He went to his office and spent the day trying to concentrate on the Deatherage case.

The night presented a unique and bitter irony. Nate had scheduled a dinner meeting for that night with Clarence Shifflett, the same private investigator who had uncovered his affair with Rosaline. Clarence was a retired deputy sheriff in his mid-seventies. He was the best investigator in the county, but his effectiveness had diminished as he aged. His main drawback was his failing eyesight. The lenses of his glasses looked like the bottoms of pop bottles. Anything more than ten feet away was an amorphous blur to him. The Division of Motor Vehicles had declared Clarence legally blind and stripped him of his driver's license. He couldn't travel without help, but he was the best in the business working from an office with a telephone.

Nate had hired Clarence to investigate Darlene Updike's background when he first took on the Deatherage case. As it turned out, Clarence had been working for Howard Raines at that time, investigating Nate. Nate was angry that Clarence had not disclosed the conflict of interest, and he planned to fire him after he got the report about Updike.

Nate walked into Sally's Diner at six. The place was packed. He looked across a sea of oxblood leather chairs and pinewood tabletops. Colonial sconces and cheap prints of fox hunts hung over the booths along the walls. The diner catered to retired blue-collar types, Marlboro smokers, and women with big hair. They filled every booth and sat shoulder to shoulder on bar stools along the counter. Nate breathed in the aromas of fried chicken, grilled steak, and baked potatoes, all mixed together with cigarette smoke.

Through the smoky haze, he saw Clarence at a booth in the back, hovering over a bowl of chili. Clarence was a short, wiry man who always wore a brown sweat-stained felt hat pulled down low over his ears. He spooned a mouthful of chili, raised his head, and looked around the diner. His glasses magnified his eyes and made him look like a giant praying mantis.

Nate slid into the booth across from him. Clarence straightened his glasses and squinted at him. "Nate. I didn't see you come in. You're late. I started without you."

"I'm not hungry." Nate got the attention of a waitress and ordered a cup of coffee.

Clarence looked uneasy. "Howard says he told you what I found out about Miss Partlow."

Nate nodded.

"I'm sorry, Nate."

"You should have told me you were working for Howard when I hired you for the Deatherage case."

Clarence pushed the bowl of chili aside. "I was afraid you wouldn't hire me if I told you."

"That's no excuse."

"You're right, Nate, but I'm awfully short on work. It's tough to make a living when everybody thinks you're washed up."

Nate stared down at his coffee cup and didn't say anything.

"I hated to take that job, given all the cases you and I worked together in the old days, but Howard offered me a young attorney to drive me around. I crave time in the field. I've had a rough go of it since the state took my driver's license."

Nate's resentment toward Clarence began to dissipate. Clarence's age was gradually robbing him of opportunities to do the job he loved, and there was nothing he could do about it.

"I had to do my best for Howard," Clarence said. "He's been mighty good to me, but I wish I hadn't found that woman."

"I wish I hadn't found her, too," Nate said. There was an awkward silence. "What have you got for me about Darlene Updike?"

Clarence looked as though he wanted to say more, but he let it go. He picked up his notepad and held it inches from his face. "Her full name was Darlene Charlotte Updike. Born July 9, 1943. One month short of twenty-four when she was murdered. Her last job was at The Fox Paw in

Albany, New York. She worked there from April 1965 to October 1966."

"What kind of business is that?"

"A restaurant with a bar. Some kind of nightspot with live entertainment. In the old days, I would've gone up there for a look-see, but I can't do it now. All I'm good for is to call people on the phone. I called The Fox Paw and talked to the manager. He said Updike was a waitress. He said she didn't do too good a job. Most nights, she was late for work or didn't show up at all. The manager said he put up with her bad ways because she was a looker." Clarence lowered his notes and frowned at Nate. "She was pretty fast and loose from what I found out. My guess is this manager took advantage."

"Why did she leave The Fox Paw?"

"The manager said she had a drinking problem. He was willing to put up with that, but he says she started using drugs and he wouldn't tolerate it. He claims he caught her in a back room one night shooting drugs into her arm, so he fired her. I think that was a lie. I think he fired her because she stopped sleeping with him, but that's just a hunch."

"You got this manager to tell you about her drug use over the phone?"

Clarence's face crinkled into a Teddy Roosevelt grin. "When you're chained to the phone, you have to be resourceful. I told him I was a Virginia Alcohol Control Board agent. I said the state caught her selling liquor to minors when she was a clerk in a state-run outlet. Told him I wouldn't bother him if he gave me the truth about her because what she did in his bar in New York wasn't in my jurisdiction, but if he held back information I'd tell my regulatory buddies with the New York State Liquor Authority to investigate his place. He was worried about losing his liquor license, so he was real cooperative. That's what his kind does when they're scared. They tell you all the dirt on everybody else to distract you from finding out about their own crooked ways."

"Where did she work before The Fox Paw?"

"She quit high school when she was in the tenth grade. She ran through a series of odd jobs – waiting tables, answering phones for a doctor, bagging groceries, clerking in a clothing store. She never lasted more than a couple months at any one place until she got the job at The Fox Paw. I couldn't find any record that she worked after The Fox Paw fired her."

"Did you check the rehab centers?"

"They won't give out information about patients no matter what I tell them."

"Any criminal record?"

"No, but she was arrested a couple times for drunk driving."

"Why isn't there a record?"

"Her father cleaned it up."

"How do you know that?"

"I checked with the court clerk in Albany for lawsuits where Darlene was a party. There were none, but the clerk found an old civil suit where her father, Daniel Updike, was a plaintiff. The clerk sent me copies of the court file. Interesting case. About ten years ago, Updike sued his neighbor for putting up a fence that violated a homeowners' association rule. It turns out Updike is a lawyer. He represented himself in the suit and he beat the neighbor pretty good. The neighbor had to pay Updike's expenses and take down the fence. The neighbor is Robert Fleming. I called him." Clarence grinned again. "Bob's the type who holds a grudge."

"What did he tell you?"

"Bob said Darlene was a hellion, a drunk and a drug addict. Hard drugs, but he didn't know what kind. Bob said she was out all night every night. When she bothered to come home, she was blind drunk or worse. He said Darlene got at least two DUIs, and he suspected there were others he didn't know about. I told Bob there was no record of the DUIs. Bob said that was because her father had the Albany police chief in his back pocket, but that wasn't the most interesting tidbit Bob had to offer."

"What else?"

"The girl had a fight with her father after the last DUI and she moved out. That was about three years ago. She moved back in with her folks a year later, a year before she was killed. When she moved back in, she had a baby boy with her, her baby boy."

Nate paused, surprised. "Who's the father?"

"Bob didn't know. He thinks Darlene didn't know either. I suspect The Fox Paw's manager might be the culprit, but that's a wild guess. Bob said that illegitimate baby tore up Darlene's folks. Daniel Updike is a big-time Catholic, and the baby was the scandal of his parish. He quit his church over the way they treated Darlene."

"Where is the baby now?"

"With Darlene's folks. Bob said Darlene took off and left the little boy with her folks a couple months before she turned up murdered in Bloxton."

"You mean she ran away?"

"I don't think so. Updike told Bob that she was down south with relatives, taking a break from the baby, but Bob thought the Updikes sent her somewhere to work on her drug problem."

"Did Darlene's parents tell Fleming anything about the murder?"

"Bob said they were shocked and torn up, like you'd expect. Darlene's father tried to do himself in. Swallowed a bottle of sleeping pills. The doctors pumped his stomach and saved his life. He spent a few months in a mental institution last fall. Bob said the Updikes have never recovered from the murder. I've heard you can't get over the death of a child, but I don't rightly know, thank the good Lord."

"Did you talk to the Updikes?"

"I called them and spoke to Darlene's father. With all he's been through, I couldn't lie to him. I told him who I worked for. He said he wouldn't talk to anyone who worked for Deatherage. I can't blame him."

"You have anything else on Darlene?"

"That's it."

Nate was astonished by Clarence's discoveries, considering his confinement to his office. "Nice job, Clarence. You earned your fee and then some."

"Thanks, Nate. What's your next step?"

"I'm going to Bloxton day after tomorrow to dig for more information."

Clarence scooted up on the edge of his seat. "I know I have no right to ask you for work after what I did to you, but take me with you. I guarantee you I can find a truckload of information for you in Bloxton."

"Sorry, Clarence. I can't use you."

"Come on, Nate. Take me to the local watering holes and turn me loose. I'll find out more in a few hours than you'll figure out in a month."

Nate didn't say anything.

"Please, Nate. I crave time in the field something awful. Take me to Bloxton."

Nate's plan to fire Clarence melted away. He couldn't bring himself to judge him harshly. After all, when it came to ethics, Nate hadn't been a paradigm of virtue. "All right. I'll pick you up Wednesday midmorning."

Clarence's face broke into a broad smile. "Thanks, Nate. You won't regret it."

"Use the day tomorrow to do a background check on Randolph Swiller. Do one on Judge Edbert Herring, too, but make sure no one tips him off to your investigation."

"I'll get on it first thing."

Nate thought about Deputy Jones and the incongruity between his reputation as a war hero and his apparent falsification of evidence. "Do you know of any way to get access to military personnel records?"

"What branch of the service?"

"The army."

"The army's personnel files are stored in a records center in St. Louis. I've got a contact there who owes me a favor. What are you looking for?"

"There's a deputy sheriff in Buck County. His name is Darby Jones. They say he's a war hero, but I'm not so sure."

"When did he serve?"

"He was drafted. I'm not sure when, but I'd guess by his age it was 1962 or '63. He's rumored to have fought in Vietnam."

Clarence scribbled on his notepad. "I'll call my contact tomorrow."

"Okay. See you Wednesday morning." Nate stood to leave.

"Nate."

"Yeah?"

"Thanks for not holding it against me – what I did for Howard."

Nate nodded to Clarence and walked out of the diner. He stood in the street and breathed in the warm night air. A nightingale sang in Beauregard Park. Nate looked for the nightingale and thought about Rosaline. He wished he'd never met her. He wished he hadn't sunk to the bottom of a sea of whiskey. He wished he could wipe away the last few years and live them over again the right way.

Chapter 19

The Lawyer

Wednesday morning was scorching hot. The mercury stood above ninety when Nate drove down a dirt road and across a one-lane bridge that arched over Little Bear River. Clarence Shifflett lived alone in an unpainted little cinderblock house with a green tin roof that sat back from the road on the banks of the river. Clarence stood on his front stoop dressed in a shiny brown suit, a string tie, and his trademark felt hat. Unruly shocks of silver hair stuck out from the hat rim. He was clutching a big black briefcase to his chest with both hands.

Nate drove to the house and stopped. Clarence squinted at Nate. "That you, Nate?"

Nate leaned across the seat and opened the door. "Get in."

Clarence climbed in and set the case on his lap.

"What's in the case?"

"Tools of the trade."

Nate drove the winding road to Bloxton. The heat cooked the asphalt. The mountains shimmered on the horizon. "Did you find anything on Jones?" he asked.

"My contact in St. Louis found his personnel file. The rumors about him are true. He served in Vietnam, and he was one helluva fighter." Jones' story seemed to have had an effect on Clarence. Uncharacteristically, he recited what he had learned about Jones from memory without reference to his notes. "Jones was drafted in 1961. When he'd served his time, he reenlisted and volunteered for combat duty. The army sent him to Vietnam with the first wave of American troops that fought the North Vietnamese. He fought at a pitched battle on the Drang River in November, 1965. His platoon was ambushed from two sides in a clearing near a creek bed. Jones was shot in the thigh in the first minutes of the fighting, but he couldn't retreat from the field because his platoon was cut off from the rest of the US forces. His platoon held off the enemy forces for two days and nights before their battalion reached them and pulled them back. Over half the platoon was killed. Jones fought the entire battle with a shattered femur. He killed scores of North Vietnamese troops and the army gave him a lot of the credit for the platoon's survival. He got a Purple Heart for the wound and a Bronze Star for bravery. His leg wound was so serious they ruled him medically unfit for combat and sent him back to the states. He was discharged in 1966."

Nate was surprised. Given what he'd learned about Jones' corruption of the evidence in the Deatherage case, he expected his reputation to be a myth, but if anything, the rumors understated his heroism. It didn't add up. "Did your source see anything at all in his record that looked off-color?"

"Nothing. His record is clean."

Nate shook his head. "All right. What did you find out about Swiller?"

"I tracked Swiller back to Albemarle County through the DMV records. I called a retired deputy there, one of my old buddies. He gave me a lot of scuttlebutt on him." Clarence struggled with his case to extract a notepad. He held the pad close to his eyes. "Swiller's people were rich landowners in Albemarle County all the way back to colonial days, but he didn't live up to his family name. He was a gadfly as a young man and he didn't improve with age. He barely graduated from the University of Virginia. Took him six years. His daddy's money got him into Washington and Lee Law School, but he didn't do much better there, graduating at the bottom of the class in 1930. He opened a law office in Charlottesville the next year, but he was more interested in the whiskey bar than the legal bar. In the thirties and forties he racked up a long record of convictions for drunk driving and drunkenness in public. In the fifties his boozing began to mess up his law business. His clients filed a pile of bar charges against him. Mrs. Dietrich at the state bar looked up his record for me. Nice lady."

"Those records are confidential."

"Judge Blackwell chairs a committee looking to write new legal ethics rules, you know. Mrs. Dietrich somehow got the idea she was talking to the judge."

Nate grimaced. "I wonder how she got that impression."

Clarence chuckled. "Mrs. Dietrich said Swiller showed up drunk at a trial and the case had to be postponed. That was in 1956. The Virginia State Bar's disciplinary board gave him a written reprimand. It happened again in '57 and another time in '60. The disciplinary board pulled his lawyer's license for three months after that third one. Mrs. Dietrich said they usually see that kind of pattern with the lawyers who drink too much. She said whiskey is the downfall of many – " Clarence caught himself. "I'm sorry, Nate."

"Just tell me what happened to Swiller."

"His drinking got worse. In '61 he flat didn't show up for a trial. The disciplinary board pulled his license for six months. Then in '62 he didn't show up the last day of a jury trial. The court issued a bench warrant on him. The Albemarle County sheriff's boys found him passed out drunk on his kitchen floor. The judge had to declare a mistrial, assign the case to another lawyer, and retry the whole thing. The disciplinary board was mighty pissed about that one. They took his license for a year and told him they would disbar him for good if he slipped up again. He didn't give them the chance. He shut the doors on his law practice in Charlottesville and drank his way through his inheritance. By the summer of '63 he ran out of money and declared bankruptcy. In November '63, the disciplinary

board's suspension wore off, and shortly after that, he showed up in Bloxton to represent the well-known murderer Creighton Long. He moved to
Bloxton, opened a law office in a building near the old freight yard, and
handled criminal cases there till he died. Kept to himself in Bloxton, I
guess. Nobody I called there knew much about him."

Nate shook his head, mystified. "I don't understand how Swiller got
the Long case."

"I don't follow you."

"Long was an indigent defendant. The case was notorious. I'm sure
defense lawyers from all over Virginia volunteered to represent him for
the publicity. Yet Judge Herring told District Judge Gwathmey to appoint
Swiller, a bankrupt broken-down drunk coming off a string of suspen-
sions. It doesn't make sense."

"It makes sense when you know Judge Herring's background."

"What do you mean?"

"It was hard to find much on the judge because you didn't want me
to talk to anyone who might tip him off, but I found out enough to guess
why he gave Swiller that big case. The judge went to Washington and
Lee Law School. He graduated in 1930, just like Swiller."

"Washington and Lee's a small law school. If the judge and Swiller
were classmates, they knew each other."

"They knew each other all right. The postal records show the same
address for them while they were in law school – 33 University Circle,
Apartment 3B."

"They were roommates."

"They were, and I'm guessing they stayed in touch after law school.
If I'm right, they were friends for more than thirty years when the judge
appointed Swiller to represent Long. Is it legal for a judge to appoint his
friend to represent people in the judge's own courtroom?"

"There's no rule against that, but if the judge persuaded Swiller to
lose the Deatherage case or other cases on purpose, they engaged in a

criminal conspiracy. What I don't understand is why Judge Herring would risk his career to convict Deatherage or anyone else."

"I was in law enforcement for forty years. I've seen people commit serious crimes for every kind of reason. From what I've heard about this judge, his motive for rigging the outcome of this case might be power."

"Why do you say that?"

"Judge Herring is the chief judge of the circuit and the only circuit judge in Buck County. He didn't get into that position by accident. He worked and schemed to get to the top. Power is its own reward for a man like that. Maybe he can't get enough by following the rules."

Chapter 20

The Mattresses

Nate and Clarence arrived in Bloxton at half past noon. "Is there a restaurant where all the truckers stop to eat?" Clarence asked.

"There's a place called the Grill on Ewell Street near the state road. I've noticed trucks parked in front of it every time I've been here."

"If the truckers eat there, it'll have the best food in town and it'll be popular with the locals. Drop me off there."

"Okay," Nate said. "There's another place I'd like you to look at. Deatherage told me he met Updike at a restaurant called the Coal Bin. I drove by it last time I was here. It's on Water Street about three blocks from the Grill."

"I'll get directions from the help at the Grill and walk down there for supper."

The Grill was a little white frame building in a gravel lot. Three tractor-trailer rigs, an oil tanker, and a cement truck were parked in front of it. Nate dropped Clarence off there and agreed to pick him up at seven at the Coal Bin.

Nate wanted to find Henry Crawford. He might have seen or heard something that would lead to the identity of the murderer. Nate drove every street in Bloxton looking for him. No luck. He went to the abandoned warehouse and searched it. Crawford wasn't there either. He stood in front of the warehouse and thought about the man who attacked him and removed Crawford and the mattresses from the warehouse. That man might be holding Crawford somewhere, keeping him away from Nate. It wouldn't be difficult. A steady supply of liquor would keep the old drunk out of sight. He was probably somewhere in the county, but Nate didn't know where else to look. Without help, he was at a dead end.

Nate squinted at the sun. The temperature had risen into the high nineties. Streams of perspiration trickled down his back under his shirt. He wiped sweat from his face and stared at Odoms' house. Odoms was the logical person to reach out to for help, but Nate felt uncomfortable doing so. In Buck County, Odoms was the most vulnerable class of citizen. He was poor and black. He had no reason to help Deatherage and Nate had no right to drag him into a contest with the local authorities. Nate stared at Odoms' house for a long time. He could think of no one else in the county he trusted. He crossed the yard and knocked on Odoms' door.

Odoms opened the door and grimaced. "I hoped I'd seen the last of you. What you want now?"

"Have you seen Henry Crawford?"

"Ain't seen him for days."

"Where do you think he might be?"

"He's a homeless drunk. He don't have a regular place to be."

"When was the last time you saw him?"

"About noon the day before you came here and questioned me about the killing. He was walkin down Ewell Street with a bottle of wine. He went inside the warehouse."

"So you haven't seen him since the night that red pickup was parked here."

Odoms looked concerned. "That's right, now that you mention it."

Nate wiped sweat off the back of his neck and looked at the warehouse. "If you wanted to get rid of the old mattresses in the warehouse, what would you do with them?"

"Burn em."

Nate thought about that. "Burning them would take a long time."

"Not if you poured gas on em. I'd guess a half hour to an hour."

"Lots of smoke. It would attract attention."

"That's true. Black smoke. Lots of it. People would see it for miles around. Smell it closer by. So what?"

"I don't think the man who took the mattresses would risk drawing attention to a fire. If you couldn't burn them, what would you do?"

"Haul em to the county dump."

Nate nodded. "Where's the dump?"

"Other side of Bloxton."

"Show me where it is. Ride with me."

"Why you so interested in those mattresses?"

"Somebody knocked me out that night you saw the red pickup. While I was down, he got Crawford out of the warehouse and removed the mattresses. For some reason, he doesn't want me to get a good look at them. Burying them would be a big job. Burning them might attract attention. The county dump seems like a logical alternative for quick disposal."

"Why would somebody hide the mattresses from you?"

"They may have evidence of the murder on them, Updike's hair or fibers from her clothes or an old bloodstain."

"Why you botherin me about this malarkey?"

"I don't know my way around Buck County. I need help. You've been straight with me. I trust you. I don't trust anyone else here."

"Why should I help you? I don't care what happens to Deatherage."

"Henry Crawford is missing. You seem to be the only person who cares about him. Whoever took the mattresses may be holding him against his will."

Odoms seemed to reflect on Nate's points. "All right, damn it. Wait here." Odoms left and returned with a pistol in his hand.

"You won't need a firearm," Nate said.

"You don't know what you're up against, lawyer. I'll take you to the dump, but that's the end of it. You're on your own after that."

About five miles outside Bloxton, Odoms pointed to a wooden sign with the words "County Dump" scrawled in white paint. Nate turned onto a dirt road that cut a path through scrub pines. A rusty pipe stretched across the road, blocking access.

Odoms said, "You got to pay a dollar to the man."

Nate gave Odoms a dollar. He walked across a clearing to a shack. An old black man came to the door, and Odoms paid him. The old man limped to the gate, unlocked it, and waved Nate and Odoms through. Nate drove down the dirt road and rolled the car to a stop on a shelf of land that overlooked a gaping ravine. Odoms and Nate walked to the lip of the ravine. The stench of rot soured the air. A flock of sparrows flew out of the dump, momentarily blotted out the sun, and streaked a dark line across the sky. All manner of castaway items lay at the bottom of the ravine – rusted bed springs, broken furniture, hollowed-out hulls of junk cars, rusty refrigerators and stoves, boxes and bags of trash. They scanned the surface for several minutes.

"Don't see the mattresses," Odoms said.

Nate returned to the car, retrieved a pair of binoculars from the glove compartment, and walked back to the cliffside. He peered at the trash through the binoculars for a long time. "It's only been a few days since they disappeared. If they're here, they should be on the surface."

"Lemme have a look," Odoms said. Nate handed him the binoculars. Odoms searched for a while longer but finally gave up. "They ain't here."

"Looks like we guessed wrong," Nate said.

They returned to the car and drove away from the dump. Nate drove through the gate and stopped at the paved road. "Where else could someone hide those mattresses?"

"It's a big county. Could be anyplace."

"Maybe you were right with your first guess. Maybe he burned them. It was late at night, very dark. Maybe he wasn't worried about the smoke."

"Could be." Odoms stroked his jaw. "There's another place to dump trash. It's easier to get to. You don't have to go through a locked gate, and there's less chance somebody will see you there."

Odoms directed Nate to drive west to Dealeton. Just past the town, they turned off to a dirt road. The car crested a rise and a manmade canyon opened up before them, stretching out for several hundred yards. They drove down a road that was cut into the cliff walls of the gaping hole. The road rounded the huge hole and descended to the bottom of a pit. Two thirds of the way around the wall, Odoms told Nate to stop the car. He got out and went to the edge of the road and Nate followed. Trash thrown from the road cascaded down the slope and formed great piles of debris at the bottom.

Odoms said, "Red Diamond Rock Products dug this quarry years ago. When all the rock was gone, they laid off their workers, pulled out of the county, and left this big hole behind. It's illegal to do it, but some people throw their junk in there. There's no gate to block your way. You don't have to pay here. You could throw those old mattresses in this hole and figure nobody would notice em or come here lookin for em."

They scanned the piles of junk and Odoms saw the mattresses first. Five mattresses were strewn along the slope of the biggest mountain of trash. From the high spot on the road, they looked like wrinkled postage stamps.

"How do we get down there?" Nate said.

"We follow this road to the bottom and drive along the flats to the base of that pile of junk."

The mound of trash looked small from the road above it, but as they drove across the bottom of the quarry, the mountain of cast-off goods loomed higher. When they rolled to a stop at the foot of the mound, Nate guessed the pile of trash was sixty feet tall.

Odoms craned his neck to look at the top. "Ten years' worth a junk mounts up."

The trash hugged the wall of the pit and stretched down a long steep slope to the bottom. The mattresses were not visible from the quarry floor, but based on the view from above, Nate guessed they lay close to the top of the slope.

Odoms and Nate awkwardly picked their way up the mountain of junk. Nate's foot broke through the seat bottom of an easy chair. He cursed, kicked free of the chair, and climbed on. Farther along, Odoms stumbled over a rusty metal bed frame and fell to his knees. He struggled to his feet, mopped his face with the belly of his shirt, and squinted at the sky. "Hot as hell." When they finally reached the mattresses, they sat down to catch their breath.

Odoms said, "What are we lookin for?"

"If Updike was killed on one of these mattresses, it should still have an old bloodstain on it."

Nate and Odoms rose and inspected the closest mattress. It was filthy. Stains of various colors and shapes marred both sides. Some of the stains were dark, but Nate couldn't tell if they were bloodstains. They looked at three more mattresses, all of them filthy and covered with stains. Nate was hot and winded. He stood with his hands on his hips, sweating and breathing hard. The last mattress lay behind Odoms. A stain on it caught Nate's eye. It was centered in the top half of the mattress. It was dark red and it glistened in the sun. Nate pointed to it. "That looks like dried blood."

Odoms grabbed one end of the mattress and tried to turn it, but it was heavier than the others. He dropped it, covered his nose with his hand, and stepped back. "God almighty. There's trouble here. I know that smell. Grab the other end and help me."

Nate grasped the end of the mattress and they flipped it over. The lining ripped open. A cloud of vapor billowed from it and an oval-shaped melon-sized object fell out of the tear in the mattress. It was maroon, purple, and blue. It was framed by matted hair streaked with dried blood.

Nate staggered backward and fell. He sat up on his haunches and vomited. Odoms leaned over the mattress and looked at the protruding head. He walked over to Nate and sat down beside him.

"I smelled that rot in Korea," Odoms said. "You don't ever forget it."

"Is it Henry Crawford?"

"You can't tell by his face. He was beat too bad, but the hair and the beard are Henry's." Odoms wiped his mouth with his sleeve. "Had to be a cold man killed Henry. He was just a poor old drunk who couldn't crawl out of his bottle."

They sat for a while without saying anything. Then Odoms said, "What you gonna do about Henry?"

"Notify the sheriff."

"I don't wanna be part of it. They'll put Henry's killin on me. I'm the nigger in this mess."

Nate agreed. "I'm sorry I dragged you into this. There's no need to expose you. I'll tell the sheriff I found him on my own. I'll keep you out of it."

Chapter 21

The Sheriff

Nate took Odoms home, found a telephone booth beside the Esso station, and called the Buck County sheriff's office to report the discovery of Crawford's corpse. A secretary told Nate Sheriff Feedlow would meet him at the quarry.

Nate returned to the quarry floor. He got out of his car, leaned against its fender, and waited. It was midafternoon. The heat was intense. Buzzards circled overhead and the odor of rancid garbage rose from Nate's stained clothes. The stench of Crawford's rotting cadaver and the sight of his bloated face haunted him.

He thought about Crawford's murderer. The killer's disposal of the body was reckless and foolish. Tossing the mattresses in the quarry made some sense; they were difficult to dispose of and the quarry was remote. He'd probably assumed it was unlikely anyone would search for them, and if someone did, the quarry was not an obvious place to look. But stuffing a corpse in a mattress and tossing it into the quarry was another matter. The stench of a dead corpse was unmistakable. Wild carrion birds would be drawn to it. The likelihood of discovery was much greater. Nate thought the killer must have panicked and made a foolish choice in haste. He was convinced that he was inexperienced.

Nate pondered the murderer's motive. Crawford was in the warehouse at the time of Darlene Updike's murder. Maybe he saw the killing and maybe his murderer was also Updike's killer. But why would Updike's murderer wait a year to kill Crawford? More likely, the murderer was part of the conspiracy to convict Deatherage. He'd attacked Nate to prevent him from finding out that the conspirators covered up Crawford's presence in the warehouse the night of the murder and then had to kill Crawford to prevent him from identifying Nate's attacker. Deputy Jones seemed a likely suspect.

Sunlight glanced off the windshield of a patrol car traveling the road cut into the quarry's wall. The car reached the quarry floor, sped across the flats, and pulled up next to Nate. Buck County Sheriff Hubert Feedlow stepped out of the car. He was in his sixties, tall and slim with a pale complexion, a long narrow face, and close-set green eyes. His jaw ballooned with a chaw of tobacco. He wore a tan uniform and holstered a service revolver on his hip. He spat on the quarry floor and touched his hat. "Long time no see." The sheriff squinted. "Ugly scar."

"I was in a car accident."

"So I heard tell." The sheriff wrinkled his nose. "You smell like you ought to be bagged up and throwed away."

"I climbed this pile of garbage. I got it all over me."

The sheriff's thin lips parted in a wry smile. "You'll have to take your bath before Saturday this week." He looked up at the mound of junk. "You picked a mighty hot day to climb this pile of trash. The dispatcher said you found a dead body."

"The body's up there on top, stuffed inside an old mattress."

"What the hell's it doin in a mattress?"

"I don't know."

"What's the body doin on top of the trash pile?"

"I don't know."

"Well, what the hell do you know?"

"I know the dead man was Henry Crawford."

"Henry? Why would anybody kill Henry? Better yet, why would

anybody stuff that poor sumbitch in a mattress and haul him way the
hell out here?"

"I don't know."

The sheriff looked suspicious. "Why were you crawlin around in the
trash on a day hot enough to boil your brains out?"

"I'm working on the Deatherage case."

"What's Henry got to do with Deatherage?"

"He was in the warehouse the night Darlene Updike was murdered."

"First I heard of it. Who says so?"

Nate was caught unprepared by the question. He'd promised to conceal
Odoms' involvement. He hesitated. "Crawford told me he was there."

"When did you talk with Henry?"

"Last week."

"Where?"

"In the warehouse."

"What else did Henry say about the murder?"

"Someone hit me and knocked me out before he could tell me anything."

"News to me. How come you didn't file a complaint with my office?"

"The injury wasn't serious, and I was busy with the case."

Feedlow looked skeptical. He spat tobacco juice and wiped his lip with
the back of his hand. "Why did you come lookin for Henry at the quarry?"

"When I saw Crawford, he was lying on a pile of mattresses. The person
who hit me removed them from the warehouse. I've been searching for
Crawford and the mattresses ever since. I thought maybe the person who
hit me hauled them to the county dump. I came here looking for them."

"This ain't the county dump. Who told you about the trash in the quarry?"

Nate hesitated again. "I don't remember, but it seems to be common
knowledge in the county. I guess I heard about it from someone when I
was here last week."

"You guess." Feedlow's wry smile returned. "A smart lawyer like you
ought to be able to come up with a better story than that."

"What do you mean?"

Feedlow squinted at Nate and then looked at the pile of trash. "Well, I sure as hell don't want to climb that big heap of trash, especially on a day hotter than the fires of the devil's homebase. I sent one of my deputies to fetch Mac Somers. We'll wait for him. You can show him where Henry is. I'll supervise from down here."

Nate wasn't surprised by Sheriff Feedlow's lack of enthusiasm. Nate had served on statewide criminal task forces with him and knew him well. Buck County paid its sheriff the minimum required to fill the job, and in Hubert Feedlow, it got what it paid for. He did what he had to do to stay in the job and nothing more, but he wasn't stupid. Buck County was filled with tough men. Throughout Feedlow's thirty years as sheriff, rivals had accused him of negligence, others claimed he was corrupt, and a few had threatened violence against him. He'd fought off every challenge. He was a survivor: cunning and resourceful.

Another patrol car made its way down the wall and across the quarry floor to the trash pile. Two men stepped out of it, a short chubby man in civilian clothes and a young deputy sheriff. Nate recognized the deputy from Country Faire. He extended his hand to Nate. "Darby Jones, sir." His grip was firm and he looked Nate straight in the eye.

The short chubby man was Malcolm Somers, the local medical examiner. Nate knew him from his days as a prosecutor. Somers was in his fifties and wore a seersucker suit, a string tie, and a straw hat. His face was drenched in sweat. He nodded to Nate. "Good to see you again. What have we got here?"

"A man's been murdered," Nate said. "His body was stuffed in a mattress and dumped on this trash pile. The body's near the top."

"How do you know the man was murdered?" Somers said.

"When you see him, you'll know."

"Hold your horses," Feedlow said. "I don't recall anybody electin you sheriff. Mac, you go up there and take a look. You think somebody murdered the poor sumbitch, I'll declare this a crime scene and we'll rope it off."

"Who's the victim?" Deputy Jones said.

"Henry Crawford," Nate said.

Jones flinched. "Why in the world would someone kill Mister Crawford?" He seemed shocked and disturbed.

The sheriff said, "You go with Mac, Darby. See what you can find up there."

Somers and Jones began climbing the mound of trash. On the difficult, awkward climb, Jones exhibited a pronounced weakness in his left leg. Twice he fell to his knee on that side and had difficulty returning to a standing position.

The sheriff and Nate stood next to one another at the foot of the mound of trash, watching Somers and Jones. The sheriff spat on the quarry floor. "I wouldn't make much of what Henry said if I was you. Henry was drunk on rotgut most of the time. The rare times he was sober, he didn't know who he was or where he was. If he was anywhere near the warehouse when the girl was murdered, which I doubt, he probably didn't know what county he was in. You dirtied up your pretty clothes for nothin."

Nate didn't say anything. The sheriff kicked an empty paint can that lay at the bottom of the trash heap. The can rolled across the quarry floor, hit the tire of the sheriff's patrol car, and came to rest. "You shouldn't have come out here to this dump," the sheriff said.

"What do you mean, Hubert?"

"You poke around in the wrong places in this county, you'll be sorry you ever hooked up with Kenny Deatherage."

"Is that a threat?"

The sheriff smiled and shook his head. "No threat. Just friendly advice. The rules are different in Buck County. It don't pay to stir the pot here."

"Who sets the rules in Buck County? You?"

The sheriff didn't respond, but Nate was afraid to press him further.

Somers and Jones picked their way down the slope. Just before they came into earshot, the sheriff said, "I'm not powerful enough to set the rules. From what I hear, you ain't either. They tell me you tried to set the rules in Selk County, and it didn't work out too good." He looked at Nate's scar and smiled.

Jones and Somers reached the quarry floor out of breath and covered with sweat. Somers took off his hat and mopped his face and neck with a handkerchief. "The man's been murdered. Someone beat him to death. The killer made a clumsy mess. He cut the mattress open, crammed the body inside, and fastened the mattress lining together with a staple gun. The staples tore loose, and the dead man's head broke free of the fabric."

"Is it Crawford?" the sheriff said.

"I don't know. His face is mutilated beyond recognition. I'll notify Roanoke. We'll need Shirley West to do an autopsy and investigate the murder."

"It's Mister Crawford," Jones said. "I recognize his hair and beard." Jones was pale. He went behind his patrol car and retched. He struggled there for a good while. He was clearly in distress, but given Jones' combat record, Nate doubted the gore had sickened him. It seemed more likely he was upset by the cruelty of the killing. Up to that point Nate had thought Jones was the best suspect for Crawford's murder. He had a motive to conceal the mattresses, and unlike the judge, he was physically capable of following Nate to the warehouse, attacking him, and hauling Crawford's corpse to the quarry. But Jones' reaction gave Nate pause.

The sheriff smirked. "Get hold of yourself, Darby. We got work to do."

Chapter 22

The Suspect

The sheriff left Deputy Jones in charge of the crime scene, and he and Nate returned to Bloxton and met in the sheriff's office. The room was small and furnished with nothing but a desk and two chairs. The sheriff sat in his chair with his boots propped on the corner of his desk, spitting into a Styrofoam cup. Nate sat across from him. A rotating electric fan was perched on the desk, swinging back and forth slowly.

"You wanted to talk," the sheriff said.

"Deatherage says he found Updike's corpse sprawled on mattresses in the warehouse. I want Shirley West to investigate the ones I found at the dump to see if there's evidence that Updike was murdered on them."

"Deatherage is lyin about that, but you'll get your wish. The mattresses are evidence in the investigation of Crawford's murder. I told Mac and Darby to haul em to Mac's lab. If Shirley finds somethin that connects em to Updike, we'll let you know."

"Thanks. I have another small request. Do you remember Eva Deatherage's complaint about a robbery of her craft shop last summer?"

"I remember it. Never caught the thief."

"I'd like to see the case file."

"Why?"

"The robbery may be connected to Updike's murder."

"I can't see how."

"Eva is Deatherage's mother. The robbery occurred around the time of the murder. Maybe there's no connection, but I want to make sure."

The sheriff shrugged. "I suppose it can't hurt to let you have a peek at the file." He sauntered lazily to his secretary's desk just outside his office door. The secretary was a plump middle-aged red-faced brunette who looked as though she might faint from the heat. The sheriff spoke to her. She gave Nate an aggravated look, heaved herself out of her chair, padded on bare feet to a file cabinet standing against the far wall, retrieved a manila folder, and handed it to the sheriff. Feedlow walked back to his desk and gave the file to Nate.

Nate looked at it. There was one piece of paper, Eva's complaint. "Is this all?"

"Never got a lead. There was nothin to put in the file."

The original complaint in the file was identical to the carbon copy Eva gave Nate, except the original was dated June 1, two days before the murder. The carbon copy bore a date of June 12. Nate suspected the 2 had been removed from the original. He held the complaint up to the light, but he couldn't detect any trace of the 2. "Could I have a Xerox copy of this?"

The sheriff took the complaint from Nate and held it up to the light. "There's nothin on this form about your case."

"I'd like a copy, just to be thorough."

Feedlow smirked. "You're a lawyer through and through, wastin my time and makin extra work for me and my people."

"Where's your copying machine? I'll do it myself."

"Twyla already hates your guts for makin her haul her carcass to the file cabinet in this heat. You screw up her copyin machine and we'll have another murder case on our hands." The sheriff took the form to the secretary and spoke to her again. She gave Nate a more severe scowl, waddled to a copying machine standing near the front door, and made the copy for Feedlow.

He returned and handed the copy to Nate, and Nate put the copy in his briefcase. "One last question," Nate said. "At the quarry you said the rules are different in Buck County. What did you mean by that?"

The sheriff's lips stretched into a tight smile. "I was just jawin to hear myself talk. Don't make too much of it."

"There's one set of rules in Virginia. You can find them in the Virginia Code. If anyone in Buck County broke the law to convict Deatherage, there are no rules here that will protect you."

Feedlow's smile fell. "From what I hear, you ain't qualified to warn others about breakin the laws."

"You're wrong about that. I'm especially qualified. I know better than anyone what it costs you."

Feedlow nodded. "Well, then, thanks for the warnin, and here's one for you. Don't go anywhere till we figure out more about Crawford's killin."

A chill ran through Nate. "Why?"

"You're a material witness. Don't leave Buck County without my permission."

"I planned to return to Jeetersburg tonight."

"Change your plans."

"You have no right to hold me here."

"You can stay voluntarily or I can hold you for questionin. We got a nice soft bed for you back there in cell number one."

"You have no grounds to hold me."

The sheriff spat in the cup and wiped his lip. "You were a commonwealth's attorney. Tell me what you think of these grounds. You said you talked to Henry last week. You said he disappeared last week. Mac said he'd been dead for about a week. You found the body in a place no one would normally look for it. You gave me a cock-and-bull story about why you looked for Henry at the quarry. The word is you broke a passel of laws in Selk County, you have a drinkin problem, and you have a hair-trigger temper that caused you to rough up your wife last fall. Henry was beat to death. What do you think? Do I have grounds to hold you?"

Nate searched Feedlow's face for clues of his intentions. Was the sheriff part of a conspiracy in Buck County to frame men for murder? Was he moving Nate into the queue as the next target? The sheriff stared at Nate, his face blank, chewing his tobacco like a cow chewing cud. Bored, languid. "So what'll it be, Nate?" he said. "The Black Gold Motel or cell number one?"

"I'll stay in Buck County until tomorrow night. If you haven't questioned me by then, I'm heading home."

Nate left the sheriff's office, drove down Ewell Street to the Coal Bin, and picked up Clarence. He filled Clarence in. Clarence was more than happy to remain "in the field." At the Black Gold Motel, Clarence worried that he might lose effectiveness in gathering information if people in Buck County knew he worked for Nate, so he hid in the car while Nate checked in with Drinkard.

Room number three was a sweatbox that evening. Clarence sat on the bed and mopped his face with a bathroom towel. Nate sat in the room's only chair. "What did you find out today?" he asked Clarence.

"The Grill was a disappointment. I sat at the counter with a farmer named Frank Gentry. I told him I was an undertaker from Wise County on my way back home from a funeral in Salem. We talked about recent deaths and funerals in Buck County, and I worked him around to Updike's murder. At the mention of her name, he turned red as a tomato, paid his tab, and skedaddled. I moved down the counter and sat with a John Deere mechanic, Herman Doyle. We got around to Updike and I got the same result. He got skittish as a white-tail deer and scurried out the door."

"Drinkard mentioned those two men. He said they spent nights with Darlene in a room at this motel."

"That fits with what a lawyer named Daryl Garth told me."

"When did you talk with Garth?"

"The luncheon trade was petering out at the Grill when Garth came in and sat next to me. Kind of a simpleton, this fellow Garth. He was in the middle of telling me gossip about the murder when he suddenly seemed to realize what he was doing, stopped in midsentence, and hopped out the door like a scared rabbit."

"Garth represents one of the other death penalty defendants. What did he tell you before he fled?"

"He said the men in town were tight-lipped about Updike because some of them fooled around with her. He claimed the gossips say Gentry and Doyle both partied with her, and their wives would be none too pleased to find out about it. I asked Garth a couple questions about Deatherage. He started to say something about Swiller and the judge and that's when he caught himself and ran off. He knows something, but he's afraid to say it."

"I should talk with him. I'll call him and set up a meeting. Did you learn anything at the Coal Bin?"

"I hit the mother lode at that place. I used that same undertaker cover. A waitress named Tilly Garrison took the bait and ran with it. Nice little girl, this Tilly. Darlene spent a lot of time at that restaurant and Tilly got pretty friendly with her. Here's the bombshell: Darlene stayed at Judge Herring's house while she was in Bloxton."

Nate took a moment to digest that fact and then said, "Did this Tilly know why Darlene stayed there?"

"Tilly asked, but Darlene wouldn't tell her. Tilly was surprised by it. She said the judge was a well-known teetotaler and Darlene got fall-down drunk every night she was at the Coal Bin. Darlene told Tilly the judge pitched a fit and threw her out of the house whenever she came home drunk."

"That fits with information I found here last week. Darlene rented a room in this motel seven different nights. Drinkard said she was always drunk when she checked in, but I don't understand why the judge took Darlene into his home in the first place. I wonder if the Herrings are related to the Updikes. Did you do a background check on the Updikes?"

"Like I told you before, I did a court records check on Darlene and found that civil case her father filed. That's all I've got on him." Clarence held his wristwatch up to his eyes. "Seven thirty. All the agencies have shut down for the day. The best I can do is call from here first thing in the morning. We need to act fast. This case is getting dangerous. Who do you figure killed Crawford? Deputy Jones?"

"I don't know. Jones seemed surprised and sickened by Crawford's murder. His reaction to it was convincing."

"Could the judge be the killer?"

"I don't think the judge is physically capable of attacking me, killing Crawford, and hauling the corpse and the mattresses to the quarry. Maybe he directed someone else to do all that. I thought his henchman was Jones, but Jones' reaction doesn't fit. Nothing I've found tells me who else might have killed Crawford."

"Well, one thing seems clear. Your boy Deatherage was framed."

Nate nodded. "It looks like the judge, Swiller, and Jones worked together to ensure his conviction, and maybe Sheriff Feedlow and Mac Somers were working with them. Maybe even George, although everything I know about him says otherwise." Nate was about to ask Clarence more about Updike's local boyfriends, Doyle and Gentry, when there was a knock at the door.

Clarence said, "I better get out of sight." He went into the bathroom and closed the door.

Nate opened the door. Deputy Jones stood in the doorway.

"Hello, Deputy."

"Howdy, Mister Abbitt. Can I come in?"

Nate stepped aside and Jones walked in. "I have some questions about Mister Crawford." Jones sat in the chair, took off his hat, and wiped sweat from its headband. Nate sat on the bed. "Mister Crawford's body was in an awful state. The heat, you know. The maggots and such. Mister Somers said someone hit him across the eyes with some kind of big club."

Jones was watching Nate closely. Nate showed him nothing. "How did you come to find Mister Crawford's body in the quarry, Mister Abbitt?"

"Deatherage told me he saw Updike's body on mattresses in the warehouse. Someone removed the mattresses from the warehouse last week. I found them in the quarry, but I didn't expect to find Crawford stuffed into one of them."

"Deatherage is lying. There were some old mattresses in the warehouse the night of the murder, but they were at the back wall, nowhere near Miss Updike's body. Why were you looking for them? What good would they do your case?"

"Some types of forensic evidence have a long life."

"How did you know they were at the quarry?"

"I guessed."

"Pretty good guess. What did you base it on?"

"Someone knocked me out in the warehouse last week when I found Crawford. When I came to, Crawford and the mattresses were gone. I figured the man who took the mattresses didn't want me to look at them. I guessed he either destroyed or discarded them. The dump was a logical place to look."

"That makes sense, but you didn't go to the dump. You went to the Dealeton quarry. Who told you the locals dumped their trash there?"

"I don't remember who told me about the quarry, but everybody in the county knows about it. I've talked to a lot of people here about the Deatherage case. One of them must have mentioned it."

"Convenient you don't recall who told you. That way I can't check it out."

Nate gave Jones a hard look.

Jones said, "Why didn't you file a report with us about the assault on you in the warehouse?"

"I was busy, and the injury wasn't serious."

"It also prevented us from investigating your story. Who do you think hit you?"

"I don't know."

"It couldn't have been Mister Crawford, I suppose."

"Crawford was in front of me when I was hit. The man who hit me followed me into the warehouse and attacked me from behind."

"And you have no idea who he was?"

"I have some ideas, but I'm not ready to share them."

"Why not?"

"I'd rather not say."

Jones frowned. "You're not giving me much to work with, Mister Abbitt. You'd rather not say. You don't remember. Maybe you can answer this question. How did you come to know Mister Crawford?"

"I didn't know him. I went to the warehouse to look at the scene of the murder. Crawford was there, and I approached him."

"And you talked to him?"

"The man who attacked me knocked me out before I could speak with Crawford."

"You didn't talk to Mister Crawford?"

"That's right."

"And you never met Mister Crawford except that one time?"

"That's correct."

Jones put his pad and pencil in his shirt pocket. "I guess that's it for now." He stood and put on his hat. "If you get around to deciding to share your ideas about who attacked you or if you start remembering things you don't remember now, give us a call." He stepped out the door and turned back to Nate. "I have one last question. How did you know the name of the dead man who was stuffed in the mattress at the dump?"

"What?"

"You said you only saw Mister Crawford the one time. You didn't speak with him. So how did you know who he was? How did you know his name?"

A bead of sweat slid into the trench of Nate's scar. It stung. "I didn't mean to say I didn't speak to him at all. I spoke to him for a few moments. He told me his name and then someone hit me over the head."

"You just told me you didn't speak to Mister Crawford."

"I misspoke."

"You told Sheriff Feedlow that Mister Crawford said he was in the warehouse when Miss Updike was murdered, but on your second run-through on your story with me you said Mister Crawford only got to tell you his name before you got knocked out. You seem to be having trouble keeping your story straight. So which is it? Did you lie to Sheriff Feedlow or to me or to both of us?"

Nate reddened. "Lying requires a conscious intent to deceive. I didn't lie. I mistakenly gave you the impression I hadn't spoken to Crawford at all. I meant that someone hit me after I learned his name and he answered a few of my questions."

Jones' frown returned. "I don't think you made a mistake, Mister Abbitt. I think you changed your story about talking with Mister Crawford. I think there's a lie in there somewhere, or maybe two or three lies. Are you trying to hide something?"

Nate considered revealing Odoms' help, but decided the risk to him was too great. He'd persuaded Odoms to help, and Odoms asked for nothing in return. Nate couldn't bring himself to abrogate his promise. "I didn't change my story. I made an honest mistake in my choice of words. Don't make more of it than it warrants."

Jones turned and stared at Nate's car. "Mind if I take a look inside your car?"

"What are you looking for?"

"I don't rightly know, but you don't have anything to hide, right?"

Nate went outside with Jones and unlocked the car. Jones looked at the interior. He searched the glove compartment. He removed the bench seats, both front and back, and crawled around on the floorboard. When he was done, he stood beside Nate. "Clean as a whistle. Mind if I look in the trunk?" Jones stuck out his hand. Nate handed him the keys.

Jones unlocked the trunk. He removed the spare tire, tire iron, and jack. He lifted the trunk floor carpet and felt around underneath it. He poked into the cavities over the tire wells. He put everything back in its place and closed the trunk. "Trunk's clean." He took off his hat, wiped sweat from his face, and let out a long breath. "Jehosophat, it's a hot one." He put on his hat and handed Nate the keys. "Stay close by, Mister Abbitt. I'll be talking to you again soon." He got into his patrol car and drove off.

Nate went back in the room. Clarence sat on the bed, wiping perspiration from his face and neck with a bathroom towel. "What was Jones looking for in your car?"

"I have no idea. I think he just wanted to intimidate me."

"It sounded like he's fixing to pin Crawford's murder on you."

"I agree."

"We better find the truth quick before the crooks who run this county do you in."

Chapter 23

The Beginning

The next morning Clarence called his agency contacts to inquire about Daniel Updike. Nate phoned Daryl Garth and Garth agreed to meet him. Nate drove to the other end of Ewell Street to Garth's office, a square little cinderblock building sitting alone in an asphalt lot. It didn't look like a law office. Two oval concrete platforms rested on the asphalt side by side in front of the building. On the wall to the right of the door a rectangle of cinderblocks newer than the others had been patched into a space as large as a garage door. Nate opened the office door to find a room with a bare concrete floor. The faint aromas of motor oil and lubricating grease confirmed his suspicion that the building was formerly a gas station.

In the office, a big man in his mid-thirties with blond thinning hair was hunched over a desk, poring over documents. He looked up and blanched. "Can I help you?"

"I'm Nate Abbitt."

Garth flashed a wide smile and stood. "Mister Abbitt." Garth's blue suit was shiny and too small for his heavy body. His gut strained against the buttons of his white shirt. He bounded over to Nate and extended his hand. "I met you once. I didn't recognize you with that, uh, I mean that . . ." Garth frowned at Nate's scar. "Well, like I said, I met you at a seminar in Richmond. The Fourth Amendment and the exclusionary rule. Your lecture was the high point of the weekend."

"Thank you," Nate said. He looked around for a place to sit.

Garth lurched across the room and dragged a wooden straight-backed chair to his desk. "There you are. Have a seat."

Garth returned to his chair and smiled at Nate. "I'm excited to meet you. I've read all your articles. That one in the *Virginia Law Review* about jury selection helped me win a robbery prosecution – well, almost win it. I'm privileged to meet a lawyer of your stature." It was apparent Garth didn't know about Nate's downfall. He was probably the only lawyer in the state who hadn't heard it. Clarence's assessment appeared correct. He was a simpleton.

His eyes focused on Nate's scar again. "I'm sorry for being rude. I mean . . . I noticed your, uh . . . ."

"I was in a car accident."

"Oh." Garth continued to gawk, his mouth hanging open.

"You're probably wondering why I called you."

"Oh. Well, yes. What's this about?"

"I understand you succeeded Randolph Swiller on the Jimmy Washington case. I represent Kenneth Deatherage. I'd like to compare notes with you."

Garth flinched. "Compare notes? About what?"

"I'm sorry for being blunt, Mister Garth, but I don't have much time. Circumstances force me to get right to the point. Swiller didn't put on a defense in the Deatherage case. I suspect he lost the case intentionally at Judge Herring's behest. I want to know if Swiller failed to represent his clients in his other capital cases. I know you looked at all the files. I figure you're suspicious, too."

Garth's eyes widened. "Who told you I looked at the files?"

"I saw your name in the evidence logs."

"Oh . . . well, I was just looking . . . uh . . . you see, I don't know anything about the cases, really."

"Come on, Mister Garth. You reviewed the record in the Deatherage case. Swiller laid down for the prosecution. My guess is he did the same in the other capital cases, and I think that's what you learned when you reviewed the files."

"Well, uh, I don't know. Laid down for the prosecution. That's a serious thing you just said there. I don't know about that." Garth pulled at his collar and coughed. "You have to be careful what you say in Buck County, Mister Abbitt. Allegations like that could get you in trouble."

Nate looked around Garth's office. He had no secretary. The room was bereft of furniture except for his desk and the miserably uncomfortable chair Nate occupied. "I understand your situation, Mister Garth. It's hard to earn a living practicing law in Bloxton. You can't risk the added burden of alienating the powers that be."

"Well, yes. I can't, uh, take the risk that you might – "

"I won't draw you into combat with Judge Herring. All I want from you is information."

"There's only one circuit court judge in Buck County, Mister Abbitt. No lawyer can survive here if he gets on the bad side of Judge Herring."

"I won't tell anyone I talked to you. I promise I won't expose you as a source."

Garth looked doubtful and worried.

"Men's lives are at stake," Nate said.

Garth rubbed his eyes with the palms of his hands and stared at Nate with a tortured expression. "I know that, Mister Abbitt. I know it all too well." He looked at Nate fearfully and let out a long breath. "What do you want to know?"

"How did Swiller get appointed to represent Creighton Long?"

"I don't know for sure." Garth fell silent.

"Come on, Mister Garth. Open up and tell me what you know. All of it."

Garth hesitated again. "Give me your word you'll never tell anyone I talked with you."

"You have my word."

Garth slumped in his chair with his hand over his eyes. After a short while, he took a deep breath, sat up straight, and seemed to gather his courage. "All right. Here's what I know about Swiller's appointment to the Long case. Every lawyer in Bloxton put in the word with District Judge Gwathmey's clerk that he wanted the case. Big-shot lawyers from out of town volunteered, too. Judge Gwathmey appointed Swiller. We were all surprised. None of us had ever heard of him."

"I've been told Judge Herring instructed Gwathmey to appoint Swiller."

"That's right. Judge Gwathmey secretly told one of the lawyers in town that he had never heard of Swiller before the Long case. When Judge Herring told him to appoint Swiller to the case, he tried to push back, but Judge Herring wouldn't listen to him." Garth tugged at his collar and cast his eyes around the room. They finally settled on Nate. "Everybody in Buck County does what Judge Herring tells them to do. Judge Gwathmey knuckled under. He had no choice." Garth passed his hand across his forehead and wiped off sweat on his shirt. "Anyway, Swiller showed up in Bloxton for the first time for the preliminary hearing. He opened an office in one of the abandoned buildings at the freight yard. Judge Herring owns that building. One of the other lawyers in town found out that the judge and Swiller were friends in law school and that Swiller's legal business in Charlottesville failed. We figured Judge Herring ordered Judge Gwathmey to appoint Swiller because he was Judge Herring's friend and he needed business."

"Was there more to it than that?"

"Later on, we guessed that the judge wanted Swiller to do him a favor."

"What sort of favor?"

Garth loosened the knot of his tie. "Remember, I never said this myself. It was the other lawyers. They said the judge asked Swiller to lose the Long case."

"Why would the judge do that?"

"To help the people of Buck County. Creighton Long killed five little boys. He tortured them, molested them, cut their throats, and watched them bleed to death. The sheriff's men found Long's diary. Long wrote about the pleasure he got from what he did to the boys. The diary was damning evidence against him, but there was a problem."

"What sort of problem?"

"The sheriff didn't get a warrant before he searched Long's apartment, and he didn't have probable cause. The sheriff was under tremendous pressure to solve the crimes. When they found the fifth boy's body in the abandoned coal mine, the sheriff still had no leads and no suspects. People in Buck County were wild with fear and anger. They called for the sheriff's head on a platter. He was desperate. He launched a door-to-door warrantless random search. They found Long's diary in a sweep through the boarding houses at the base of Skink Mountain near the mine."

"The diary was inadmissible."

"Like you said at that seminar in Richmond, the Fourth Amendment prohibits warrantless searches unless the government has probable cause. Evidence gathered from an unconstitutional search has to be excluded from trial to ensure the government won't storm into everybody's house whenever they feel like it. The search of Long's apartment didn't fit any of the exceptions to the exclusionary rule, so it looked to all of us like the defense would be able to keep it out of the trial. That was a hell of a problem for the prosecution. The diary was the only evidence against Long, and the prosecution couldn't convict him without it."

"I see. Judge Herring told Swiller not to object to the diary."

"I don't know what Judge Herring told Swiller. All I know is Swiller didn't raise the Fourth Amendment issue at trial."

"Is it possible Swiller was so incompetent he missed the issue?"

"The unconstitutional search that produced that diary was the talk of the town before the trial. Swiller knew it was inadmissible. Judge Herring knew. Everyone in town knew, but Swiller didn't object and the judge admitted the diary into evidence."

"Didn't anyone raise a question about Swiller's failure to object? The newspaper reporters, the other lawyers in town?"

"We all kept mum. We knew the judge had taken matters into his own hands, and we were glad he did it. We didn't care about Long's constitutional rights because we wanted him to pay for what he did to the little boys."

"The admission of that diary may have been the first step down a road to the conviction of innocent men in this county."

"That's why I reviewed the files of all the other capital cases. The cases followed a pattern. Judge Gwathmey appointed Swiller to represent the accused in each case. Swiller didn't put on any defense in the Long and Deatherage cases. He seemed to try harder in the other cases, but his efforts were inept. Judge Herring did nothing to protect the defendants from Swiller's malpractice. George Maupin presented powerful cases each time. The jury convicted all four men and voted for the death penalty for each one of them."

"Tell me about your case, the Washington case."

"Jimmy Washington is a hard-luck story. Since the coal mine closed down and Red Diamond Rock Products pulled out of town, there are only a few jobs, and young Negro men are the last to be hired. Jimmy got his girlfriend pregnant and married her when he was seventeen. He needed to support his family, but no one would hire him so he took the only job he could find. He enlisted in the army. The army shipped him out to Vietnam. He picked up some bad habits over there, namely drinking and brawling, and he came home with a chip on his shoulder. He got into trouble with the law – a string of DUIs, convictions for drunkenness in public, disorderly conduct, a couple of minor assaults – misdemeanors for the most part, nothing real serious, but he caused enough mischief to earn a reputation as a good-for-nothing troublemaker. His wife, Shirleen, stayed with him and tried hard to reform him. Jimmy's friends say he was beginning to pull out of his tailspin when Joe Hitt, a local farmer, was murdered. Hitt was white. Jimmy is colored. Hitt was a member of the Klan. He and Jimmy got in a big fight in the Coal Bin's parking lot the night Hitt was killed. People pulled them apart, but they were wild with anger. They yelled racial stuff at each other. Afterwards, Hitt went to the Dealeton quarry to drink. His body was found on the quarry floor by one of his drinking buddies the next morning."

"Jimmy Washington was the prime suspect."

"Yes," Garth said. "The prosecution claimed Jimmy followed Hitt to the quarry and killed him."

"How was Hitt killed?"

"The local medical examiner originally thought the cause of death was a knife wound to the chest, but there were abrasions and bruises on Hitt's throat. An autopsy revealed that his larynx was crushed and his hyoid bone was fractured."

"He was strangled."

"Yes, and the stab wound was *post mortem*."

"Why did the murderer stab him after strangling him to death?"

"George Maupin argued that Jimmy wasn't sure Hitt was dead, so he stabbed him. The knife wound turned out to be the clincher with the jury. The sheriff's men found a pocketknife in Jimmy's house with the tip end broken off. The medical examiner said that knife matched perfectly the wound in Hitt's chest."

"The knife seems like conclusive evidence of Washington's guilt."

"Jimmy swears he didn't own a pocketknife and he never saw the one they found in his house. His wife and kids and friends all say he never carried a pocketknife."

"They're lying to protect him."

"I don't know. It doesn't add up to me. Jimmy's a troubled young man, but he's smart, plenty smart enough to throw that knife away rather than leave it in a drawer in his house like a big sign saying 'I'm the killer.'"

Nate recalled Deatherage's comment about the scarf: "I might as well put a sign on my chest says 'Killer.'" Nate said, "Was Darby Jones the deputy who investigated the murder?"

"Yes."

"Did Jones conduct the search of Washington's house?"

"Yes. How did you know that?"

"My guess is Jones is another part of the pattern in these cases. Maybe he stabbed Hitt *post mortem* with the pocketknife and then faked finding the knife in Washington's house." Nate told Garth about the scarf in the Deatherage case.

Garth leaned back in his chair and frowned. "You know, a strange thing happened when I interviewed Jones before the trial. For the most part, the meeting was the same as other interviews with law enforcement officers, just a straightforward account of the evidence Jones had gathered, but when I was finished with my questions, he didn't make a move to leave my office. So I said, 'Okay, that's all I have for you.' But he still didn't move. He just sat there glaring at me. Made me very uneasy. He finally stood up and said, 'I have one more thing to say. You tell Washington he should be ashamed of himself. He's a disgrace to the uniform. He wasn't fit to serve.' Then Jones stomped out of my office."

Perhaps, Nate thought, Jones was a misguided patriot who thought his job as a deputy was to rid the county of the men he considered to be criminals. "Jones was a good soldier," Nate said, "a volunteer for combat, and a war hero. Maybe he can't tolerate men he perceives to be weak or corrupt, especially a disgraced Vietnam veteran like Washington."

"I don't know. I suppose you could be right, but that doesn't explain Judge Herring's behavior. Why would Judge Herring be involved in framing Washington and the other men?"

"Maybe the judge wanted to ensure convictions of men he was convinced were guilty, and Jones was a willing accomplice. You said the judge used Swiller to convict Creighton Long to protect Buck County. Maybe the judge convinced Jones they should rig the other cases to protect the county's law-abiding citizens from murderers."

"I can understand why the judge rigged Long's trial," Garth said. "He was a serial killer of children, and he was about to get off on a legal technicality. But Jimmy Washington, Kenny Deatherage, and the others were just run-of-the-mill defendants. They could have been innocent for all the judge knew. Why would the judge deny these men a fair trial?"

"Pieces of this puzzle are missing. We have to find them to answer that question."

"I don't think you understand what you're up against, Mister Abbitt. Judge Herring's influence is immeasurable. He can destroy his enemies with the clap of his gavel, the stroke of his pen. Anyone who attacks him risks his career. Maybe his life." Sweat dotted Garth's forehead. His eyes were fearful.

"Don't worry, Mister Garth. I won't tell anyone you helped me." Nate stood and extended his hand. "Let me know if you find out anything more about the capital cases."

Chapter 24

The Tire Iron

It was late morning when Nate left Garth's office. The temperature had climbed into the nineties. The sun baked the asphalt parking lot and oil was pooling in its low spots. The inside of the car felt like the belly of a furnace. Nate rolled down all the windows, started the car, and quickly drove out of the lot. Sweat poured down his face and drenched his shirt. He headed down Ewell Street to rejoin Clarence at the motel, but he slowed when he saw Clarence walking on the sidewalk, clutching his briefcase to his chest. When Nate pulled to the curb, Clarence sucked in his breath and stumbled backward.

"Clarence. It's me. Nate."

Clarence squinted at him and scrambled into the car.

"What are you doing on the street?" Nate said.

Clarence was breathless and sweating. "Jones came to the motel looking for you. I was lucky to get away."

"What did he want?"

"He came to arrest you for Crawford's murder. You better get off the road before he sees us."

Nate turned off Ewell Street and coasted down an alley that ran between two rows of dilapidated buildings. He parked in the shade behind an abandoned building with boarded-up windows. A mangy dog stood by an overturned trash barrel at the end of the alley. The dog looked at Nate's car and trotted away. There was no one in sight.

"Tell me what happened," Nate said.

"A car pulled up outside the motel room. Someone tried to get in, but I had the door locked. I heard Drinkard ask the man at the door what he wanted. I recognized Jones' voice when he answered. He said he was looking for you. He said you beat Crawford to death with a tire iron they found at the quarry and he had come to arrest you for murder. Drinkard said you drove off first thing this morning. Jones said he wanted the key to the room so he could search it. Drinkard ran off to get the master key. I was afraid Jones would hold me for questioning if he found me in your room, so I crawled out the bathroom window and hotfooted down the dirt road behind the motel to Ewell Street. I couldn't see, so I followed the sidewalk till you came along. I didn't even know which way I was headed." Clarence shook his head. "I've got a bad feeling about Jones' search of your car yesterday. Did he take your tire iron?"

"He looked at it, but he put it back in the trunk."

"You better check to see if it's there."

Nate got out of the car and looked in the trunk. He didn't see the tire iron beside the spare tire, where it had been before the search. He removed everything from his trunk, looking for it. The tire iron was not there. He got back in the car. "It's gone."

"I figured as much. He stole it. He's going to frame you with it the way he framed Deatherage with the bloody scarf."

"He didn't take it when he searched the trunk, and it's been locked since then. I've had the car keys the whole time."

"Did you give your trunk key to him to unlock it?"

"Yes."

"He used wax or clay to make an impression of your key. I've done it a few times. You hold something soft, like wax, in your hand, and you press the key into it. Later you make a duplicate from the impression in the wax. He made a duplicate key, unlocked your trunk last night when we were asleep in the room, and stole the tire iron. You're too close to the truth. They have to stop you." Clarence took off his hat and wiped sweat from his face with his shaking hand. "It's just a matter of time till the deputy finds you. We've got to close this thing out right now or you'll go to jail for murder."

"We don't have enough evidence to close it out. Did you learn anything new on your phone calls this morning?"

Clarence put his hat back on and got his notepad out of his case. "In all the excitement I almost forgot. An old buddy of mine in the postal service gave me Daniel Updike's addresses going all the way back to his first residence, more than forty years ago. There was another bombshell in there." Clarence held his notepad close to his glasses. "In 1929 Daniel Updike lived at 33 University Circle, Apt. 3B, in Lexington."

"That rings a bell."

"That's where Swiller and Judge Herring lived when they were in law school. Updike, Swiller, and Judge Herring were all roommates at Washington and Lee."

"The judge and Updike were close friends."

"Right. That little tidbit gave me a reason to call Bob Fleming again. You remember him?"

Nate nodded. "Updike's neighbor, the one who doesn't like him."

"Right. I asked Bob if he ever heard of Judge Herring. Bob said the Herrings used to visit the Updikes years ago. The Herrings are big-time Catholics, like the Updikes, and here's the kicker – the Herrings are Darlene Updike's godparents."

Nate raised his eyebrows. "So Darlene Updike was in Bloxton to visit the Herrings."

"You bet." Clarence flipped back a few pages on his pad, pointed to a line of his notes, and held it up to Nate. "And remember Tilly, the waitress? She said Darlene stayed at Judge Herring's house except when she got drunk and he threw her out. Maybe the judge was trying to help her with her drug and alcohol addiction."

Nate leaned back and looked out the window. He suddenly understood the judge's need to convict Deatherage. "The judge's goddaughter was killed in his own county right under his nose. He drove out to Dealeton that day and talked with Eva Deatherage about her son. She said he cried. Eva thought he was worried about Buck County's residents, but he was looking for something else out there. He wanted confirmation that Deatherage was Darlene's murderer. Eva gave it to him. She told him her son had a history of choking and torturing animals and that he once tried to choke her. That removed all doubt from the judge's mind."

Clarence shook his head and frowned. "Deatherage never had a chance. I'm surprised George Maupin didn't object to the judge trying this case. George is known all over the state as an honest prosecutor."

"George didn't know about the judge's relationship to Darlene. The judge issued a ruling in the case to discourage him from finding out about it. My guess is no one in Buck County knew about it except Swiller and Jones and whoever else conspired with them."

"We should take what we've found to George. He's a good man. He's got the power of the state behind him as commonwealth's attorney. He can protect you while he investigates these crimes."

Nate stared at the old brick wall of the abandoned building beside the car. Some of the bricks were crumbling, and red dust piled at the foot of the wall. Nate recalled the look of fear on George's face when they discussed the judge. He remembered George's warning not to take aim at the king unless you knew you would kill him. "George won't move against the judge without solid evidence that would knock him off the bench."

"We've got a lot of dirt."

"We don't have enough to bring him down. We can prove he presided over the trial of a man accused of murdering his goddaughter. That's a violation of the rules of judicial ethics, but it's not a crime. Besides, it's almost impossible to remove a judge from the bench in Virginia if he doesn't want to step down. The only way to force a judge out is to convince the House of Delegates to impeach him, and then the Virginia Senate has to try him and vote him out. No judge in Virginia has been removed in over fifty years. The last time anyone tried, the judge involved had bribed a man and the House of Delegates impeached him for it, but the Virginia Senate wouldn't vote him out so he retained his judgeship. Judge Herring has a long clean record and a good reputation. We don't have anywhere near enough evidence to force him off the bench."

"But the judge was in cahoots with Swiller and used Jones to falsify evidence."

"We can't prove that. We suspect the judge told Swiller to throw the Deatherage case and told Jones to lie about the bloody scarf, but all we can prove is that Swiller and the judge were law-school roommates. We don't have hard evidence of anything beyond that. Swiller's dead and Jones will lie to protect himself. We don't have enough."

Clarence swiped his hand over his mouth. "There's got to be a way. What about Eva Deatherage's criminal complaint? It proves the scarf was in her store when Darlene was murdered."

Nate shook his head. "I thought of that, too, but it doesn't work. Jones can claim I altered the date on the carbon copy to implicate him and save my own neck in the Crawford investigation. Eva Deatherage has no independent recollection of the date of the robbery. She can't back me up. And that evidence goes against Jones. It doesn't prove the judge was involved with him."

"Jones had no motive to frame Deatherage. The judge must have told him to plant the scarf."

"That's our assumption, but we can't prove it. We need more evidence."

"We can't search for more evidence. Jones will arrest you if you show your face in Bloxton, and I can't do legwork without help. I think we ought to take what we have to George Maupin and let him run with it."

Nate thought about George again. "I don't think George can help us. He won't take the risk of accusing the judge of a crime without rock-hard evidence and a virtual certainty the judge will be removed from the bench."

Clarence snorted. "Damn." They were quiet for a while. Then Clarence said, "Let's go outside Buck County. Judge Blackwell has no reason to fear Judge Herring. He won't believe this poppycock about you killing Crawford. He respects you." Clarence hesitated. "At least that's the way it used to be."

Nate looked at a pile of brick dust at the base of the wall. A bluebottle fly scurried over the dust and then flew away. From Nate's meetings with the judge about sobriety, the judge knew every despicable act Nate had committed while drinking, and Nate had confessed his recent relapse. The judge might well believe Nate got drunk, lost his temper, and killed Crawford, especially in the face of apparently solid forensic evidence. The judge protected Nate from prosecution twice, but he warned Nate that he would face the harsh consequences of his actions alone if he slipped and fell again. "I can't go to Judge Blackwell on this one, Clarence. I've drawn from that well too many times."

Clarence cursed again. "Maybe I could dig up something more on the phone if I knew what I was looking for. What do we need to nail the judge?"

"I don't know. Time is short, and people in this county are afraid of him. Our best shot would be something that would force him to resign. We need evidence so strong and embarrassing that he would rather step down than have it publicized. At this point, I doubt anything other than a confession would do us much good."

The dog that Nate saw earlier peeked around the corner of the building and stared anxiously at them. He lowered his head, crept back to the overturned barrel, and pawed through the trash.

Clarence turned to Nate with a curious expression. "Have you ever worn a wire?"

Chapter 25

The Confession

Nate and Clarence drove out of Bloxton just after noon in search of a place to hide so that the sheriff's men would have no opportunity to arrest Nate for Crawford's murder. Heat rose from the road and the blue mountains on the horizon paled to gray in the haze. Nate looked for a location where they couldn't be spotted from the road and where there was some shade to protect them from the blazing sun. About five miles out of town, he found a deserted lumber mill that met his requirements. He drove into the lumberyard and parked in a shed filled with corroded band saws, pulleys, and chains. A rusted-out logging truck hulked against a wall in the shadows. Cobwebs stretched across its busted windshield.

Clarence got out of the car and carried his case to a rotting workbench and Nate followed. The pungent scents of decayed wood and sawdust filled the shed. Clarence placed his case on the bench and opened it. A pistol was jammed in a pocket on the inside lid of the case.

"I didn't know you carried a gun, Clarence."

"Smith and Wesson. Good weapon."

"Have you ever fired it?"

"Not at a live target. I go to a firing range every so often to keep sharp."

Nate imagined Clarence peering through his thick lenses at targets he couldn't possibly see. Nate marveled at the old boy's refusal to give in to the infirmities of old age. Nate looked at the jumbled contents of the case – handcuffs, thumb cuffs, leg manacles, a ring of keys, a flat file, a walkie-talkie, a tangle of electric wires, and other gadgets he couldn't identify. Clarence withdrew an object that looked like a miniature transistor radio, a small tape recorder, and a set of earphones.

Clarence took off his hat and used a handkerchief to wipe sweat from his hatband. "I never had occasion to use a listening device when I was with the sheriff's office," he said, putting his hat on again. "After I retired, an old buddy at the FBI gave me this setup and showed me how to use it. This thing is a microphone and transmitter. You tape it to your body. It picks up sounds near you and sends them by radio signal to this battery-powered recorder. The recorder makes a recording of the sounds. We'll strap the mic to you and go see the judge. You tell him what we found out, and we'll see what he says. I'll run the recorder and listen in with earphones from a hiding place nearby."

Nate looked at the devices askance. "Operations like this require experience and planning. We have no experience and no time to plan. This could blow up in our faces."

"I can't think of another way to get what we need to protect you from the judge, but you're right that it's risky. Things could go real bad. You're the one facing the murder rap. It's your call."

Nate picked up the miniature transmitter and turned it over in his hand. A chain saw buzzed somewhere in the distance. A hot breeze blew through the shed, ruffling Nate's collar. "I'll give it a try, but let's plan it out as best we can."

They spent the afternoon discussing the logistics of taping the judge. They thought it would be too dangerous to approach him in the courthouse. He would have ready access to the sheriff's men there and would have Nate arrested as soon as he appeared. They decided to approach the judge at home, where he would be isolated from the sheriff's men and others. They thought a late night visit had the best chance of catching him with his guard down. But beyond those broad details, they realized they didn't have enough information to plan the taping. Nate knew the location of the judge's farm, but he had never set foot on the property. They had no map of the land and no floor plan of the house.

"We'll improvise when we get there," Clarence said.

"Winging it could get us killed. We don't know the house. We don't know how many rooms there are or their layout. We don't know where the judge sleeps. Suppose he has a gun or employs a bodyguard or an armed security guard. What if one of the sheriff's men guards the property? How do we deal with the judge's wife or a visitor or guest? There are too many variables. It's too risky."

"You're right about all that, but the way I see it you only have three options. You can turn yourself in and try to beat the Buck County justice system. You can run and hope they never catch you. Or you can approach the judge tonight and hope things break in our favor."

Nate knew Clarence was right. Trying to tape the judge was the best of three bad choices. They hid in the shed at the lumber mill the rest of the afternoon, tried to anticipate the many problems that could arise, and tried to devise ways to deal with them. The sun set and night fell and they talked on. It cooled down a bit from the heat of the day, but the night was still warm and sultry.

At half past ten they drove to Judge Herring's farm. Nate turned off the state road onto a paved driveway and stopped the car just inside a stand of white pines. "I'll walk ahead to scout the terrain," he said. "Wait for me here."

The paved driveway ran down a steep hill through a dense forest. The moon was full but the trees blocked out most of the light. At the bottom of the hill Nate came to a little wooden bridge that crossed a trickling creek. Frogs croaked and crickets sang. Stalks of mint on the creek bank gave off a fresh scent. Beyond the bridge, the road climbed another hill. Scores of fireflies winked on the face of the hill. Nate crossed the bridge and climbed the road. At the top of the hill, a white plank gate blocked the road and fencing stretched out on both sides of it. The gate was pad-locked. This was as far as the car could go.

Behind the gate, moonlight bathed a broad manicured lawn. A stately two-story colonial home stood in a grove of tall oaks, maples, and sweet gums. The paved road circled a fountain in the center of the lawn. Box-woods lined a brick walkway that ran from the fountain to a wide front porch. A light shone in an upstairs window. The other windows were dark.

Nate looked at the area around the gate. There was a grassy flat place beside the driveway behind a stand of fir trees. A car parked there would sit about fifty feet from the house and would not be visible from it.

He retraced his steps to the car and reported what he had seen to Clarence, then turned off the headlamps and drove the car slowly down the hill, across the bridge, and up the opposite hill. He steered the car to the grassy spot behind the fir trees and cut the engine. They sat in the car for a while to see if anyone heard or saw the car approach the gate. No one appeared.

Clarence tested the recorder. Nate spoke into the mic. The devices were ready.

Nate said, "How long will the battery have power?"

"Longer than we'll be here."

"We're farther from the house than I would like."

"If we're fifty feet away like you said, we should be fine."

Nate started to get out of the car. Clarence said, "One more thing. We need a signal, code words that mean you're in trouble and you need me to come running."

Nate paused, thinking. "I'll use Deatherage's full name. If you hear me say Kenneth Deatherage, I'm in trouble."

"Kenneth Deatherage. That's good."

Nate looked at Clarence's glasses. The moonlight was bright, but Clarence couldn't see well in full sunlight. "Can you see to find the house if I call you?"

"I'll follow the driveway's pavement till I see the house. I'll make it." Clarence put on the earphones.

Nate got out of the car, walked to the gate, and climbed over it. He turned back to Clarence. "Can you hear me?" Clarence stuck his arm out the window and waved.

Nate walked to the nearest shade tree, stood behind it, and scanned the lawn and the woods bordering the yard. There was no one in sight. He felt a nudge at his calf and looked down to see a black-and-tan hound. Nate's heart skipped a beat. The dog slid his muzzle down Nate's leg to his shoe and then shifted to his other leg. He expected the dog to take a chunk out of him at any moment. The dog looked up at him and whined. Nate didn't move. The dog whined again. He extended his hand. The dog licked it. He knelt beside the hound and rubbed his ears. The dog wagged his tail. "Good boy. Good dog." Nate spoke aloud to Clarence. "There's a dog in the yard, Clarence, but he won't hurt you."

Nate crept across the lawn to the house. The dog trotted along behind him. He climbed the steps to the porch. The dog stayed at the base of the steps, looking at him and wagging his tail. Nate peered in a window. The interior of the house was dark except for a wedge of light that poured through an open door on an upstairs landing. The light fell across a spiral staircase and illuminated part of an entry hall. It was late. He guessed the Herrings were preparing for bed.

Nate looked back at the yard. There was a garage off to the right of the driveway and fountain. Its door was open. He could see a black car in the shadows. There were no other vehicles in the road or the garage.

He heard the sound of voices upstairs, of the judge laughing. Nate thought he might be able to sneak into the house while the Herrings were distracted. He turned the doorknob. The door was locked. On reflection, he didn't know what he would have done if it hadn't been. Sneaking into the house served no purpose. The judge wouldn't confess to a prowler.

Nate didn't know what to do. Forcing the door would only provoke the judge to react defensively. Knocking seemed to be his only viable choice, but when the judge saw him on the porch, he would likely refuse him entry and call the sheriff. Nate could overpower him when he came to the door, but the judge wouldn't confess to an assailant, either. The idea to tape-record him was ill-conceived from the start. There was no rational plan that would render the desired result.

The light upstairs went out. Nate cursed under his breath. He must act now or walk away. He felt he had no choice, even though he could envision no successful outcome. He took a deep breath and rapped the door knocker. The clanking pierced the silence of the night and jarred his nerves. He waited. Nothing happened. He rapped again. The light upstairs came on. Someone lifted the curtain on a window beside the door and looked out. The porch light came on and the door opened. Judge Herring stood in the doorway in a housecoat and slippers. He didn't appear to be armed.

"Mister Abbitt? What are you doing here?"

"I need to talk to you, sir."

"It's past eleven."

"I'm sorry about the lateness of the hour, Your Honor, but I have to speak to you about the Deatherage case."

"I don't conduct judicial proceedings at home, Mister Abbitt. See me in chambers in the morning." The judge seemed irritated, but not alarmed.

"The matter I came to discuss is urgent. We must talk tonight."

"No, sir. You'll have to wait until morning." The judge started to close the door.

"I know about you and Darlene Updike."

The judge stopped cold and looked at Nate. "What are you talking about?"

"Darlene Updike was your goddaughter. You directed Randolph Swiller to throw Deatherage's case so you could sentence Deatherage to the electric chair."

The judge's face betrayed nothing. He looked up at the landing and back at Nate. He stepped out on the porch and closed the door. He looked at the driveway. "I don't see your car, Mister Abbitt."

"I left my car on the hill. The gate was locked."

"You're quite right. I forgot about the lock." Crimson flushed the judge's jowls. He let out a long breath and took off his glasses and pinched the bridge of his nose. "I don't like the locked gate. It seems unneighborly to me. Sheriff Feedlow insisted I install it. He worries that someone might harm me. I've never fretted about it. I trust the people of the county to respect my privacy, but the sheriff was intractable so I relented and installed the damn thing. I don't lock the gate, though. Betsy must have locked it tonight when she returned from choir practice. She shares the sheriff's concerns." The judge looked at Nate and smiled slightly. "You don't intend to harm me, do you, Mister Abbitt? At least not physically?"

The judge's wistful demeanor disarmed Nate. He didn't know what to say.

The judge gazed at the gate. "The sheriff isn't satisfied with the gate and the padlock. He says they aren't sufficient to keep a determined intruder at bay. He wants to install an electric fence and man the gate with an armed guard. I suppose you've proved the sheriff's point, Mister Abbitt."

The black-and-tan hound hopped up on the porch and trotted to the judge, wagging his tail. "The sheriff says Socrates is too docile to serve as a watchdog. It seems he's correct on all counts." The judge rubbed the dog's back. "Not to worry, Socrates. I won't hold you to the sheriff's standards. In my book you're a good dog in all respects."

Nate thought he saw a tear course down the judge's cheek, but his face was turned away from the porch light and Nate wasn't certain. "You'll have to forgive me for being somewhat shaken, Mister Abbitt. I feared this day would come. I even dreamt about it, but now that it's here, I don't know what to do. I suppose no one is ever prepared to expose his failings to the world." He glanced at Nate's scar. "I'm sure you understand, Mister Abbitt."

Nate was confused by the judge's implicit admission. He'd antici-
pated arrogance, defiance, even violence, but his assessment appeared
to be wildly off the mark.

"I suppose we should go inside and talk," the judge said. He opened
the door and stepped into the entry hall and Nate followed.

A stairway swept around a crystal chandelier to the landing on the
second floor. An elderly woman stood in her housecoat on the landing,
looking down at them. "Who is it, Edbert?"

"It's all right, Betsy. It's Mister Abbitt, a lawyer from Selk County.
He's here about one of my cases." The judge bowed his head and swallowed. He lifted his face to his wife and managed a wan smile. "You go
on to bed, dear. I'll come along shortly."

Betsy Herring looked at Nate anxiously. "All right, but don't be long."
She padded down the hallway to the bedroom.

The judge stared after her. Then he led Nate through a doorway off the
entry hall into an office. The walls were lined with bookcases filled with
legal treatises. The judge shut the door behind Nate. Nate thought about
Clarence and said, "I like the layout of your entry hall. It's convenient
to have your office to the right of the front door."

"Let's dispense with the small talk, Mister Abbitt. You've got me
hanging by tenterhooks." The judge limped across the room to a mahogany
desk and sat in a burgundy leather desk chair. He gestured for Nate to
sit in a matching easy chair on the other side of the desk. "I assume you
intend to reveal my bias against Deatherage to the world," he said.

Nate sat in the chair. "When I file my appellate brief, Your Honor, I'll
be required to state grounds for overturning his conviction."

"It's ironic you still refer to me as Your Honor. Indeed, you may be
the last person who will address me that way." The judge opened a desk
drawer, withdrew a cigar box, and extended it to Nate, who declined the
offer. The judge lit a cigar and puffed a cloud of smoke to the ceiling.
"Smoking a fine cigar usually calms me in stressful times, but I suspect this

one won't produce the desired effect, given my circumstances. I assume you intend to approach the circuit's legislative delegates, inform them of my crimes, and encourage them to initiate impeachment proceedings."

Nate paused. "I don't know. I haven't considered what steps I should take beyond those required to defend Deatherage."

The judge covered his eyes. "No matter. Impeachment won't be necessary. The publicity and disgrace that will flow from the revelations in your brief will be sufficient to destroy me." The judge removed his glasses and pinched the bridge of his nose again. After a few moments, he said, "Do you understand why I didn't disqualify myself from the case, Mister Abbitt?"

"You wanted to be certain Deatherage was convicted and sentenced to death."

"Precisely. Deatherage beat my goddaughter. He raped her while he strangled her with a garrote. Her suffering was intense and prolonged. He feasted on her pain. Execution in the electric chair is too good for him. The Supreme Court's ambivalence toward the death penalty has forced the state courts to refrain from executing defendants for the time being, but I expect the death penalty to be vindicated and reinstated. When that day comes, I wanted to ensure that Deatherage would be one of the first in Virginia to sit in the electric chair, but even then his suffering won't compare to my goddaughter's ordeal."

"Deatherage may not be her killer."

"Spare me your legal sophistry, Mister Abbitt. I'm certain Deatherage is guilty. That doesn't excuse what I did. I abused my power. I deserve to be punished and disgraced, but I'm not sorry for it. I would do it again if given the chance."

"It will cost you your career."

"I don't care about my career. I'm ready to step down from the bench. I've seen too much misery. I'm tired of it." The judge looked in the direction of the upstairs bedroom. "I don't care a whit about myself, but there's my beloved Betsy. She doesn't deserve what lies ahead." There was a long silence. Then the judge stared at Nate. He leaned forward, a pleading look on his face. "I have no right to ask you, Mister Abbitt, but is there no place in your heart for mercy for my Betsy? Is there no way we can work out something between us that won't destroy her life along with mine?"

"I don't know what I can do for her, Your Honor. What do you mean?"

"I'm not sure what I mean. This is uncharted territory for me." The judge looked at his cigar pensively. "Perhaps I could step forward on my own and admit my bias in the Deatherage case, explain my relationship to Darlene to my constituents, step down from the bench, and take retirement. Perhaps there would be no need to reveal my arrangement with Randy. My admission of bias would likely result in the reversal of Deatherage's conviction and your duty to your client would be fulfilled." The judge looked at Nate, his expression tense but hopeful. "Rumor has it that Harry Blackwell was merciful to you in similar circumstances. He allowed you to resign. He didn't have you indicted. He didn't expose your crimes to the world. Can you do the same for me now?"

Nate struggled to regain his equilibrium, reminding himself that a ruthless man could be artfully deceitful. He realized the judge's concern for Betsy gave him leverage. The judge might be willing to confess to Nate to spare his wife humiliation and ignominy. Nate said, "Maybe there's a way to fulfill my duty to my client and preserve your interests, but I'll need to understand the full scope of your misconduct."

"Of course. I'll tell you whatever you want to know."

"You convinced Randolph Swiller not to present a defense of Deatherage, correct?"

"Yes."

"Why did Swiller do your bidding?"

"Randy, Darlene's father, and I were old friends and Randy knew Darlene. He wanted to send Deatherage to the electric chair for the same reasons I did."

"Swiller's affection for Darlene wasn't his sole reason for helping you. Your conspiracy with Swiller predates the Deatherage case."

The judge sighed heavily, and there was a long pause. Then he said, "You're a fine lawyer, Mister Abbitt. I hoped enough time had passed for the world to forget what I did to Creighton Long, but it appears you have left no stone unturned."

"Why did you rig the case against Long?"

"Creighton was a fiend. He lived in our midst for years, pretending to be a respectable member of the community, a bank teller, a Little League coach, a Sunday school teacher, for God's sake, all the while preying on defenseless children. The sheriff's search of his apartment turned up a diary that proved he was the killer, but the search was unconstitutional. The diary was inadmissible, but I couldn't free Creighton to kill again. The people of Buck County rely on me to safeguard their interests, so I made an arrangement with Randy. You understand what I did, don't you, Mister Abbitt? You once bent the laws to secure a conviction."

"I was wrong to do it. The defendant wasn't guilty."

"I wasn't wrong about Creighton. He killed five children."

"Why did Swiller help you in that case? Did you bribe him?"

"I didn't pay Randy to help me." The judge hesitated. "Perhaps that's not entirely true. When Creighton was arrested, Randy needed work. I set him up in practice here in Bloxton. I have great influence over the district judge here, Toby Gwathmey. Toby's predecessor died when the general assembly was out of session. During such times the chief judge of the circuit has the power to appoint an interim district judge. I appointed Toby. That gave him preferred status with the local legislators when the general assembly reconvened. I recommended him to the local house of delegates and senate members. They accepted my recommendation and the general assembly elected him to the district judgeship. He owes his judgeship to me. I told him to appoint Randy as Creighton's defense counsel, and he agreed to do so."

"Was Judge Gwathmey aware of your efforts to convict criminal defendants through the use of Swiller?"

"No. Judge Gwathmey wants to be a circuit court judge some day. He curries my favor and does my bidding, but he's not corrupt. He's merely ambitious. I convinced him to appoint Randy as Creighton Long's defense counsel, and I gave Randy an office free of charge in a building I own. That was the extent of my arrangement with Randy."

"But you made sure Judge Gwathmey appointed Swiller to represent all the capital defendants in your jurisdiction. Did you ask Swiller to lose those cases, too?"

"No, but Randy didn't prepare the cases. He didn't care."

"Why did you tell Gwathmey to appoint Swiller to represent those defendants?"

"Randy threatened to expose our arrangement concerning Creighton. He didn't want money for his silence. He wasn't an evil man. He wanted work. He wanted to feel useful, I suppose. Successful, perhaps. He demanded that I use my influence over Toby to deliver to Randy the lion's share of indigent criminal defense work in Buck County. I agreed and made sure Toby gave Randy the cases he wanted. That's all Randy asked of me, but it was almost more than I could bear. When Toby appointed Randy to represent those defendants at my direction, I stole their Sixth Amendment right to competent counsel. My conscience hid behind the fact that Randy's clients were guilty, but guilty men have rights, too, and I swept those rights away. Otis Banks, Carl Gibson, James Washington. Those cases have haunted me. I was actually relieved when Randy died. I thought my ordeal had come to an end and my violations of my oath of office had escaped detection. Then you appeared here tonight."

"Did George Maupin know about your conspiracy with Swiller?"

"No."

"Did George know you were Darlene Updike's godfather?"

"George knew nothing about Darlene. I granted a motion *in limine* to exclude all evidence about Darlene's background, hoping to prevent anyone from discovering my relationship to her. My plan worked until you took the case."

"What was Darlene Updike doing in Buck County in the first place?"

"She was addicted to alcohol and drugs. She had a child out of wedlock two years ago, which inspired her to clean up her life for a short while, but she soon fell back into her old ways. Darlene's parents, Daniel and Rachel, my lifelong friends, were at their wits' end. I suggested to Daniel that Darlene stay with Betsy and me for a while in hopes I could steer her to the drug rehabilitation center in Roanoke."

"But you weren't able to convince her to mend her ways."

"She was incorrigible. The first week she stayed with us I caught her using drugs in this house. I threw her out and told her she could not return until she was clean. She stopped using drugs here in Buck County as far as I could tell, but she drank heavily. Several nights she came home drunk and I turned her away until she sobered up. In fact, I banished her from my home the night Deatherage murdered her." The judge's voice broke.

Nate waited a respectful time and said, "You visited Darlene in her motel room the night of her murder. What were you doing there?"

"I had given up on her. I talked with Daniel. We agreed Darlene was lost to us forever. He asked me to talk to her about her son, Nicholas. Daniel was afraid Darlene would destroy the boy's life. He asked me to try to save the boy."

The judge opened his desk drawer and withdrew a pistol. Nate was stunned. He expected the gun to fire at any moment, and said, "Kenneth Deatherage. Kenneth Deatherage."

The judge looked at Nate with raised eyebrows.

"Kenneth Deatherage is my client," Nate said. "I owe Kenneth Deatherage a duty. I'm required to protect Kenneth Deatherage's interests."

"I have no quarrel with your conduct, Mister Abbitt," the judge said. "You have every right to expose my corruption in order to protect your client." He placed the pistol on his desk and rummaged through his drawer.

Nate leaned back in his chair and the tension drained away as he realized that the judge meant him no harm. He was simply looking for something in his drawer. Then his relief was replaced by anxiety. He had used the code words. Clarence would believe Nate was in trouble. He imagined Clarence stumbling over the gate in the dark and staggering toward the house, but he had no way of telling him to stand down without revealing to the judge that someone was listening. Their lack of experience had hurt them, he thought. Experience would have taught them to agree in advance to a second code-phrase to cancel the call for help.

"Here it is," the judge said. He extended a document to Nate. Nate put aside his concern about Clarence for the moment, took the document, and reviewed it. It was an agreement signed by Darlene relinquishing custody of her son and consenting to his adoption by her parents. "Darlene gave Nicholas to her parents," the judge said, "when I met with her in the motel, but the agreement became moot when Deatherage murdered her. That agreement has remained in my desk drawer since that night. No one knows about it but me. And now you. After she signed it, I begged her to come home with me, but she refused. She was drunk and miserable, consumed by self-loathing." The judge pointed to the pistol on his desk. "This gun was Darlene's. I saw it on the bedside table in her room that night. I feared she would take her own life. I took it away from her and talked with her for almost an hour. She promised me she wouldn't hurt herself and she agreed to go home to Daniel and Rachel the next morning." The judge's eyes welled with tears. "If I hadn't taken the gun, Darlene might have used it to defend herself. She might be alive today."

When the judge regained control, Nate said, "Tell me about your collusion with Deputy Jones."

"What are you talking about?"

"You persuaded Jones to lie about the bloody scarf in the Deatherage case."

The judge looked confused. "I don't know what you're talking about."

"Jones testified he found a scarf in Deatherage's pocket. That was a lie. You told him to falsify evidence against Deatherage."

"I did nothing of the kind. I've done some shameful things, but I'm not so low as to corrupt the sheriff's office."

Nate sat up on the edge of his chair. "Jones had no motive to manufacture evidence against Deatherage. You had the relationship with Darlene Updike. You had the motive."

"I swear to you I don't know anything about false evidence against Deatherage. I relied on Randy to help me. The case against Deatherage was strong. There was no need to manufacture evidence."

"You had Crawford killed because you were afraid he would tell me he was in the warehouse the night of Updike's murder."

The judge's eyes widened. "I didn't have anyone killed. I'm not a monster."

Nate was confused. "You told Drinkard to call you when I arrived in Bloxton. Right after he called you, someone knocked me out and killed Crawford."

"I asked Drinkard to tell me when you arrived because I was afraid you'd discover my bias in the case. I asked the sheriff to have someone watch you. Feedlow had someone follow you the morning after you arrived, but he said you were conducting a routine review of evidence and he dropped his surveillance. I didn't tell anyone to attack you."

Nate's theory of a wheel of conspiracy with the judge at the hub was breaking apart. The judge had to be lying. "You told the county file room clerk to call you whenever anyone looked at the trial exhibits. You sent Jones to Country Faire to check on me right after I looked at them."

"Darlene's driver's license was an exhibit in the file. Her home address in Albany was on the license. I wanted to be able to warn Daniel if it appeared that someone was about to contact him so he would be sure to conceal his relationship with me. The clerk told me you looked at the file and he said you concentrated on an exhibit you thought was sold at

Country Faire. Your interest in Eva Deatherage's craft shop frightened me because I thought you might discover an *ex parte* conversation I had with her about her son's guilt. I asked the sheriff to find out what you discussed with her. He sent one of his men to interview her, but she refused to talk to him." The judge cast a worried look at Nate. "I assure you, Mister Abbitt, I had nothing to do with manufactured evidence and I know nothing about Crawford's murder. What in God's name has been going on in my county?"

A door slammed in the entry hall, followed by the sound of scuffling and a loud thud. Socrates bayed. The door to the office burst open and crashed against the wall. The judge jumped to his feet. Clarence stood in the doorway, his felt hat low over his eyes, his thick glasses streaked with sweat. He squinted at the judge and sucked in his breath. He widened his stance and pointed his pistol at the judge with a straight-armed two-fisted grip. "Drop it or I'll shoot!"

The judge looked down at the burning cigar in his hand. He turned toward Clarence and lifted the cigar. "Who are you and what – "

Clarence's gun exploded. The judge fell, knocking over the desk chair and collapsing on the carpet. Clarence leveled his gun on the judge's prone body. Smoke floated up from the barrel. The sulphuric aroma of gunpowder filled the room. "Get his gun, Nate. I can't see it. If he makes another move, I'll have to shoot him again."

It took Nate a moment to regain his presence of mind. Then he rose and walked around the desk. The judge lay sprawled on the floor, his arms and legs askew, a bloodstain spreading across the chest of his housecoat. His cigar lay beside him. The carpet smoldered under its glowing ash. Nate knelt and put his hand to the judge's throat. There was no pulse. His eyes were lifeless.

"How bad is he?" Clarence held the gun on the judge, his hands shaking, his magnified bug eyes blinking behind his thick fogged-up glasses.

"He's dead."

All the air went out of Clarence's lungs. His arms fell to his sides, and he dropped his gun. "Lord almighty. He gave me no choice. Why did he aim at me? I had the drop on him."

Nate picked up the judge's cigar, placed it in an ashtray on the desk, and stamped out the burning spot in the carpet.

"You saw it, Nate. He pointed his gun at me. He was ready to fire. I had to shoot."

A woman's voice called from the landing. "Edbert? Are you all right?"

Clarence looked up at the landing. "Oh, Lord."

Betsy Herring ran down the stairs and rushed across the entry hall. Clarence caught her at the door. She struggled against him, craning her neck to see over his shoulder. "Edbert!"

"No, ma'am. You don't want to go in there. You don't want to see it." Clarence pushed her into another room off the entry hall.

Nate could hear her sobs across the way. He sat down on the floor beside the judge's corpse and leaned against the wall. Socrates' baying trailed off. Betsy's cries devolved into whimpers. Later, sirens wailed from the state road. Betsy must have called the sheriff when she heard the shots. The sirens screamed down the judge's private road and stopped at the top of the hill. The sheriff's men were in the process of opening the locked gate, Nate guessed. The moment was nigh when he must make a choice between a harsh truth and a benign lie. As it seemed was so often the case of late, the truth was his enemy. The lie was his friend. He had made this choice too many times. He had to stand. He had to act before the sheriff arrived.

Nate forced himself to stand. He looked out the window. He saw the flashing lights of patrol cars parked beside the fountain. Sheriff Feedlow and two of his deputies got out of the cars. Socrates trotted to the sheriff's side. The sheriff and his men ignored the dog and strode to the porch. Nate heard the front door open and the tread of boots rushing across the entry hall. He heard the voices in the other room – Clarence's old scratchy pipes and Betsy's soft cries.

Nate pulled the sleeve of his suit jacket over his hand and nudged Darlene's pistol off the desk. It fell to the carpet beside the judge's out-stretched hand. Nate rounded the desk and stood by the bookcase on the opposite wall.

Sheriff Feedlow entered the office, glanced at Nate, knelt, and put his hand to the judge's throat. He straightened up, went to the office window, and looked out. He took off his hat and slapped it against his thigh. After a short while, he smoothed out the crown of his hat, put it on, and turned to Nate. "Clarence Shifflett told me what he claims happened. It's your turn."

"The judge pointed his gun at me. Clarence kicked open the door and told the judge to drop the gun. The judge turned his gun on Clarence. Clarence shot him."

The sheriff picked up Darlene's pistol with a handkerchief and broke it open. "It's not loaded."

"Clarence and I had no way of knowing that."

"We'll see about that."

The sheriff went back to the window and stared out at the night. There was a long silence. "You asked me the other day who set the rules in Buck County. The judge set the rules. He didn't follow the law to a tee, but his way was better than the law. He was a decent man. He did a lot of good around these parts. You and Clarence are in a lot of trouble."

Chapter 26

The Recording

Clarence sat on the stairs in the entry hall, holding his head in his hands. Nate sat beside him, watching paramedics roll Betsy through the door on a gurney and carry her to a van in the driveway. Malcolm Somers had arrived earlier. He was in the judge's office with the corpse. George Maupin had appeared shortly after Somers. George and Sheriff Feedlow stood outside on the porch, talking. They came into the entry hall and walked over to Nate and Clarence. "You two have a lot to answer for," the sheriff said.

George put his hand on Nate's shoulder. "Why didn't you bring your suspicions to me?"

"I didn't want to pit you against the judge without hard evidence. We came here to get that evidence, but we didn't mean to harm the judge. The situation spun out of control."

The sheriff said, "That's a polite way to describe murder."

"Hold on, Hubert," George said, "We'll deal with the judge's death when Mac completes his preliminary investigation." He turned to Nate and drew a heavy breath. "Hubert tells me he has evidence implicating you in Crawford's murder."

"It more than implicates him," Feedlow said. "It proves he's the killer."

Nate said, "The evidence is false."

"Bullshit."

"Calm down, Hubert," George said. "Let's hear what Nate has to say."

"There's a problem in Buck County with rigged prosecutions and false evidence," Nate said. "That's why we came here tonight."

George swiped his hand across his face. "This entire situation is surreal – these accusations against the judge, his death, accusations of murder against you. I hardly know what to believe."

"We recorded my conversation with the judge. Listen to the tape. You can believe what you hear on it."

"Where is the tape?" George asked.

"We have it," the sheriff said. "It's in the dining room."

"I want to hear it now. Lives hang in the balance."

"You better hope that tape backs you up," the sheriff said to Nate, "because I don't believe a word you've said."

They all moved into the judge's dining room and sat at one end of a large dining table. A crystal chandelier hung over the table and filled the room with bright light. Nate looked at the tape recorder with trepidation. The tape was double-edged. It would prove the judge conspired with Swiller to convict Long and Deatherage, but it would also prove he did not threaten Nate with Darlene's gun. The sheriff would learn that Nate lied about Clarence's claim of self-defense. Nate was guilty of obstruction of justice, and his lie about Clarence would hurt his credibility in claiming he was being framed for Crawford's murder. Nate was on the horns of a dilemma. The tape helped him in one murder case and hurt him in the other.

The sheriff handed the recorder to Clarence. Clarence pressed play and the tape rolled. Nate's voice described the encounter with Socrates. There was silence while Nate stood on the judge's porch trying to decide what to do. The conversation with the judge finally began. George took notes. When the judge admitted he told Swiller not to defend Deatherage, the sheriff took off his hat, ran his hand through his hair, and grimaced. George said, "What the hell was Eddy thinking when he hooked up with that fool?" Later, when the judge described his relationship with Darlene, George's fist tightened around his pen. "I should have looked into her background despite that damned motion *in limine*."

Further along, the tape replayed Nate shouting "Kenneth Deatherage," followed by several sentences in which Nate used Deatherage's full name. Muffled sounds followed and then dead air. The reel spun round and round, but there was no sound. Almost a minute of silence passed.

Nate leaned forward. "The judge and I were talking during this part. Why isn't the recorder playing what we said?"

Clarence said, "I don't know." He turned off the recorder and inspected the reel. He returned it to the spool and played it again. The same result occurred. "I don't understand." Clarence frowned at the recorder. "That last part where Nate said 'Kenneth Deatherage' – that was my signal he was in trouble. I jumped out of the car and ran to the house. The recorder must have stopped taping after I left the car. Maybe I knocked it over or something went wrong with it when I got out. I don't know."

The sheriff shook his head. "You boys should be ashamed. You conducted this operation like rank amateurs."

George had a troubled look on his face. "All we have to tell us what happened after that tape went dead is your word, Nate."

The sheriff scoffed. "His word ain't worth a damn to me."

"Let's hear him out, Hubert. What did you and the judge talk about after the tape stopped recording?"

"I accused the judge of conspiring with Deputy Jones to falsify evidence against Deatherage."

George blanched.

The sheriff said, "What in hell makes you think Jones phonied up evidence?"

"I have documents that support my claim." The sheriff's men had brought Nate's briefcase to the dining room along with the tape recorder. Nate retrieved from it the original and the carbon copy of the complaint

Eva Deatherage filed. Nate explained the connection between the scarf and the theft and pointed to the altered date on the original complaint.

George held the documents up to the light.

The sheriff said, "You say these papers prove Darby changed the date on the original, but there's another possibility. You could have changed the date on the copy."

"I don't have a motive to alter the date."

"You have a damned good motive. Darby found evidence that says you killed Crawford. If you can prove he phonied up evidence in the Deatherage case, you might get off the hook for Crawford's murder." The sheriff took the original and copy from George and inspected them. "These papers are inconclusive, but I know a way to pin down the date of the theft. I keep a personal duty log. There'll be an entry in my log of the date I talked to Eva. My log's in my car. We'll see who the liar is." The sheriff walked out of the room.

Nate's anxiety mounted. The sheriff was Jones' boss, and he was close to Judge Herring. If he was a conspirator, his duty log would show a false date and Nate would likely be convicted of Crawford's murder.

The sheriff returned with a black notebook with a worn cover. He leafed through the notebook, settled on a page, and stared at an entry. "Eva reported the break-in on June 12, more than a week after the girl's murder. That scarf was still in Eva's shop when Darby said he found it on Deatherage. Darby lied. Nate's tellin the truth." The sheriff looked at Nate with a surprised expression, and his hostility toward him seemed to evaporate.

George said, "All right, Nate. You accused the judge of telling Jones to plant the scarf. What did the judge say about that?"

"He said he didn't know anything about it."

"His denial was a lie."

"I don't think so. I don't think he conspired with Jones."

George frowned. "He admitted he used Swiller to rig the Long and

Deatherage cases. It's a short jump from Swiller to Jones. Eddy turned crooked during the prosecution of Long four years ago. It figures he drew Jones into his corrupt scheme some time after that trial."

"I thought so, too, before I spoke to the judge, but when I confronted him with my accusations, he seemed to know nothing about Jones' crimes. I think Jones acted independently. They both corrupted Deatherage's trial, but my guess is neither of them knew about the activities of the other."

"I don't buy it," the sheriff said. "Darby ain't smart enough to pull that off by himself. He's a follower, not a leader. He takes orders and does what he's told as good as anybody I've worked with, but that's his limit. Good as his army record was, he was never promoted in rank because he can't make decisions on his own. He wouldn't try to frame Deatherage by himself. He wouldn't know how to go about it. Someone smarter than Darby told him what to do and how to do it." The sheriff stroked his chin. "It would have been easy for the judge to recruit Darby to help him rig a case. Darby's a true believer. He wants to protect the citizenry, but he don't question what people tell him to do. If I told him to attack a wall of fire, he'd jump in with both feet. The judge was the biggest authority figure in the county. If he told Darby to frame Deatherage to protect the county from a killer, there's no doubt in my mind he would follow orders. It stands to reason the judge is the one who got Darby into this big mess."

"Maybe," Nate said, "but the judge admitted he used Swiller to rig convictions. He had nothing more to lose by admitting he conspired with Jones."

The sheriff leaned back in his chair and seemed to consider that. "That's a good point. Knowin the judge as well as I did, I think he would have wanted to make a clean breast of all his crimes once you found out what he was up to." The sheriff paused, thinking. "The judge had almost no contact with Darby and he didn't know him well. I doubt he would have trusted him with his secrets about these cases. I agree with Nate. The judge may not be the one who gave Darby his orders, but somebody told him what to do. He ain't smart enough or mean enough to act alone. Someone else is mixed up in this scheme."

"Did the judge implicate anyone else?" George asked Nate.

"No."

"We need to know how far this rot has spread," the sheriff said. "Let's take a leaf out of Nate's book. Let's put that transmitter on Nate and tape-record a meetin between him and Jones."

George's eyes widened. "Have you lost your mind, Hubert? We can't put more lives at risk. Besides, we can't use Nate to tape Jones. He's a suspect for Crawford's murder."

"Darby lied about the scarf in the Deatherage case. That casts a cloud of suspicion over his claims about Nate. That's the problem with this mess. We can't trust anything Darby's told us, and he's been square in the middle of every criminal investigation in this county for the last couple years. We need to get to the bottom of the lyin right now or we won't be able to enforce the laws."

"No," George said. "I won't allow it."

The sheriff's back stiffened. "You're in charge of prosecutin crimes. I'm in charge of investigatin em. Darby's my deputy. I need to know what he did and who he did it with. I'm goin forward with Nate and the tape recorder." He turned to Nate. "We'll put you together with Darby tonight, before he hears about the judge."

George jumped to his feet. "You can't do this, Hubert. This is crazy."

The sheriff turned to Clarence. "Put a new reel of tape in that recorder and make sure it's workin right. Nate and I will head over to Darby's house right now."

George held up his hands. "Hold on now. There's a legal problem here. Nate and Clarence are private citizens. They can record a conversation without violating the Constitution. This time, you'll be in charge, Hubert. This taping is an act of the state. It's unconstitutional without a warrant. Normally, I'd get Eddy Herring to issue a warrant, but I can't very well do that tonight."

"Call Judge Blackwell," Nate said. "He'll issue the warrant."

George grimaced. "All right. I'll get old Harry Blackwell out of bed, but don't go near Jones until I get that warrant, Hubert. Wait for my call telling you I have it, or you'll poison any evidence you might find. Don't run off half-cocked like you did in the Creighton Long case. None of this would have happened if you had played by the rules back then."

"And Long would've killed more little boys."

"Maybe, but heed my advice this time. Don't charge over to Jones' house before I give you the green light."

"All right, but get your damned warrant before dawn. I want Nate to talk with Darby before he hears the news about the judge."

"It'll take me a few hours at most." George looked at Nate. "We've still got a loose end here, Nate. What happened at the end of your conversation that caused the judge to draw his gun on you?"

Nate had to lie. "There was a great deal of noise in the entry hall when Clarence rushed into the house. The judge picked up his gun then. He may have thought someone was breaking in. I don't know. Clarence kicked open the door to the study. The judge was pointing the gun at me at that time, but that may have been unintentional. He turned the gun on Clarence and Clarence shot him."

George looked skeptical, but he gathered his notes and put them in his briefcase. "Until we know how this mess with Jones sorts out, you're a suspect in the Crawford murder, and we need to complete our investigation of the judge's death before I can decide what to do about it. I'm sure you understand, Nate, you're under a cloud of suspicion."

George turned to the sheriff. "Lock Nate and Clarence in jail tonight until you hear from me about the warrant. When you and Nate finish taping Jones, put Nate back in jail until we can review whatever Jones tells you." George shook his finger in the sheriff's face. "Remember, Hubert, if you approach Jones before I get that warrant, you'll destroy our case against him."

Chapter 27

The Setup

It was three in the morning when Sheriff Feedlow locked Nate and Clarence in opposite cells. It was hot, humid, dark, and dead quiet. Clarence stretched out on his cot and rhythmic snores soon cut through the silence. Nate couldn't sleep. He replayed his meeting with Judge Herring, combing his memory for signs of the judge's involvement with Jones. He found none. The judge's words, demeanor, and actions were consistent. He'd conspired with Swiller to convict Long and Deatherage, but he seemed to know nothing about Jones' crimes or Crawford's murder.

Nate rolled over on his back and stared at the ceiling. It was clear that Jones falsified evidence against Deatherage and probably against Jimmy Washington, but based on his reaction to the discovery of Crawford's body, Jones was not involved in Crawford's murder. The sheriff was convinced Jones could not have acted alone. Someone in Buck County conspired with him but not with the judge, and that person was likely Crawford's murderer.

Malcolm Somers might be involved with Jones. That would explain how Jones got access to B+ blood to stain the scarf. On the other hand, Somers didn't impress Nate as particularly smart or creative. He seemed more of a follower than a leader. Nate thought it was possible he was part of a broader conspiracy, but Nate didn't think Jones took direction from him.

George had said he understood what Nate did in Selk County. "The burden on the prosecution is too great. The standard of proof is too high." Nate pondered the possibility that George was Jones' mentor. Nate had yielded to temptation. Maybe George was no better.

Nate turned over on his side on the hard cot. Moonlight cast a shaft of gray mist through the window. He stared at the striped shadows of the bars on the floor. Clarence's snoring droned on.

Nate was confident George was not Jones' mentor. He might be capable of falsifying evidence against a man he considered to be guilty, but he couldn't have murdered Crawford. Very few men were hard enough and cold enough to beat a helpless man to a bloody pulp. Everything he knew about George from their days in law school to the present convinced him that George was not capable of such cruelty.

Nate sat up on the edge of the cot and looked at the cell block door, thinking about the sheriff asleep in his office behind it. Nate had worked with Sheriff Feedlow many times, and he knew the sheriff was a hard man.

He went to the window and looked outside. The stars shone brightly. The full moon hung low over the horizon, just above the mountain range.

The sheriff could be cold and ruthless, and yet he had decided, over George's objections, to go forward with a taped conversation between Nate and Jones, supposedly to root out the corruption in Buck County. But the sheriff had never exhibited a passion to eradicate corruption before. Feedlow's record of fighting crime was spotty, but he was a master of self-preservation. Perhaps his decision to tape Jones had nothing to do with discovering who'd conspired with Jones, and everything to do with self-preservation.

A car's headlights rounded the turn on Ewell Street. The light splashed into Nate's eyes and swept past the jail. An owl hooted in the darkness. Nate searched the shadows of a gum tree for the bird of prey but couldn't see it.

Nate replayed the night's events, searching for signs of deception in Feedlow's words and actions. There were no obvious indications of deceit, but the sheriff was shrewd. He'd dismissed George's concerns about the risk of violence posed by a taped meeting with Jones, but the risk was great. Jones was a deputy. He would be armed. If the sheriff was the man who told Jones to falsify evidence, Nate's death would halt the investigation and the sheriff would survive.

Nate gazed out the window. A crescent of pale haze appeared on the horizon, the first hint of the approaching dawn. The cell block door clanked and the light came on. Nate turned to see Sheriff Feedlow at the door of his cell, a chaw of tobacco bulging from his jaw and a half smile on his thin lips. "Time to go. George got his almighty warrant. Darby gets up at dawn to start his shift. We have a half hour to catch him unaware."

The sheriff escorted Nate to a patrol car. About ten miles out of town, he turned off the state road to a narrow dirt road. "Nobody lives down this road except Darby. There won't be anybody around to get in our way."

The car heaved and pitched over a deeply rutted road that tunneled through dense sumac, honeysuckle, and blackberry vines. Nate saw a break in the brush ahead. The sheriff stopped the car, cut off the head-lights well short of the break, and spat out the window. "We'll walk from here so Darby won't hear the car. I don't want him to have time to think before you talk to him."

The sheriff reached across Nate to open the glove compartment and withdraw a pistol. He offered it to Nate.

"Why do I need a gun?"

"I said I'd make sure nobody got hurt when we taped Darby, but the truth is I can't control the situation. Darby keeps his service revolver next to his bed. He'll bring it to the door. I'll try to cover you, but once you're inside his house he'll have a clear shot at you. I figured you'd want to protect yourself."

Nate stared at the gun. If the sheriff was Jones' conspirator, he wouldn't care whether Darby killed Nate or Nate killed Darby. Either way, the sheriff could shoot the survivor and claim they'd killed each other, and his complicity in the scheme would never see the light of day.

The sheriff thrust the gun at Nate. "Go ahead. Take it." Nate took the gun.

The sheriff handed Nate the transmitter and the original and copy of Eva Deatherage's complaint. "Here's the way I see it. We'll leave the tape recorder runnin in the car. I'll find a spot by the house under a window and I'll try to cover you from there. When you get inside, tell Darby you want him to see some papers before he jails you. Show him the dates on the complaint forms and tell him you gave copies to Clarence and told him to take the forms to the law if anything happens to you. Tell Darby you're willin to make a trade. You'll get off his back about the Deatherage case if he gets off your back about Crawford, but you need to know who else is mixed up in his scheme so you can protect yourself."

"It might work."

"If you got a better idea, say so."

Crickets and tree toads sang. A breeze stirred. The pungent odor of mowed grass drifted in the car window. Nate pointed the gun at the sheriff. "Give me your gun."

The sheriff's smile fell. He wrenched the gun from Nate's hand. Nate rubbed his wrist and groaned.

"You don't know much about guns, do you?" The sheriff released a clasp on the hammer of the gun. "That's the safety. You can't fire the gun until you release the safety. What the hell are you tryin to pull?"

"If you helped Jones falsify evidence, you want him to kill me or me to kill him. You'll kill the one who's still standing and your crimes will stay in the dark."

"You're a lawyer all the way. You lawyers think everybody is as crooked as you are, and you make things complicated when they're plain as day. Your situation is simple, Nate. Everyone thinks you're a murderer. I'm the only one willin to give you a chance to prove you're innocent."

"That's what you want me to think, but you could be setting me up."

"Why would I bother to set you up? Hell, I could kill you right now if I wanted to. Lawyers." He shook his head. "Well, I tell you what. I'd like to know who's the brains behind Darby's crooked doins, but I won't lose any sleep if I don't find the sumbitch. It's not that important to me. You're the one who's in trouble. If you don't want to take the risk to tape Darby, I'll drive you back to the jail and lock you up safe and sound. It's up to you. What do you want to do?" The sheriff waited.

Nate considered the sheriff's description of his dilemma and concluded he was right. He had no choice. He taped the transmitter to his chest and got out of the car. The sheriff set the recorder on the seat and turned it on. "I'm gonna trust you with this gun, but I won't hesitate to shoot you down if you turn on me again. You understand me?"

Nate nodded gravely. The sheriff handed the gun to him and Nate eased it inside his belt at the small of his back. He and the sheriff walked along the dirt road to a clearing where a small frame house sat beneath a pair of huge sweet gum trees. The yard had been mowed the day before and the smell of cut grass filled the air. Outbuildings sat on one side of the house. A patrol car and a pickup truck were parked in one of the sheds. The house was dark. The sheriff said, "We're in luck. He's not up yet."

They walked to the front stoop. Blades of wet grass stuck to their shoes and morning dew splattered their trouser cuffs. The moon dipped below the mountains, and shafts of sunlight speared the sky on the eastern horizon. They stopped under one of the sweet gums. The sheriff drew his gun, pointed to his left, and whispered to Nate. "I'll find a window where I can see you when you get inside. Gimme a minute to get there." The sheriff crept around the house.

Nate leaned against the gum tree and wiped his brow with his sleeve. His legs trembled. He stepped up on the stoop, took a heavy breath, and knocked on the door. No one came. He rapped again harder. "Deputy Jones!" No response. He looked in a window. Dark forms squatted against the opposite wall. He could make out a sofa, a desk, a table with a lamp.

The sound of hurried footsteps came from the left side of the house, and the sheriff suddenly rounded its corner, his gun pointed skyward. "Get away from the window," he shouted.

Nate stepped back. "What's going on?"

"Stay back." The sheriff kicked the door open and disappeared inside. Nate heard his steps running to the rear of the house. Nate leaned inside the doorway. The first light of dawn seeped in the windows and cast a gray hue over the room. He saw the sofa and the desk he had spied from the window. He stepped inside. A recliner sat beside a window to his left. Dim light fell on bare feet draped over the footrest. He lurched backward and grabbed for his gun. It slipped out of his hand and clattered on the floor. He backed into a wall and knocked a lamp off a table.

Nate peered into the shadows until he was sure of what he was looking at. A man was sprawled on the recliner, wearing nothing but his undershorts. His flesh was pale, his legs thick and strong, his chest bulging with muscle. A shotgun lay across his legs. His face and the top of his head were blown away. Blood was splattered in an oval pattern on the plaster above him. A bloodstain on the chair's headrest framed what was remaining of the man's head, and blood was pooled on the floor around the recliner.

Nate sat on the sofa and put his head between his knees. Nausea came. He lurched out the door and vomited. When he was done, he sat on the ground under one of the gum trees. The sheriff came out of the house and sat on the stoop. "You see Darby?"

Nate nodded.

"Pretty bad." The sheriff pulled the chaw of tobacco out of his mouth and threw it across the yard. "When I looked in the window and saw he was shot, I thought the killer might still be here, but no one murdered him. His own shotgun is lyin in his lap. It's been fired. The doors were locked. No signs of a break-in. It's a suicide. Open and shut case."

"Why would he kill himself?"

"Someone told him about the judge, I reckon."

"Who could have told him? The judge has been dead only a few hours."

"Gossip runs through these mountains faster than a deer runnin from a pack a wolves. Lots of people could have spread the word – the boys on the rescue squad, people at the hospital who tended to Betsy, Mac's help in the medical examiner's office. Whoever it was must have called Darby just before we got here." The sheriff scowled. "That damned warrant caused this. The body's still warm. We got here minutes too late."

"He didn't seem the type to take his own life."

"I didn't think so either. I thought he would stand and fight and try to claim what he did was good for the county. The last thing I expected him to do was take a coward's way out. I didn't think he was mean enough to kill a poor old drunk either, but it looks like he killed Crawford and couldn't live with the guilt and shame." The sheriff stood. "I've got to call Mac Somers and get him out here. I'll take you back to jail."

Chapter 28

The Aftermath

Later that morning lying on his cot in the cell, Nate fell into a fitful sleep. He awoke that evening at dusk to sunlight shining through the bars to stripe his face. He was drenched in sweat. The air was heavy and close. He sat up on the edge of the cot. Clarence was sitting on his cot in the opposite cell.

"What time is it?" Nate said.

"I don't know. Hubert took my watch."

Nate went to the window and looked outside. The sun had set, but there was still a peach-colored glow in the western sky. Nate returned to the cot and mopped sweat from his face with the end of a sheet.

"What do you think they'll do with us?" Clarence said.

"I don't know."

They didn't say anything for a while. Then Clarence said, "I've been going over it in my mind all day. I kicked the door open. I saw you. I saw the judge standing over you with the gun in his hand. I told him to drop it. He turned and pointed his gun at me and I shot him. I keep going over it, trying to find the place where I went wrong."

Nate didn't say anything.

"The judge said something right before I fired," Clarence said. "I couldn't understand what he said. You hear it?"

"He said, 'Who are you?'" Nate went to the window and looked outside. A cornfield stood across the road. A breeze rustled the stalks, a dry coarse sound.

"I'm too old for this line of work," Clarence said. "I've been trying to deny the effects of my age, but it's clear to me now. My failing body parts don't fit the job requirements. With my weak eyesight I aimed at the biggest part of the judge's body to make sure I hit him. Hubert told me the bullet went through his heart." Clarence took off his hat and ran his hand through his hair. "I wish to God it had turned out some other way." Clarence lowered his voice. "His wife was mighty torn up."

"Let it go, Clarence. There's nothing we can do to change what happened."

Night fell. Clarence stretched out on his cot. His rhythmic snoring resumed.

Nate lay awake for hours. Before dawn he fell asleep. He dreamed about the rainy night when he wrecked his car. He lay on his back in the dark in the pouring rain. Four bodies lay near him in the grass. Darlene Updike, Henry Crawford, Judge Herring, Deputy Jones. Crawford, Judge Herring, and Jones were dead. Darlene was alive. She lay beside Nate. She grasped his hand. Her hand was small and soft and cold. "Please stop," she said. "Please. Please don't." Her eye was swollen. She bled from her mouth. She turned her head to look at Nate. "Please don't. Please stop." She wasn't Darlene. She was Christine. "I hate you."

Nate awoke with a start. An oblong shape eclipsed the light in the cell. Nate's eyes came into focus to see Sheriff Feedlow bending over him, his wide-brimmed hat shading his face and blocking the light. "Wake up, Nate. Let's go."

"Where are you taking me?"

"I'm releasin you." The sheriff led Nate out of the cell block and into his office. Clarence was already there, standing by a window, looking outside. The sheriff handed Nate his watch, wallet, and cash. "You're free to go."

"What about Crawford's murder?"

"My men searched Darby's house. They found a ring of keys and a drawer full of molds for making keys. One of his keys fit the lock on the trunk of your car. In Darby's shed they found a cotton swab with blood on it. Mac Somers says the swab came from his lab. It has Crawford's blood on it. One of the keys on Darby's ring unlocked the door to the lab. You were right. He was fixin to frame you for Crawford's murder."

Nate let out a long breath.

"George says he can't make a case against you and Clarence for the judge's killin either. There's no evidence to disprove your claim of self-defense." The sheriff handed Nate his car keys. "Your car's parked out front. George said to tell you to go see him before you return to Selk County. He wants to talk to you about the Deatherage case."

"Thank you, Sheriff."

"Don't thank me. This was George's decision. I don't agree with it."

"I'm sorry you feel that way."

The sheriff stared hard at Nate. "I've been in law enforcement a long time. I've questioned a lot of men. You get a feel for the truth after a while. I don't know what went down in the judge's house, but I know you're lyin about it. When you finish with George, go home. Don't come back here. You're not welcome in Buck County."

Nate didn't argue. He and Clarence went out to Nate's car and got in. Nate sat for a moment, thinking about how close he had come to being indicted for murder.

Clarence said, "Are you all right?"

"I'll be okay, I guess. How about you?"

Clarence pulled his hat down low over his eyes. "I'll never be the same."

Nate and Clarence drove to the Buck County town square in silence. Nate left Clarence sitting on a park bench under the statue of Captain Bloxton and walked to the county office building. George's secretary ushered him into George's office. George sat at his desk. He was dressed formally, as though he was headed to court, in a three-piece blue suit and a dark red tie. He looked up at Nate and smiled. "Nate, come in and have a seat."

Nate sat in a chair across the desk from George.

George said, "I called the clerk of the Virginia Supreme Court of Appeals yesterday. I advised him that Judge Herring admitted on tape that he convinced Swiller not to present a defense of Deatherage at his trial in order to ensure his conviction. I told the clerk to inform the justices that I want to stipulate to an order reversing the conviction and remanding the case to the circuit court for a new trial. I made a copy of the tape recording and sent the original to the clerk along with a letter summarizing the evidence of corruption you discovered." George handed Nate a copy of the letter and the stipulation, and Nate looked them over. The letter urged the court to reverse Deatherage's conviction on the grounds that the trial judge deprived Deatherage of his right to legal representation.

Nate was stunned. There was no provision in the Virginia Code or the court's rules for such informal contact with the court. Appellate rules required Nate to present the argument about Deatherage's Sixth Amendment right to competent counsel in his appellate brief. George would normally have opposed Nate's arguments in a reply brief. The court would have heard oral arguments on the issues and later rendered a decision. The entire process would have consumed months, and with the extensive forensic evidence against Deatherage, the outcome would have by no means been certain. George was attempting to short-circuit the process by conceding the issue before Nate had even raised it. The decision seemed rash and unprecedented. "I've never heard of a prosecutor contacting the court this way," Nate said.

George shrugged. "There's no rule authorizing it, but I figured you wouldn't object. It's indisputable that Swiller didn't defend Deatherage. I see no purpose in wasting the court's time and my energy arguing about it. I'd rather get on with prosecuting him again."

George's action was so irregular that the court might very well deny his request, but it was true that Nate had no reason to object to it. Nate wondered if George's surprising generosity extended beyond the Deatherage case. "What about the other capital cases?" he asked.

"The judge made no admissions about the other cases. There are no grounds to reverse those convictions."

"Swiller was their lawyer. He was incompetent, and Judge Herring did nothing to protect the rights of those men."

"Yesterday I called each of the lawyers who replaced Randy and told them what you uncovered about the Long and Deatherage cases. They can take whatever actions they deem appropriate to protect their clients, but I won't help them. What the judge and Jones did in the Deatherage case was illegal, but that doesn't change the facts of the other cases. All the men on death row from Buck County are murderers. If I'm required to retry them, the outcome will be the same. They'll be convicted and they'll die in the electric chair. That goes for Deatherage as well. I'm confident I'll convict him a second time."

"The Deatherage case is weak. You don't have the smoking gun. Without the bloody scarf, you can't prove beyond a reasonable doubt that Deatherage killed Updike."

"The forensic evidence is powerful. Odoms puts Deatherage at the window where the body was found. Deatherage fled the scene."

"Crawford was in the warehouse at the time of the murder. He could have killed her. He's dead. You can't put him on the stand and ask him what happened that night."

George paused. "What proof do you have that Crawford was in the warehouse?"

Now that Judge Herring and Deputy Jones were dead, Nate felt he could reveal Odoms' role in Nate's investigation to George without endangering him. Nate said, "Willis Odoms saw Crawford leave the warehouse right after the murder. Crawford's presence there creates a textbook case of reasonable doubt."

George looked concerned. "We're not in law school studying textbooks, Nate. We're in the real world. You know Deatherage killed that girl. If he gets out, he'll kill again. You should be careful what you present to the jury. If you free Deatherage, the next murder will fall on your shoulders."

Nate took a moment to digest George's words. "That attitude is what brought me down in Selk County and that same attitude brought down Judge Herring and Jones here in Buck County. I have a duty to defend Deatherage. I'll call Odoms to the stand. A jury will decide whether Deatherage goes free or goes to the electric chair. I won't make that decision."

George shrugged. "I didn't mean to imply you should compromise your duty to defend Deatherage. Your clients deserve your best effort, but rest assured I have ample untainted evidence to convict Deatherage again." George stood. "Much as I'd like to spend more time with an old friend, I'm sure you understand I have a lot of work to do and I'm pressed for time." He extended his hand. Nate stood and shook it.

In the hallway, Nate stopped and looked back at George's office. In their first meeting about the case, George had been tired and fearful of Judge Herring. The night of the judge's death, he was tense and nervous. Now, he was relaxed, confident, and almost arrogant. Nate understood the change to some degree. Judge Herring's grip on the county had squeezed him for a long time and his death gave George newfound freedom and authority, but the change also troubled Nate. Despite his disclaimer, he'd clearly suggested that Nate should withhold evidence that might exculpate Deatherage. Nate worried that George was going to have to learn his own hard lessons.

Chapter 29

The Hero

Judge Herring's death was big news. The Virginia press swarmed over Buck County. Someone disclosed the details of the judge's corruption, Jones' falsification of evidence, and Nate's pivotal role in the investigation. Reporters called Nate, but he made no comment.

The newspaper stories and television coverage that eventually came out didn't bear much relationship to the truth. The press portrayed Judge Herring as completely corrupt. They described Jones as a well-intentioned but dimwitted soldier whose wooden understanding of good and evil and right and wrong made him susceptible to the misguided direction of a powerful authority figure like Judge Herring. As the story gained momentum, the judge became a criminal mastermind who preyed on a broken-down alcoholic defense attorney and a simpleminded patriotic deputy to send men to death row solely because he didn't like them.

Judge Blackwell's advice that Nate's work would help him regain some of what he had lost came to fruition in the news coverage. Citing an unnamed "official in local law enforcement" as their source, reporters characterized Nate as a hero. None of the stories mentioned the rumored reasons for his resignation from his commonwealth's attorney position. His checkered past didn't fit the theme the media advanced. In the news stories, he was a savvy former prosecutor who switched sides late in his career to defend innocent indigent criminal defendants. He was portrayed as a man who was especially sensitive to corruption and abuse of the justice system because of his long tenure as commonwealth's attorney. The stories credited his prosecutorial expertise, guile, and ingenuity for dethroning the self-coronated king of Buck County, and in the process, the media anointed him as one of the state's most talented criminal defense attorneys. Some of the details publicized about his investigation, such as the reference to the judge as the king of the county, led Nate to conclude that George Maupin was the media's unnamed source.

Nate didn't feel like a hero. Judge Herring was dead. Betsy Herring was living in a personal hell through no fault of her own. Clarence Shifflett was a broken man. Deputy Jones was dead. Some unknown public official, who directed Jones to falsify evidence and murdered Henry Crawford, was still on the loose. Nate felt responsible for these tragedies, but he did nothing to undermine his reputation as a hero in the hope that the publicity would impress the only person who mattered to him.

That hope was dashed on Monday morning at the final settlement conference in his divorce case. Howard and Christine met with Judge Greene in chambers first. The judge then sent them to wait in the courtroom while he met with Nate. Nate and the judge sat across from one another at the conference table. "As I feared," Judge Greene said, "your affair with Miss Partlow has embittered Christine since our last meeting. Howard says she's no longer willing to settle the case. At this juncture all I can do is set a trial date. I'm sorry, Nate."

"There's no need for a trial. I'll give Christine whatever she wants."

"What do you mean?"

"She can have everything – the house, the farm, the bank accounts, all of it. I'll pay whatever amount of alimony she wants."

"Are you sure you want me to convey an open-ended offer like that? Christine is angry and hurt. She may demand the lion's share of your future earnings."

"I don't care about the property or the money."

Judge Greene tapped his knuckles on the conference table. "Very well, then. I'll present your offer to Howard."

"There's one condition. I want to talk to Christine alone before a divorce decree is entered. I want to talk to her this morning in this room, just the two of us."

The judge paused. "I don't believe your condition will be acceptable to her."

"Those are my terms. She gets whatever she wants. I get nothing except a meeting with her."

"I'll talk with Howard."

Judge Greene left the room. Nate went to a window and looked outside. The sky was clear and azure blue. He recalled the first time he saw Christine, his first dates with her, their wedding day. They were so young then. Now they were growing old. More of their lives was behind them than ahead, and so much had happened between them – Nate's crimes, his affair with Rosaline, the drinking. He wished he could go back to that first day at the cross-country meet. He wished he could live it all again and do it right this time. He wished he could give Christine the love and respect she deserved.

"I have a counterproposal from Christine." Nate turned. The judge stood by the door. "Because you offered to release your interest in the property, Christine doesn't want alimony."

"What about the meeting?"

"She will agree to meet with you, but only under certain conditions which are not negotiable. She won't meet with you alone. Howard, the bailiff, and I will be present. The meeting will be here in chambers. Now. For no more than fifteen minutes. You will sit on the far side of my conference table. She will sit on the side closest to the door. The bailiff will stand at the head of the table. He'll be armed. If you make a move toward Christine, the bailiff will have instructions to subdue you."

"I won't hurt her."

"She's not willing to meet without the bailiff standing over you."

"What I have to say to Christine is private."

"I'm sorry, Nate. Those are her conditions."

Nate went to the conference table and sat down heavily in the chair closest to the wall. "I accept her conditions."

The judge went out in the hall. The bailiff, Franklin Spears, entered the room. He was a black man in his forties. He was short, solid, and strong, with a shaved head. He had served as Judge Blackwell's bailiff for years, and Nate knew him well. He shook Nate's hand with a firm grip. "Mister Abbitt."

"Hello, Franklin."

Franklin propped his hand on the butt of a pistol holstered at his hip. "Mrs. Abbitt's gonna come in now. She told me she had some trouble with you. She said you broke into her house, pushed her around."

Nate looked down and swallowed. "I was drunk. I made a terrible mistake. I'll regret it till the day I die."

"Mrs. Abbitt wants you to understand there won't be no trouble here today. I want you to understand that, too. Do you understand that, Mister Abbitt?"

"Yes. I understand."

"Good." Franklin moved to the head of the conference table. "Put your hands on top the table and keep em there long as Mrs. Abbitt's in the room."

"You know me better than that, Franklin."

"I knew you once, Mister Abbitt, couple years ago. I don't know you lately."

Nate folded his hands on top of the table.

Franklin nodded to Judge Greene. The judge opened the door. Howard Raines entered the room with Christine clutching his arm, her eyes on the floor. Howard led her across the room to the table. She sat down and held on to Howard's arm until he pulled it away gently and stepped back.

Judge Greene and Howard retreated to a spot near the door and looked away from Nate and Christine.

Christine's eyes remained downcast. Nate drank in the sight of her. He hadn't seen her in so long, and he wanted her back so much.

Judge Greene said, "You have fifteen minutes, starting now."

Nate tried to forget the others in the room. He struggled to find a starting point. There was so much he wanted to say, so much to atone for.

"Get on with it," Christine said. "I won't sit here one more second than I have to."

"I don't blame you."

Her eyes flashed. "Don't patronize me."

"I wanted to tell you . . . I know I've done . . . Christine, I'm so sorry for all I've done to you."

"Is that what this meeting is about? An apology? Save your breath. There's nothing you can say to excuse what you've done. Besides, your words mean nothing. You're a liar."

"Our marriage wasn't a lie."

"That's precisely what it was, a lie that spanned thirty years."

"The truth is I loved you for – "

"You never loved me. You loved yourself."

Nate looked down and shook his head.

Christine said, "Don't think you can play the role of the aggrieved bad boy who wants to be good again. You never loved me. Our marriage wasn't about me. It wasn't about us. It was about you – what you wanted, when you wanted it, and how you wanted it. You never loved anyone but yourself."

"I understand why you feel that way. I failed you. I hurt you."

"Oh, please, spare me your false pity. I'm way past the sappy tricks you played on me for so long."

Nate struggled to maintain his composure. "Christine, please."

"You don't get it, do you, Nate? You don't understand who I am, who I've become because of you. It must be difficult for you to make the adjustment. You manipulated me for thirty years. You think you can still say the right words, cobble together a few artful phrases, make a superficial apology, and I'll fall into place where you want me, like I always did. Well, that day is gone, Nate. I know who you are now. It took me a long time to see the real you. I suppose I was the last person in Selk County to find you out, but I know you now. I know you and I hate you."

"I can understand your bitterness."

"No, you can't. You can't begin to understand my bitterness." Christine's lips trembled. "I met with her, you know, your secret love."

Nate put his hand over his eyes. Franklin tapped the table. Nate returned his hand to the table.

"What's the matter, Nate? Does it trouble you that Rosaline and I met? Why? You should have known she would come to me some day. You drove her to me. You lied to her. You told her you loved her. You promised her you would leave me to be with her. You broke her heart. She told me everything, Nate, all of it. We discovered how much we have in common. You lied to both of us. You stole both our lives." Christine's eyes glistened. "We both loved you." She wiped tears away. "And we both hate you now."

"I'm sorry about Rosaline."

"You're sorry all right. You're sorry you got caught." Christine almost broke down. She put her hand to her mouth and struggled to hold herself together.

Nate felt helpless and hopeless.

There was a long silence. Then Christine said, "Do you have anything else to say to me, Nate?" She looked at her watch. "You've got eight minutes. After that, I get my greatest wish. I'll never see you again."

Nate gathered what strength and resolve he had left. "Let me talk for a few moments. Don't cut me off. Please."

"Don't tell me what to do."

"Just listen to me. Please, Christine. Hear me out without interruption. Give me a chance to say my piece."

Christine's eyes were as hard as stones. "Fine. I'll sit here while you talk to yourself if that will bring an end to this ordeal."

Nate confronted the look of hatred on her face and said, "All the years we spent together I loved you."

She rolled her eyes.

"I loved you," he said, "whether you believe it now or not. The years went by. Too fast. I looked up and I was suddenly old and something went wrong. I guess I wanted to be young again. I don't know. I didn't understand what was going on inside me then and I don't understand it now. All I know is I was afraid. And desperate. I drank. I drank to silence the screams of panic inside my head. I drank more and more, but I couldn't drink enough to drown my fears. I did terrible things when I drank. I hurt you when I drank." Nate's voice failed him. "I'm so sorry for all of it."

"That doesn't wash, Nate. You weren't drunk the entire time you carried on with Rosaline and lied to me and concealed it from me. You can't blame what you did on alcohol. That's too easy."

"I'm not saying the drinking caused the harm. I chose to drink. I'm responsible for what I did, but I wasn't myself when I drank. I would never have hurt you if I had stayed sober."

"You're lying again. You're lying to yourself to ease your guilt. Think about it, Nate. Why did you choose to drink? If you were afraid or confused or whatever it was, why didn't you talk to me? We were husband and wife, a team, partners in life. If you loved me, why didn't you turn to me with your fears? You didn't. You turned away from me. You shut me out."

"I was ashamed of my weaknesses. I was afraid and I didn't want you to know I was afraid. I turned to the bottle for courage. It was a bad choice. My drinking got out of hand, and I lost myself."

"Too easy, Nate. The bottle doesn't explain Rosaline. Why did you turn to Rosaline?"

Nate hesitated. "I don't know why I turned to Rosaline."

"You're lying, Nate. You know why. I know. Rosaline knows. She and I discussed it when she came to see me. Your selfishness drove you into her arms, your need for a new thrill to feed your boundless ego. You wanted someone new to admire you. You wanted someone new to see you as her hero, and you didn't care who you hurt to get what you wanted. You didn't think about her or me or anyone but yourself. You wanted a new conquest to boost your opinion of yourself, so you chased and caught Rosaline and she gave you what you wanted. She admired you and loved you. Until you tossed her away." Christine hesitated, gathered herself, and said, "I loved you, too." Her voice was low, quavering. "And you hurt me. You hurt me so much, but I didn't know who you were then. I believed your lies then. Now I know who you are and you can't hurt me anymore." Christine took a deep breath and looked at her watch. "Time's up." She pushed her chair back from the table.

"I'm sorry, Christine. I'm sorry I was so selfish. I'm sorry I hurt you so much and failed you in every way, but you've got to believe me. I love you. I've always loved you."

"Really, Nate? Did you love me that stormy night when you forced your way into our home. You wanted to hit me that night. You almost did. I could see it in your eyes. Did you love me then, Nate?"

"I . . . I don't . . ."

"What, Nate? You don't know what to say? You? The grand-master wordsmith? The great trial lawyer who could convince a jury to believe black was white? You, of all people, are at a loss for words. Amazing, isn't it? Did it ever occur to you there's a reason for your uncharacteristic incoherence? The reason is clear. Clear to me. Clear to everyone except you. Your case has no merit, Nate. You have no merit. You are guilty, and there is no well-crafted argument, there is no impassioned plea, there are no words that can save you from the awful truth. We had a good life and

I loved you, but it wasn't enough for you. You ruined our lives, Nate. You – not some strange force that took you over, not some overwhelming fear of your age, not some mysterious psychological breakdown, not some mind-altering guilt-absolving sea of whiskey – you and you alone destroyed our lives. You and you alone did that to both of us, Nate, and you can never make up for it! Never!" Christine shouted the last words and a sob burst out. She put her hand over her mouth and stifled the sobs that would have otherwise followed. She stood and walked to the door.

Nate stood.

Franklin put his hand on the butt of his gun. "We won't have no trouble, Mister Abbitt."

"Christine," Nate said, "please don't leave me. I love you, Christine. I have no right to love you, but I do." She stopped at the door, standing between Howard and Judge Greene, her back to Nate. "I love you," he said, "more than anything in the world, and I want you back. I want you back so much. Please forgive me, Christine. Please take me back. I'll do anything you ask. Anything. Please, Christine. Please take me back."

For a precious instant Nate thought there was a chance. Then she walked out the door and she was gone.

Howard stood at the door, looking at Nate. Tears ran down Howard's cheeks. He followed Christine. Judge Greene stood with his back turned to Nate. Franklin put his hand on Nate's shoulder and eased him back into his chair. Then Franklin and Judge Greene left the room.

Nate cried, deep wracking sobs. Memories flooded over him, a panorama of scenes of his life with Christine. They rolled by like a movie reel on high speed. He wanted to slow down the images and drink them in, but they were compressed into a short stream of fleeting moments – ephemeral, transitory. Too soon the images ended with her last words to him. "You and you alone destroyed our lives and you can never make up for it! Never!"

Thirty minutes later, Judge Greene read the terms of the settlement into the record and entered a decree ending the marriage of Nathan Allen Abbitt and Christine Smith Abbitt.

Chapter 30

The Wife

In the days that followed the media frenzy, prospective clients came to Nate's door in droves, and he turned no one away. He worked sixteen-hour days, seven days a week. When he came home to his apartment each night, he hoped exhaustion would speed him to sleep, and when it did not, he got out of bed and worked at his kitchen table all night long. Memories of Christine always lurked in the shadows of his mind. In idle moments they tormented him and drove him toward whiskey, but each time he resisted by turning to the only thing he had left – his work.

The Deatherage case plodded through the court system that summer. The Virginia Supreme Court of Appeals refused to dispose of the case based on George's informal letter attempting to concede the appeal. Nate promptly filed his appellate brief, and George filed a statement of non-opposition in reply and waived oral argument. The court then reversed Deatherage's conviction and remanded the case to the Buck County Circuit Court for a new trial. While Nate and George waited for the Virginia General Assembly to elect a new judge to the Buck County Circuit Court, they prepared the case for trial. Sheriff Feedlow was true to his word and turned the warehouse mattresses over to Shirley West and the Virginia medical examiner's lab in Roanoke. With the passage of time and all the movement of the mattresses, the chance that any evidence of the murder had survived was slight. As Shirley had warned Nate, hair and fibers don't normally cling to fabric, but she had a stroke of luck when she looked under the buttons that held the mattresses together. Clamped to a mattress by a button she found fibers that matched Darlene Updike's blouse. The fibers gave Nate a powerful argument that Darlene was raped on the mattress, instead of on the warehouse floor.

The fibers, coupled with Odoms' testimony that Crawford was in the warehouse during the attack on Updike and that Crawford normally slept on the mattresses, weakened the commonwealth's case, but Nate thought the other forensic evidence against Deatherage was so powerful there was still a good chance a Buck County jury would convict him unless Nate could offer them a viable suspect and an alternate theory of the murder. He decided to approach Frank Gentry, Larry Lamb, and Herman Doyle, the men Drinkard had said had one-night stands with Updike, to see what he could shake loose.

While Nate was preparing questions for these men, Daryl Garth called him. Garth's wife was a nurse at the Buck County Medical Clinic. Garth said she had treated Kenneth Deatherage's father-in-law for an asthma attack the previous day. He told her George Maupin came to his house to question Deatherage's wife, Claire, about the murder. She'd refused to talk and he threatened to subpoena her to testify at trial. Claire's father wanted Garth to help them by trying to keep her off the witness stand.

"I can't do anything for her," Garth said. "She can't pay my fee, but I thought you'd be interested to know the commonwealth's attorney may subpoena her."

"Thanks for letting me know," Nate said.

"Maybe you can pay me back by giving me some help with the Washington case."

"I'll do what I can. I'll give you a call when the Deatherage trial is over."

George's attempt to question Claire Deatherage implied she must know something that might bolster his case. Evidence of the corruption of the judge and Deputy Jones had developed so rapidly that Nate had never gotten around to questioning her about the case, but he definitely needed to now.

On a sultry afternoon in late July, Nate turned off the state road east of Bloxton onto a narrow paved road bordered by farmland on both sides. A few miles in, the pavement ran out and the road carried on over a rutted dirt surface. Just past an End State Maintenance sign, Nate came to a clapboard house sitting among hardwood trees. The house was in bad shape. Felt roof tiles had worn away exposing patches of black tarpaper subroofing. Several upstairs windows were broken. The yard was a dust bowl pocked with clumps of weeds.

Nate parked in front of the house and climbed rickety steps to stand on a creaking wooden porch. A hole had rotted through the porch planks just to the left of the front door. The rheumy eyes of an emaciated old dog panting feebly on its side gazed up at Nate indifferently from the shadows under the porch.

The front door stood wide open. Nate stepped into an entry hall. "Anyone home?" No one answered. The entry hall was barren of furniture. There were doors to other rooms to his right and left. A stairway with a broken banister climbed along the back wall to a second floor. A pool of liquid stained the floor beside the front door. Flies swarmed over it and fed on its crusty edges. A sour smell filled the air.

A woman's voice from inside the house called out. "Put the damn melon rind down. I'm not gonna tell you again." A red-faced toddler stumbled through the door to Nate's left. The child wore nothing but a rag diaper that was wet and brown in the seat and sagged between his legs. The little boy stopped and looked up at Nate. He was filthy. Tear tracks streaked through the dirt on his cheeks. His round face and red hair resembled Kenneth Deatherage, but his owlish brown eyes belonged to someone else. The child bent his knees, balled his fists, and urinated through his diaper. A puddle pooled on the floor between his feet. He tippled past Nate to the porch and worked his way down the steps on his hands and knees.

The woman's voice called out again. "Harmon!" There was a pause. "Goddamn it." A short young woman in a plain brown dress that hung loosely on her slight frame padded on bare feet into the hallway. She looked at the puddle of urine and cursed. When she saw Nate she put her hand to her breast and let out a little cry.

"I'm sorry I startled you, ma'am," Nate said. "The door was open. I called out but no one answered."

The young woman had damp auburn hair that was pressed to her fore-head in front and frizzy and sticking up like a bird's tail-feathers in back. A clear slick substance, likely cooking lard or vegetable oil, was smeared on her chin. She was small and thin. She had the body of a teenager, but her face belonged to a woman older than her years. Her round brown eyes had a wounded look in them. "We can't pay. I told the other bill collectors the same. We don't have no money. We're livin on the dole."

"I'm not here about money, ma'am. Are you Claire Deatherage?"

The young woman stared at Nate's scar. Her tense face softened. "What happened to your face, mister?"

"I was in a car accident."

"Are you all right?"

"I'm fine, ma'am. It's just a scar. Are you Mrs. Deatherage?"

"What do you want with her?"

"I'm an attorney. I represent Kenneth Deatherage."

"I heard about you. You're the one wants to get Kenny out."

"I take it you're Mrs. Deatherage?"

"I used to be, but I went back to Moses when they put Kenny away. I'm Claire Moses now."

"Moses is your maiden name?"

"Yes, sir. My daddy's Tinker Moses. He's not here. He's got the empy-sema. The rescue squad came and got him last night cause he couldn't breathe without them tubes they put in his nose. They took him back to the hospital, but they won't keep him long. He can't pay." Claire craned her neck. "You see Harmon come through here?"

"The little boy? He went outside."

Claire walked out on the porch and Nate followed. "Drop that handful a dirt right now or I'll come down there and smack you good!" Harmon squatted in the yard with a fist full of dirt. His face was scrunched up in a stubborn frown.

"Drop it!"

Harmon flinched and opened his fist. He began to cry.

"Shut up, goddamn it! Shut the hell up right now or I'll smack you good!"

Harmon swallowed a sob and stuck his dirty thumb in his mouth. He waddled around the porch to a side yard. A chicken ran from under the porch, clucking and squawking. He squealed and laughed.

Claire pushed a strand of hair back from her face. "Sumbitch eats dirt like it's candy. Drives me plum crazy."

"I'd like to ask you a few questions about your husband, ma'am."

"I told the law all I know about Kenny back when he killed that girl. You're not gonna get him out, are you?"

"Who did you talk to?"

"Darby Jones."

"What did you tell him?"

"They say you're the one who caused Darby to get killed. They say you killed the judge, too."

"I didn't kill them."

"They say you came here to get Kenny out and you don't care what happens to the rest of us. Why do you want to set him free, mister?"

"I'm his attorney. That's my job."

"Don't you care what happens to us? People say you don't care, but you don't look like a hard man."

"I owe your husband the best defense I can provide. That's the law."

"Then the law's wrong, mister. Maybe you don't know what'll happen. If Kenny gets out, he'll come here first and he'll do to me what he did to that girl. He told me so before they took him off to the state jail."

"He threatened you?"

"He said if I know what's good for me I'll keep my mouth shut, but I know him. He don't trust me to keep quiet. If he gets out, he'll shut my mouth for good."

"Shut your mouth about what?"

Claire walked to the far side of the porch. Nate followed her. She gazed at Harmon. He stumbled into a patch of weeds, pulled a handful of dry stalks out of the ground, and waved them in the air, laughing. "I won't say what Kenny told me."

Nate decided to come at the subject indirectly. "Deatherage said you and he had a fight the night of the murder."

"It wasn't a fight. It was a beatin."

"Why did he beat you?"

"He don't need a reason. He beats me for the fun of it."

"Did you have an argument that night?"

"Same one we always had."

"What was the argument about?"

"Kenny was gone more'n a week. Then he came here all liquored up and acted like he'd never left. He wanted it, like always. I was worn out from wrestlin with Harmon all day. I wouldn't give it to Kenny. He knocked me down and got on top of me on the kitchen floor right in front of Harmon." Claire's eyes teared up. "Choked me while he did it. If Daddy hadn't pulled him off me, he woulda killed me."

"He choked you?"

"Kenny choked off my air and made me pass out when he took my favors. That's how he liked it. He didn't do it to me when we first met. He was nice to me in the beginnin. Then he did it to me once just after Harmon was born when I didn't want to give it to him. He did it more and more after that. It gave him pleasure to choke me when he took it from me." Claire scowled at Harmon. "Drop it! I told you a hunnerd times. I'll smack you up side your head you eat one more mouthful a dirt!"

Harmon dropped the dirt, waddled to a rusty tractor, and sat in the weeds under the rear axle.

"What happened after your father pulled Deatherage off you?"

"Daddy put the twelve gauge on Kenny, and he ran off." Claire's eyes clouded. "Don't you see what happened, mister? He came here first. I wouldn't give it to him, so he found that girl. She wouldn't give it to him either, so he took it from her and he choked her, just like he did me, and he killed her. The girl died instead of me."

"Did you tell Deputy Jones that he choked you?"

"I won't tell you what I told Darby."

"I understand George Maupin questioned you about the murder?"

"He came here last week. He wanted me to talk in court. I told him I wouldn't do it." Claire looked at Nate's scar. "He's not like you, mister. He's a hard one. He wouldn't leave me alone. Daddy had to run him off. I didn't tell that hard man nothin."

"He can subpoena you."

"Yeah, he said that, too, but I don't care. I won't go to court. I told him so."

"You won't have a choice. If you don't comply with the subpoena, the law will find you and take you to the courthouse, and you'll be forced to answer George Maupin's questions at your husband's trial."

Claire's eyes widened. She grabbed Nate's sleeve. "But I can't. Kenny'll kill me. I swear to God. Don't nobody care that he'll kill me?"

"I'm sorry, ma'am, but the county can force you to testify. I need to know what you'll say on the witness stand."

"How did that hard man find out what I know? I didn't tell him nothin."

"If you tell me what you know, maybe I can do something to help you."

"You got to keep me out of that trial, mister. Please."

"I'll try."

"I knew you weren't the bad man everybody said you were. That ugly scar's not who you are. You don't have the look of a bad man."

"What do you know about the murder?"

Claire paused. "I know Kenny killed the girl."

"How do you know that?"

"He told me. He said he killed her because of me."

Anger flashed through Nate. He had tried to convince himself that Deatherage was innocent. The forensic evidence coupled with Eva Deatherage's stories about Deatherage's strangulation fetish made Nate skeptical, but the corruption in Buck County gave him hope that someone else killed Darlene Updike. Now that hope was dashed and he knew Deatherage had played him for a fool. Deatherage was a sadistic rapist, a murderer, and a very good liar, as Nate had suspected all along.

"Are you all right, mister?"

Nate reined in his anger and pulled himself together. "Exactly what did Deatherage say about the murder?"

"Kenny said he never woulda choked the girl if I had given it to him like a wife's supposed to do. He said it was my fault he killed her and my fault he went to jail."

"When did he tell you this?"

"The day after he killed the girl. Darby Jones caught him and locked him up. Kenny used his phone call to yell at me to get my sorry ass down to the jail. I went down there and talked to him through the bars. I was glad he was locked up cause he was mighty hot with me. He said I got him in a world of trouble and me and Daddy better come up with the money to get him a crooked lawyer to spring him outta jail or he'd come lookin for me when it was all over. Course, me and Daddy don't have no money and we don't have no way to get no money."

"George Maupin knows Deatherage confessed to you. That's why he wants to call you as a witness."

"I didn't tell him."

"Did you tell anyone?"

"The only one I told was Darby Jones."

"When did you tell him?"

"I didn't tell Darby nothin the first time he came here, but Daddy told him about the beatin Kenny gave me that night before he killed the girl. Darby came back another time. He said it was a crime for Kenny to beat me. He was real nice to me that night. He brought me flowers – daisies. We sat on the back porch and talked for a couple hours. He had a jug a hooch and we drank most of it. He was sweet to me, the way Kenny used to be."

"And you told him about the confession?"

"Darby promised to keep it a secret. He said he'd make sure I wouldn't have to go to court and tell what I know. He said he would fix it so Kenny never got outta jail."

"Did Jones tell you about stealing a scarf and putting blood on it?"

"No, but I heard about it from the gossips. People say Darby made up stories about Kenny so the court would send him to the electric chair. If it's true, Darby did it as a good deed for me and Harmon and Daddy."

"Did Jones tell you about anyone who helped him put Kenny in jail?"

"No."

"Did he say anything to you about the murder of Henry Crawford?"

"He said it was a terrible crime to kill a poor old drunk like that."

"Did he know who killed Crawford?"

"No, but he said he'd find out who did it and he'd make sure Henry's killer paid for it with his life."

Nate looked across the yard at Harmon, still squatting in the weeds under the tractor, tracing his finger in dust on a tractor wheel, and Nate thought about Deatherage. The Deatherage case had turned into Nate's worst legal nightmare. Ethical canons required Nate to do his best to free Deatherage, but he wasn't sure he could force himself to do it now that he knew Deatherage was guilty.

Claire put her hand on Nate's arm. He looked down at it. It was a small hand, like Darlene Updike's hand. Like Christine's hand.

"Please, mister. Don't let em take me down to the courthouse. Kenny'll kill me for sure. Please help me, mister."

Chapter 31

The New King

A week later on the first Monday in August, the clerk of the Buck County Circuit Court called Nate and told him that the Virginia General Assembly had elected George Maupin as Judge Herring's replacement. She said Judge Maupin had recused himself from the Deatherage case and the circuit's acting chief judge had assigned the case to Judge Wigfield, the presiding judge of the Starkey County Circuit Court.

Nate knew the selection of judges was based in large part on who you know, rather than what you know. A candidate had to be endorsed by the legislative delegates who represented the residents of the circuit. Once the delegates advanced a candidate, he was interviewed by the Courts of Justice Committee, but the interview was usually a mere formality. If the local delegates supported a candidate, the committee almost always certified him. He then had to be elected by a majority vote in both houses of the General Assembly – the House of Delegates and the Senate of Virginia – but the election was normally a foregone conclusion. Most legislators didn't know the candidates outside their circuit, so they voted for any candidate endorsed by the local delegates and certified by the committee. Election to a circuit judgeship depended upon one thing: cultivating a good relationship with the circuit's local legislative representatives.

Nate thought about George Maupin all day. In the middle of the night Nate lay awake in bed in his apartment, still thinking about George. It was hot. He rose and opened the window. Across Lee Street in Beauregard Park someone hacked and coughed. A garbage can clattered on the pavement. Nate leaned on the window sill and stared at the night.

He thought about a conversation he had with George when they were in law school. At the end of their first semester they studied together for final exams. One afternoon they took a break and went to a coffee shop. They sat across from each other in a booth. It was early in December. Nate watched snow falling outside a window by their table. He took a sip from his cup. The coffee was hot and smelled good.

"What made you decide to go to law school?" George had asked.

Nate shrugged. "I don't know. I was an English major. I'm pretty good with words." He paused. "The truth is I couldn't think of anything else to do." They were quiet for a while. Then Nate said, "What about you, George?"

George stared out the window and didn't answer for a long time. Then he said, "My family got pushed around a lot when I was growing up." He looked at Nate. "Respect was the main reason, I guess. People respect lawyers." Nate saw something in George's eyes. Then George took a sip of coffee and looked away and their conversation moved on.

George's background was a subject of gossip among the students. One of them told Nate George's father had been "a laid-off coal miner, a deadbeat, and a drunkard" who drank himself to death and left George's family to fend for itself. In a culture where pedigree often counted for more than talent, George started every race from way behind everyone else. He came to law school with no money and no influence and with his father's shortcomings as the first thought that came to everyone's mind when he entered a room, but he persevered and overcame tremendous economic and social handicaps. What Nate thought he saw in George's eyes that day in the coffee shop was steely determination, and he'd admired him for it. Recalling the intensity of that look now, Nate wondered if he had misread it. He wondered if what he saw that day was ambition, unbridled and unrestrained, born out of poverty and desperation.

Nate stared into the darkness of Beauregard Park and thought about George's election to the bench. George had been nominated for the circuit judgeship by his local representatives, interviewed by members of the selection committee, recommended by them, and then elected by both houses of the legislature. The process took time. It had to have started more than a month ago, almost immediately after Judge Herring's death. And George would not have been considered by his legislators for the judgeship in the first place unless he had invested significant time and energy months beforehand positioning himself with them as an acceptable replacement.

Nate went back to his bed, sat on the edge of it, and held his head in his hands. He craved a drink. A pint of Old Crow he'd bought during his relapse stood at the back of the cupboard over the sink. He hadn't mustered the resolve to throw it away. He was afraid to touch it. Once he had his hands on it, he wasn't sure he could resist it. He had stayed away from it so far, but its presence had haunted him.

Nate went to the cupboard and opened it. The bottle of Old Crow stood there guarding his addiction to alcohol, liquid amber winking at him in the moonlight. He grabbed the bottle and unscrewed its cap. The liquor's vapor filled his nostrils. Its tendrils slithered into his lungs and splintered his brain. He pressed the bottle's mouth to his mouth. The trace of bourbon on the bottle's lip stung his lips.

Nate's hands shook. He set the bottle on the counter, leaned over the sink, and gagged. He moistened a dishrag with tap water and cooled his face. He stood there for a long time. Then he poured the bourbon down the drain. Nate stared at the drain's black hole. Some of the whiskey was still in the trap of the sink. He could smell it. He could disconnect the trap and suck the whiskey from its elbow. He wanted to do it, and there was a time in his life when he would have done it, but he pushed away from the sink. He dressed, walked from his apartment to his car, and drove to his office. He sat at his desk and opened a case file.

That morning, before the first court session began, Nate went to Judge Blackwell's chambers. When he entered, the judge was sitting in a chair beside his bookshelves, poring over a legal treatise. He removed his reading glasses and smiled at Nate. "Congratulations. Your work on the Deatherage case is the talk of the state. I'm proud of you."

Nate didn't respond.

The judge's smile fell. "Is something wrong, Nathan?"

"I think so."

"Have a seat." The judge closed the book and pointed to a chair.

Nate sat down. "I'm worried, Harry, about what happened in Buck County."

"I understand your concern. Edbert Herring's demise is a tragedy. Your role in his death must weigh on you, but it wasn't your fault. Edbert caused his own destruction. You did your job. You defended your client from a corrupt system."

"I'm concerned about the circumstances leading to my appointment to represent Deatherage. I don't understand why the court selected me."

"The court selects attorneys from a list of volunteers. You know that full well."

"I placed my name on the list one week before I was appointed to the case. The list was long. Some of the attorneys volunteered a year earlier than I did. Why did I jump to the top of the list?"

Judge Blackwell appeared uncomfortable.

Nate said, "You told me the chief justice called you about me."

"Yes."

"What did he ask you?"

"He heard the rumors about your resignation. He wanted to know the details."

"What did you say?"

The judge sighed. "I lied. I told him you resigned voluntarily, took a year's sabbatical, and decided to do criminal defense. I told him the rumors about you were libelous falsehoods circulated by your political enemies. I told him you would be an excellent choice for the Deatherage case."

"Why did you recommend me for the Deatherage case? You didn't know anything about the case. It wasn't in your circuit."

The judge shifted in his chair. "I'm not sure what I . . . I don't know – "

"The chief justice didn't call you, did he?"

"Well, I talked to him by phone. I don't know what you're driving – "

"You called him."

"What difference does it make?"

"Why did you call him about the Deatherage case? You had no connection to it."

The judge didn't answer.

"George Maupin asked you to make the call, didn't he?"

"Why is this important, Nathan?"

"It's very important to me and to the Deatherage case. Did George ask you to call the chief justice to persuade him to appoint me to the case?"

"Well, I suppose there's no harm in telling you, since your representation of Deatherage worked out so well. You're correct. Mister Maupin asked me to recommend you to represent Deatherage."

"The bastard."

The judge blanched. "Is something wrong, Nathan?"

"Did George ask you not to tell me about his conversation with you?"

"Yes. He thought you might resent it. He said he wanted to help you recover from your problems. He thought the case would present you with a professional challenge and an opportunity to earn a reputation as a defense lawyer, but he thought you would regard his efforts on your behalf as an unwelcomed act of charity or a meddlesome interference with your recovery. You've been quite proud during this rough patch, Nathan."

"George advanced my name specifically for the Deatherage case and not for any of the other death penalty appeals involving Buck County defendants?"

"Yes. He said your experience was a particularly good fit for the

Deatherage case. Judging by your performance, I'd say he was correct."

Nate shook his head. "George knows me well."

"What?"

"He knew I would uncover Judge Herring's bias and expose it. He knows you well, too. He knew you would want to help me, and he knew you would honor his request to keep his conversation with you confidential."

"I don't understand, Nathan. Have I done something wrong?"

"George has done something wrong. Or he's done many things right, depending on your perspective."

"I don't understand."

"It's a long story." Nate looked out the window, thinking. "The night Judge Herring died you issued a warrant authorizing the recording of a conversation between me and Deputy Jones."

"Mister Maupin called me at home in the middle of the night. He woke me from a sound sleep. I authorized the taping over the telephone."

"What time did he call you?"

The judge went to his desk and looked in a file. "I authorized the taping at four forty-five that morning. I always make a note of the exact time I grant a warrant in case someone later challenges the state's action."

"George left Judge Herring's house about two thirty. Two hours passed before he called you."

"If you say so. Is there a problem with the warrant?"

"No."

"What's going on, Nathan? You seem quite troubled."

"I'll fill you in later. Thanks for your help, Harry." Nate exited the judge's chambers and stood in the hallway, thinking about George's actions. Nate knew almost everything George had done now, but there was still one piece of the puzzle missing. Nate thought he knew where to find it.

Chapter 32

The Murderer

George Maupin's farm was a few miles east of Bloxton. Nate arrived there late in the morning. It was a beautiful summer day. The oppressive hot spell of the previous weeks had broken. The sky was clear and a cool breeze blew across the pastureland bordering the highway. Nate turned off the state road onto a long paved driveway lined on both sides by a white plank fence and evenly spaced sycamore trees. At the end of the driveway was a farmhouse and a shed and, behind them, a barn and a silo. Angus and Hereford cattle grazed in the field behind the barn.

Nate rolled to a stop in front of the house as Gracie Maupin came out on the porch. She was a stout woman with stringy gray hair styled in a bowl cut. She wore a loose-fitting gingham dress, and she was barefooted. She wiped her hands on a dish towel and stared at Nate's car. When he got out of the car, she scowled and said, "You're not welcome here."

"Is George at home?"

"Get off my property."

"I need a minute of your time, Gracie."

"Your brash ways killed Edbert Herring. You destroyed his good name and Betsy's cherished memories of him. Get off my property or I'll call the law."

"I'm sorry you feel that way. Does George own a red pickup truck?"

"I'll give you five seconds to get in your car and drive off."

Nate stood his ground.

Gracie said, "I'll fetch the sheriff to arrest you for trespass." She marched inside the house.

The shed to the right of the house was a long low building constructed with wooden planks supported by creosoted posts. It was open along most of its front side and Nate could see bales of hay stacked against the back wall and a tractor in the shadows. A hay baler and a hay rake were parked beside it. There was no truck.

A door with a metal handle at its base fronted a closed-off part of the shed. Nate walked over to it and lifted the door. Hay dust, grit, and dander floated in the sunlight that fell across the tailgate of a red pickup truck. The smell of gasoline hung in the air. A mouse kicked up a trail of dust and disappeared under a bale of straw. Nate stood just outside the shed and stared for a long time at the letters framed in a rectangle on the tailgate. "Chevrolet."

He walked around to the driver's door and looked at it. He ran his hand over a big deep dent below the window. The truck fit Odoms' description of the pickup parked at the warehouse the night someone attacked Nate. It was the last puzzle piece.

Nate walked back to his car and stood beside it. He looked at the shed and the truck and thought about his next step. Prudence said he should fear for his safety. No one knew what George had done except Nate, and George had been ruthless in covering up his crimes. Yet, Nate wasn't afraid of him. He couldn't shake the notion that there had to be some shred of decency left in him and that their friendship still counted for something, but even if he was wrong about that, he didn't care about his personal safety. He had nothing more to lose. If George came after him, so be it. A man with nothing to lose had nothing to fear.

Nate thought the most logical next step was to confront George with what he had discovered and try to convince him to give himself up. The smart play would be to wear a wire. Clarence Shifflett was the only man

Nate could ask for help in setting up a taped meeting with George.

Nate looked back at George's long driveway. A solitary crow flew across the pasture and alit on a top branch of the nearest sycamore tree. The crow's feathers ruffled in the wind and the tree limb swayed.

Given Clarence's state of mind, it would be cruel to drag him back into the fray. Besides, arranging to wear a wire would take time, and time was against Nate. As things stood, he had the advantage of surprise, but it wouldn't last long. George would soon learn Nate was at his farm asking about a red pickup truck.

The crow in the sycamore cawed raucously, spread its wings, and flew across the pasture. Nate watched it shrink to a black speck on the horizon and disappear. He looked at the red pickup in the shed one last time, then got in his car and sped down the driveway.

Nate parked his car on the curb near Captain Bloxton's statue and walked to the courthouse. The court was in recess during the noon luncheon break and the courtroom was empty. Nate found a warren of offices behind it, walked past a startled secretary, and opened the door to Judge Maupin's chambers. George sat behind a desk with a phone to his ear.

He looked up and smiled. "Forget it, Hubert. He's here in my chambers." There was a pause. "No. I don't need your help." He hung up the phone.

The secretary stood beside Nate, glaring at him. "I'm sorry, Your Honor. This man barged into chambers before I could stop him."

"That's all right. He's a good friend. Leave us alone, please."

The secretary pulled the door closed behind her.

"Gracie called the sheriff. Betsy Herring and Gracie are close friends. I know it's unfair, but Gracie blames you for what happened to Eddy. The truth is a lot of people in Buck County still respect him, and they blame you for his death. No amount of reasoning seems to persuade them otherwise. Have a seat."

Nate sat in a chair across the desk from George.

George said, "What were you doing at the farm?"

"Looking at evidence."

"Evidence of what?"

"I know everything, George. You used me. You manipulated the process so I'd be appointed to the Deatherage case."

George winced. "Old Harry Blackwell told you I advanced your name for the case, didn't he? Damn it to hell. I wanted to keep it hidden from you." George smiled. "You're so damned proud. Look, maybe I shouldn't have meddled in your affairs, but I couldn't stand by and do nothing. You were down and out. You needed work. I asked Harry to recommend you for the case. I was trying to help you."

"You didn't do it to help me. You did it to advance your own ambition. You knew I was desperate to regain my reputation, desperate enough to run the risk of taking aim at the king, something you were afraid to do on your own."

George leaned back in his chair, looked down at the floor, and pursed his lips. A long time passed. "For the sake of argument, let's say I suspected something was wrong in the Deatherage case. Let's say I was reluctant to accuse the judge of wrongdoing and I hoped you would find the truth. What's the harm? You removed a corrupt judge from the bench. You reformed your public image. Everyone is a winner."

"You didn't mention the biggest winner. You. You got the black robe."

"All right. Let's throw that into the mix, too. I still say what's the harm."

"There was a great deal of harm. Men were murdered."

George nodded. "I see your point. I feel bad about Eddy Herring. It's a shame Clarence shot him. I didn't see that coming and I wouldn't have wished it on Eddy, but let's not forget that he broke the law. He corrupted the justice system in this county. He paid the ultimate price for his crimes, but they were his crimes, not mine or yours."

"What about Henry Crawford? He did nothing wrong. How do you justify his murder?"

"Justify it? I can't justify it. The man was an innocent victim of an evil criminal."

"There's no point in maintaining your act. I'm on to you. You murdered Crawford."

George was motionless but his face turned crimson. "For the sake of our friendship, I'll try to forget you said that."

"You knocked me out, beat Crawford to death, and tossed his body in the quarry like a piece of garbage."

Beads of sweat dotted George's bald head. He glared at Nate. "You've been through a lot. I'll take that into account, but I'll give you fair warning. Before you make accusations against me, you might consider the vulnerability of your situation."

Nate was in no mood to heed warnings. "When you thrust me into the Deatherage case, you knew I'd expose the judge's wrongdoing. You knew simple background checks of Darlene, her father Daniel, Swiller, and the judge would expose the judge's bias. But you thought I'd stop there. You didn't expect me to discover your crimes – witness tampering, suppression of evidence, obstruction of justice, subornation of perjury. You counted on Jones to intimidate Odoms so he wouldn't reveal Crawford's presence in the warehouse the night of the murder and you thought Jones would have the good sense to keep Crawford away from me, but as Hubert said, Jones wasn't the smartest soldier in the army. He let you down and I found Crawford, and you were there behind me that night. You attacked me and knocked me unconscious."

Nate paused, hoping George would open up, but George said, "You're talking nonsense, Nate, foolish vile accusations with no basis in fact."

Nate continued, "I can understand how you justified your crimes initially. You saw what the judge did to Creighton Long with Swiller.

That made it more acceptable to you to violate the law to reach results you thought were just. You cultivated Jones to help you convict men you thought were guilty, and your conviction rate skyrocketed. You told yourself you were performing a public service. I can understand all of that, but I can't understand what you did to cover up your crimes. George, you committed cold-blooded murder, for God's sake."

George held up his hands, his palms facing Nate. "Stop this nonsense or I won't ever forgive you, no matter how good a friend you are."

"I can't stop it. Maybe we could have worked something out if all you'd done was rig prosecutions, but when you killed Crawford you made it impossible to save you."

"This is ridiculous. I had nothing to do with Crawford's murder. I had no reason to kill him."

"You killed him to conceal your crimes. You told Jones to make sure Crawford kept quiet about being in the warehouse the night of the murder and you told him to keep the mattresses out of the case so no one would test them for Updike's and Crawford's blood, hair, and clothing fibers. You knew I would have to spend the night in the Black Gold Motel in order to attend the meeting with you the next morning. You were anxious about what I might look into, so you came to the motel to watch me and you followed me into the warehouse. When I found Crawford, you were afraid I'd learn that you and Jones suppressed evidence. You panicked, and you attacked me to keep me from talking to Crawford."

"Jesus, Nate. You know me better than that."

"You're not the man I thought you were. The man I knew couldn't have killed anyone, but you killed Crawford. You killed him to conceal your crimes. Crawford saw you assault me. He was an unreliable drunk and you couldn't take the risk he would tell someone about the assault. You knew that revelation would lead to the unveiling of all your crimes."

George looked down at the floor and didn't say anything.

"You murdered Jones, too," Nate said.

George flinched. "Don't say these terrible things. It hurts too much to have a good friend turn on me like this."

"Don't play games with me. You're the Judas in this story. You warned the sheriff to stay away from Jones until you could get a warrant from Judge Blackwell. You left Judge Herring's house at two thirty. It takes ten minutes to drive to your farm and another ten minutes to find Judge Blackwell's phone number and call him. You should have called the judge no later than three, but you didn't call him until four-thirty."

George brushed his lip with a trembling hand. Nate waited, hoping he might open up, but he didn't say anything.

"Jones trusted you," Nate said. "You were his mentor, his commanding officer in civilian life. You told him he was serving the greater good by falsifying evidence against guilty men, and he followed your orders like the exemplary soldier he had been in Vietnam. He opened his door to you that night with no idea what you intended to do. My guess is he trusted you until the moment you put the barrel of his shotgun to the base of his chin. You made his murder look like suicide, and you hurried home and called Judge Blackwell to get the warrant."

George swiped his hand over his bald head and down his face. He heaved his heavy frame out of his chair, went to his liquor cabinet, poured himself a shot of whiskey, and drank it. He drank a second shot. He poured a glass of straight whiskey and carried it back to his desk and sat down.

Nate said, "Whiskey won't help. I know. I tried it."

George turned the glass up, gulped down half of the whiskey, set the glass down on his desk, and let out a long breath. "All I did was prosecute and convict guilty men."

"Crawford was guilty of nothing and Jones' only crimes were the ones you persuaded him to commit. You murdered them."

George drained the rest of the whiskey and returned the glass to his desk. He stared at the empty glass for a few moments. Then he straightened his tie, smoothed down the hair rimming his bald pate, and looked

Nate straight in the eye. "The gist of your wild accusations seems to be that I was Jones' conspirator. I was not. Judge Herring directed him to commit crimes. Your accusations have no evidentiary basis. You have no proof I did anything improper."

Nate was disappointed. He had hoped some part of the good friend he had known still lived inside George. He had hoped those remnants of goodness would be caught off guard by Nate's discoveries and George would falter, but after exhibiting some initial vulnerability in the face of Nate's aggressive attack, he seemed to be recovering. It made sense he would be tough to break. George's ascension from the depths of poverty to the catbird seat in Buck County was due in part to his refusal to give an inch, no matter how daunting the challenge he faced.

Nate still held out hope he could break loose an admission from George's rock-hard determination if he could intimidate him with the threat of prosecution and exposure of his crimes. He knew he didn't have evidence to support an indictment against George, but he hoped a good bluff might cause him to make a mistake. "I can prove you conspired with Jones," Nate said.

George tensed. "How would you propose to prove such a slanderous lie?"

"You've decided you'll call Claire Deatherage to the witness stand in the second trial because Jones told you Deatherage confessed to his wife, but you didn't use her as a witness in the first trial because Jones promised her she wouldn't be required to testify. He couldn't have made that promise unless you agreed to it. You agreed to keep her off the stand on the condition that Jones lie about finding the scarf on Deatherage."

George relaxed. "You're half correct. Jones told me about Deatherage's confession and I agreed not to call Claire as a witness, but my reasons were innocent. I didn't know he stole the scarf. I thought it was legitimate evidence and it made the case airtight. Jones told me Claire was deathly afraid of Deatherage, and I thought she would be an unreliable witness. I didn't need her testimony in the first trial. Now, with the scarf out of the case, I plan to call her to the stand."

Nate moved on quickly. "There's evidence proving you killed Crawford."

"What sort of evidence?"

"You hauled Crawford's body and the mattresses to the dump in your pickup truck. A forensics team will find traces of his blood in the truck body, fibers from his clothing, strands of his hair."

George smoothed down his tie, hooked his hands into his belt, and smirked. "This time of year I spray pesticide on my apple trees. I haul barrels of malathion in my truck from the fruit growers' co-op to my farm. If I don't wash out the truck body afterwards, the poison contaminates the feed I haul to my cattle and makes them sick. I scrub down the truck with disinfectant to cleanse it of malathion. I washed out the truck body last week."

"How convenient."

"Convenient or not, my truck is clean."

Nate had only a few cards to play, and all of them were low-numbered. He decided to tell George someone had seen his truck at the warehouse but to withhold Odoms' name to protect him from George. "There's a witness who saw your truck at the warehouse the night I was knocked out."

"You mean Willis Odoms."

Nate froze.

A wry smile crossed George's face. "I'm not stupid, Nate. When you told me Odoms saw Crawford walk out of the warehouse right after Darlene Updike's murder, I had a conversation with him. It occurred to me during that meeting with him that he might have seen my truck at the warehouse close to the time you say Crawford disappeared. After all, Odoms lives next door to the warehouse and he keeps a wary eye on it. So I asked him if he saw my truck."

"You intimidated him. You threatened him."

George shook his head. "I did nothing of the sort. All I did was clear up a misunderstanding. Willis is like most colored folk. He means well, but he gets confused. When he talked to you, he made an innocent mistake about the date he saw my truck at the warehouse. My pickup was parked there the night before you arrived in Bloxton. I knew you'd want to take a look at the warehouse, so I walked through it to refresh my memory of the details of the murder. When I told Willis I visited the warehouse the previous night, he agreed he might have seen the truck that night instead of the following night."

Nate leaned back in his chair. Game over. At least for now. "You've covered your tracks well, George." Every move George had made since Nate appeared in the case had been carefully designed to protect his position. "You know, you caught me off guard when you called the Virginia Supreme Court of Appeals' clerk and sent the court that amateurish letter trying to concede the appeal in violation of the court's rules. At the time, I couldn't understand why you were so willing to give up the appeal, but now I understand. You wanted me to back off before I discovered your role in the corruption, and you got what you wanted. I stopped investigating the case and focused on the appeal. But you know me, George. Now that I know the truth, I won't give up until I find evidence that proves your guilt."

"You might consider how well I know you. I know you rigged five criminal prosecutions. I know you suborned perjury in one of those cases. I assume you committed additional felonies to rig the others." George's face hardened. "I know Harry Blackwell is an accessory after the fact to your crimes, and Harry must have committed felonies to cover up what you did. If you push me, I'll expose his felonies along with yours."

A chill ran through Nate. "You're good at this," he said. "When you convinced Judge Blackwell to recommend me for the case, you knew we might come to this point. You counted on my affection for him to keep me in check." There was a long silence. Nate searched George's face. "Tell me, George. If Jones had survived, would you have framed me for Crawford's murder? Would you have asked the court to sentence me to death?"

George was quiet for a while. Then he said, "You and I have been friends for a long time, but we're different men. You had it easy. Your daddy died when you were a young man, but he left you money to pay for your schooling. You sailed through law school at the top of the class. You became the commonwealth's attorney of a prosperous county at a young age and your county paid you well. Your cases made you famous. The legal community hoisted you on its shoulders and paraded you around the state."

George leaned back in his chair. "My daddy was a drunk. He died when I was six. He left my mother and sisters and me with nothing. Nobody helped us. We worked like dogs to get by, scratching in the dust for every penny. Sometimes we'd creep into our neighbors' houses and steal food so we'd have something to eat. You don't know what it's like when your last meal is two days behind you and you don't know when the next one will come along. You don't know what it's like to be dirt poor."

George's eyes glistened. His lower lip quivered. He brushed it with his hand and coughed. Nate gave him time to recover. Then he said in a soft voice, "Growing up in hard times doesn't excuse murder."

"The term 'hard times' doesn't do justice to what my family went through." George bit his lip and was quiet for a while. Then he said, "You know, Nate, I always liked you, but I envied you, too. You were the golden boy in law school. You commanded the respect of Judge Blackwell the first time you stepped into his courtroom. Your conviction rate was always higher than mine. I wondered what it was like to have so much handed to you, to have people treat you like an equal without questioning your background, to appear before a judge who seemed to think you were a saint." George sighed heavily. "Well, the world turns, doesn't it? You hit bottom there for a while, and I'm on top now. I've finally gotten a taste of what you've had all your life. I wear the black robe. My word is the law in Buck County. People stand up when I walk into the courtroom. They address me as Your Honor. They do what I order them to do." George took a deep breath and his expression hardened. "Look, Nate, we both know you have no evidence to prove I committed any crime. Be careful what you say and do when you leave this room. I worked mighty hard to get here, and I won't give it up without one hell of a fight."

George's secretary opened the door. "Parties and counsel in *Clayton v. Hobart* are in the courtroom, Your Honor. The jury's in the box."

"Thank you. I'll be there in a minute."

The secretary pulled the door closed.

George stood and put on his robe, looking at Nate. "When we first met about the Deatherage case, I advised you not to take aim at the king unless you could kill him, but you're courageous and you took aim at Eddy Herring and you brought him down. Now I wear the crown. I'm not Eddy. He was soft. I'm not. I came up the hard way, and I'll do anything required to stay on top. Anything. If you come after me, our friendship won't be a consideration, and only one of us will be standing at the end of the contest." George rounded the desk and opened the door. "I've said all I have to say, Nate. I apologize for giving you the bum's rush, but I have to take the bench."

Nate walked to the door, stopped beside George, and looked him squarely in the eye. He didn't see his old friend. He saw ice and steel.

George said, "I'm sorry it's come to this."

"So am I," said Nate.

Chapter 33

The Plea Agreement

Nate's prospects of finding more evidence against George were bleak. He could identify no allies in Buck County who would help him. George had assumed control of Judge Herring's power base and no one in the county was willing to cross him. Nate resolved to bide his time and search for an opening over the coming months, hoping that more evidence or a Buck County counterweight to George's influence would emerge.

Meanwhile, Nate again immersed himself in his work to find refuge from his misery. The Deatherage case moved forward. The new trial was assigned to Judge Lathrop Wigfield of the Starkey County Circuit Court. Hayesboro was the county seat.

Judge Wigfield scheduled the Deatherage trial for the beginning of November. Daryl Garth was appointed acting Buck County commonwealth's attorney, pending a special election. He withdrew from the Deatherage case because of the conflict created by his conversations with Nate about the evidence. Judge Wigfield assigned the prosecution of Deatherage to the Starkey County commonwealth's attorney. Nate met with the prosecutor about the case twice in September. The certainty that Deatherage was guilty weighed on Nate's conscience. Claire Deatherage's plea for his help weighed on him, too, and Darlene Updike's resemblance to Christine wreaked psychological havoc on his motivation to defend Deatherage. During Nate's third and last meeting with the Starkey County commonwealth's attorney, Nate succumbed to all these influences and made a decision about Deatherage he knew he had no right to make.

In October, the state moved Deatherage from the state prison to the Starkey County jail in Hayesboro in anticipation of the trial. Nate drove to Hayesboro to meet with Deatherage. The Starkey County Jail was a one-story red brick building surrounded by a pine forest on the southern end of town. Nate pulled into the parking lot and parked under a tall white pine. It was a cool fall day. Drizzle misted from a gray sky. Nate got out of the car, walked across the lot, and went inside. The front door opened into a small lobby where a bald, middle-aged deputy sheriff stood behind a counter on the opposite wall. To Nate's left, another deputy, a young man with greased coal-black hair combed into an Elvis Presley ducktail, sat reading a magazine next to a gun case racked with pump-action shotguns.

Nate approached the counter. "Nate Abbitt here to see Kenneth Deatherage."

The deputy behind the counter smirked. "You're the one who brought down the boys in Buck County. Well, you won't pull any tricks on us. We do things on the up and up." He pushed a ledger across the counter. "Sign in."

Nate signed the ledger.

"Elwood, get off your ass and show the man into the cell block."

Elwood dropped the magazine and heaved himself to a standing position. He dragged his boot heels to the counter, picked up a key ring, unlocked a metal door behind the counter, and held it open for Nate.

Nate was surprised the deputies gave him access to Deatherage without any security precautions. They didn't ask him for identification, search him, or inspect the contents of his briefcase.

Nate went inside the cell block. There were four small cells, two on each side, with a narrow aisle running between them. Each cell was furnished with a cot and a toilet stool sitting under a barred window. The stench of urine lay heavy in the air. Deatherage was the only prisoner. He was stretched out on a cot in a cell to the right of the door. He looked up at Nate and smiled. "About time you showed up, lawyer."

Elwood dragged a metal folding chair to a spot outside the bars of Deatherage's cell and left them alone in the cell block. Nate sat in the chair and handed Deatherage a document and a pen through the bars.

"What's this?"

"It's a summary of a plea agreement."

"What's it say?"

"The prosecutor will reduce the charges against you to second degree murder. You will plead guilty, and the prosecutor will recommend a sentence of twenty-five years. With good behavior, you'll be out in fifteen."

"Is this some kind of joke?"

"You're facing the death penalty. This is a good agreement for you."

"I don't get it. You proved Judge Herring and Jones framed me. You found out Henry Crawford was in the warehouse when the girl was killed. You can tell the jury he might have killed her. He's dead. He can't deny it. There's no way they can convict me. Why in hell would I agree to rot in jail for fifteen years?"

"The forensic evidence points to you alone as the murderer. You had an argument with Updike the night she was killed. You were at the scene of the murder and you fled. There's a substantial risk you'll be convicted and sentenced to death if you go to trial on first degree murder. This deal eliminates that risk. Take the deal."

"But I didn't kill her."

"You're lying."

"I'm not lyin. I didn't kill her."

"I know you killed her."

Deatherage looked suspicious. "How do you know I killed her?"

"You don't need to know how I found out, but I know for a fact you killed her."

Deatherage studied Nate's face. "You talked to Claire." Nate waited as Deatherage watched him closely. Nate's expression betrayed nothing, but Deatherage apparently guessed the truth. He slammed his fist into the cot. "I shoulda wrung her neck when I had the chance. Who else knows what I told Claire?"

"The prosecutor knows."

"Damn her to hell and back." Deatherage spewed a string of curses. He rose from the cot, leaned against a wall, crossed his arms over his chest, and stared at the floor. Nate waited. After a while, Deatherage looked at him quizzically. "I thought there was a rule that a wife can't talk in court against her husband."

Nate had hoped Deatherage wouldn't be aware of the spousal privilege, but he had been imprisoned with men who had learned the basic rules of evidence the hard way and they had apparently taught him a few tricks. "There is a privilege," Nate said, "but it may not apply to your case."

"Why not?"

"It's difficult to explain to a non-lawyer."

"Give it a try. Fifteen years of my life are on the line."

The truth was the spousal privilege could probably be used to block Claire's testimony about Deatherage's confession. The best argument Nate could imagine in favor of admitting the confession was weak, but Nate presented it to Deatherage in its strongest light. "There's an exception to the privilege in cases involving domestic violence."

"What's that got to do with my case? I wasn't married to the girl."

"You raped and strangled Claire the night before you killed Updike and you threatened to kill Claire if she told anyone about your confession."

Deatherage scowled. "What's that got to do with it? The case ain't about that. It's about the girl's murder."

"That may not matter. Sympathies don't run in your favor in this case. The judge may be inclined to rule against you."

Deatherage looked skeptical. "Sounds like you're not sure about this."

"It's not absolutely clear, but there's a significant risk the privilege won't bar Claire's testimony."

"Well, I sure as hell won't agree to do fifteen years over somethin's not clear. I want you to fight it. Shut Claire down. Don't let her tell the jury nothin."

"I can't fight it."

"Why not?"

"Because Claire told me about your confession. I know you're guilty."

"What the hell's that got to do with it? You're not the judge and jury. You're my lawyer. You're supposed to do what I tell you, and I say shut Claire up."

"I can't do that. I won't do it."

"It's not your decision. I'm the one on trial. I'm the one has to pull the time."

"I know you killed Updike. I won't stand by you while you lie to the court. I'm an officer of the court, and I have an ethical duty to be truthful."

"The court? Who gives a damn about the court? What about me? Don't your high-and-mighty rules say you have to give me a fair shake? What's the point of havin a hotshot lawyer if he don't protect you? You can beat this case and you know it."

"I won't discuss this further. You'll agree to the guilty plea, or I'll file a motion to withdraw as your counsel on the grounds that you won't follow my advice."

"Well, ain't that noble? I suppose you think you're too good to defend scum like me. Let's see, now. You framed a ree-tard, and the boys in state prison claim you and one of your buddies shot Judge Herring and fixed it so you wouldn't get blamed for it. You killed a judge, but you're too good to be my lawyer."

"We're done here."

Deatherage grabbed the bars of the cell. "You can't leave me high and dry. You're my lawyer. You're supposed to help me."

Nate snapped his briefcase shut and stood.

Deatherage's face was twisted with rage. "Deeks told me about your girlfriend, you know."

Nate stared at Deatherage.

"That's right, lawyer. Even the jailbirds know you cheated on your wife. Deeks told me about your pretty little secretary, how you screwed her in your office right under your wife's nose."

"You and Deeks deserve each other. You both belong in hell." Nate rapped on the cell block door.

"Go ahead and walk out on me. I'm sick and tired of your high falutin talk about the truth. You want to know the truth, lawyer? The truth is you belong in here with me. The only difference between you and me is you won't tell the truth about yourself. You break the laws when it suits you and you tell yourself you're not a crook because you think you know better than the law what's right and wrong."

Nate looked at Deatherage.

Deatherage said, "Don't think I'm so stupid I don't know what you're pullin on me. All your fancy talk about your standards and rules is a pack of lies. You could get me off if you wanted to, and that's what your fancy lawyer rules say you're supposed to do. You're breakin the rules by walkin out on me, and you're doin it because you think you know what's right. You're just like the crooks in Buck County you brought down. You're part of it, part of the rotten system, just like them. You're no better than Judge Herring and Swiller and Jones. You're just another crooked lawyer who thinks you have the right to decide who goes free and who goes to jail. Well, I won't let you put me back in state prison. I won't go back there, and I'll find a way to pay you back for walkin out on me, by damn. Mark my words. I'll find a way."

Elwood opened the door. Nate walked through it while Deatherage shouted curses at his back.

Chapter 34

The Escape

Two weeks later, Judge Wigfield granted Nate's motion to withdraw from the Deatherage case. The change in counsel forced a postponement of the trial, and Deatherage remained incarcerated in the Starkey County jail during the delay.

A few days after Nate's withdrawal from the case, Wiley Rea, Nate's successor as Selk County commonwealth's attorney, called Nate and asked him to meet at Sally's Diner the next morning. Nate asked Rea what the meeting was about. He said he'd prefer to discuss the matter face-to-face.

The next morning when Nate arrived at Sally's Diner at the appointed time, Wiley Rea sat in a booth in the back away from the other customers. He was a slim middle-aged man with neatly combed, thinning gray hair parted down the middle. He wore a seersucker suit and one of his trademark bowties, this one navy blue. When he looked up at Nate, light glanced off the lenses of his wire-rimmed glasses. Nate slid into the booth and a waitress brought them coffee.

"I took the liberty of ordering coffee for both of us," Rea said. "I assume coffee is the strongest drink you imbibe these days."

"That's none of your business."

"No need to be sensitive about it. It's common knowledge you're a former drunk. I stress the word former."

"Get to the point. Why did you want to see me?"

Rea took a pack of Parliaments from his suit pocket and lit one. "When I was appointed acting commonwealth's attorney, Harry Blackwell met with me. He told me his recommendation was the reason I was given the job and he would require me to clean up the mess you left behind. He explained in detail your abuses of your power as a prosecutor and he handed me the files of five cases I would be required to retry. He then ordered me not to indict you for your crimes and not to tell anyone what you did."

"You're the commonwealth's attorney. You have the discretion to indict anyone you please."

A wry smile crossed Rea's face. "Many years ago, when I was a young man, I made mistakes. Harry Blackwell is the only person who knows about them."

"What sort of mistakes?"

"Big mistakes. Stupid mistakes. Mistakes only an inveterate drunk could make. Mistakes only a judge can forgive. As a result of my mistakes, coffee is the strongest drink I imbibe these days."

"Your issues with Harry are no concern of mine."

"Ah, but you're wrong about that. You see, Harry made clear to me that my mistakes would become public knowledge if I indicted you for yours."

Nate leaned back, surprised. Extortion was a felony. The judge had taken greater risks to protect Nate than Nate realized. He wondered again why. He lifted his cup to his lips and looked around the room. A young couple sat on the same side of a booth near the door, their heads close together, the boy whispering to the girl, the girl giggling.

Rea pointed his cigarette at Nate. "I've honored the judge's demands. You're a free man because of me. You owe me."

"I owe you nothing. I didn't ask you to do anything."

"You used Judge Blackwell to force me to refrain from prosecuting you. I've done what you wanted. I waded through the swamp of corrupt prosecutions you created and I drained it dry so no one will discover it in the future. But make no mistake. I know every detail of your crimes. I have all the evidence neatly organized and summarized and stored in my files. The statute of limitations hasn't run on your felonies, but the statute has long since expired on my peccadilloes. I could file an indictment against you tomorrow, and you would go to jail and I would not be prosecuted no matter what Harry told the world about my past. If Harry fulfilled his threat to expose me, I'd lose my reputation but not my freedom."

"Why destroy your reputation over me?"

"Harry Blackwell is a harsh master. I want freedom from the lash of his whip."

"I can't help you with that."

"You can help me a great deal. You hold the key to my release."

"What are you talking about?"

"Information. I want information."

"About what?"

"I want the reason Harry Blackwell spared you. I want the secret that drove him to commit felonies to protect you."

"Ask Harry."

Rea scoffed. "Harry's too shrewd to tell me his secret. He knows I'd use it to my advantage against him. For decades I searched high and low for compromising information about him that would provide the key to unlock my chains, but I found nothing substantive. You would think at the very least that an eighty-year-old lifelong bachelor would have yielded to temptation over the many years – consorted with a prostitute, preferred the company of a man, engaged in an illicit relationship – but all I found were wisps of gossip that he had an affair with a married woman when he was a young man and was jilted by his lover, an ancient rumor that his heart was broken and it never mended and he never married because of it. There were no details about his tryst, no name, no description, no dates of engagement, no stories about what they did together." Rea took a sip of coffee, swallowed, and grimaced. He looked out the window beside their booth. Nate looked outside, too. It was a warm fall day. The wind blew. Golden and auburn leaves floated out of the oak trees in Beauregard Park, fell into Lee Street, and skittered across it to pile against the curb.

Rea turned back to Nate. The lines in his face relaxed a bit. "Look. All I want is the information required to make Harry back off. I won't go public with it. I just want him to let up on me. That's all."

"There's nothing I can do for you."

Rea's eyes blazed. "Don't lie to me. When Harry convinced the board to appoint me as commonwealth's attorney and told me I couldn't prosecute you, I knew you knew his secret and you used it against him. I pressed Harry hard about it when he met with me about you, and I learned a lot from the fear in his eyes. His secret is old and deep inside him and he's mortally afraid of its exposure. Indeed, I'm certain what you know about him is exactly what I need to be free from him, but he'll never tell me." Rea jabbed his cigarette at Nate. "You must tell me. That's my price for my continued silence about your crimes. I want Harry's secret. I want to know why he protects you. I want you to tell me what you're holding over his head. If you don't tell me, I'll take you down even if I go down with you."

They fell silent when a waitress appeared at their table with a pot of coffee and refilled their cups. She was a stout redhead with a scar over her eye. She glanced at Nate's scar and moved to another table. When she was out of earshot, Nate said, "I can't pay your price. I don't know the reason Harry protects me."

Rea scooted up on the edge of his bench seat. "Don't play games with me. You must know. You've used it for years to advance your career as a prosecutor and lately to shield you from disbarment and prosecution."

"I didn't ask Harry to help me. He acted on my behalf of his own volition. I'm as mystified by it as you are."

"I don't believe you."

Nate stood and tossed a dollar bill on the table. "Then file your in-dictment."

As Nate walked to the door, he glanced at a television above the counter. A still picture of Kenneth Deatherage stared back at him. He stopped cold. Video images of the Starkey County jail followed.

Nate sat on a stool at the counter and asked a waitress to turn up the volume on the television. "Breaking News" flashed across the screen. A reporter said Deatherage escaped from the Starkey County jail the previous night. Videotape of the sheriff's press conference rolled forward. The sheriff said Deatherage had complained of an upset stomach after dinner. He vomited. A deputy called the hospital while another deputy went into Deatherage's cell to help him. Deatherage stabbed the deputy with a makeshift knife, a ball-point pen filed down to a sharp point. The deputy died from the wound to his throat. A photograph appeared on the screen and below it "Deputy Elwood P. Morris, age 28."

Nate instinctively reached for his pen in his inside coat pocket. It wasn't there. He remembered handing Deatherage a pen to sign the plea agreement, but he didn't remember retrieving it before he left the jail.

The sheriff's press conference continued. He said Deatherage stole the disabled deputy's service revolver and keys and unlocked the cell door. He shot a second deputy in the lobby. Another photograph appeared on the screen of a deputy Nate did not recognize. The sheriff said Deatherage stole a shotgun from a gun case in the lobby and fled. The second deputy survived the gunshot wound and called for help. The Starkey County sheriff's office and the state police launched a massive manhunt, but no sign of Deatherage had turned up. He had been free for twelve hours. The photograph of him reappeared on the screen while the reporter read a description of him.

Wiley Rea appeared at Nate's side. "Isn't that man your client?"

"My ex-client. I withdrew from representing him."

"Apparently a wise decision." Rea stared at the screen as the reporter launched into an explanation of the history of the Deatherage case and Nate's role in bringing down Judge Herring and securing a new trial for Deatherage. A photograph of Nate flashed on the screen.

"That picture must be ten years old," Rea said. "You've got a lot more mileage on you now." He turned to Nate. "This news report is timely. Think about what I said. You have a lot to lose. Your reputation has been restored by this Buck County affair, but I can destroy it with the flick of a pen. I'll give you until the end of the week to tell me what you have on Harry Blackwell. If I have no word from you by Monday morning, I'll file an indictment against you and call a press conference." Rea walked off.

Nate turned back to the television. The reporter moved on to a weather report. Nate asked the waitress for a telephone. She pointed to the end of the counter. He dialed the Selk County sheriff's office.

"Where are you?" Sheriff Coleman Grundy said. "I've been looking for you."

"I'm at Sally's Diner. I just saw the news. Do they have any idea where Deatherage is?"

"We know he fled Starkey County. He stole a car in Hayesboro last night. This morning we found the car at a motel in Pocahontas in Tazewell County. He attacked a man in the motel parking lot and stole the man's '61 blue Ford pickup truck. We're assuming he's still driving that Ford pickup, but we have no clues about his location."

"Call Sheriff Feedlow. Tell him Deatherage might be headed to his wife's house. Deatherage threatened to kill her."

"I talked to Feedlow. He put armed guards on her house last night. There are road blocks on all the state roads into Buck County."

"Tell Feedlow to guard Deatherage's mother and a man named Willis Odoms."

"Feedlow's got men guarding the mother. I don't know about Odoms. I'll call Feedlow again. Can you think of any other place he might go?"

Nate thought about his conversations with Deatherage. "He's angry with everybody connected with his trial. They all live in Buck County, but he's smart enough to know law enforcement will be waiting for him there. I don't think he'll risk it."

"You should join me here. I'll brief you on what we know. Maybe you'll remember something he said that will help us find him."

"I'll be there in a few minutes."

Nate hung up the phone and went to his car. He drove down Lee Street toward the sheriff's office, recalling his conversations with Deatherage. His last words to Nate came to mind – "I'll find a way to pay you back" – and it dawned on Nate that he might be Deatherage's next target.

Nate pulled to the curb and thought about his contacts with Deatherage. He didn't think Deatherage knew where he lived or worked. His office address was on letters he sent to Deatherage, but Deatherage said the guards wouldn't give him the mail because he wouldn't sign for it. Nate was certain he never gave Deatherage his home or business addresses during their meetings. Then Jimmy Deeks flashed through Nate's mind. Deatherage talked with Deeks about Nate in the state penitentiary. Deeks knew where Nate lived when he was commonwealth's attorney, on the farm in Whippoorwill Hollow.

Nate spun the car into a U-turn and raced the ten miles from Jeetersburg through Whippoorwill Hollow to the farm. After what seemed like an eternity, he slid to a stop in front of the house. A blue Ford pickup truck sat in the driveway. He ran toward the house. The mare whinnied from the corral. He stopped and looked down there. Chloe was saddled and bridled, the reins dangling to the ground. She trotted from the barn to the fence-line, tossing her head. Foam drooled from her mouth. Nate saw no sign of Christine or Deatherage around the barn. He ran to the fence-line to get a closer look at Chloe. He saw a spot of blood on her saddle. He turned and looked at the house. He saw a spatter of blood on the grass ahead of him. Nate ran up the hill to the house. The front door stood open. He crept up the porch steps and looked inside.

Deatherage was across the room at the dining table in front of a row of windows. He sat in a chair facing the front door with his feet propped on the table, smiling at Nate. "No need to sneak around. Come on in. It's your house."

Nate stepped inside and looked around the room and up the stairs toward the bedroom. "Where is she?"

Deatherage rocked on the back legs of the chair. "She's takin a rest. Might be a pretty long rest." He chuckled.

Nate scanned the area around Deatherage. There was no weapon out in the open.

"We seem to like the same kinda women," Deatherage said. "Your wife's little, like Claire. Darlene Updike was little, too. I like em little. It's easier to make em do what you want when they're little. It was easy to snatch Darlene outta her bed in the motel and drag her into the ware-house. It was easy to snatch your wife off that horse and drag her up to your bedroom. They fight like hell and yell and scream at first, but you hit em hard and they quiet down and stop fightin. Yes, sir. I like em little. Course, your wife's a bit long in the tooth for my taste, but she ain't bad for an old lady."

Nate's throat was tight, his mouth dry. He looked at the upstairs land-ing, at the door to the bedroom, imagining the hell Christine had suffered at Deatherage's hands.

"Don't worry," Deatherage said. "I gave her a good time up there. I don't think she's had a man for quite a while."

"What have you done to her?"

"I guess you could say I put her to sleep."

Nate grasped the banister to steady himself.

"You don't wanna go up there. You don't wanna see that big mess. It's fun while they last, but it's hard to look at em when you're done with em."

"Did you kill her?"

"I'd say so, but it's hard to tell. You'd be surprised how long it takes to choke a woman to death. Took almost three full minutes for Darlene. Takes longer for a normal-sized man cause he can fight you more. Joe Hitt lasted four minutes and thirty-five seconds. I know. I timed him. That's a damned long time in a life-or-death struggle."

Nate couldn't remember who Hitt was. He could think of nothing except Christine. Nate had turned this monster loose on her and he had killed her.

"Sometimes they pass out and you think they're gone," Deatherage said. "Then they wake up and you get to choke em again. My wife's good at that. Your pretty little wife pulled that trick the first time I choked her, but I'm pretty sure I did her in that second time. You never know, though. I ain't a doctor. I can't always tell for sure if they've given it up for good. They surprise you sometimes and come around again. Your little wife might have one or two more go-rounds left in her for all I know."

Nate swooned, tightening his grip on the banister to keep from collapsing.

Deatherage said, "You see, I built up this powerful need to cause you some serious aggravation. You're the one who brought this whole mess down on both of us, you know. All you had to do was get me outta jail and I wouldn't have come here lookin for you. I wouldn't have done all this here killin. But you didn't get me out and the next lawyer they sent wasn't good as you and he couldn't figure out how to get me out so I had to get myself out. I had to kill the deputies down there in Starkey County. I had to steal some poor old lady's car and her husband's duds. I had to run like a sumbitch. I had to kill a poor old farmer in Pocahontas cause he wouldn't let me have his dirty old rattletrap pickup truck without a fight. Some people are hard to figure. I sure as hell wouldn't have died for a broken-down pickup truck. Anyway, all that hard work put me in a damned mean mood when I got to Jeetersburg." Deatherage shook his head. "Then I got worried that you wasn't where I figured you'd be. Deeks told me you lived on this big old farm way out in the hollow and the phone book says you live at P.O. Box 355 on the state road so I had to sneak all the way out here with half the state police lookin for me. Then the damned mailbox out there says Christine Smith. I almost drove off before I saw her on that horse canterin around the corral and it came clear to me. She threw you off the place after you ran around with your girlfriend and all. Well, I walked right up to her and asked her if she was your wife and she didn't answer but a look came across her face that told me I was right." Deatherage chuckled again.

Nate looked upstairs. Part of him wanted to go up there, but another part of him didn't want to see what he would find there.

"She's up there in the bed. Her and me had a high old time, but I had to rush things along when I heard your car pull up out front. It's too bad because we were gettin to the good part, you know, the part where I twist the rope just a little bit tighter and the lights go out in her eyes but she's not quite dead and her body's still warm and soft and all. I wanted to drag it out, but I had to finish her quicker than I liked so I could come down here and give you a proper greetin."

Nate leaned over and propped his hands on his knees. His breath came in short bursts.

"Don't pass out on me. I'm not through with you yet. I want you to know what I told her before I killed her."

Nate looked at Deatherage. He wanted to kill him. Deatherage smiled at Nate. Then something caught Deatherage's attention and he looked up at the landing and flinched. Nate looked up.

Christine stood on the landing. Her eye was blackened, and her lip was split. Blood matted her hair and streaked down her forehead into her eyes. A red laceration ringed her neck. Her blouse was torn open and she was naked below the waist. She held a pistol in both hands. She pointed it at Nate.

Nate whispered, "Christine."

Deatherage brought the feet of his chair down on the floor and stood.

He stared at Christine, wide-eyed, but his look of fear fell away when he saw where she was aiming the gun. His smile returned. "Well, I'll be damned. Your little wife had one more go-round left in her after all."

Tears were streaming down Christine's cheeks. Her hands shook. The gun was trained on Nate.

"She's kind of pissed at you, lawyer. You see, I told her about the good times you had with your girlfriend. I told your old lady what you said about how she got old and dried up, how she didn't look good any more, how you wished she was dead so you'd be free to run off with your new girl. Go ahead and shoot him, sugar-pie. He sure enough gave you good cause to do him in."

Christine glanced at Deatherage and then looked back at Nate, her fists clutching the gun, her hands shaking violently, sobs bursting through her clenched jaw.

Nate couldn't speak.

"I told her all the tricks you and your new girl did in bed, the ones your little wife never would do with you. I told her how you and your girlfriend sneaked in this house one time and did it right up there in her bed." Deatherage chuckled. "Pull the trigger, honeybunch. You can get away with it. Everybody will think I shot him, and I sure to God won't turn you in."

Christine straightened her arms and thrust the pistol at Nate. The gun barrel danced in the air. She whimpered.

Deatherage laughed. "And I told her how you said you hated her guts and you stopped lovin her years ago and – "

Nate was looking at Deatherage when the first shot rang out. A window behind Deatherage shattered. He jumped backward. The second shot hit the wall behind him. He jerked his head around to look at the bullet hole, looked back at Christine, and raised his hands. "Hold on now." The third shot struck him in the chest. He grabbed his chest, staggered backward, and fell against the window frame, his face contorted with pain.

"Wait. Wait now." The fourth shot hit him in the right eye. His head jerked backward and he crashed through the window, dragging the curtain with him, and he fell out of sight. The fifth and sixth shots hit the wall above the window. Christine pulled the trigger twice more. The hammer pounded harmlessly against the firing pin. She stepped back to lean against the wall and slid down to sit listlessly with her back against it.

Nate went to the broken window. Deatherage was sprawled on the ground below it, his arms and legs askew. The bullet hole where his eye had been spurted blood, and a bloodstain leeched across the chest of his shirt. Shards of glass, splinters of the window's frame, and remnants of a sheer window curtain were strewn over his carcass. His legs twitched. The blood flow from his eye diminished and then stopped. He became still.

Nate turned and looked at Christine. She sat on the landing, the gun still clutched in both hands, crying. He climbed the steps and knelt beside her. He pried her fingers loose from the gun and looked at it. It was his pistol, bought many years earlier when he first became commonwealth's attorney. He set the gun on the floor and put his arms around Christine and held her. "I'm sorry, Christine. It's my fault he attacked you. He hurt you to hurt me."

Sirens wailed in the distance. "Did you call the sheriff, Christine?" She didn't answer. She didn't look at Nate. She didn't move. He went downstairs and searched the dining room. He found no weapon. He looked out the window at Deatherage's body. He assumed Deatherage had no weapon on him or he would have used it to defend himself. Nate quickly searched the entire first floor and found nothing. He ran up the stairs into the bedroom. The bed had been stripped of its covers. A bloodstained pillow lay at its head and blood was splattered on the mattress. On the floor he found Christine's torn clothing and a makeshift garrote – a strand of rope knotted around a horse whip. He searched the room hurriedly, but he didn't find a gun.

Nate returned to Christine. "Deatherage had a pistol and a shotgun. Where are they?" She didn't answer. "Where is Deatherage's gun?" She didn't respond. No presence dawned in her eyes. She was somewhere else. The sirens wailed through Whippoorwill Hollow toward the farm. He looked at the broken window frame, the bullet holes in the plaster. The pistol lay on the floor beside Christine. He picked it up and slipped it inside his belt. He shook her. Her eyes came into focus. They pooled with tears. "Stop crying, Christine. There's no time." She stopped crying. "Listen to me, Christine. I'm going to tell you the story of what happened here. Listen to me carefully. You don't have to remember much, but you have to remember it well. Every time someone asks you what happened, you have to tell this story. You have to tell it the same way each time."

Her eyes filled with tears again.

"No, Christine. The time for crying has passed. You must be strong. Your mind must be clear. My story will be the truth about what happened here. You must remember it. Do you understand me?"

She wiped the tears from her eyes.

"Do you understand?"

Her eyes cleared. She nodded her head.

Nate told Christine the story as the sirens wailed outside the house.

Chapter 35

The Plea

Nate sat on the bottom step of the stairs. Selk County Sheriff Coleman Grundy stood at the front door gripping the stock of a pump-action shotgun, his potbelly straining against the buttons of his shirt, his hat pulled down low over his eyes. Medical emergency personnel rolled a gurney out the door. Christine lay on the gurney under a blanket. She looked at Nate. He nodded to her, but she didn't respond. Her eyes were clear. The fear and anger were gone, but no other feelings seemed to have replaced them. Maybe she was numb, he thought, the way he was numb after his downfall. He hoped so.

Sheriff Grundy propped the shotgun against the wall and watched the paramedics roll the gurney to a van. The van pulled away from the house, its lights flashing. The sheriff looked at the dining room window, looked at Nate, and frowned. "Messy situation we have here, Nate. I won't bother to explain your rights to you. You know them better than I do. You know you don't have to answer my questions."

"I shot him."

The sheriff took a deep breath and looked at the shotgun leaning against the wall. "We found this twelve-gauge in the corral. There's blood on the barrel. There's blood on the saddle of your horse. I figure Deatherage hit Christine over the head with the shotgun when she was on the horse. He dropped the shotgun in the corral and dragged her across the field to the house. Is that what happened?"

"I don't know. When I got here, they were inside the house."

The sheriff stroked his ample belly and made a sour face. "We found the service revolver Deatherage stole from the Starkey County deputy tangled in the bedcovers up there in your bedroom. There's no gun on Deatherage's corpse." The sheriff hesitated. "I know you understand how important the answer to this next question is, Nate. I'll repeat – you don't have to answer my questions."

Nate waited.

"Did you think Deatherage had a weapon when you shot him?"

"No."

The sheriff winced. He looked upstairs. "There's a big mess up there. It looks like Deatherage did terrible violence to Christine. Did you catch him in the act of raping and choking her?"

"He was sitting at the dining room table when I got here. Christine was in the bedroom, unconscious, but I didn't know that. I didn't see her."

"Be careful what you say, Nate. There are three bullet holes in the wall around the windows. Deatherage was hit twice. Your pistol is empty. He was unarmed. A good lawyer will have a hard time making a case for self-defense."

"It wasn't self-defense."

The sheriff grimaced. "There's no need to say words in the heat of the moment that you'll regret later."

"Deatherage told me he had killed Christine. I wanted to kill him. I knew she kept my pistol in the drawer of that table." Nate pointed at a table by the front door. "I got the pistol out of the drawer. I fired all six shots at him."

The sheriff stared at Nate for a long time. Nate looked down at the floor and said nothing. The sheriff pulled open the drawer of the table. "Seems like an odd place for Christine to keep a gun. You'd think a woman who lived alone in the country would keep a gun in a table beside her bed where it'd be handy if a prowler broke in the house at night."

Nate's mind raced to find a convincing lie. He remembered the night of his closing argument to Christine. "I shoved my way into this room and pushed her around the night of my car accident. She's not afraid of prowlers. She's afraid of me. She keeps the gun there in that table to protect herself from me."

The sheriff frowned. He was quiet for another long spell. Then he said, "Doesn't make sense to me, but I suppose it might make sense to Christine." The sheriff walked to the dining room window and looked outside at Deatherage's body. "Where was she when you shot Deatherage?"

"She was unconscious in bed upstairs. She told me Deatherage choked her until she passed out. She said she regained consciousness and called your office for help. That must have happened a few minutes after I shot him. I didn't realize she was alive until I went upstairs to the bedroom just before your men arrived."

The sheriff put his hands on his hips, looked up at the landing, and shook his head.

Nate waited with his heart in his throat.

After a long pause, the sheriff said, "I guess I believe you." He walked over to Nate. "I have no reason not to believe you, do I?"

"I knew he didn't have a gun. I shot him because I wanted to kill him."

The sheriff heaved a heavy breath. He reached for the handcuffs snapped to his belt.

"You won't need those," Nate said.

The sheriff pursed his lips. "No, I suppose not."

That night Nate sat on a cot in a Selk County jail cell. Howard Raines sat on a folding chair in the cell. Howard rubbed his temples and sighed. "If you allow me to put on a defense, no jury will convict you. For God's sake, the man tortured your wife."

"Christine's my ex-wife."

"That's the third time tonight you've reminded me of that fact. Why?"

"I'm facing reality."

"You've picked a fine time to come to grips with your marital status. We need to craft a defense. In case you haven't noticed, your life is on the line. In the morning you'll be arraigned for first degree murder and you'll be required to enter a plea. "

"I'll plead guilty."

"Have you taken leave of your senses, Nate?"

"I shot Deatherage. At tomorrow's arraignment I'll plead guilty."

"You shot him, but you know as well as I do that doesn't mean you're guilty of first degree murder. You must have feared for your life when you pulled the trigger. Perhaps you saw him reach into his pocket or raise his hand toward you. Maybe the glare of the sunlight coming through a window behind him blinded you. You thought you saw a gun in his hand. You fired in self-defense. You knew he was a ruthless murderer so you emptied your gun to make sure you disabled him. All we need is a plausible story. The jury will believe anything you say. They'll want to believe you. You're a hero. You saved Christine's life. You killed a vicious murderer."

"Deatherage didn't have a gun. I admitted that to the sheriff."

"I'll move to exclude your comments to Cole Grundy. He didn't inform you of your rights before he questioned you. He told me he would concede that point in court. He wants to help you. Judge Blackwell wants to help you. You've always had an edge with him. Everyone sympathizes with you in this case. We all want to help you, but you don't seem to want to help yourself."

"My plea is up to me. Not Judge Blackwell or Sheriff Grundy or you. I've made my decision. I'll plead guilty tomorrow."

"Damn it, Nate! We can construct a solid basis for self-defense. Christine can testify about what Deatherage did to her. Jurors will hate the man."

Nate grabbed Howard's arm. "Christine won't testify. There will be no trial. This case will be closed by the end of the hearing tomorrow. I shot Deatherage. I killed him. I meant to kill him when I shot him. Tomorrow morning I'll plead guilty with you by my side or without you."

Howard looked down at Nate's fist gripping his arm. Nate let go of it and went to the window, his back turned to Howard. He didn't want Howard to see the anxiety in his face. A cursory investigation would expose his story as a lie. A simple paraffin test would show no gunpowder residue on his hands. The angle of entry of the bullets in the wall would show the shots were fired from the upstairs landing, not from the front door as he claimed. If he was ruled out as the shooter, it would be clear that Christine killed Deatherage. Nate could read Sheriff Grundy. The sheriff knew Nate was covering for Christine and he was willing to allow him to take the blame, but the slightest doubt about Nate's guilt might force the sheriff to conduct an investigation to protect his office from criticism. Nate's guilty plea would eliminate that risk. "I'll plead guilty in the morning, Howard. Will you stand with me?"

"Will you at least allow me to negotiate with Rea for a plea to a lesser offense?"

In the heat of the crisis, Nate had forgotten about his conversation with Wiley Rea. The consequences of Nate's bad choices as commonwealth's attorney seemed to be never-ending. "I don't want to run the risk."

"What risk could be greater than pleading guilty to first degree murder?"

Nate couldn't answer Howard's question truthfully, so he didn't respond.

Howard said, "If you allow me to work on Wiley, he'll likely agree to voluntary manslaughter with a recommendation of a short sentence, maybe even a suspended sentence with probation."

"You can talk to Rea about a lesser plea, but if he offers even the slightest resistance, you are to terminate the discussion immediately."

"He's a prosecutor. He won't roll over. I'll need to threaten him with bad publicity for an overzealous prosecution of a local hero."

"You will not pressure him. If he offers resistance, you will back off."

Howard heaved a deep sigh. "Of course, even if Wiley were to agree to voluntary manslaughter, that's a felony. At best, the bar association's disciplinary board will suspend your license to practice law for a long stretch. The board might even disbar you. I suppose you've thought about that."

Nate nodded.

Howard shook his head morosely. "All right, damn it. I'll do the best I can with my hands tied behind my back."

"Thank you, Howard."

Howard closed his briefcase and turned to leave.

Nate said, "How is Christine?"

"Doctor Davis said her physical injuries aren't critical, but he's worried about her mental condition."

"Did you speak with her?"

"Yes."

"Did she say anything about what happened?"

"She doesn't remember anything after Deatherage forced her into the bedroom. The next thing she recalls is regaining consciousness and calling the sheriff. I guess she's lucky in that respect."

"She's not lucky. She had the misfortune of marrying me."

"You're not making sense tonight. You're confusing the issues of your broken marriage with this sordid tragedy. They're separate matters."

"They have the same root cause. Me. I ruined her life," Nate said in a soft voice. "I berated her and belittled her. I slept with Rosaline for more than a year and lied to Christine about it the whole time. And I'm responsible for Deatherage's attack. He raped and choked her to get at me."

"A big part of me hates you for what you did to Christine, but what Deatherage did to her is not your fault."

"I withdrew as Deatherage's counsel for selfish reasons. He told me he would pay me back. He attacked Christine to get back at me. I caused the attack."

"I've represented people like Deatherage all my life. He was a psycho-pathic lunatic. You can't hold yourself responsible for anything he did."

"I didn't make Deatherage who he was and I didn't force him to do the vile things he did to Christine, but my actions put him in my house." Nate turned his back to Howard. "I shot him and I killed him and I will plead guilty to murdering him in the morning."

Chapter 36

The Arraignment

Nate's arraignment was the first matter on the Selk County Circuit Court's morning calendar. The bailiff unlocked the courtroom at eight. By eight thirty every seat in the courtroom was occupied. The bailiff set up folding chairs at the end of each aisle, but there still weren't enough seats to accommodate the spectators. People stood along the side and back walls three and four rows deep.

Nate waited in the hall behind the courtroom with Sheriff Grundy. The sheriff didn't require Nate to wear cuffs or manacles, and Howard had brought him a suit to wear instead of the prison garb.

At nine, the sheriff led him into the courtroom and ushered him to the defendant's table. He looked across the sea of faces in the gallery. He knew most of them. He had indicted a few of them. Some were victims of criminals he had prosecuted. Some were witnesses in his cases. Others had served as jurors. A few were personal friends. He searched their faces. There was concern and respect. He saw no animosity.

Howard joined Nate at the defense table. Howard had negotiated a favorable plea agreement. Nate would plead guilty to voluntary manslaughter.

Wiley Rea sat at the prosecution's table. His resentment toward Nate was palpable, yet Howard said Rea agreed to recommend no jail time. Howard whispered to Nate that Judge Blackwell reviewed the proposed plea agreement earlier that morning. "The judge didn't say much, but I think we're in the clear. You should be released on probation at the end of this hearing."

The bailiff called the courtroom to order. Everyone stood as Judge Blackwell climbed the steps to the bench and eased into his chair. "Be seated, please." The clerk called the case. There was a long silence. The judge stared at Nate. The judge's eyes were sad and tired. "I understand, Mister Abbitt, you're prepared to enter a plea of guilty to voluntary manslaughter."

"Yes, Your Honor."

"I assume you understand the consequences of such a plea."

"Yes, I do."

"Very well, then. How do you plead to the charge of voluntary manslaughter?"

"Guilty, Your Honor."

The judge turned to Rea. "I'll hear from you concerning sentencing, counsel."

Rea recited his part in the proceeding flawlessly, albeit without passion or conviction. He recommended that Nate receive a five-year sentence, that the sentence be suspended, and that he be placed on probation for the five years. Rea summarized the mitigating circumstances of Nate's crime, Deatherage's brutal attack on Christine, and Nate's belief that Deatherage had killed her. Rea said the commonwealth was satisfied that Nate's crime was an isolated occurrence, the product of unique circumstances, committed in the heat of passion in response to extraordinary provocation.

The judge turned to Howard Raines. Howard summarized Nate's clean record and his contributions to the community as a former commonwealth's attorney. Howard submitted letters from Sheriff Grundy and other Selk County civic leaders vouching for Nate's character. Nate was surprised when Howard read a letter from Circuit Court Judge George Maupin praising Nate for exposing the Buck County corruption. Nate understood George's letter. The letter was addressed to the court, but its message was intended for Nate. It told him to keep quiet about George's crimes. It reminded him that George was a powerful man who could influence his future both positively and negatively.

Howard brought his presentation to a close and sat down. The gallery waited for the judge's ruling. There was no sound in the crowded courtroom. The judge looked at Nate for a long time. There was more emotion in his face than Nate expected to find there. He and Nate had been friends for many years and recently their weekly counseling sessions had forged a close bond between them, but the judge's expression betrayed more affection than seemed warranted. He looked grief-stricken, devastated.

"Please stand, Mister Abbitt."

Nate stood. The judge picked up his gavel and started to pronounce Nate's sentence, but he hesitated. He set the gavel down, put his hand over his eyes, and leaned back in his chair. He was motionless for a long time. He dropped his hand and gazed at Nate. His eyes were tortured, his emotions bared. Nate recognized something in the judge's eyes, something unspoken but unmistakable, something Nate had only seen in the eyes of one other man in his life. At that moment, he knew the reason the judge had invested so much time and energy in his welfare and protected him and risked his own good name and freedom in the process. At that moment, Nate knew the judge's secret, and it took his breath away. His knees buckled. Howard embraced Nate and held him up.

"I regret that I cannot rule on this matter," the judge said. "My relationship with the defendant is too close. I am biased in his favor. My inherent conflict of interest requires me to recuse myself from sentencing this defendant. I will ask the circuit's chief judge to transfer this case to another court for sentencing. This hearing is adjourned." The judge rapped his gavel and descended from the bench.

Nate spent a week in the Selk County jail waiting for the assignment of his case to another circuit court judge. Howard was nervous. He said Nate's sentence would depend on the proclivities of the new judge. The chief judge transferred the case to Judge Wigfield of Starkey County, the judge who had been assigned to the Deatherage trial.

Howard was optimistic. He thought Judge Wigfield's familiarity with Deatherage's crimes would work in Nate's favor. It did not. Judge Wigfield refused to accept Wiley Rea's sentencing recommendation. In his ruling, Judge Wigfield acknowledged the brutality of Deatherage's crimes against Christine and Nate's long tenure as a public servant, but he condemned Nate's decision to take the law into his own hands. The judge said, "The defendant fired six shots at the victim while the victim was unarmed. It is undisputed that the defendant was under no imminent threat of physical danger. Even under the compelling circumstances of the immense provocation in this case, to reward the defendant's willful violent conduct by releasing him to probation without serving a single day in confinement would be an endorsement of vigilantism and anarchy." The judge sentenced Nate to six months in state prison and to five years' probation.

Chapter 37

The Release

The warden considered Nate to be at risk in the general population because Nate was a former prosecutor. Nate occupied a private cell in a cell block housing other inmates who were considered nonviolent and at risk. They came from the upper strata of Virginia society – a former member of the state legislature from Kilmarnock who sold his votes to real-estate developers for cash delivered to him in brown paper bags, a Baptist minister who embezzled a small fortune from the largest church in Virginia Beach, an ex-policeman from Norfolk who sold drugs he confiscated in the cases he worked.

Nate didn't mix with his cellmates. He passed the time in his cell alone. The first few weeks he was physically and emotionally exhausted. He slept the days away. Those were the easiest days. After that he couldn't sleep. There was no work to distract him. There was no whiskey to numb his pain and blur his mind. There was no escape from his memories. His thoughts were clear and vivid and brutally honest.

Nate replayed the scene of Deatherage's death in his mind's eye many times. He saw the look on Christine's face when she stood on the landing pointing the gun at Nate, the agony in her eyes, the torrent of tears, the shaking of her hands as she fought the temptation to shoot him. He saw the continued firing of the gun at Deatherage after he had fallen through the window and even after the bullets were spent. He saw the vacant expression on Christine's face when she was carried from the house on a gurney.

She killed the wrong man, Nate thought. Deatherage raped and choked and tortured her, but Nate was the source of her misery. Deatherage ravaged her body. Nate broke her heart and spirit. When Christine fired the gun at Deatherage, Nate knew she was thinking of him and all he had done to her.

During the early days of his prison sentence, Nate came to terms with Judge Greene's advice about his marriage. The look in Christine's hurt-filled eyes when she leveled the pistol on Nate extinguished his last spark of hope that he could ever regain her love. He finally accepted that she was lost to him forever. In the pitch-black darkness of every night in his cell, he wept for the death of his life with Christine.

Over the weeks and months that followed, Nate endlessly replayed the scenes leading up to the shots Christine fired at Deatherage, and he eventually remembered Deatherage saying he killed Joe Hitt. Nate's memory of Hitt clarified. When Nate met with Daryl Garth, Jimmy Washington's attorney, Garth said Washington was convicted of killing Hitt. Garth said Hitt was strangled, Deatherage's "special pleasure," as Eva, his mother, had said. Jimmy Washington was on death row awaiting execution for Hitt's murder.

Nate told Howard Raines about Deatherage's confession to Hitt's murder. Howard told Garth, but he had withdrawn from representing Washington when he became acting commonwealth's attorney. Howard took the case and prepared an affidavit about Deatherage's statement to Nate, which Nate signed. It wasn't long before Howard discovered that Deatherage and Hitt had a history of bad blood between them, dating back to days they spent together in reform school when they were teenagers. Howard submitted an application for a pardon to the governor of Virginia, and a few months later the governor granted the pardon.

The *Richmond Times-Dispatch* published a series of stories about Jimmy Washington's wrongful conviction. The stories criticized George Maupin for prosecuting and convicting an innocent man for a capital offense based on contradictory and suspect evidence. One of the stories castigated George for ignoring the similarity between the *modi operandi* of the murders of Darlene Updike and Joe Hitt, strangulation by ligature and manual strangulation. The theme of the *Times-Dispatch* stories was repeated by newspapers and television stations all over the state. The unflattering notoriety besmirched George's reputation and drained power from Buck County's new king. Nate was glad to see it. It wasn't enough to satisfy him, but it was a start. He hoped he would have the opportunity someday to finish the job of introducing the real George Maupin to the world.

One of the *Times-Dispatch* stories included a picture of Washington embracing his wife and children after his release from prison. The article depicted Nate as a hero for extracting a confession to Hitt's murder from Deatherage and for saving Christine's life. An editorial in the *Times-Dispatch* asserted that he was wrongly incarcerated and called upon Judge Wigfield to commute his sentence. He threw the editorial away, but he kept the picture of Jimmy Washington and his family.

Three months into Nate's sentence, the Virginia State Bar's disciplinary board suspended his license to practice law for six months, the same time as his jail term. The chairman of the disciplinary board, a defense lawyer from Richmond Nate had once opposed in an armed-robbery case, enclosed a handwritten note with the board's formal notification. He informed Nate that the board's sympathies ran with Nate. He said the board gave Nate the shortest suspension it could justify, given the seriousness of his felony. Nate would be able to resume practicing law as soon as he was released. The note closed with a heartfelt expression of the chairman's admiration for Nate's "courageous assault upon the fortress of corruption in Buck County."

Without the distraction of a caseload or any other means to deflect his thoughts, the long empty days in the penitentiary forced Nate to confront his worst deeds. He lied to Christine, belittled her, demeaned her, and cheated on her. These were his most despicable acts. He tried hard to blame them on a mixture of overwhelming compulsions. Fear of death, fear of aging, despondency, depression, whiskey – they were the real culprits, he told himself. They robbed him of his judgment and sensibility. They crowded out all other thoughts and feelings and took control of him. He wanted to believe he wasn't guilty of these cruel deeds, but no amount of reflection or rationalization could convince him of his innocence. Christine was right. There was no guilt-absolving compulsion that forced him to destroy her life. Scared or not, drunk or not, Nate, and Nate alone, made the decisions and took the actions that broke her heart. There was no justification for what he did, no valid reason, no good excuse. He was guilty. Open and shut. And no rehabilitation or penance could rescue him from a life sentence of remorse for what he had done to her.

He had rigged prosecutions against five defendants. He'd tried to tell himself that his motives were noble, that he falsified evidence to take violent criminals off the streets, but he knew that was a lie. His motives were entirely selfish. He wanted to escape the burdens of his job. He rigged prosecutions to free up time to drink and to pursue his affair with Rosaline. Deputy Jones' effort to prove Nate killed Henry Crawford taught him the harsh consequences of his indifference to the rights of the accused. As with his cruel treatment of Christine, there was no justification for his crimes as commonwealth's attorney.

The morals of other questionable actions he took were not as clear to him. He pondered the lies he'd told about Judge Herring's death and about killing Deatherage. He told these lies to protect Clarence Shifflett and Christine from being charged with crimes that Nate's actions had set in motion. These lies were felonious. They constituted obstruction of justice. Also open and shut. And yet, he could not convince himself they were wrong, and if presented with the same circumstances, legal or not, moral or not, he knew he would tell the same lies again.

The moral character of his decision to withdraw from Deatherage's defense was the most difficult for him to analyze. The code of legal ethics was clear. His duty to defend Deatherage was paramount. It should have taken precedence over his personal opinion of Deatherage's guilt. A good defense attorney would have used the spousal privilege to block Claire Deatherage's testimony about Deatherage's confession, and even if she had been allowed to testify, a good defense counsel would have tested her truthfulness on cross. Kenneth Deatherage beat his wife. She was afraid of him. She wanted him out of her life. Her testimony against him would keep him in jail and away from her. A competent defense attorney would have exploited these facts to attack her credibility.

Nate believed Claire Deatherage, but he knew it was not his role to judge her credibility. That judgment belonged to the jury alone. The decisions he had made as a prosecutor to circumvent judges and juries to convict criminal defendants were clearly wrong. The same should be true of decisions made in his new role as defense counsel, but in the Deatherage case, he could not ignore his firm conviction that Claire told the truth about Deatherage's confession. At first Nate didn't know why he could not force himself to stand by Deatherage, but during his time in the state penitentiary, the truth about his withdrawal from the case stepped forward slowly from the shadows. Darlene Updike looked like Christine. Deatherage was guilty of murdering Darlene. Nate was guilty of destroying Christine's life. He tried to tell himself he was drunk and didn't know what he was doing when he hurt her, but that was no excuse. Deatherage drank two jars of bootlegged alcohol the night before he murdered Updike, but she suffered greatly at his hands and died just the same. Nate thought Deatherage was right when he told Nate, "The truth is you belong in here with me," and, "The only difference between you and me is you won't tell the truth about yourself."

That was true when Deatherage said it, but Nate's time in jail changed him. He admitted the truth about himself. He couldn't defend Deatherage because he couldn't defend himself. He withdrew from the case to avoid the pain of reliving his own crimes, and it led to the most disastrous tragedy of his life.

Nate's mother visited him in prison twice a week, bringing him cakes, cookies, magazines, and books. During the visits, Nate sensed a tension in her that she'd never shown him before. At first, he thought she might be stressed by his surroundings. The visiting room was a cramped gray windowless room strewn with tables and chairs. A defective fluorescent light flickered on and off. The room stank of sweat and ammonia. The inmates and their visitors were loud and profane, and Nate thought his mother was depressed to see him dressed in a khaki prison jumpsuit like the other convicts.

During one of her visits, Nate said, "Does it bother you to see me here?"

"It doesn't please me, but it helps to know you don't belong here."

"I'm sorry you have to come here. I'm sorry for all I've put you through."

"Don't be silly. You're a hero for what you did to that man. The judge was wrong to put you in jail. Everyone says so."

"That's not what I meant. I don't regret what happened to Deatherage. I'm sorry for the mistakes I made before he came along. I'm sorry I drank myself into so much trouble. I'm sorry I dishonored my position as commonwealth's attorney. I cheated on Christine and I broke her heart. I'm sorry I embarrassed you and hurt you. I'm sorry for all of it."

His mother placed her hand over Nate's hand. "We've all made terrible mistakes. I've done things I regret. I've caused grief to those I love." She fell silent.

"Visiting me is too hard on you. You shouldn't come here again. I'll be okay. I'll be out soon."

"That's nonsense. I enjoy my time with you."

"No one enjoys time in this place. Don't come here again. There's no need."

Her eyes pooled with tears. She clutched her purse and stood. "I'll see you Tuesday."

In the next few visits she filled every moment with small talk. She spoke of her intended spring garden plantings, repairs to the house, the death of her neighbor's cat, recipes for the food she brought Nate, the weather. She talked without respite, as though a single moment of silence would break her down. In each successive visit, she talked faster and louder and seemed more anxious. A half hour into one of her monologues Nate interrupted her in midsentence. "Is something troubling you, Ma? You seem worried."

"Of course not. Why would you say such a thing? We're having a nice conversation and you jump in and – "

"We're not having a conversation. You're talking, but you're not saying anything."

She burst into tears. "I'm doing my best. What do you want from me?"

He waited until she regained her composure. Then he said, "These visits wear you down. You don't need to come here."

She left without another word.

Two weeks passed without a visit. Then a guard told Nate he had a visitor and escorted him to the visiting room. Nate's mother appeared at the door and walked across the room with a pronounced limp. There was a bruise on her forehead, and her eyes were red from crying.

Nate helped her to a chair and sat beside her. "What happened to you, Ma?"

"I fell and sprained my ankle."

"How bad is it?"

"It's not bad. I can manage."

"Did you go to the doctor?"

She nodded. "Doctor Davis said to stay off my ankle for a few days. That's why I didn't come to see you for a while."

"How did you fall?"

"I missed that last step on the back stoop again. I fell into a low spot by the flower bed. Anyone but a feeble old woman would have jumped up and gone about her business, but I couldn't get up. I squirmed around every which way but it was no use. I gave up and laid there for a long time. My head hurt and my ankle throbbed. I was too embarrassed to cry for help, but the pain overwhelmed my pride. I yelled for Clara but she didn't come. I screamed and screamed some more." She shook her head. "I was so helpless."

"Your back yard is a good one hundred yards from Mrs. Templeton's house. I'm not surprised she didn't hear you."

"Oh, believe me I was whooping and hollering loud enough for Clara to hear me, but she's such a vain old biddy. She won't wear her hearing aid. She thinks it makes her look old. If she hadn't put it on at noon to watch *The Guiding Light*, I suppose I would have died of exposure in my own back yard."

"I'm surprised Mrs. Templeton was able to help you up."

Resentment darkened Nate's mother's face. "Clara didn't help me up. She wouldn't try. I begged her to take my hand, but she wouldn't do it." Nate's mother spoke in a singsong voice, in mimicry of her neighbor. "'I can't lift you up, Abigail. I'll fall and we'll both be stuck out here in the garden with no one to help us.' Clara insisted on calling the rescue squad. Don't call anybody, I told her. Just let me take hold of the hem of your dress. But no, she wouldn't hear of it. Stubborn old witch."

"She was right, Ma."

She brushed away tears. "You don't understand how humiliating it was. There was such a big ruckus, those loud sirens and flashing lights. A crowd followed the ambulance to the house, hoping to see some sort of tragedy, I suppose. I told the two young men I could walk to their truck if they'd just give me a little help, but they were as stubborn as Clara. They insisted on lifting me onto a gurney and rolling it through that big crowd of gawking strangers, people who hear the sirens and chase down ambulances to catch sight of blood and gore. Vultures. Busybodies and gossips. Of course, they couldn't wait to tell everybody about poor old Mrs. Abbitt, so feeble and weak she fell down and couldn't get up. By now the whole county knows I'm too old to help myself."

Nate's mother cried. He placed his hand on her shoulder. After a while, she cried herself out. "I suppose some good came from this ordeal. It forced me to face up to my age. I can't live alone forever."

Nate was struck by how old she looked. For so long, she'd defied her mortality with good health, vigorous exercise, and an indomitable spirit, but that morning she looked depressed and defeated. For the first time in Nate's memory, she looked her age.

"Do you still want me to move into that rest home you spoke to me about?"

"I don't know. Are you considering it?"

"I guess so. I've been a stubborn old woman for too long, I suppose. If you still want me to, I'll take a look at that place. I want you to look at it again, too, when you get out of here. I'm not saying I'll move in, but I'll think about it. You and I will discuss it and we'll decide together what I should do."

"All right, Ma. If that's what you want."

She folded her hands on the table, sat up straight, and seemed to gather herself. "Nathan, there's something I want to talk to you about." She stared at her hands. "I've kept a secret for many years. I've kept the truth from everyone, including you. I've told myself it was best for you that you didn't know the truth, but that was a lie. It was best for me, but not necessarily for you. My fall forced me to think about my secret in a different light. Only one other living soul knows the truth, and I realized that when I die the truth may die with me and that's not fair to you. You deserve to know the truth, no matter how much it may hurt me to tell you."

Nate knew what was coming. He steeled himself.

"You brought up the subject of your father's death when you came by the house – "

Nate cupped his mother's hands in his hands. "Don't, Ma."

"What?"

"Don't do this. There's no need."

"You don't know what I want to tell you. You have a right to know – "

"I don't want to know."

"But Nathan – "

He put his fingers over her lips. "Whatever your secret is, it doesn't matter now."

She pushed his hand away. "You don't know what I want to tell you." She frowned. Awareness dawned on her face, quickly followed by shock, and then fear. "Did you learn the truth somehow? Do you know?"

"I know you and Dad took good care of me and raised me right. I know you both loved me." He hesitated long enough to be sure his voice wouldn't quaver. "I know I loved Dad and I love you."

Abigail broke down. She wept for a long while. When she stopped crying, they sat together without saying anything for another long time. When she left the prison that day, the tension between them was gone.

For the last few weeks of his sentence, Nate spent most of his time in a room with other sequestered prisoners in front of a television, but he didn't see the shows that played on its screen. He saw the people he loved.

He saw his father. He tried his best to recall all the precious memories. His father was unfailingly kind and loving, from Nate's first memory of him until the day he died. He was gentle and soft-spoken. He never lifted a hand against Nate in anger or frustration and never once raised his voice.

Nate saw his parents together and thought about his lifelong puzzlement at an apparent distance and coldness between them. They were polite to one another. They talked to each other when required to deal with the practical logistics of living together. They dined together at the supper table every night, but there was very little meaningful conversation between them. For the most part, they talked to or about Nate. They weren't angry or sarcastic or cruel to one another and he never heard a cross word between them, but he could recall no evidence of genuine affection between them either. He never saw them kiss, not even a peck on the cheek. He never saw them embrace or hold hands. He searched his memory for a single instance when they touched each other in an open expression of affection, but no image came to him.

As scenes on the television screen played on, Nate saw his mother. He felt her hand flinch when it rested on his hand at the kitchen table the day he told her about the judge's deathbed promise to his father. He saw her pause when he asked her about the friendship between the judge and Nate's father. He saw her avert her eyes. He heard the strain in her voice when she answered.

Nate saw Judge Blackwell on the prison's television screen, too. He thought about all the good advice and counsel the judge had given him. He recalled the many kindnesses and favors with nothing asked in return. He saw the judge sitting beside Nate's bed when Nate regained consciousness the night of the car accident. He remembered the tears the judge shed as he sat there. He heard the judge's voice. "Thank God, son. I was afraid we'd lost you." He thought about the felonies the judge committed to protect him from indictment. He recalled the judge's response when Nate questioned his relationship with Nate's father. The judge said, "We were good friends once before you were born." Nate remembered that all Wiley Rea could find out about the judge was a vague rumor about an affair with a married woman and a broken heart.

Nate remembered a debate in a sociology course he took at Jefferson State. The issue was whether genetic traits or environmental circumstances exerted greater influence over a person's actions in life. He favored the environment at the time, but during his last days in prison, he wondered if psychological weaknesses were passed along in genes. It would be less painful for him to think he betrayed Christine because he was pro-grammed from birth to do so. It would be less devastating to have lost everything he cared about if his genetic makeup precursed him to make the pivotal mistake of his life. A belief in genetic predestination would have eased Nate's conscience, but in the end he knew he couldn't escape responsibility for his failings. His environmental influences were too strong and too good.

As he gazed at the television screen, Nate saw Christine when she told him about her deathbed conversation with his father. "Your father said you brought more joy to his life than he deserved. He said you are the proudest achievement of his life. He said he loves you." And later. "He said he feared there would come a time in your life when you might doubt him, when you might need to be reassured about how much he loved you." That moment had come during Nate's sentencing hearing before Judge Blackwell. Nate's father's love remained an enduring truth. It had survived an untold story of conflict and turmoil and heartbreak. It had survived his father's death. And it had survived Nate's discovery of the truth. Having lost everything else that was meaningful to him, Nate clung to his father's love during his final days in prison.

Nate's last day of incarceration was May 16, a little more than a year after he first met Kenneth Deatherage in Visit A – Max Sec. He awoke that morning after dawn and lay in his bed thinking about his release. He approached it with a sense of dread. He didn't know what he would do when he got out. Returning to the practice of law did not appeal to him. As a defense lawyer, he had regained much of what he had lost. His work on the Deatherage case restored his reputation in the legal community. He had climbed a long steep road back to integrity, respectability, and sobriety, but the prize he treasured most was not at the summit when he arrived there. Without that prize, his achievements were empty, worthless.

At nine o'clock, a guard came to his cell, returned his civilian clothes to him, and waited for him to change. As the guard walked Nate down a hall to the last checkpoint, Nate thought he might return to the base of the steep hill and rest there. He might go back to the run-down hotel on the edge of the slums in Hayesboro. He might crawl inside the bottle and numb his pain and mark time until his time was all used up.

A guard at the counter in the lobby stared at Nate's scar. Then he said, "You got all your clothes, right?" He referred to a checklist. "Jacket, shirt, slacks, drawers, belt, socks, shoes. You got everything?"

Nate nodded.

"Personal belongings," the guard said. "Let's see." He rummaged through a wire-mesh basket. "Wallet. Sixty-eight dollars cash. Money clip. Watch. Ring. Here you go." He shoved the basket across the counter. Nate put on his watch and pocketed his wallet and cash. He looked at his wedding ring and then put it in his pocket, too.

"Is that it?" the guard said.

Nate nodded again.

The guard handed him the checklist. "Sign here."

Nate signed his name.

"Okay. You're done. You're free to go. Good luck."

Nate looked at a door with an Exit sign above it. Returning to the run-down hotel in Hayesboro suddenly seemed foolish. There was no point in going back there. It was a dead end. There was no point in going anywhere. There was no point in living.

"You're all done," the guard said again.

"I don't know where to go," Nate said under his breath.

"Aren't you going with the lady?"

"What lady?"

"The lady who came to pick you up. People who come for the pick-ups aren't allowed to wait in here. I told her to wait in the parking lot."

Sunlight poured in a window beside the exit door, its mullions casting neat rectangular shadows on the linoleum floor. Nate went to the window and looked outside. An asphalt parking lot stretched away from the building. The lot was bordered on its far side by a forest of white pines. Five or six cars were strewn around the lot. To the right of the prison door about thirty feet away sat Christine's pickup truck. She was leaning against its front fender, looking down at the ground, her arms folded over her chest.

Nate went to the door. It was made of metal, painted battleship gray. A chrome bar sliced across it waist-high. Nate put his hand on the bar. It was smooth and cool to the touch. He pressed the bar down and pushed the door open. Sunlight washed over him and fresh air rushed into his face. The scent of pine floated in the air and the faint sound of birdsong came from the forest.

Christine looked up at Nate. Her eyes glistened and her mouth was pinched into a tight line. The wind blew a strand of raven hair across her face. She pulled it back behind her ear. Nate stepped outside, let the door close behind him, and walked toward her.

Acknowledgments

My heartfelt thanks to Meghan Pinson of *My Two Cents Editing* for her expert guidance, advice, and encouragement. She is smart, thorough, fearless, and great fun to work with.

The cover is adapted from *Double Sunset, 2009* by Devon Oder. Thanks to Jono and Anne Marie Singer of Singer Design Studio for their good work on the presentation and appearance of the book.

Thanks to those who consented to read and critique my story in its various stages of development, especially Jack, Mike, Nancy, Daniel, Josh, Devon, and Chelsea, whose enthusiastic encouragement spurred me on.

Stanley Klein provided extensive advice and insight about the laws, procedures, and courts of Virginia. Thanks to Mike Holleran for convincing Stan to fit me into his busy schedule. Virginia's laws have changed significantly since the late 1960s, especially regarding divorce proceedings and the removal of judges. I did my best to set the story within the framework of the laws in effect at that time, taking liberties with the rules in a few instances to advance the plot more efficiently. Any and all errors are my fault.

Last but not least, I greatly appreciate the time and energy that fellow author Pamela Fagan Hutchins and her husband Eric Hutchins devoted to my book. Their two key suggestions changed the tone and quality of the story so much for the better.

Biography

Ken Oder grew up in White Hall, Virginia, at the foot of the Blue Ridge Mountains. He received undergraduate and law degrees from the University of Virginia and moved to Los Angeles, California, in 1975 to join the law firm of Latham & Watkins. He practiced law there until 1993, when he left the firm to become an executive at Safeway, Inc. He retired from Safeway in 2003. He and his wife, Cindy, have three children and two grandchildren. They live in California.

CPSIA information can be obtained at www.ICGtesting.com
Printed in the USA
LVOW06s1722140715

446203LV00016B/1102/P